AF487777

THE LEGEND OF CASTLE COVE
by G. M. Donley

The Legend of Castle Cove
Published by Miscagon, Cleveland Heights, Ohio

ISBN (print paperback): 979-8-9876725-3-2
Library of Congress Control Number: 2024906408

Design by Miscagon
Printed in USA
First edition April 2024

For EB, Drew, and Gwen

PERIPHERAL VISION

When most people think of a ghost, they picture either Charlie Brown with a bed sheet over his head, or maybe Jacob Marley waking up Ebenezer Scrooge one Christmas Eve, or those terrifying bloody girls in the elevator in "The Shining." But, of course, we are not like that really. We could never be so obvious. This is why we show up when you are half asleep or not quite paying attention: so that you can never be sure, so that you think perhaps it was nothing and you're going crazy. It might be just a blade of grass shimmering in the sunlight. This is how it has to be. Specifically speaking, there is a particular Irish type of ghost, a Taibhse, which sounds a lot more exotic than "ghost," does it not? I won't even tell you how to pronounce it. Perhaps I've never said it aloud.

"We have found our Holy Grail," Bret pronounced with a warm yet solemn intonation like the deep voice of the disembodied fellow who does the previews for sensitive foreign movies. Then he folded the screen of the laptop halfway down, lifted the blue plastic pitcher, and poured a half-glass of water. Bret watched his own hand tilt the spout back up and noticed how the crisp striped cuff of his shirt was sticking out just the right amount under the sleeve of the olive-green summer suit—a suit that said "professional" but wasn't so expensive or ostentatious as to upstage this audience of board members. Two seats to his left, he could see Dave Jameson shifting his hands through his papers as if working up to say something, but he knew it would be half a minute at least before Jameson had composed his opening phrase, and that was why Jameson would never get this job, even though both of them knew he was smart enough: the guy just couldn't pull the trigger. Immediately to his right was Christine, who was more of a threat. He glanced over just in time to see her roll her eyes. It was a subtle gesture, calculated to look involuntary, but she was well aware that it would be seen by more than a few in the room. She was a good protégée, damn her. The air was silent but for the low mumble of a horn being played somewhere. Amusement parks always have a lot of tuba players hanging around. And clarinetists, but that piercing sound, implausibly, doesn't seem to carry as far as the rumbling tuba. After sipping twice, Bret set the glass down next to the laptop and picked up the yellow pad and placed it down again near the middle of the conference table.

He liked to do that—not say anything, just utter those dramatic few words, then deliberately go through the motions of putting the various things in their various places, and carefully pour himself a glass of water and take a slow drink (having made sure to set up the pitcher and a glass appropriately ahead of time). It has the ritualistic rhythm of the priests initiating the Holy Communion. That's no accident. By the time the attendees were certain that he had indeed finished, a full minute of silence could have passed. This lends the words a certain gravitas. He looked up at his audience, gave a subtle nod of affirmation in their direction, and sat down. A flicker caught his eye.

Note: I can claim neither credit nor responsibility for this flicker; it was just a flicker like any other flicker.

Bret glanced to his left. A sliver of sunlight reached across the table from a gap in the vertical blinds and reflected off the top of the water in the pitcher. Next to that, he saw that Jameson had a small stack of papers under his official briefing and one of them was sticking out enough that the headline was partially visible: DISCREPANCIES AND MISREPRESENTATIONS IN . . .

Circled around the other side of the Round Table, a half-dozen heads nodded. He'd gotten them again. So much was in the presentation. And in having the nerve to just go for it.

Jameson cleared his throat. Bret knew Jameson was looking for an opportunity to spill the beans about just how much in the hole they would be a week from now. He had kept Christine at work late last night massaging the door figures and minimizing marketing outlay in order to provide a suitably upbeat printed report to the board. He had made sure to effusively praise Christine for preparing it, and made sure her name was at the top of it. If Jameson was going to bring up any funny business here, he was going to take Christine down with him. Bret stood up to leave. "Thanks everyone!" Jameson swallowed whatever word it was he was about to say. Bret leaned down to Christine. "Listen, Chrissie, dear, would you reach out to Dave with those numbers you worked up? We want to be sure you can stand behind everything in there, right?"

"What do you mean?" She asked from her seat, her voice low, eyes steely.

"That your numbers match his," Bret said.

"You know those aren't my numbers, Bret," she hissed through clenched teeth. She and Bret both knew now that she was cornered for the moment. She would have to stop Jameson from speaking.

"Excuse me," said Jameson, pulling out his stack of papers. The milling crowd turned his way.

"Dave," said Christine in a solid, bright voice. "Let's go over a couple things."

He froze, staring at her. She smiled. "Come here, have a look at this," she said. "It's pretty cool." The crowd turned away and meandered toward the door. Jameson deflated and tucked the papers under his arm. Bret patted Christine on the back and strode away, whistling.

On the way out of the conference room, Sylvia Scharff, Bret's boss and managing director of King Arthur's' Kamelot Inc., put a hand on his forearm and said in a low voice, grinning, "You do know how to put it over, Mr. Sheehan."

Bret feigned a surprised look.

"But you know as well as I," she continued, "that we've got a couple of high hurdles ahead of us and we won't clear them on bullshit alone."

"No," he thought quickly, "but if you pile enough up on the front side it makes it the jump a lot easier."

She laughed, clapped him on the shoulder, and turned down the hall toward her office. "Follow me. I'd like you to meet a few people. International delegation here on a junket with the Great Lakes convention bureau. They want to know how we do it."

He chuckled to himself. Sometimes it was almost too easy.

Sylvia Scharff stopped and shook the hand of a slick-looking guy in a cheap blue suit. "Nice to see you, Tom," she said. "Mr. Sheehan here will give you the ten-minute spiel."

The guy in the suit suppressed a momentary flash of disappointment and turned to Bret. "Nice to meet you, Mr. Sheen."

"Sheehan," he shook the guy's sweaty hand. "Bret."

"Sorry, Mr. Sheehan." The guy stepped back. "I must have been thinking of that actor."

"Charlie Sheen?" Bret offered.

"Martin, I think," the guy answered. "Well, never mind." He turned to motion toward the dozen or so people behind him. "These folks are here to start a three-week tour through Ohio, P.A., Michigan, and Indiana to see how we do regional and international tourism. We've got people from, if I remember right, England, Ireland, Spain, France, Belgium, Germany, Italy, Bahrain, Indonesia, Taiwan, and the Philippines."

Bret said hello and scanned the faces, trying to guess which one went with which nation as he began the canned spiel. Well, the short Asian guy was Taiwan. "Welcome to King Arthur's Kamelot." Two women looked like they could be either Indonesia or Philippines. "We like to think we've recreated the spirit of the Round Table right here in River County." The two tweedy guys were surely Ireland and England, with the shorter, baldheaded one with the shiny black eyes probably Ireland because his face was ruddy while the other guy's was pale and pasty. "There's a concept that people who study literature call suspension of disbelief—which means that the reader sometimes has to accept some implausible things before they can really get into the story." The striking dark-haired woman with the Gallic nose and tastefully exposed lacy bra scalloping had to be France. "Finding the Round Table out here is certainly implausible, but we make it come to life with magic—the magic of adventure." Bahrain? Where the fuck is Bahrain? "The very first magical experience happens long before the visitor approaches the gate." That grim-looking guy with the slicked-back hair—Belgium, Germany? Italy? "But let's go back to the beginning, when, before any of this magnificence you see around you came to pass, there was a simple idea." Spain? Or maybe one of the Philippines/Indonesia ladies was Spain or Italy? Bahrain?

ON THE WAY HOME, he stopped at the Tops market to buy a bottle of California Mosel and a little shrink-wrapped mixed bouquet of flowers for Leslie. "What do you think of this bottle?" he asked the young lady at the deli counter, because she was the employee nearest the wine section.

"It's pretty," she said. Her name tag read "Sh'Nelle."

"And that's a pretty name," he said. "Sounds like Chanel Number Five."

"Thank you," she said.

"Have you got flowers here?" he asked.

"Aisle 3 near the end by the customer service desk."

"Thank you very much." He smiled and bowed. The flowers were arranged in a cooler case next to boxes of chocolates. The overhead sign didn't say so, but Bret understood that this was the "sorry I fucked up" section of the grocery store, as in, I forgot our anniversary, or I'm sorry I started that stupid fight, or I know I'm late to dinner again.

He hadn't been very attentive to Leslie recently, what with the launch of the new attractions. Then again, it was always like that this time of year. By now, she would have figured that out. Priorities. In the driveway, he removed the sticky plastic from the flowers and re-wrapped the stems in a sheet of crisp gold foil, a sample left by a printing company representative who had visited on a sales call earlier in the day. This kind of personalizing touch could make such a difference in impressing someone. He peeled the price tag off the wine bottle, stuck it on the old flower wrapper, and shoved the crumpled plastic under the seat. He looked up at the wall. The second-floor light was on, so she'd already gotten home.

"I've returned from the ends of the world to claim your hand, my darling," he called up the stairs. He heard a strange swishing sound as he climbed, and realized the residual adhesive on the flower wrapper had stuck the crumpled plastic to the heel of his shoe. That wouldn't look too good. He stooped down and removed the wrapper from the shoe, quickly, in case she appeared at the top of the stairs. Then he shoved it in his pants pocket and continued walking.

The parakeet greeted him as he entered the room. "Later, dude." The stupid bird watched too much television. They probably shouldn't have named it Oprah. The light by the window was on, but the rest of the place was dark. Dark and empty. There seemed to be things missing.

"Les?" he called.

"Later, dude," said the parakeet. Bret glanced over at the bird's cage near the window and noticed that a small sheet of paper was taped to the cage door. He walked over and saw that it was a lavender envelope, invitation size, with two words written across it in Leslie's careful hand, on two separate lines. "Good Bye."

"Later, dude," said the bird.

"Would you shut the fuck up?" He smacked the cage. Bird shit and millet scattered all over the floor.

It is not my place to editorialize, but by this time, you might have come to a judgment that Bret Sheehan could be characterized as what the humans call a man with temperamental and perhaps intersocial issues. I have heard some use the specific term "asshole" in evident reference this man's character. But what is character, and what is simply behavior? What separates the two? Whether expressive of character or behavior, it is a charming term, broadly evocative. A distillation of the human entity to a single expressive orifice.

BRET NOTICED A GLINT in the corner of his eye. He was sitting in a shady portion of his Uncle Michael's assisted-living room, looking over toward the bed. The flicker might have been sun hitting off something outside the window, but the skies were overcast. Anyway, he noticed it.

This time, indeed it was I.

"Fool yourself first and everyone else will follow," the old man propped himself on his elbows and leaned off the edge of the bed to face Bret. "That's what I say."

"No," Bret replied, "that's what I say." The essential thing in believability was to be consistent. Being consistent while telling the truth is easy: you don't have to get your story straight if you just tell the truth. But being consistent while perpetuating a fiction, or even a moderately elaborated version of the truth, requires constant attention. Since Bret found himself in a profession—indeed, a mode of living as he saw it—that involved a considerable degree of audience manipulation, he found it useful from time to time to ask himself a question: "What would Bret do?" He would hear his own voice saying this aloud in his head. If the contemplated action would be consistent with the carefully curated character of Bret, then he could be confident that whatever it was would be believable to his audience.

First impressions are rarely lasting impressions, I have heard some say. I do not recall my first impression of Bret, but I can say that, to this moment, the impression has remained consistent, though not, I must say, associated with any particular orifice. Now if it were I speaking to a man lying in a convalescent bed, his mind in fog, his corpus not so far from departing this form, would I be concerned with who is being fooled? Due to my nature, this is a moot conjecture—I do not speak. I listen, I consider, I attempt to influence.

"Beg pardon?"

"I just said, Uncle Mike, that you never say that. I say that."

"Say what I'm saying?"

"That bit about fooling yourself." The door to the hall was open. Bret had a vague sense that somebody had quietly but errantly stepped into the room, realized the mistake, and continued on down the hall. Bret noticed his jacket collar was sticking up, so he reached back and folded it down into place. "In my line of work, that's what you have to do."

"Oh, so you've got yourself a job, now, eh?"

"Same job I've had these last five years, Uncle Mike."

"It's about time, that is."

"Director of Marketing and Constituent Services for King Arthur's Kamelot." This was the routine. Uncle Michael didn't seem to remember much of anything, so Bret would repeat it all every Sunday afternoon when he came by to see the old man. That was the secret of getting the crowd on your side: ask them what they want and give it to them. If they want to hear the same story over and over, so be it. King Arthur's Kamelot was the fourth biggest-drawing theme park in the southern Great Lakes region. It was Bret's job to help dream up new attractions and programs, and then ignite and fuel the necessary "buzz" that would get the crowds to file between the two huge stone (well, mold-formed concrete, really) watch towers and plop down their $66.95 for a day of edutainment, sunburn, and deep-fried snacks. "We just opened Lancelot's Return, the tallest steel-track out-and-back thematic roller-coaster in the world."

"Oh, so he's returned, has he? Watch out!" Uncle Michael's frosted-over blue eyes opened wide. "What else?"

"Well, we've got that, and the Gardens of Guinevere continue to draw the picnic-packers. We had an interesting situation at Viking Invasion last week. Couple gentlemen on the Celtic side swapped their foam clubs for wooden ones and started beating the crap out of two jocks from the Cornwall football team. Looked like a payback to me. Anyway, then two friends of the jocks figure out what's going on and jump the line to get in and join the fray, but old Ian McCloud (he's about six-eight, two-eighty, ferocious red beard), he won't have people jumping line, so he grabs one of 'em by the t-shirt as they run past him and the shirt rips and then the kid goes ballistic screaming about how it was his special shirt commemorating the time he won the pancake eating contest over at Riverside last year. 'How many?' Ian says. 'What?' goes the kid. 'How many pancakes?' says Ian. 'Thirty-seven in ten minutes,' says the kid. 'Hmph,' says Ian. 'Now get the hell out of here.' And he throws them all out."

"He fought them off at the wall of the fort for seven hours, they say," said Uncle Michael, lying back down. A long silence followed and Bret thought the old man had dozed off. One thing he liked about visiting Uncle Michael was that there was no need to keep up the character of Bret. No need to be consistent with himself. He could be audience instead of actor. Paying attention was optional because most of the conversation was nonsense anyway. He had been stopping in most Sundays for the past five years, ever since the family had decided it was time to move Michael out of his little bungalow out east and put him in assisted living. Since Bret lived very close to the retirement home, he couldn't not visit at least every once in a while without looking like a shit. So he made the gallant gesture of graciously setting aside his Sunday afternoons to visit Uncle Michael. It had been a chore at first, but he told himself it was worth it because he knew it bought him some family-guilt/indebtedness points he could cash in later, and because he thought it made him look noble when mentioning it offhandedly to his girlfriend or work colleagues. And yet, despite these less-than-altruistic initial motivations, he looked forward to these hours. There was no stress—just being together and talking, or not talking. "Then death was on him." Uncle Michael spoke again, his eyes remaining closed. "They burned his body and returned the blood and bones to water and stone. Took the ashes up the mountain and cast them into the holy well as they do."

"Hmm?" Bret asked. He'd been staring out the window and thought he must have missed something.

THE CIRCULAR CONCRETE BENCH around the flower patch, next to the Catch a Holy Grail game, was Bret's favorite place to sit and watch. From here he could see the back end of Lancelot's Return if he looked straight ahead, just above the aqua blue slide where right now a steady stream of local middle-schoolers was circulating up the stairs and down the eight lanes as fast as they could, leaping onto their burlap sacks at the top and purposely toppling over at the bottom so as to interfere with the kids beside them. The girl running the slide wasn't supposed to allow that, officially, but everyone knew that was why it was fun, so she scolded mildly and let it continue. Good instincts. She'd go far.

To the right was the Fun House, where disheveled teenagers emerged, usually in pairs. Boys would be guffawing and slapping each other on the back, girls would be squealing and leaning into each other, and mixed-gender pairs usually either held hands and hugged or the girl barked a few icy words at the boy. For the last minute or so, though, the only person to come out was a fifty-ish man, more than a little heavy, wearing Bermuda shorts and a light green polo. He stopped for a minute, disoriented, then waddled off toward the midway.

And to the left was the bottom of the big hill of the park's old wooden coaster, whose track at that place took an abrupt left turn. On the ground under the curve was a good place to find earrings, pens and pencils, hats, and other assorted trinkets. And just to the left of that was the swing ride, popular with those who wanted a milder experience. The swings were only half-filled today, mostly moms and younger kids. Tuesdays were usually slow and, besides, the season wouldn't really get going for another couple of weeks. It was only thanks to the after-school discount promo he had dreamed up that they had half the crowds they had today. The wood tracks creaked as a car rumbled down and around the turn.

As usual when he sat here, Bret wore the nondescript dark green windbreaker, shapeless jeans, and Cleveland Indians cap that allowed him to be in the middle of the crowd without calling any attention to himself. Since his seat was at the end of the midway, he could see anyone approaching from the eastern part of the park where most of the more adult rides were, and also the back of anyone headed to that area from the midway. Three girls passed just now on his right. They walked abreast and all wore the unofficial uniform of the day: a bright cropped shirt and tight, low-cut jeans. A few paces behind them, three boys followed. Baggy cargo pants hanging down below the waist of their boxers, and shapeless t-shirts, and the slow, foot-dragging bowlegged shuffle walk. These were all examples of PPP "Passive Performative Presentation." This was Bret's term for the intentional nonverbal communication of group identity affiliation within and between social groups through choices of apparel and physical comportment. He had always intended to write this up for a scholarly journal, but to do that he would have to somehow get past his resentment of scholars and their so-called standards.

Bret remembered first coming here when he was a child. The park had been sold twice since then and most recently re-themed as King Arthur's Kamelot—one of half a dozen parks with variations of that name in the country—but the demographics really hadn't changed: equal parts blue-collar school kids, families on the cheap, and hormone-fueled teens and twenty-somethings. Tattoos were a lot more common now, though, having moved up in the world from ex-military men and biker gangs first to alt-rock hipsters, and now to anybody under 40. And piercings. Who knew where those came from? In the seventies the uniforms had been different, too. Young men of this crowd would have worn tight Levis and tight glossy polyester shirts half unbuttoned to bare the chest and had wallets attached with loose-hanging chains. Women wore tight Levis too, or occasionally tight running shorts. At that time it was considered bad form to show one's underwear, so the uniform often included a tight tank top, whose thin straps provided the premise for not wearing a brassiere lest the straps might show. That mode of public display, Bret theorized, had been replaced by another now. Today all these girls wore bras, usually padded ones designed to manufacture cleavage, and it had become normal to show bra straps or even the whole damn thing. An example walked past: a loose white sleeveless muscle shirt over a black bra. Thanks, Madonna. Comparing and contrasting PPP from sequential eras proved an invaluable exercise whereby Bret could trace the social ancestry of self-selected tribes and thereby predict the market responsiveness of today's sample based on the documented behavior of previous iterations of that same tribal group. In the case of the sample he was now observing, the key group motivators were signals of rebellion against establishment expectations and a simultaneous conformity to a shared language around sexual objectification of the female and symbols of male power; the PPP expressed the accepted shorthand for those messages. For the young men, showing the inch or two of boxers or briefs marked them as just a little bit dangerous (via rap music and because of the reference to jailed men having their belts taken away) and also suggested that the pants might come off easily should a sexual opportunity arise. He scanned the passersby for another of today's universal signals, a bit of thong underwear sticking up above the waistband. There, that curvy young lady with the gray stretch jeans.

Bret's eyes were lingering a bit too long on the young people's bottoms, and in order that his inconspicuousness might rest uncompromised, I conjured up a distraction. He was going to need to get more serious soon.

Bret felt a shadow flit over and he looked up as another car whooshed by: rumbles and creaks with screams overdubbed. That never changed either, nor did the smell of creosote on the wooden timbers, the oily heat coming off the chain pulls, the faint little tunes always audible in the background. In recent years, King Arthur's Kamelot had made some headway in drawing visitors from beyond the adjoining counties, but this was still more or less the same park it had been for decades. These new folks would visit and maybe have a good time, but he sensed that the new visitors felt either that the place was just a little bit seedy—which it was—or that they were too obvious as outsiders. In any case, they usually didn't come back. The park had a new name and a few new rides, but the same characters populated the place—the offspring of the characters who had populated it when he was a kid, who were, presumably, the offspring of the same characters from the fifties. And so on back to the day when the first ride went up and the first chain-smoking tooth-deprived nomad from that region of the world that breeds all the carnies took hold of the big wooden stop/go lever.

It did not strike Bret as implausible that you could take a few dozen acres of farmland, build a bunch of contraptions on it, then charge people money to come spend the day there. And charge them to eat overpriced junk food, charge them for games of not-much-chance, charge them for souvenirs, charge them for parking. All to come hang around in an old cornfield for most of a day, getting sunburned and nauseous. That's the power of imagination. Imagination could take you out of the cornfield you worked in all day, put you in another cornfield all day, and get you to pay for it. Most people yearned to escape their cornfields but were also afraid to venture into places unknown: what they really wanted to escape to was a comfortably familiar place amped up with some risk-free thrills.

A glint of light caught his attention and he looked down to see a silver gum wrapper reflecting the sun between his shoes.

It would be a misnomer to call myself a "ghost of Michael" or indeed a ghost of anyone. The circumscribed lifetime of any human is but a minute fragment of the continuum of consciousness. And thus, a person such as Bret, having an awareness in the foggy recesses of his comprehension that his uncle Michael was nearing the corporeal conclusion, might sense what might be labeled a "ghost of Michael" even while Michael still lived. Phenomena such as this, of course, put the lie to the idea that a ghost might appear the moment a certain person dies. It is rather, I propose, that a surviving person might naturally at that time begin to actively look for what might be termed a ghost in an effort to stay connected with the lost person. Of course the continuum of consciousness was there already and always has been and will continue forever, but it can also be convenient to let people feel they are somehow in conversation with the so-called departed. In my role, I am charged with preparing the way, managing the transition, cleaning up loose ends. It is perhaps similar to what the humans hire a wedding planner to undertake. Except that wedding planners can gain wisdom through experience, and on the other hand each human death is a once-in-a-lifetime—so to speak—event. As soon as one learns how to do it, one is dead. One birth is bracketed by one death—no further elaboration after that closing parenthesis.

"BOONE, YOU'RE A STIFF!" Bret yelled. Down on the field, Aaron Boone tossed his bat and helmet down and stomped to the dugout while the occupants of all three bases trotted in with resignation to get their gloves.

Next to Bret, Dave Jameson shook his head. "One big hit in one big game for the Yankees and the Indians think he's God's gift to baseball." Christine and the intern Leslie sat further down, talking to each other and ignoring the game completely.

"What we need is another total effing sociopath like Albert Belle," Bret replied. "It's not enough to respect the hitter. He's gotta scare the crap out of you. Because he's completely whacked. Beer?"

"My round," Jameson said, standing up. "Want a good one or pisswater?"

"Pisswater," Bret said, "but it's on me. Not the piss, the beer—you know what I mean. Ladies," he leaned over. "Buy you a beer?" Bret was pretty sure that department expense accounts had been invented to made it easy for managers to come across as generous; the paltry raises could be blamed on some distant computer rigged in corporate favor.

"No, I'm good," Christine said. The intern shook her head, too.

In the tunnel out to the concourse, Bret ran into the rest of his staff coming in—Val and Vicki from group sales and Rich and Julie from the ticket office. "Hey guys," he called as they passed, "we're about halfway up on the left side. You'll see Dave and Christine up there with the intern. Want anything?" He could see that they were all carrying food and drinks already, and they all shook their heads, but it looked good to ask.

"Four Bud Lights and a carrier," Bret asked the server, who glanced up at a TV monitor as the crowd could be heard groaning.

"There's always next year," said the server.

"Giving up already?" Bret said as he stepped away. "It's only the first week of May."

"You got it," the guy replied. "Next!"

He carried the four beers back up to the seats and handed one to Christine and one to the intern, who protested mildly but then accepted. He sat next to Jameson. "So what went wrong?"

"The usual," Jameson replied.

"They just suck?"

Jameson nodded.

THE NEXT WEEK, as he turned the car into the lot behind the nursing home, Bret thought he saw something moving quickly behind the trees to his left, but when he got out of the car and peered over there, nothing. Probably just a reflection on the window.

In fact, I was trying out a new apparition style, myself on a silvery gray steed. Knowing the earthly hours were numbered, I had set about practicing. Many people do not entirely understand the relationship between the corporeal self and the extracorporeal. How could it be, such a person might ask, that a ghost of a person could appear when that person is still alive? Such a question betrays a fundamental misunderstanding.

"Hey Uncle Michael," Bret said when he got to the room. Bret scratched his cheek. He'd taken off Thursday and Friday and the four-day beard was beginning to itch a lot. "You got any deer or big animals running around the woods out here?"

"Deer? Dear." He patted Bret on the forearm and grinned his toothless grin. "You know you can count 'em to go to sleep."

"Don't most people count sheep?"

"You'll see no sheep here. Now back in Castle Cove, I tell you, we had sheep. Never know where one turns up." He turned and propped himself up to look out the window. "Look out there, my boy," he said after a long pause.

"What?"

"No sheep."

Bret scanned the landscape. Uncle Michael was right. A sheepless vista, the shadow of a cloud approaching across the lawn.

My presence here obviously does not mean necessarily that the corporeal body with which calls a taibhse to action has died. It does, however, generally mean that death is nearby.

"But back in Castle Cove," he said, "that was a different story."

"Oh?"

"It was the same story, just a long time ago," said the old man.

I was particularly proud of the next effect, wherein I was able to get Bret's attention with a slight flicker, and then to deftly step aside as he mistook his own reflection for a ghostly apparition. These are the kinds of moments I live for. For which I live. If I am in any real sense alive, that is.

"Mmm." Bret was only half listening because he was distracted by what he was sure had been the face of a man peering through the window, a face crowned with disheveled salt-and pepper hair and encircled by short patchy whiskers. And black eyes. He felt a little twitch in his belly. But after a fraction of a second, the window frame was vacant again. Maybe it was just the shadow of a cloud. A tree outside the window was shaking in the breeze, casting its flickering shade over the glass. A jet was rumbling past somewhere out there. Time to hurry up before the traffic got too bad. "Hey, I can't stay too long today, Uncle Michael. Big goings-on at work this week and I have to get some stuff ready. Lancelot's Return doesn't seem to be catching on like we thought and they want to reevaluate the marketing strategy."

"He'll come back," said Uncle Michael. "He can't help to do it. In his blood, in his bones. The sea and the seals and the stones and the love he left behind."

"Whatever. Besides, he's French."

"All the same. He'll be back."

"It's kind of tough, because on the one hand, he's coming back because of Guinevere, but if you base the whole thing on that, what does it say to the females—we want them to ride, too. So we came up with this nuanced messaging where he's coming back for Arthur out of loyalty and for Guinevere out of love, but he can't bear it when he's back so he has to leave again. And come back again. So the TV promo spots—have you seen them? They were in heavy rotation about 6 weeks ago on the History Channel and Fox—the TV spots do this flash-cut thing where you see Lance galloping out through the castle gate into the mist, then it cuts to the car rolling out of the station. Then he climbs a high mountain pass, and of course the car crests the hill and starts down. Then halfway through the spot, he starts getting thought bubbles of Arthur and Guinevere and stops riding. Meanwhile the car gets to the top of the turnaround hill, then starts rolling backwards. Then he's galloping through the wind and rain and blazing sun until he's back inside the gates of Camelot. Then you see the exhilarated riders climbing out of the car so the next batch can get in. Friggin brilliant. But I don't know, I think what with the economy in the tank and maybe some negative feelings about the French on account of the war, it just hasn't started to buzz yet."

"We all have to go back," said Uncle Michael.

"Or maybe the problem is I never really believed it myself, you know? I always say you have to fool yourself first, but I never quite was able to get it out of my mind that you're going backwards halfway through, and what does that say about Lancelot? See what I mean? Look, I gotta go. I promise next week I'll stay longer."

Uncle Michael lay back down on the bed and cleared his throat.

As he hurried down the back hall, Bret heard the sound of someone following, faintly squeaking and clanging, but when he glanced over his shoulder as he turned into the foyer to leave the building, no one was there. Bed pans and nurse shoes? It was an odd sensation, of someone almost there. He observed himself as if from above: a man stopped in a hallway, glancing back at something that wasn't there. The man looked like he had something weighing on his mind. Was it that obvious?

Obvious to whom? One might ask. Nothing appeared out of the ordinary to me. But then I have my own preoccupations.

LESLIE'S NOTE HAD SAID she'd stay in touch, but Bret suspected otherwise. Things just weren't going that way. In fact, there seemed to be a definite momentum in the opposite direction—that is, away from good.

He didn't have a good feeling about this meeting, either, but what could he do? His eyes met Sylvia Scharff's as their corridors merged and they headed for the conference room. She fixed his gaze and nodded. He looked down. He'd forgotten to put on his polished cordovan power shoes.

Knowing that Jameson and Christine would have conferred by now and planned a joint strategy, he had sent them both off on short notice to a hospitality conference in Atlanta. With them out of the way, he might pull it off.

He went through the routine as he'd planned, but the faces weren't receptive this time. This was what happened sometimes when facts started intruding. People lost their patience and their willingness to believe. And once they'd lost their willingness to believe and to persevere in the face of adversity, the likelihood of his persuading them of anything dropped through the floor. Outside, he could hear a tuba at it again, but it was plodding awkwardly through the notes. Must be another new kid. As if in sympathy, he felt his own confidence wavering. What would Bret do? He turned up the drama. It was go for broke time.

"Did Lancelot quit at his first obstacle? No!" he boomed across the table. "He didn't quit at his tenth obstacle! Did Guinevere give up hope just because society wasn't ready to accept her love? No." He knew that was pushing it a bit, since she was the king's wife and all, so he didn't dwell on it. "Sir Gawain! He forged gallantly ahead! These are not times for doubt and second-guessing, but for resolve and unity. It must be all for one and one for all!" He held the pose for a second too long. Thunk.

"Would you come with me for a moment, Bret?" Sylvia Scharff led him down the hall after the meeting and closed her office door behind them.

Some things are difficult to explain. A ghost is in a way a version of the extracorporeal living person but not quite the same as the extracorporeal person. This is because the person is affected by living in the world in ways that the ghost is not. Thus, the ghost has the benefit of greater objectivity. A good analogy might be that it is as if I have observed parts of Michael's life on television or in a movie, without having lived it myself in the same way that Michael's extracorporeal self has lived it. It's not surprising that I might have tuned out for parts of it and missed a few bits. Indeed, as I reflect, it seems I know more about Bret than about Michael. Such are the mysteries of my station. A ghost image is not the image itself, but the ghost of it. A ghost's job, as I understand it, is to manifest the story of life beyond any corporeal form, and yet because this expression is completely intangible, there is never certainty about . . . about whether the extracorporeal form exists, let alone why. I confess, it confuses me. And the manual is not much help. If I could even find it.

"I GOT HERE EARLY to make up for last week," Bret said as he made sure the big metal door eased shut. He looked across the room and noticed Uncle Michael was fuzzy. Damn, he'd forgotten his glasses in the car. "And I can stay a while. Nothing to prepare for next week."

"Fine day, it is. Three in a row." Uncle Michael never quite shook some of his County Kerry inflections, so "three" came out as "tree" with a soft trilling of the "r." This was one of the things Bret remembered from early childhood: the sound of Uncle Michael pronouncing the number three. Later, in their school years, the cousins came up with the notion of purposely asking Uncle Michael to solve simple math problems whose answers included the number three, just to hear that sound. The old man, who had been propped up looking out the window, turned back toward Bret. "Won't be long, now."

"What won't?"

"Time to go home." Uncle Michael motioned out the window with his thumb.

"But I just got here." Bret pulled a chair aside the bed.

"Back to the land of my blood and bones."

"You're not going anywhere, Uncle Michael. They'll take care of you here for life."

"True, that is."

They sat silent for a few minutes, watching two school-age kids taking turns throwing a stick for a big collie on the large open lawn to the east of the building. Probably their parents were visiting someone here and the kids were just killing time. It reminded Bret, for some reason, of a time maybe twenty-five or thirty years ago when he had been forced by his parents to go on a day-long fishing excursion with Uncle Michael. A few snippets remained vivid: the aluminum rowboat carving a silent curve in still water before nudging into the long grass with a crackly whisper; Uncle Michael saying that the reason he always looked over his shoulder every few minutes was to check the sky for approaching weather; not getting a single fish-nibble all day.

Young Bret had started that day grumbling, sour to the whole idea. Uncle Michael either didn't notice or didn't let on. He was a lot sharper back then, so probably the latter. After the second hour of sitting on the thwart while his uncle rowed from spot to spot, waiting ten minutes with the lines in the water, then setting off again, he gave up on staying angry and decided to revel in the boredom. He lay down in the bow and stared up at the windless hazy blue sky. Michael let the boat drift out into the middle of the meandering lake.

"When I was a lad," Uncle Michael had said after a long silence, "there was nothing I loved more than to row out along the Kenmare shore toward the sea. Mind you, it was dangerous. Wouldn't take more than but one wrong wave to lift you up and smash you down on the rocks—for that shore was not gentle like this one, but nearly every bit of it jagged stone. Pretty as paradise, but deadly too.

"One day, though, the seas were like this. Flat like you'd struck it down with the back of a skillet. The sky like this too, so full of damp and heat that you couldn't tell if it was blue or grey. And not a breath of air. I made my way, with the aid of the current, all the way to Lamb's Head. I fancied a peek at the Skellig Rocks, you see, and one could see them only once past the headlands. Well, see them I did, their sharp edges sticking out of the sea against a mass of the darkest storm clouds, lightning flashing about the peaks.

"I turned about and began to stroke for home with all my breath, but I knew it wasn't much use. The current was against me still, and though I knew how to dodge it by sheltering behind rocks and islands, that would not be the proper place to find myself once the heavy seas arrived. So I pulled and pulled, but kept an eye behind so that I could aim myself out into the open water just before the storm arrived. I suppose I might have just made for shore straight away and waited for it to pass, but I would have been missed at home and, truth be known, I wasn't supposed to have taken the boat out in the first place. So, while I didn't want to perish in the storm, I also didn't want to get into trouble. And don't forget those were unfamiliar shores. How was I to know if I could find a safe harbor? So I clung alongside the rocks as long as I dared, until I felt the wind shift and the air turn cooler. Now the breeze was behind me and could help to push me home. I turned away from the shore. I noticed a seal heave itself into the sea from a rock to my left, apparently with the same idea of getting to open water.

"But then the storm came on with such sudden violence that it was all I could do to keep upright in the crashing seas. The sheets of rain robbed me of any sense of where I was going, except that I felt confident in continuing with the wind behind me, though that was more treacherous going in a small boat. I looked over me shoulder every few seconds to see what was ahead. One time when I did that my stomach fell almost out of me, for a great disastrous rock loomed black in my path. There was no way to go round. A second later, it was gone, washed clean over, then there it was again, much closer than before, the foamy streams of white water pouring off it. I realized in that moment that the only hope for my survival was to get on top of the next wave that overwashed the rock and pray that there was not another rock just beyond. And I realized that this most important wave was cresting under me right now—if I didn't catch it, I was a few seconds from dead. I heaved at the oars with every muscle in my back and arms, strained my shoulders till I could feel them beginning to tear, and braced my feet against the thwarts and gunwales in order to get my legs into it was well. Two four six eight ten twelve fourteen sixteen!—I burned off as many strokes as I could as fast as I could and the little boat suddenly surged and knocked me off my balance. I fell in the bottom just as I felt the shallow keel thump against something, then the water crashed over me. I knew I had to get up and retake the boat or else we'd swamp or be overturned and I could feel that we were already turning sideways to the seas. I jumped up and pumped the oars in opposition and praise the Lord she responded. I had two or three more looks back at that black rock, ever smaller as the wind pushed me inland away from it.

"Then the storm was over as quick as it came up, except for the breeze, which helped me home that day and dried my clothes so that when I walked in for tea, no one was the wiser. Took me a few weeks before my arms recovered. Could barely lift a spoon."

Bret had always liked that story. By the end of the old man's life, he had heard the tale in one version or another at least twenty times, always ending with "could barely lift a spoon," but that day becalmed in the rowboat had been the first. He'd replayed it so many times in his head that he could almost swear that it had been himself who had been in the little boat and not Uncle Michael. He could even feel the ache in his shoulders. To this day, he never trusted still water to stay that way.

The old man's breaths rose evenly in his chest. Did he even remember that story himself now? Did it matter? Others would pass it on. Change a few details.

Bret broke the spell. "Well, I got fired."

"That so?"

"Time to go in a new direction, quote-unquote."

"To the land of my blood and bones. Blood and bones, water and stone."

"What? No, the company wants to go in a new—never mind. I tell you what's getting me. Not that I lost a job. That happens to everybody. No, it's that all the people there who acted like they were my friends, they just melted away. Like it was all some kind of hologram that just ceased to exist once the light was turned off. We were just all at the ballgame, what, two weeks ago? Had a great time. I was buying beers for everybody. Now where are they?"

"Nice to see you today," said Uncle Michael.

"Hmmm?"

"Fine day for it." His voice was almost all breath. Something was different. Michael had slipped again. Every once in a while, Bret would show up and the old man was a little more gone.

"Yeah," Bret said. He looked around the room. "People just don't bother to look below the surface sometimes—I think that's the problem."

The old man grabbed his hand and squeezed it with surprising vigor. "You'll help me, will ya not?" The blear evaporated from his eyes for a moment. "Help me get back."

"Back where?" he asked.

"Home. Back home."

"You can't go anywhere, Uncle Michael. You know that."

"Soon, it will be." He motioned vaguely with his hand. "My blood and bones," he coughed.

"You really think I could take you back there? It wouldn't be easy."

The old man nodded three times.

"Okay," he paused. How he might transport a bedridden invalid across the Atlantic was a detail that remained to be worked out, but people had arranged similar voyages, he felt sure. More to the point, whether or not he actually took the old man back to Ireland didn't matter. What Uncle Michael wanted to hear was a promise, and Bret knew all about giving the audience what it wanted. "Okay, I will. I promise."

"Tank you, tree times tank you." He smiled and leaned back. "One more time I'll say it for you: tank you. That's tree." The old man either coughed or chuckled.

"You know, I wish we could take a trip now," Bret said. Uncle Michael closed his eyes and smiled. Bret continued, "I've got a decent severance package and some outplacement counseling if I want it. Thought I might take a break first, before jumping right into the job hunt. With Leslie out of my life and no kids or anything, there's not too much holding me back, I guess. Might be good to get away, get a little perspective. Recharge the batteries. Prepare for new conquests." Bret shivered as the words came out. He never took vacations to unfamiliar places. And anyway, the likelihood of traveling anywhere with Uncle Michael was zero, so no harm in building up a little scenario to give the old man something to dream about.

Uncle Michael gripped the rails at the bedside and shakily pulled himself up a few inches. "After tree fine days, it's time to go. But 'tis a rare thing, tree fine days."

"How many days?" he asked.

"Tree fine days." His voice was soft as a breeze.

Bret smiled at the trilling sound and at the hunch that Uncle Michael had been aware of its effect and happy to oblige all these years. And he smiled because he realized it had indeed been three fine days in a row, glorious sunny spring days, half cool half warm, bursting with bird songs and flower smells. It had been at least 18 months since the old man had even been out of bed. "How do you get there?" he asked.

Uncle Michael grinned and motioned over his shoulder with his thumb, then he lay back down. A few sparse white chin whiskers trembled a little as he exhaled through his nose.

THREE
FINE
DAYS

When Uncle Michael had motioned out the window, Bret glanced up that way and noticed a figure at the far end of the open lawn, deliberately walking toward the building. In itself, this was not unusual. People walked toward buildings all the time. But there was something peculiar about the profile of this person: what looked a long weapon in his left hand, the blade flashing in the sun. A gardener with a rake or something.

In fact, Bret was used to seeing this kind of thing, too, at work. The park was crawling with local teenagers dressed up in ersatz medieval battle garb, most of them selling cheese fries or mopping the bathrooms. Maybe that was it! Perhaps the company had reconsidered and had sent some kid out here to let Bret know he was invited back to the Round Table. Maybe this past weekend had been a record-breaker. Maybe all the advance marketing for Lancelot's Return had suddenly paid its dividend! Maybe he could tear up that resume he should have just revised, but hadn't yet.

But no, the blade didn't seem quite right. The way it glinted didn't look like molded plastic. Then he noticed an animal standing next to the big sycamore at the far corner of the clearing. Was that a horse? Or just a deer? No horses at the park. Too messy. He imagined a jousting tournament taking place on the wide green. It would be perfect: thundering hooves, violent clashes, blood and mud. Two riders would collide and fall with a great clatter. Then one of them would get up to search for his next adversary, and he would start walking toward Bret, and he could see a steel breastplate over tan sleeves and dark brown trousers, and a bloody hand clutching a broken halberd. Bret would be armored too. Back at the park, everybody wore fake metal armor, which was actually made of lightweight ABS plastic by a company that manufactured replacement hubcaps. That was another of Bret's ideas. The Chinese factories didn't care what they were making—just give them the specs and the shipping details and a percentage up front and order a sufficiently massive quantity and you could very cheaply outfit a whole amusement park in matching fake armor. Ten thousand sets of half-armor (you'd never get the rigid legs to fit right, so half armor over tights was a sensible compromise) for $77,500, which worked out to less than $9 unit cost, even after R&D and design fees and shipping and defects and a plane trip to China. Waterproof, too. And they did a brisk business selling the extras to the public for $74.95 with a pair of red or blue tights. He could remember the exact moment of inspiration: one day he ran over a piece of scrap metal near the railroad tracks while taking the back way into the park, got the jack out to change the flat, and realized that the hubcaps were made of plastic, not the heat-treated matte finished aluminum alloy he had always assumed them to be. So when he got into the parking lot a little later, he did a quick inspection of a few other vehicles. Some had real alloy wheels and no hubcaps at all, but he found quite a few upscale cars—a Lincoln, an Audi, and two Lexi in just the first row—with plastic hubcaps that looked very convincingly metallic from just a few feet away.

Boom! he thought. Armor. We could get a hubcap factory to mass-produce us cheap plastic armor. And it worked. But did the company remember things like that now? No.

About a dozen feet outside the window, the walker stopped walking and paused. Yeah, a gardener, probably. But still something odd. Maybe he saw Bret looking out the window. At times like this, a person would anticipate feeling a sudden chill or tingling up the neck or something, but he experienced only puzzlement. The man stood outside the window—it was hard to know how long, a few moments—until, abruptly and arbitrarily, he shrugged his shoulders and trudged off to the left and out of sight.

Honestly, I do not know what that was. Sometimes you introduce a little apparition here and there, and then people start seeing things all on their own. There may be a reason for it, I do not know.

It was at this point that Bret fixed upon Uncle Michael's blue eyes: half-closed, gazing at nothing, lashes still. Bret leaned down and held the back of his hand where the breath had recently been, then touched the forehead—still warm. But the old man was gone.

"DON'T WORRY YOURSELF, SIR," the assistant manager said when he called the office. "Happens all the time. It's the only way out of here, ya know." The statement was true, Bret knew, but even to a jaded performer like himself, it seemed a bit callous. The massive Mrs. Griddle appeared a few minutes later with a nurse and a wiry little fellow in a striped blue and gray jumpsuit. She had on the same kind of tent-like floral garment she had invariably worn whenever he had seen her, this one a riot of yellows and greens. The nurse confirmed his analysis: Uncle Michael had stopped breathing some time ago, and there didn't seem to be anything going on in the way of vital functions. His limbs were beginning to stiffen. Bret wondered fleetingly who the manager was, or if there was only the assistant manager, Mrs. Griddle. He'd never seen anyone else who seemed to be in charge of anything. Then again, he usually came on Sundays.

The wiry little guy wrestled Uncle Michael out of the bed and onto a stretcher, then pulled the sheet up over the old man's grinning face. "My condolences, chief," he said as he wheeled out the door past Bret. Mrs. Griddle stayed a few minutes so she and Bret could work out the arrangements for the funeral home and, more pressingly, for getting Uncle Michael's few remaining possessions out of the room. There was always a waiting list to get into the wing where they had the full nursing care. He squinted to read the forms she asked him to sign. Michael was an old man whose time had long since come and gone, but Bret felt shocked by the sudden absence. Leslie's departure, in contrast, had affected him more like the combination of vague sadness and relief that comes with the end of a mediocre romance novel.

BRET CAME BACK LATER that afternoon and cleared out the room. Aside from a dresser and an upholstered chair, there was nothing but a cardboard box on the bed, into which the staff had packed various loose items, and a stack of boxes that had been in the closet as long as he could remember— probably since the day Uncle Michael had moved in here half a decade ago. Bret replayed in his mind those last days, trying to sort out the truth from the nonsense. All he could hear in his memory was his own voice talking. The time he spent with Uncle Michael, what was it really? He had spent virtually every minute talking about himself. And now the old man was dead. At least, he confirmed to himself as he replayed it in his mind, he had not been actually talking out loud at the moment Uncle Michael took his last breath. But still . . .

He lifted the last of five boxes into the back seat (because that last one wouldn't fit in the trunk) and went back inside to leave the donation form with the front desk. Neither he nor anyone else really needed that ratty easy chair, nor the chest of drawers, so he signed them over for charitable donation. The Salvation Army would be by to pick them up in the morning.

He steered the silver-blue Taurus slowly down the long winding drive toward the main road. Ahead, he heard the sound of a car horn. A few seconds later, a black Mercedes coupe crested a rise and sped past in the opposite direction.

Just a normal deer coming up.

And a second after that, he slammed on the brakes and swerved to avoid a large deer leaping onto the drive. Its hooves skittered out from under it and its rear legs splayed, but then it regained its composure and bounded off into the forest. It looked terrified, like it was trying to escape something. Bret peered off to the left into the woods. Trees, leaves, glints of sunlight. Running away from nothing.

In the rearview mirror, he watched the black Mercedes disappear around the bend. He sat still for a little while, engine idling. There was no way to spin this. Even though he had been with Uncle Michael in body, his mind had been elsewhere, occupied with nothing but Bret, Bret, Bret, Bret, Bret, and more Bret. It was as if the old man had died alone. Fine day, indeed.

MEMORABILIA

When, after the corporeal decease, the ghost assumes a more free-floating, self-determinative aspect, there is a lot of work to do to get things in order. One can never be quite prepared for this, though one knows it is coming. It may be like giving birth to a child in that way. Indeed, perhaps the manual can be seen in some ways as akin to a misplaced book like "What to Expect When You're Expecting," aimed at first-time mothers, because just as each first birth is the only time that mother has had that experience, each death is also a first-time experience. Although in this case, the title might more appropriately be "What to Expect When You're Dead." No ghost is an expert at this process for having done it before because no one dies more than once—so the manual is really the only guide one has. Provided one could find it. Though even then one might wonder who devised the manual. Myself, I was quite startled by this sudden sense of "unmoored-ness," and I resolved to more firmly attach myself to someone or something to prevent myself from drifting completely out of the picture.

Bret stacked the five boxes along the kitchen end of the sun-washed living room where Leslie's piano had been. The rectangular unfaded place on the wall was a startling indication of how long she had been here. The relationship hadn't seemed that implausible. But the way she'd said "It just isn't working" on the phone that night when she finally called him was exactly the same way a creative writing teacher might say "It just isn't working" to a student, as if the story of Bret and Leslie had been doomed from the start by plot defects and sloppy character development.

He walked into the kitchen, poured himself a glass of cheap Mosel, and cleared a small space at the edge of the table so he could eat the gyro he'd picked up on the way home.

He looked over at Oprah the parakeet, who had been watching the whole exchange. "There now," he said.

"Would you shut the fuck up?" said Oprah.

"Same to you asshole," he shot back.

"Same to you asshole."

He unwrapped the foil and began to work out a strategy for eating the gyro, at which time he perceived that he had two beverages, the Mosel he had poured himself as well as the Dr. Pepper that had come with the gyro. He decided that wine would count as part of dinner and the Dr. Pepper would be dessert. He downed the entire glass of wine. Or maybe that was the appetizer.

"Would you shut the fuck up?" said Oprah.

"I didn't say anything," he replied.

"Same to you asshole."

He put the sheet over Oprah's cage. When was Leslie going to come by and pick up the damn bird, anyway?

He began sorting. Most of the files on the table were manila folders containing documents related to the constant succession of marketing projects he'd undertaken during his six years with King Arthur's Kamelot. A few days before that last fateful meeting, he'd had to arrange with Nikki, the maintenance chief, to leave the back gate unlocked so he could come by the service entrance after closing time to pick up the three plain cardboard boxes in which he'd stashed the files. The reason he gave was that an important client wanted an after-hours tour, which Nikki accepted with a wink and a nod, but he knew that if he'd given the real reason it probably wouldn't have worked. Of course, he could have just walked through the little door that was behind the old depot—that was always open—but it was more fun to involve some accomplices in the crime. He wasn't even sure why he wanted these old things. It wasn't as if any of it had any inherent substance or value. It was just one line of bull after another. Yet, that was his career. What else was there to show for it? Finest vintage bullshit.

So he began pulling out the key items from the key files and eventually had compiled a pretty good documentation of his presence at King Arthur's Kamelot in the three boxes. Memos, proposals, sketches, contracts, newspaper clippings. Of course, in the office file cabinets he'd left all the labeled file folders that still contained all the remaining materials, so that it would look like nothing was missing. He amused himself by imagining his successor looking through those papers and trying to figure out what had gone on based on insignificant peripheral documents that implied the existence of the meaningful documents that were not there any longer. One Monday morning about a week before he got fired, he had stacked the three boxes out next to the back dumpsters so he could come pick them up that evening.

It wasn't exactly a surprise, in other words, when he lost the job. He had never left a job in this way—he'd always departed on his own terms, moving up or at least sideways after he felt as if he'd stayed long enough. In each of his three jobs prior to Kamelot, that amount of time had been about four years. That was long enough to come in, wow the management for a while, gather a handful of feathers for the resumé, then move on just as the higher-ups were beginning to become skeptical. There was always a grace period with the higher-ups because their egos were invested in the apparent success of the people they hired. The lower-downs, without fail, figured it all out within a few weeks of his arrival, but they were powerless and so he came to enjoy their frustration, even feed off it. Pretty soon, though, they would either quit or resign themselves to the situation. The tension would abate and he would have to get his energy from somewhere else. But for some reason, he'd stayed longer at King Arthur's. Maybe the job was too cushy. Maybe he'd lost the hunger. Maybe he was just tired. For whatever reason, during the past year, his image among the senior staff had gone from golden boy to fall guy. That was just the flip side of claiming credit when things went well—taking the blame with things went wrong. But he knew it was more than that. It was that his act had worn thin with too many people, and beneath the act he had nothing. He'd known he was on the way out for a few weeks at least. That "something" was missing, a kind of conviction that was prerequisite in this line of work. Whatever it was, it seemed to him that he was losing it, and the evidence could be seen everywhere. People weren't riding the new attractions. Bret's ideas weren't rising to the top as they were supposed to. Girlfriends weren't sticking around.

It takes some premeditation to move a full upright piano out of a second-floor flat. You have to call the movers, and they have to work you into their schedule, and it's usually a couple weeks before they can get around to it. So Leslie had been planning to leave for a while. He'd been vaguely aware of that, too. And yet, though she'd had plenty of time to be organized, she still left behind an assortment of things: the back issues of *Ovation* she'd kept telling him she needed to keep, her purple rain jacket and an expensive floral silk suit in the front closet (the ones he said made her look like someone from a French movie of the 1960s), a drawer full of white pantyhose, things like that. Oddest of all was in the bathroom, where she'd left, neatly stacked on the little table beside the bathtub, a complete outfit: pair of black pumps, black bikini and matching bra, tartan skirt, blue linen blouse. The skirt and blouse, he was pretty sure, were what she had been wearing on their first official date after the press club dinner six years ago. The shoes he didn't remember, the underthings he certainly hadn't seen. These items, he felt sure, she had left on purpose. He concluded they were remnants of a surface she had fabricated for his benefit and now she didn't need them anymore. She was letting him know he'd been scammed. Touché.

She'd left the bird, too. Was Oprah also some kind of stage prop?

Maybe it was just that the effort of remaining compatible had become too tiring. Each of them had impressed the other with a calculated presentation, a strategy that was pretty effective from a medium distance, but very difficult to sustain up close. They were quite similar in that way, he reflected bitterly: two superficially talented but essentially insubstantial people who looked better from a distance.

No, she'd been pulling away for a while. Bret's charms weren't working on her anymore, either. Come to think of it, relationships with women seemed to last about four or five years, too, just like the jobs. Was this going to be the rest of his life? Four years and out, four years and out, four years and out? He worked it out quickly in his head. If he retired at 65, that would be another six or seven jobs. If he lived to 80, another nine or ten girlfriends. That could get old. It already was old. He poured another glass of wine.

This life was like an elaborate cardboard model that had been assembled with a glue that had gradually dried out and lost its adhesive power. He had come to the queasy realization that if the glue was bad, it meant that the whole contraption was in peril. What had seemed to be solid and reliable fixtures broke loose and tumbled away. Pretty soon the history he had built for himself would be little more than a pile of scraps suitable for nothing but the recycling bin. Then what would he do? Start over? With what? On what foundation? Was there any real Bret?

The pervasive black mood that had been welling up around his foundation for the past few weeks was almost up to the windowsills. Soon it would start spilling into the living area.

One of the most consequential and, I am realizing, terrifying decisions a ghost makes is around issues of attachment—which might mean being buried asleep (more or less) for eternity or burned up tomorrow—or to "haunt" a place a deceased used to live, or to follow some living person about, or to detach altogether and float freely. Each option has its perils and potentials. In my case, I had already promised to lead Bret on his journey, but I had been procrastinating and was still lingering in a cardboard box that had been in Michael's closet, where I had "lived" ever since Michael's death began to become imminent. A ghost will often have a home base during transitional periods rather than be wandering around aimlessly lest a critical event might be missed. For myself, the thought of being permanently detached from any person, place, or thing, exchanging connection for a certain kind of freedom . . . I cannot say that such freedom would constitute liberation. To what end?

MOST OF THE CONTENTS of the first box from Uncle Michael's room were well-worn woolen goods: some socks, a few sweaters, a walking hat, a pair of coarse-woven slacks with suspenders. Two tall rubber boots. Mothballs scattered throughout. Bret put the hat on and sifted through the second box which, like the first, had been stored in the bottom of the closet in Uncle Michael's room. This one contained documents and photographs. A duplication of a ship's log from 1928 (the USS Celtic) recording a passage from Liverpool to New York. Uncle Michael's 1963 US passport with stamps for Dublin airport, Cherbourg, France, and Cork, Ireland. A small stack of black-and-white photographs bound together with string. A document noting that Michael Sheehan was born 23 February,

1916 in Killarney, son Sean and Mary Sheehan of Castle Cove, County Kerry; a date at the top stating that the document was a copy, reissued in 1962. A church record showing a marriage of Sean and Mary Sheehan in 1916. Hmm, Bret noted—a little tight with the timing there. A family Bible from the late 1800s, wrapped in a yellowed and brittle christening dress. A couple of black-and-white portrait photographs in a hinged frame: a high cheeked, dark-haired woman gazing intensely on the left, and on the right a square-faced gent with light hair that he assumed was the same brassy red as his father's, because it looked like his hair did in black-and-white pictures. Bret had gotten the dark hair, though now it was peppered gray. He'd gotten his mother's locks, but not her slim build. He was put together thickly, about five feet-eight, like his father—even when he was at his skinniest, his face was square and fleshy. Maybe sturdy was a better word. He'd sprained one ankle a couple of times, but he'd never broken a bone.

He unbound the stack of photographs. Some looked familiar. Probably they had been hung up in that dark hallway on the second floor of the old house. A square one showing a little stone cottage set into a steep hillside, another square one from what seemed to be a curving stone parapet with hills behind. Some people having a picnic next to a rocky river, a stonework bridge above in the background (everyone formally dressed in dark suits and long dresses). A seal perched on a rock at the edge of a smooth sea. A boy and a long-haired dog posing outside the same small cottage. A group of eight or ten people seated around a long table in a dark room, many of their faces and arms blurred from motion. The dog and the boy in the foreground and what looked like some kind of old ruin in the background. Some people clustered around a park bench in a town square, an older couple, three men and one woman who looked to be in their twenties, and one woman holding an infant. With these black-and-white pictures, which seemed to have all been taken with the same camera, were two other photos of more broadly rectangular shape. In one, he instantly recognized the front steps of their grandmother's house in Massachusetts, with his father sitting on the top step, Uncle Michael (who was a dozen years older) standing on the bottom step, and the middle child Aunt Molly standing between them. In the other photograph, very small, it was impossible to tell the location because the background was little more than some out-of-focus foliage.

"Hmmm," he said aloud.

Nothing was familiar to me, though I had been inhabiting the same box with these things for such a long time.

He emptied the wine bottle, drained the glass, put on his jacket, and lurched outside into a light drizzle.

FOG

Dusk was nearly night.

Bret stepped briskly to try to clear his head: to the end of the street, across the boulevard, and onto the paved path that skirted the edge of the old city park. Slowly his eyes adjusted to the darkness, which was profound here under the tree canopy, though he could easily see the streetlights and glowing windows of the neighborhood off to the right.

The drizzle eased up, but in its place, a dense mist gathered. Soon, even though he was walking a path he had taken through this park probably fifty times at least, he somehow lost his way. The pavement disappeared beneath a puddle and never came back. Then he was walking on a hard gravel path, then mud and tree roots as the trail sloped first steeply down, then upward around the edge of a hill.

The path ended in a little-used stone stair, which he ascended with care because the accumulated leaves and twigs made the footing very slippery, and because the wine made him sluggish. At the top of the steps was a level section of path, moonlit now, that led alongside a couple of huge square boulders fifteen or twenty feet high, overhanging slightly so that they created a sheltered place where it appeared that campfires had been built and had blackened the rock. For Bret, there was something a little bit disconcerting about being alone out in the woods—it wasn't that someone or something might sneak up and attack him, or that he might get lost or hurt, or anything like that. It was that there wasn't any audience. You can't find out what motivates the rocks and trees and then use that to persuade them to your way of thinking. What they thought didn't matter. What he said didn't matter. Very scary.

The place was shaped like a natural theater. With his back near the rocks, he could imagine a small crowd seated before him, along the edge of the open space. What the hell, why not? "Welcome!" Bret called out. "Welcome to nothing!" He laughed and leaned back against the cold stone. He didn't see until he got home later that some dark soot must have rubbed off the rock onto his shoulder. "Tonight I present to you a story of a man—or at least what looks like a man—who has spent his life so wrapped up in presentation of himself that he no longer has any self at all. If he ever did. He's just a figment of his own imagination. When he stops imagining, or misses some little detail, or God knows just gets tired of keeping it up, everything starts to crumble. His job? Rubble. His lover? Poof! His so-called friends? Mere shadows. And it serves him right! He's full of shit. You must listen carefully now." He lowered his voice, speaking now to the front row. "Full. Of. Shit."

A thought had been whispering insistently through his mind, and now that thought was bellowing: What if his greatest strength was really his deepest flaw? He had relied on his gift of persuasion for so long and so completely that when the gift failed him, he was left with nothing. No one seemed to notice his lack of substance as long as he kept on the attack, took every opportunity to persuade someone of something, anything. But quite possibly, there was nothing else to him.

Was there any true, substantial achievement in his life? He scanned his memory for evidence. Only smoke and mirrors. Songs and dances. Baloney and Wonder Bread. Remember that one afternoon in high school? After he had completed a lengthy oral defense of his analysis of a book he had not read, the teacher, fully aware of what had just happened, said, "That, class, was what we call a tuba solo."

There are at least two responses to an incident like that, and one of them would be to be shamed into properly doing the research and taking a minimal amount of pride in the substance of the work. But he didn't respond that way. Instead, he became convinced that he was a gifted tuba soloist and that he simply needed to work on his technique until even a seasoned critic such as his 11th-grade English teacher Mr. Walbaum would be persuaded. That was more of a challenge than simply reading the material and regurgitating it. And he did get better at it. He prided himself on being able to spin nothing into something. He was a first-class bullshit artist. Only problem was, somewhere along the way, he had taken his eye off the truth for too long and now he wasn't quite sure what it was. Bret's beloved uncle had died four feet away from him and he had been so self-occupied he hadn't even noticed. How's that for comeuppance?

Worse, it didn't seem to matter. He often remembered reading the first paragraph of a book about the literary theory of deconstructionism back in college: there was no objective truth, only perception and cultural bias. He didn't bother reading any further, but that thought had always seemed the key to his own success as a marketer. He got an A on his final paper for that modern philosophy class, despite doing a small fraction of the required reading and skipping half the classes. Even earning his MBA had been one long tuba solo, he mused. To be fair to himself, though, he knew wouldn't be the first MBA to be an empty suit.

He stepped away from the wall and moved to the center of the open space. "Now why, you might ask, would such a man spend every Sunday afternoon sitting in a small room with a semi-incoherent uncle who doesn't even remember his name? Damn good question. Who's he fooling there? The uncle? No, the uncle is beyond foolery. Himself? That would seem in character, but it's not clear that it applies here. Some unseen audience? Some kind of shade of a man from another time and place? Or maybe the shadow man was just the grounds guy he'd seen outside the window, or somebody with a mop bucket clanking and sloshing down the hall."

He paced slowly along the edge of the patch of moonlight. "Consider the possibility," he intoned, "that such echoes, imagined or not, are connected to something real. The man has a sense that this is so, yet he cannot understand all the way. What is it? He throws his arms up in frustration." He threw his arms up.

"But back to the uncle. Does it really make sense that a man with nothing inside would devote such time to the old man? And if he did care about him, why wasn't he paying attention when the uncle died? Why has he experienced dull unease, but not sadness? At first there was a shock at the abrupt finality of the thing, yes, but true sadness has yet to set in. Why not? Have the years of acting parts completely disconnected him from any real feeling?" He stepped back into the shadow.

"But what is this? Is that a lump in the throat? Are his eyes blurring with saltwater? Could it be? Has he been wrong about himself?" He wiped the tears from his cheek and spoke louder. "Well, has he?"

"What the fuck you talking about, man?" Bret imagined the voice as coming with one of those rough characters who would be waiting for the city bus with a posse of thugs and a few tarted-up girls.

He didn't say anything at first, but then his head cleared enough to come up with a response. "Practicing. What does it look like?"

"Practicing what?" The owner of the voice stepped out of the darkness from up the hill, a bulky young black man holding a few beer cans by the plastic rings, followed by a young lady who half-hid behind him.

"My part," he said. "Drives people crazy when I practice at home, so I come down here."

"You are crazy, that's what," he said, and his companion giggled.

"No doubt," he laughed. "But I'm done anyway. I got to the end. The stage is yours." He wasn't sure if he had improvised that transition as impressively smoothly as it seemed to him at the time, or if he was just still fairly drunk and couldn't tell the difference, or both.

"Stage?" the young man laughed. "Muh-fuh bedroom. Right baby?"

The girl elbowed him and giggled. "You dream on, Marcus!"

"Well okay," Bret said. "I hope those are sweet dreams." And he started walking in the direction from which the two had emerged, figuring they must have come from someplace.

"Shit," Bret heard the boy draw out the word, and the girl's voice countered with a hissed "shut UP," then more giggling.

Beyond the boulders, another stone stair ascended into the woods. At the top, he emerged into a clearing. The lights of the city reflected dimly off the overcast sky. Suddenly, he was blinded. After three or four thumping heartbeats, he realized that the glare was thrown by the headlights of a car cresting a hill and coming in his direction, and that he was standing just outside the woods at the edge of a familiar field of grass across the street from the elementary school. He waited for his eyes to readjust to the darkness and scanned the edge of the woods. After a few minutes, he walked up to the street and headed back home.

LIGHT

Bret closed the front door behind him, turned on the hall light, and climbed the stairs. He cleared a small space on the kitchen table and walked over to the box holding Uncle Michael's pictures. He wanted to take a closer look at one particular photograph. The parakeet was clucking to itself under the sheet.

But the image of the bearded man wasn't in that box. Must have put it in one of the other boxes, he thought, and he unloaded the other two. Not there. "Well, hell," he mumbled.

Once again, he went through the contents of the boxes, more carefully this time, and once again, he could not find the picture. The overhead light suddenly seemed oppressive, glaring off the shiny wood floor and tearing through the backs of his eyeballs.

"Thirsty," he said aloud, clearing his throat. He stumbled over to the fridge to see if there was a beer stashed in the back. He stopped on the way to look over the stacks of files on the table to check if he'd left the missing picture there. It took a moment for him to register that one of the photos, of the family in the park, had landed in a small puddle of Dr. Pepper, and was now nearly soaked through. "Damn." He lifted the sheet to take it to the sink and rinse it off. "Damn."

"Later dude," said the parakeet.

"That doesn't make any sense," he retorted. Where the paper was wet, now he could see what looked like writing, bleeding through the back. He held it up to the light above the sink. Two words were written in a plain hand, printed in block letters. "Castle Cove," it read.

There must be some kind of sympathetic harmonization that happens because, just as my mind had become bleary as Bret had drunk the wine, now my attention was piqued by those two words. Castle and Cove. A ghost might imagine lingering about a castle near a cove, around a cove with a castle.

ARRANGEMENTS

It had been at least fifteen years since Bret had been in St. Michael's church, and another ten before that to get back to the days when he'd spent many hours a week here. Now he walked across the side parking lot that didn't actually look a whit different than it had back then. Ascending the six steps to the door that led to the parish offices, he realized that he scaled them in the same cadence he had always done as a young teenager. He opened the door and entered into the familiar smells—old wood, floor cleaner, coffee brewed a few hours ago. He wasn't sure whose office he was looking for, so he just walked toward the opposite end of the hall. Beyond that was the narthex where all the Sunday traffic jams occurred, and beyond that the large nave and a smaller chapel.

"Bret Sheehan," a voice called from a door as he passed. The tone was a mixture of cheerfulness and astonishment. He stopped and backtracked to the open door.

"Hello?" he called in. The tall, bearded man behind the desk had already risen and was walking toward him.

"I thought that was you. Saw you out the window. I guess I'm busted for daydreaming."

"Peacock?" he asked. "Donoson Peacock?"

"The same." The man held out a hand and firmly shook Bret's. "To what or whom do we owe the honor?"

"Ah," he paused, mentally catching Peacock up to the present from the day he'd last seen him, whenever that had been. "My Uncle Michael died. I was going to investigate the possibility of setting up some kind of service."

"Yes, we heard. May he rest in peace. He hadn't been in here for a good while, either. But of course this is still his church, oddly enough."

"Oddly enough?"

"If he was Protestant before he came to America, his family must have been just about the only ones in County Kerry. So maybe he switched from the Catholic side after he came over. On the other hand, he didn't even go to church. So why bother to switch if you're not going to church anyway? Still, we got his check every year, and he kept his membership going all this time."

"Really? Who sent the checks?"

"He did. Quite obviously. Couldn't read them to save our lives! But he'd done the same thing year-in, year-out—last year's pledge plus a hundred dollars—since the '60s, so we made educated guesses. His bank concurred."

"That amazes me," Bret said. "To talk to him, you wouldn't have thought he could remember anything like that."

"Well," Peacock tugged on his gray beard (which hadn't been gray the last time Bret had seen it), "people surprise you."

"Case in point," replied Bret, "I'm surprised a youth minister would be in the same place for thirty years."

"That would be surprising," said Peacock. "But two things: one, I'm no longer youth minister, but an associate rector; and two, I left for eight years and came back. With a Ph.D. on top of divinity school. I'm teaching college full-time and work part-time here."

"Hmm. Well, it's good to see you. As for me, I . . ." he searched for words.

"You drifted away," said Peacock. "Happens a lot. Sometimes people come back. Or they re-attach to another church someplace."

"Well, I don't know that I'm coming back, to be honest. It just seems right to do the service here."

"That's fine," said Peacock, without any hint of overtone that it wasn't fine. "Come sit down."

Bret and Donoson Peacock fully entered the room in whose doorway they had been standing and sat across the large oak desk from each other. Peacock pulled out a notebook and got a black planner off the bookshelf. "Okay . . . dates. Have a look at the calendar here. That has all the weddings and special services. Best times are weekdays during the afternoon—very little competition then. Weddings, as you'll see, tend to fill up the Saturdays, and Sunday you have to squeeze in between the late morning service and the early evening, if there's not a concert or something going on. I'd suggest you write down a few likely dates, then check them out with the family and see what will work best."

With time, I felt I gained better empathy not only for what Bret might be thinking, but for the people he knew well. This, I trusted, would allow me to more effectively enlist the cooperation of Mr. Peacock.

Bret nodded and began to look through the planner.

"Now," Peacock continued, "on to practical matters. The body has been cremated, I assume?"

"Yes."

"Good. No time pressure. Were you close?"

He thought for a minute, inconclusively, then looked up and met the man's eyes. "I don't know. I guess you would say so. We spent most Sunday afternoons together these past few years. I was nearby and didn't have any family commitments.

But the truth is I spent all of our time together talking about myself."

"Probably what he wanted to hear anyway," said Peacock. "Plus, time together is time together. No one else spent time with him?"

"Not much, no."

"Know why not?"

"Nope."

"You don't spend much time with the rest of the family either?"

"Correct," Bret said. "Don't know why that is."

"Because it's a family."

He laughed. Peacock's gift as a youth minister had been that he could always get on your side. That didn't always solve the problem at hand, whatever it might have been, but for a teenager, just knowing somebody was on your side could go a long way. Then Bret had grown older and his need for that kind of support had faded, or, more precisely, he had felt the need to make it fade. So he purposefully disconnected a bit. Then he went off to college and, as Peacock said, drifted away. Bret suddenly felt vulnerable—Peacock had known him before he became who he was, saw him turn into that.

"Look, you were there and no one else was," said Peacock. "That counts for a lot."

"I was there in body."

"You were there."

"The rest of the family didn't have the time I did. I'm sure they thought of him."

"You know what?" Peacock leaned forward. "Fuck them. You were actually in the room. Take some credit for that." Peacock tended to swear occasionally, Bret recalled. At first these had seemed like inadvertent indiscretions, but Bret had perceived over time that there was a certain pattern to the "accidental" slips: they tended to happen when Peacock wanted to come across like a regular salt-of-the-earth guy stating some obvious fact that any plain fool could see. This was especially effective with teenagers, for whom the dangerous language also held special appeal. Usually, Bret found himself agreeing.

"Okay, I do give myself credit for showing up, at least."

"But you feel that the time you spent with Uncle Michael somehow didn't count as much because you were soliloquizing all the time?"

He nodded. "Something like that. I feel like I let him down. Like if he'd been trying to say something to me, I would have missed it. Somebody's supposed to hear your famous last words."

"And you don't remember exactly what he said?"

He shook his head. "Not really. He was feeling homesick, I think. He asked me to take him back there, to the land of his blood and bones, as he called it. I promised I would, even though of course that would have been wildly impractical. But that's what he wanted to hear, so I said it. Then he died. So much for that."

"See, you were listening."

"I was just humoring him."

I deftly spun a little notion into Peacock's ear.

"You promised to take him back and you actually thought about the practicality. That's a little more than just humoring somebody. Especially since you could still do it."

"What?" Bret looked up and Peacock's eyes were sparkling.

"There are ashes, right?"

Bret nodded.

Peacock leaned forward. "So take him back."

BRET WAS USED TO SPEAKING in front of groups, but an audience of relatives at a family funeral seemed like it would be an especially tough crowd. You weren't trying to convince a bunch of middle managers to spend a little more money, but rather trying to come across as genuine regarding a person you all cared about. This could not be pulled out of thin air or spun up from a catchy phrase. But, since he was the only person who had spent much time with Uncle Michael during his last few years, he was the obvious candidate to stand up and share a few thoughts before the priest gave the official eulogy. The date that had worked for the family did not work for the Reverend Peacock, so the attending clergyman was a person Bret had not met before, and he had already forgotten the pleasant Reverend's name. Why he had been the only family member to visit was a question answered only partially by the fact of his relative geographic proximity. Others—his father (Michael's younger brother), for one, and Bret's older brother David, for another—lived within a couple of hours, but they mostly stayed away. Bret's mom liked Uncle Michael, but after the divorce she had moved to Montreal. Michael had never married or had children; Bret had sometimes heard whispered hypotheses as to why not. This topic, though obvious, did not seem suitable for a warm and fuzzy eulogy. Indeed, Uncle Michael was a fixture of the family yet also kept at something of a distance, with certain questions neither brought up nor answered: how and why exactly he had come from Ireland, how very young his mother must have been when Michael had been born—perhaps there was something vaguely scandalous back there that people deemed best left alone.

As the day approached, the task of preparing these remarks came to occupy all of his attention. It would be a symbolic endpoint, a closing statement after which things would not be the same. So the stakes were kind of high.

He decided that, rather than recounting the long career as a bookseller and occasional bartender at the James Joyce-themed local Irish pub, or trying to speak directly about the man and his qualities—the gentle humor, the melodious voice, the distracted demeanor, the sense that Uncle Michael was some kind of ambassador representing the values and interests of a mysterious and perhaps fictional faraway place—it would be best to be oblique. So he made up his mind to simply relate a small anecdote of their time together, and to let that stand for the man's character. That had the additional virtue of not presenting any life details that could be argued with or disagreed upon.

Bret walked up the aisle toward the altar. The dark gray suit felt tighter through the back than it had the last time he wore it. It wasn't the kind of suit he'd wear at work—too somber, too lawyerly—but for a funeral it was the only thing, and he hadn't even tried it on before this morning since there was no other choice anyway. Drawing on some distant memory of body language, he nodded at the cross before turning and approaching the podium from the side. He did not compose a written text, but rather had sketched a few notes on an index card and relied on his ability to improvise. That always sounded more engaging. He pulled the card out of his inner suit jacket pocket and placed it on the lectern, then looked up to scan the small crowd that had gathered in the chapel. The late morning sun angled in from the clear leaded windows to the left and the shadows of the tree branches and leaves trembled across the faces and shoulders. He looked down at the index card. Intro, recent, kids, tree, NBC.

"When I was a little boy . . ." he began, then halted. Forgot the intro. Nervous, he guessed. "Forgive me. My name is Bret Sheehan. Michael was my father's older brother." Bret nodded over to the left where his ruddy father was sitting beside his even ruddier brother David, a few rows back along the center aisle. "Uncle Michael and I spent a lot of Sunday afternoons together in the past few years, after he moved into the assisted living home. But even before that he was always around, for as far back as I can recall. Unlike my dad, who was born in Massachusetts, Uncle Michael emigrated to this country. When we were kids, we used to love to talk to him, just to hear his voice. It made him seem like some kind of fairy-tale character or something. I especially liked the way he pronounced words that began with 'T-H-R,' like 'throw' or 'through' or 'three.' He spoke these with a hard 't' followed by a slight rolling of the 'r.' I'm not quite sure where County Kerry is or if everyone from there speaks in this manner, but it was the way Uncle Michael spoke at any rate. We liked that sound so much that we would steer our conversations in order to hear it. It was sort of like the teacher we all probably had in school who could reliably be sidetracked from the lesson at hand by bringing up that one special topic, or—perhaps a better analogy—like asking Barbara Walters questions that would require that she pronounce the letter "r" in order that one might hear the "w" in its place. The easiest way to do this with Uncle Michael was to ask questions the answers to which I knew would contain, somewhere, the number 3.

"He would usually play along for a while— 'Hey Uncle Michael, what's the square root of nine? How many legs in a tripod? If two's company, what's a crowd?' Then the subject would begin to get tiresome. I would switch to 4 or 2, but they just weren't the same."

Mild chuckles.

"One afternoon I recall with particular fondness was a time when we were playing this little game, and I grew bored and asked 'What channel is ABC on?'

"'Tree,' said Uncle Michael.

"'No it's five. Three is NBC.'

"'Then you should ask me what channel is NBC.'" Some in the congregation laughed. Most at least smiled. Now what? That was it. End of anecdote. It wasn't enough. Bret glanced up. Clearly, the people expected more. What would Bret do? He saw himself leaning forward, hands clenched on either side of the lectern, frozen. All eyes in the church were on him. He liked that, usually, but this was a challenge.

He didn't panic, exactly. Indeed, something popped into his head immediately. It was just that he wasn't sure if he should go that way. But, there it was and nothing else was stepping forward. What would Bret do? Take the inspiration and go with it.

"Much more recently, during his final days, I came across something else that, I guess, was a sort of connection to his past. We were chatting and I looked up to glance out the window—some kind of movement had caught my eye."

He paused. This was the last chance to bail out. He looked around. Aunt Maureen's glassy black eyes gazed at him from the second row, peering around the massive shoulder of his young cousin Kevin, who was a high school linebacker, Bret had learned this morning.

"Outside that window I saw the strangest thing," he continued. "Or I think I did. I'd left my glasses in the car, after all." People chuckled again. A little comic relief never hurt. "I saw a man walking toward the window. I didn't think much of that, at first. But then I imagined that he was wearing some kind of chest plate armor and carrying a big weapon, and as he got closer—the window was kind of, you know, glare-y, so it was hard to see—but it seemed maybe he was dressed that way. That got my attention, so I tried to interrupt Uncle Michael, who had been talking on and on about I'm not quite sure what, but then I looked up and the guy was gone." He stopped. "No wait, I'm sorry. That's not right. When I looked back down, that was when I realized that Uncle Michael was, had—that he had stopped talking. He was still smiling, but he was gone. So just at the moment when I was looking out the window seeing this strange sight, that was when Uncle Michael passed away. Makes you wonder." Bret paused for a long time, looking out over the small gathering.

After Donoson Peacock had proposed the idea that Bret take Michael's ashes back to Ireland as a way of fulfilling his promise to his uncle, Bret had momentarily entertained the idea. But more practical concerns intervened. He really should get a job soon, despite his good severance package, so that his resume would not show a large gap. Careers could stall easily in his world. Not that he had much fondness left for this professional world at this point in his life, but a gap was a gap.

And besides, the likelihood of finding the "right" place for the ashes seemed so remote anyway.

So he had initiated the process to have Uncle Michael's ashes interred in the columbarium here at the church. Michael was gone anyway. He had died believing Bret would take him back, and that was all that mattered.

"I've arranged," Bret said at last, "to have the ashes interred here, in the church he supported for many years."

What?! I must not have been paying attention. No, no, no, that won't do. You must take the ashes back. It's my job to lead you there. What would Bret say next? I had to act quickly now. I had been taken off-guard because, contrary to what one might expect, you can't read minds—only hear what they say, just like anyone else. And you can't really talk to a living human in ways that will be taken as words. But you can reach them. So I conjured an image as vivid as I could of hills and a rocky cove and a salty breeze off the sea, and I cast it out and said 'Imagine, you are walking here, you know where to go, you are at peace, and I am leading you—this is what matters to you. Water and stone, blood and bones. This is what matters to the universe.'

Well, that sounds like a conclusion, Bret thought. There was that stumble in the middle, but it had ended well at least. He paused for a few seconds, then nodded his head and stepped away from the lectern. He didn't look at anybody as he went back to the fourth pew and sat down.

The priest stepped up and continued the service. As the concluding hymn began and everyone stood, Aunt Maureen slowly turned around and caught his eye. She winked and grinned. He stood and sang next to his father as one or both of them lost track of which verse of "Be Thou My Vision" they were on. When the hymn was done, his dad leaned over and said, "you and your mother, always good on stage," which kind of pissed Bret off but he just smiled and nodded and didn't say anything.

AFTER THE SERVICE, as everyone milled about in the parish hall, eating cookies and punch and catching up on recent news, Aunt Maureen pulled Bret off to the side. The Irish people he knew in his family came in two types: the ruddy-skinned and robust redheads and the dark wiry ones with black hair and black eyes and long black eyebrow hair. She was of the latter type. She wasn't a first aunt, but some form of more distant relation. In this family, as in many, vaguely related older relatives were just called uncle or aunt. "Blood and bones?" she whispered.

"What?" said Bret.

Bret's dad stepped up and nodded to Aunt Maureen. Bret's brother David appeared before the nod was finished, flanked by Aunt Molly.

"Water and stone, blood and bones," said Aunt Maureen, in full voice now.

Bret unsuccessfully scanned her face for a clue as to whether she was being serious or not. He quickly replayed in his mind what he'd said during his speech, and he was sure there had been no mention of blood and bones or water and stone.

"He talked about that in his last days," Bret said, "blood and bones, water and stone."

"Of course he did," she said. "And you and I, we both know what that means. It means them ashes will not be staying in this church, will they?"

Bret recognized immediately that he'd been maneuvered, the expected roles reversed, the persuader forced to act. He had a flash of anger at being outwitted. He locked on her eyes for a second or two, then released his breath with a careful smile. He shook his head slowly. "No, of course not" he said in a low voice, looking up at the others. "Just being gracious, you know, because the church had offered. But don't say anything to the rector. I don't know the man, not sure how he'd take it. But yes, I am returning Uncle Michael back to Ireland. Blood and bones to water and stone. In fact I already have my plane ticket. Our plane ticket." Now it sounded like this had been Bret's idea all along.

"May the road rise with you." Her black eyes flashed, then she took his hand, clasped her free palm on top for a moment, then released him and walked away.

I don't know where they come up with this poppycock about blood and bones, but if it makes them act responsibly, fine. I hope I am not over-explaining. Never mind me. Perhaps I like to hear my own voice.

A QUEST

It was never stated aloud, but Bret had sensed during his childhood that there was some shame in having an Irish name, as if their parents were afraid that embracing Irish heritage meant accepting some kind of label of inferiority. If his forebears had ever been Catholic, they weren't now and hadn't recently been. Some people changed their names: Sheehan became Sheen, O'Riordan became Reed. His mom wasn't even Irish, anyway. Her family was French. Celerier was her maiden name. The rest of the family, who knew where they came from? They were in America now. That was what people always said: Where you came from didn't matter anymore. The important thing was that your family had come to America to make a new start and that was just what you had done, made a new start. Who your family was before should not affect who your family would be in the future. Except for Uncle Michael. He had talked incessantly about Ireland. It was obvious that Uncle Michael really belonged back there in Castle Cove, wherever that was, rowing along the coast in a wooden dory talking to seals and sharing mystical secrets with the young people.

He scanned the Avis map. The old man's descriptions had been rich in eye-level detail, but extraordinarily vague in context or geography. All Bret knew—or thought he knew— was that it was in County Kerry, which he had recently discovered was in the southwest part of the country. A series of peninsulas angled out into the Atlantic toward the southwest. They were labeled on the map: Dingle, Iveragh, Beara. Inland, close to the foot of all three peninsulas, was the town of Killarney. That was where he'd pick up the rental car, after the train ride from Dublin. He'd made the plane reservations on the internet, immediately after getting home from Uncle Michael's memorial service. When given a choice between Shannon airport and Dublin, he chose Dublin on the basis of a rail schedule he had found in his research that indicated that a person would have to take a train to Dublin in order to get to Killarney if one flew into Shannon, and what was more, the plane stopped in Dublin before continuing on to Shannon anyway, so a person might as well get off in Dublin. Now that he looked more closely at the map, he saw that Shannon airport was in fact much closer to County Kerry, and he could have simply rented a car there and driven to Killarney. Or taken a bus. His best guess as to the location of the mythical Castle Cove was about three-quarters of the way out toward the end of the Iveragh peninsula, not far from a town called Sneem—where, happily, he had already reserved lodgings. There was a cove marked "cove" and a castle in it marked "castle."

He was also passingly curious to see Dublin: the legendary Book of Kells, a pint or two of the famous Guinness stout right from the brewery on the banks of the River Liffey. He'd found a guest house close to Heuston Station, from which all the trains to the southwest departed, and made a reservation online. The place was called Gate Lodge, and it was across from the entrance to the huge Phoenix Park at the western edge of Dublin. Phoenix seemed like a not-very-Irish name, nor a British one, so that made him curious, and the guest rooms looked suitably quaint in the pictures. Plus they served an authentic Irish breakfast. He wanted to find out firsthand what that was, an authentic Irish breakfast. Was there whiskey involved?

With this general plan, he could drop off his bags at the guest house, spend a day wandering around in Dublin, get a good night's sleep, then catch the train to Killarney. Once there, the quest would begin in earnest. He estimated he could afford to go for a month or so in Ireland without being particularly frugal. In that time, he'd be able to find some way to do something appropriate with Uncle Michael's ashes. Then, after this time-out, he could get on with life again. Hopefully not see any more strange faces in windows. And actually, as the events became more distant, he wasn't at all sure if he'd really seen anything in Uncle Michael's room. After all, he'd been under a lot of stress. But looking back at it, he rationalized the whole business—whether or not he'd imagined it—as a sign that he should embark on this quest. It wasn't a lady in a lake handing him a sword, but it would do.

Such doubts and suppositions are marks of a Taibhse on top of his game.

Bret mentally reviewed the itinerary. First fly to Toronto on a little turboprop. Then sit there in the terminal for five hours. Then fly overnight to Dublin, getting in at 7:20 a.m. and losing six hours on the way. The airlines were saying to get there three hours early for international flights, because of the stepped-up security after September 11. And because he had chosen to fly Air Canada, he actually had two international flights, each with a minimum three-hour lead time. Add to all that waiting around the two-hour bus ride to Cleveland (because he had no one to give him a ride and didn't want to pay for a month of parking at the airport), plus the walk

from Greyhound terminal to the rapid transit station, and the
train out to the airport, and it seemed he could ride a donkey
to Dublin and get there in about the same time. It all meant
getting up way too early tomorrow. He put the map on the
bedside table and shut out the light.

*I assumed that all of this meant he was ready to go. This was
my estimation. We believe we can sometimes influence thoughts
and mental images, but we can't see or hear any more than
you can. Indeed, as an extracorporeal entity, a ghost has no
eyes to hear, no ears to see, no tongue to feel—but of course these
are but data-gathering instruments for the corporeal body,
and the real seeing and hearing and feeling takes place in
the mind. A certain taste is not literally a taste, but a mental
image of a taste, an image to which a meaning is ascribed by
the mind. There's a lot of presumptuous mind-reading that
goes on. Misunderstandings can happen. What is more, the
further I have gotten from the moment of decease, the fuzzier
things have gotten in general. I cannot pay attention to so
many things at once. Speaking of the deceased, one naturally
might ponder, in such a situation, questions about the so-
called afterlife. To be clear, a ghost is not a soul or anything
like that. It is my interpretation that we are more like a clean-
up crew who stays behind to wrap certain things up. I cannot
answer whether there or not there is an afterlife. It will not
surprise you to learn that we are non-denominational. Our
business is independent of sectarian specificity. A dead Hindu
or Christian or Muslim or Atheist—they're all the same to
us, though a person of any faith (or none) may believe very
specific things about where they are headed now. I'm not here
to disabuse anyone of any such notions, only to say it is not my
business. I do know that the idea of a person, and elements of
a person's character as experienced by other people, do linger
after that person has died, among those still living. I conclude
that this is my business: the continued life of the dead among
the living. This is why we do things like persuade burned-out*

middle-aged marketing managers to take their uncle's ashes to Ireland. Or maybe he would have undertaken the quest anyway. This was a chance I could not take.

FLIGHT

Bret followed a rule about air travel: if the trip was a week or less, he would drive to the airport and leave the car in the long-term lot; longer than a week, he would get to the airport via bus and train, so as not to have to pay too much for parking. He looked out as they crossed a bridge over a deep river valley whose sheer walls were carved out of layers of flat, crumbly stone, he felt the edge of his carry-on bag to make sure the square tin of ashes was in there. He leaned his head back.

He caught himself from tipping over to his left as the bus rounded a sharp right turn. When his eyes focused, he realized they were in downtown Cleveland already. It was the height of rush hour. The bus made its way haltingly through the traffic and eventually pulled into the lot behind the old Art Deco style Greyhound station at 8:41 a.m., according to the big clock on the wall. He grabbed his two bags and stumbled through the aisle, down the steps, and into the muggy, noisy air. Perhaps one day the bus station had been a gracious and uplifting sight for weary travelers—its streamlined architecture suggested as much, at least. These days it wasn't a place you wanted to hang around much, unless you liked to bum cigarettes or creep out innocent bypassers. He hoisted his large bag out of the storage compartment and quickly began to walk to the west. He felt the morning sun hit the back of his neck as he stepped out of the shadow of the awning.

It would have been convenient if the bus station were immediately adjacent to a stop on Cleveland's rail transit system, but no. He walked the 10 minutes from the Greyhound station down to the Tower City rapid transit stop.

The 25-minute train ride to Hopkins airport offered passing glimpses of the industrial valley, the rows and rows of time-battered wood frame houses, the big brick 19th-century factory and warehouse buildings. Bret could tell they were nearing the airport as the tracks came up alongside the interstate and a procession of planes began catching and passing the train outside the right-hand windows, angling in low to land. He gathered his things and was standing at the double doors when the car squeaked to a stop and let the passengers off.

SINCE THE TERRORIST ATTACKS, the airport had begun but had not yet finished an awkward transition to a plan where most of the services were pushed outward into the concourses where no one but ticketed passengers could go. Now the central former food-court area was a huge staging space where outbound passengers stood in long, winding lines in order to be scanned and inspected and sometimes searched before going out to their gates.

Bret stood in line at the Air Canada counter so he could check his large blue duffel. There were very few customers in line. He found it amusing to identify from the other people's clothes who they were, where they were headed. Bret's own attire of khakis, subtle checked sport shirt, New Balance walking shoes, and lightweight jacket casually tossed over his shoulder, for example, said everything he wanted to say:

here was a confident, sensible traveler—someone not worth hassling and too savvy to be pickpocketed, yet friendly and approachable. The middle-aged guy just stepping up to the counter was utterly nondescript in khakis and a pale shirt—except for the Expos cap. Nobody wears an Expos cap in Cleveland unless they're headed to or coming from Montreal. The two college-age women just ahead of him were headed for some sort of hot-weather party place, as indicated by the crop tops and white capri pants, the unnatural suntans, and the loud discussion about who was in which cabana near whom during some recent sojourn. The older gentleman in front of them, who looked like he'd just stepped out of an Irish country pub, down to the tam o'shanter and the coarse tweed jacket, turned his ear toward the conversation and glanced behind him warily.

Bret chuckled to himself and took one last look in his carry-on to see if there was anything he'd better check with the other bag. Unless they were going to confiscate his fountain pen as a deadly weapon, he decided, the contents would pass inspection. He pulled his ticket out of his inside jacket pocket and looked it over to verify the times and flight numbers. The clerk called for the next customer and the line inched forward.

"Yes, I connect to Dublin in Toronto," he heard the tweedy gentleman say in the lilting way of an Irish native.

"Next please," called the man at the right end of the counter. The beach-bound girls, momentarily indecisive, approached the desk together. Definitely sisters, he decided, observing their distinctive knock-kneed shuffle. "Halifax," they said in unison.

"Will the next customer come to the desk, please?" Bret snapped to attention and lifted his things. Halifax? By way of Hilton Head.

"Toronto and Dublin," Bret said as he lifted the duffel onto the metal platform. It had occurred to him that there might be some rule against transporting cremated remains, but he had a plan: say nothing and make a dramatic emotional scene if the opportunity arose. The image of a man fighting the bureaucracy when all he wanted to do was to take his dear old uncle back to Ireland would play well. Meanwhile, the square metal container would either make it through or it wouldn't. Certainly they wouldn't just discard it. If it couldn't fly with him, perhaps he could ship it insured to the PO in Killarney or something. After he checked the bag, Bret went to stand in another line at the central security checkpoint. The obvious but carefully observed pointlessness of the roped stanchions zigging back and forth reminded him of the lines to the most popular rides at King Arthur's Kamelot, except there he was always allowed to sneak in at the front by unbuckling the rope and flashing his ID. Or had been. But the stanchion maze did have the unique feature that one kept encountering the same people over and over as the line advanced. So he got to smile and nod a few times at the Irish gentleman and, about ten customers behind, the two Canadians. Bret decided to charm them. "Where you headed?" he asked them. "Oh, back home to Nova Scotia," said the taller one. "We've spent two days at Cedar Point," said the other. "We're roller coaster fanatics. Guess how many coasters they've got there?"

Always Cedar Point and its hyped-up rollercoasters. "This year? Nine," Bret replied. "Quantity over quality. But numbers sell, don't they?" Cynically ridiculing the "rollercoaster arms race" was his usual strategy when faced with Cedar Point's dominance of the regional market, even though it amounted to insulting the visiting public. The woman shrugged and turned away. The two didn't seem charmed at all, which threw Bret off his game. Maybe because they were Canadian. The line advanced and the presumed sisters stepped up to the next conveyor. The Irish fellow had been eavesdropping and gave Bret a wink.

Bret checked his watch. Eighteen minutes had passed. The average wait for Gawain's Green Looper was 18 minutes. Just in front of him, a well-dressed businessman discovered that his Bostonian oxfords contained metal shanks. A businessman who doesn't fly much, Bret concluded. Bret kicked off his sneakers and placed them in a plastic tray. In another tray he put his jacket. And in another his wallet, change, and keys. And there was his Swiss army pocketknife, attached to the key chain.

Of course, they pulled him aside and explained the options. "Sir, it's not permitted to carry this weapon onto the aircraft. You have two choices: forfeit the knife or check it in another bag. You can check your carry-on if you like, and place the pocketknife in there." But his other bag was already checked, and he needed this one on the plane.

"Thanks, but I need the carry-on with me. Forfeit, I guess." Bret watched as the blue knife was tossed into a bin with a pile of others, its dull, inch-long blade, nail file, tiny scissors, and toothpick no longer hazards to the human race.

"Sorry about that, sir."

"Thanks for keeping us safe," Bret said. He put his shoes back on and started to head out toward concourse B.

"Mr. Sheehan?" The attendant called him. Uh-oh. Bret turned around. "Your passport, sir."

"Oh. Thank you." He walked back, took the passport, and slid it back into his inside jacket pocket.

THE PLANE WAS VERY NARROW, with just two seats per side. The roof curved so that tall persons might have trouble sitting near the window unless they hunched over. This was what the father of the two small children was doing now, leaning forward so he could look out the window and see—what?—the luggage cart, perhaps. Bret sat about two-thirds of the way back, a few rows in front of the two Canadian students, who had gone straight to the back. Everyone else sat as far forward as they could, presumably to beat the rush of all 15 people leaving the plane once they landed in Toronto. The Irish gentleman, however, sat across from Bret and began to make small talk about the tourist economy of Northern Ohio. At first Bret conversed absently, cynically poo-pooing the region as natives were prone to doing, but then he caught himself and made sure to note the many fine and little-known amenities of the area, and swore the other man to secrecy with a wink. "We like to keep it quiet, you know."

The rumble and clunk of the luggage compartment doors pulled Bret's attention back out the window. A cart had been wheeled alongside and Bret noticed with alarm that his duffel was not there among the handful of suitcases. A man tapped him on the shoulder. "Mr. Bret Sheehan?" The guy was about six-eight, with a blond crewcut. He had to hunch over even standing in the center of the aisle. "Could you come with me for a moment, please?"

What would Bret do? It was hard to tell. He didn't know this man at all yet. Best be careful. "Sure. What's the problem?" But Bret knew they were going to ask him about the canister. Outside the plane, he saw his duffel on a second cart, off by itself. He decided to be preemptive. "Oh, it's Uncle Michael, isn't it?"

"Pardon me?" Dolph Lundgren, that was who he looked like. The bad guy in *Rocky IV*.

"There's a canister in my bag containing the cremated remains of my uncle. I'm returning him to Ireland."

Oh my. This could be the end of it. Keep calm, keep calm.

"Ah, yes. That's what I wanted to ask you about. You know, technically, you're supposed to notify the airline if you're transporting remains. And if it isn't sealed under official witness, the container needs to be opened and visually inspected. Since the airline understands that this could be a very personal matter, we generally don't open such a box to verify its contents without the owner present, so if you wouldn't mind opening it up, we can finish up and you'll be on your way."

"Oh, certainly. Sorry, I didn't know."

"It's not all that common for most people, traveling with cremated remains. Don't feel bad about it."

Bret opened the bag and unwrapped the sweatshirt to lift out the canister. He removed the lid and showed the agent the lumpy light gray powder. Bret himself had not actually looked at the ashes before now. They looked literally like the scrapings from the bottom of a fireplace, complete with a few chunks of stuff that hadn't completely gone to ash.

I am certain this scenario would not be covered in the manual.

"Thank you, sir. Now we're going to tape this shut with marked security tape and I'll sign off on it and it will get straight through to Dublin." He yanked a three-foot length of yellow and black striped tape off a roll retrieved from his pocket and wrapped it a few times around the canister, then initialed it in black magic marker. "Sorry for the trouble. Have a safe journey."

Bret climbed back up into the plane and took his seat. No one looked at him, so there was no need for an appropriate quip, though he had a good one ready: "Don't put your uncle in a suitcase." Too bad. The engine whined into action.

I paid only slight attention to the flight crew's presentation on safety . . . something about the use of seat cushions as flotation devices. Ghosts are essentially floating already.

The flight followed the south shore of Lake Erie, then the Niagara River (a small bank of clouds managed to obscure the falls, to the evident disappointment of the father in front and the child seated next to him), then the north shore of Ontario. The Irish man seemed to have dozed off. The plane swooped in on a steep, curving course and touched down lightly. The sprawling Toronto airport seemed even more discombobulated by the post-9/11 security restrictions than Cleveland. There was no direct way to get from any one point to any other, so travelers were constantly moving about, taking shuttles, stopping to ask directions, or just meandering around dazed. It dawned on

Bret that perhaps this was a clever means of foiling terrorists, by making sure they had no idea where they were or where they were going. Or maybe it was just a way to ease crowding in the terminals by having people spend most of their time in buses. He lost track of his traveling companions after the customs point. The last he saw of the two women from Halifax was when they were asked why they were bringing in two large jars of dill pickles from Garrettsville, Ohio in their checked luggage. "They're not dangerous," he overheard. "Except for the garlic." The inspector rolled his eyes, said something about contraband, confiscated the pickles, and motioned them on. They shuffled off into the crowd beyond the stanchions.

I was just during these moments discovering some of the peculiarities of my situation. I could see and hear essentially what Bret would, but that was the extent of my range. If I wanted to have any influence on Bret in order to properly carry out my mission of mentoring him along his way, then it would not do too much good for me to be down in the baggage compartment. Are ghosts passengers or baggage?

BRET FOUND A STOOL at a little round table in a bar where he could watch the television news and keep an eye on the plane schedules out in the concourse. He ordered a sandwich and a beer. The waitress returned with a modestly scaled corned beef-on-rye in one hand and an enormous vessel full of beer hoisted in the other. He took a long, cold swallow. It took him 40 minutes to eat the sandwich between episodes of the newscast and glances out into the concourse, but he wasn't making much headway on the beer. It seemed, from the buzz in his head, that he had drunk more than that, but the glass was still two-thirds full. He looked back down the aisle again. His plane departed in another hour and a half. As he turned back, the waitress was topping off his beer. "Thirsty tonight, eh? Hope you've got a seat near the loo!" She chuckled and walked off. He held the glass in both hands and waved the waitress off next time she came around with a pitcher a few minutes later. "Just the check, please."

"You already paid, sir."

"Oh yes, right. Thank you."

He gave up on the beer after getting it down to half-empty, left a couple American dollars on the table, then set off for his gate. He found a seat along a wall and sat down. He folded his arms over his carry-on in his lap and leaned his head back.

"FINAL BOARDING CALL for Air Canada flight 894 to Dublin," Bret heard. Someone was shaking his arm. He opened his eyes and after a second they came to focus on the ruddy face of the Irish gentleman. "Rise and shine, sonny." Bret sat up.

"Hmm. Thanks." He stood up and stumbled after the older man to the end of the boarding line.

"Almost missed it myself," the gentleman turned and said. "They had that 'Baywatch' program on the pub telly."

Suddenly, Bret was intensely aware of his full bladder. He found his passport and plane tickets and boarding pass and considered whether he had time to dash to the nearest men's room. He looked over his shoulder to see that the entrance to the restroom was blocked with a yellow plastic sign indicating that it was being cleaned. He'd have to wait until he was on the plane. It always seemed to him that one shouldn't use the toilet on the plane while the flight was still on the ground, but he was willing to make an exception this time. The line moved at a sloshingly slow pace, even past the boarding agent, as people in first class blocked the aisles in order to fish through their bags to get themselves set up for the long overnight crossing. He loosened his belt, held his breath, tried to think about tumbleweeds and saltines—every desperate trick he could remember. "Welcome aboard, sir," said the flight attendant as Bret took another step and was officially on the plane. He nodded and smiled weakly. He could see a lavatory a few rows ahead. Just behind him he could hear a stressed whisper, "Mom I really have to go, I'm desperate." The mom replied that girl could use the lavatory just ahead even though it was in the first-class section. Only a minute to wait.

Finally, the line inched forward far enough so that Bret found himself even with the toilet. He opened the door and ducked in. No sooner had he latched the door than a small knocking began. But there was no turning back now. "Just a minute," he called out. Actually, it was a few minutes later when he emerged. The mother shot a cold glance at him as she bustled her young daughter through the door. "Frequent flier privileges," said Bret.

He had a window seat and, as luck would have it, the middle and aisle seats were taken by the same girl and her mother. Bret nodded and then magnanimously offered the window seat to the girl. The mother managed a small smile and then, as Bret had expected, said no thanks. Bret then studiously looked out the window. There was still a little bit of light in the sky as they took off, and it seemed to him over the next couple of hours that it never did get completely dark. Soon enough, that sun that never went altogether away would be rising and it would be tomorrow and he would be another day and an ocean away from where he had begun. Sometime during the complementary made-for-airplanes news programs, he began to doze off.

"Shit!" he whispered aloud, his eyes popping wide open. "The parakeet."

"Wash your mouth with soap," said the girl.

DUBLIN

The flight was long for me. I attempted to entertain myself by appearing to gallop alongside the plane outside Bret's window, but alas, it was dark and he apparently saw nothing, even though it looked to me as if he were staring directly at me. It did seem, however, that a young boy three windows back perhaps did see me. This took me aback because I had thought I was supposed to be visible only to Bret. Perhaps I had skipped over a chapter in the preparatory manual, or, more likely, dozed off. It was written with a ponderous didacticism that indicated it was meant to be taken with grave seriousness but whose effect was instead to dull the reader's attention to the point of somnabulance. I went back and found the section in question, which took some time, given the dense disorder of the manual—but at least the task consumed some time. 'The perceptibility of the ghost may be construed to be oriented to the primary image.' A lot of help that was. Written by lawyers, no doubt. In any case, I judged it prudent to discontinue the galloping act to avoid any possible impression of impropriety.

The sun was back up in no time, and Bret's head was throbbing from too much beer and too little sleep, and seven hours of stale air, and the flickering through his eyelids of the in-flight entertainment that he didn't feel like watching. Clouds blanketed the terrain as the plane descended. He didn't see Ireland until a minute or so before landing. Then there was Dublin, and the sea, and a range of mountains pale beyond. Then that was all gone and there was only the runway and the airport terminal. Bret's brain battled through the half-sleep fuzz. He'd get his bags then go find a phone to call Leslie and make sure she stopped by to pick up Oprah.

After picking up his checked suitcase and extricating a hundred and fifty euro from an ATM machine next to the baggage claim, he set about getting himself to Gate Lodge. His abiding distrust of taxicabs led him to deliberately walk across to the information area in such a way as to avoid the cab stand he could see outside the windows. Being in the persuasion business, Bret was always hyper-cautious of being manipulated himself. He didn't even want to be put in the position of having to try to say no to one of those guys. At the Information Centre he discovered that an inexpensive shuttle bus ran all the way from the airport, through downtown Dublin, and out along the Liffey River to Heuston Station, which looked as if it would be just a couple of blocks from his lodgings. Also, he recalled, Heuston Station was where his train would depart tomorrow, so he could scope out the walk ahead of time. He bought an all-day pass that could be used on any city bus, envisioning a full day of energetic touring about the city.

It set my mind at ease to have the ashes back with us. With that immediate worry put away, I began to think about ways in which I might more actively participate in our joint endeavor, which for me was settling into an unsatisfactory pattern of long intervals of excruciating boredom punctuated by moments of unbridled panic. Of course, there was no reason to expect

Bret to depart from his itinerary, and that itinerary would deliver him to within a few miles of our final destination in County Kerry, so there really was nothing I should need to worry about. But doing nothing seemed a rather passive form of mentorship. I suspect manual would have very little to say about matters such as this—full of advice about the obvious, silent about any important issue that might come up. Whoever designed the thing missed quite a few opportunities to make it useful, from what I gather. Page numbers would be nice. Maybe an index. A table of contents at least. Instead, just one long undifferentiated text, without so much as a chapter heading or even paragraph breaks. Maybe it was trying to emulate James Joyce.

The bus rolled along briskly, through a leafy suburb and then down toward the city center. Near the river, their progress slowed as the bus turned right at the gigantic customs house and inched its way along with traffic. He could see that this side carried outbound flow and the two lanes on the opposite shore of the river traveled back toward the city center. Numerous bridges crossed the river. He caught the names of a few: O'Connell, Ha'penny, Liam Mellowes.

Any body of water adds a measure of aesthetic appeal to an urban setting, he had often observed, but, from his perch on the second deck, the Liffey seemed to ooze things other than charm. Its edges were squared off with stonework and concrete, and a significant amount of debris seemed to be floating in (or half-submerged under) the water—everything from bottles and cans to shopping carts and truck tires. It was more of an open culvert than a river. He imagined it might have smelled pretty bad a hundred years ago. Or maybe it did now.

One would not necessarily think that I would have a keen olfactory sense, as I have no nose, but I can tell you that the odor of the warm summer Liffey was less than enticing as I floated outside the bus. The sense was intermingled with the aroma of boiling barley malt. Perhaps I picked this up through some sort of sympathetic harmonization with humans inhaling those smells. This is a peculiar existence, that of the taibhse.

The bus teetered around a left turn and crossed a bridge to the train station. The doors opened. He hoisted his duffel and small backpack, descended to the exit, and began to walk back across the bridge toward Phoenix Park and the Gate Lodge, his eyes on the water to the left. In this direction, the Liffey's edges reverted to a more natural state, and he could imagine it meandering in from the countryside, gradually looking more and more like a river and less like a gutter if one could follow it upstream. The water rippled around the upturned bottom of a street vending cart that appeared to have been launched over the bridge railing. Bret walked straight into the back of someone who had stopped in the walkway, knocking the man over onto his suitcase. "Oh, very sorry." Bret dropped his bag and reached down to help the other up, and then recognized him as the man from the check-in line back in Cleveland and the terminal in Toronto.

"Well, fancy that," the man replied. "Following me, are you now?"

"Sorry, no. I mean, not on purpose," said Bret. "Are you all right?"

"Quite." The man held out his hand. "Francis Rosko, sir."

"Bret," he replied, "Bret Sheehan."

"Here on business, then?"

"Business? No, more of a personal errand."

"Ah, digging out the family roots, are we?"

"Not exactly," said Bret. "Helping someone else come home."

"Eh?"

"My uncle Michael." Bret pointed at his duffel.

"Wee bit unusual." The older man stared at the bag for a few seconds, then shrugged and lifted his suitcase. He turned to Bret. "Well, if you're walking down here, you're either headed for the Gate Lodge or you're terribly lost."

"Yeah, that's it, Gate Lodge. He's not in there really, Uncle Michael. Well he is, but he isn't. It's his ashes."

"Ah, his ashes, yes. The Gate Lodge is exemplary, you'll find. I always stop here when in Dublin. Of course, I wasn't planning to be in Dublin today. Got off the airplane by mistake—force of habit, you know. I meant to continue on to Shannon, but now I'll have to take the train. Used to be I always did it that way, since the flight terminated here, but they added the leg to Shannon during the past year. That's how I found the Gate Lodge, looking for a place to sleep that was close to Heuston Station, which is the station for trains to points west. Stroke of luck, I tell you."

"You live in Shannon, Mr.—how shall I address you?"

"Just call me Rosko, R-O-S-K-O. Francis is a bit girly, people say. I don't live in Shannon, but it's the closest airport."

"Rosko, that's not an Irish name I've heard."

"Well, depends how you define Irish. It's an old name, if not a common one. Assumption is that it got stuck to a family of fishermen who worked back and forth between the southwest Irish coast, Cornwall, and Brittany in France. Town called Roscoff out there at the tip of Brittany, Rosko in the Breton tongue. There are a few of us in Cork and Kerry, been so as long as anyone can trace it back."

"You live in County Cork or Kerry?"

"Kerry."

"Kerry is where I'm going tomorrow, by train to Killarney. Then I've got a car reserved so I can drive to Castle Cove. If there is such a place."

"It's a place, not an official village, but people call it that. Won't be surprised if its fame were to grow in future, as more and more tourists are visiting the area. Not much over an hour's drive from Killarney. If you rise early in the morning, you could get out and back in a day easily. Well, perhaps we'll share a train cabin as well."

Bret realized that Rosko thought Bret was staying in a Killarney hotel, as most tourists did, when in fact he was proceeding straight on to the room he had reserved in the town of Sneem, but he didn't see any point in correcting the misimpression. They arrived at the steep steps up to a multistory brick building. "This is the place," said Rosko. "Might I suggest, after you've had a chance to unpack and have a shave, that you join me across the street at the Nancy Hands? In Parkgate Street, actually, but it's the same street as Conyngham. Names change every few city blocks. Fine pint and a savory roast."

"That would be nice, yes, if I can stay awake," Bret said.

They were greeted, after knocking a few times, by a buxom redheaded lady in a green satin dress who appeared to have run down a few flights of stairs to get the door. "Very sorry—I didn't hear you over the hoover. Nice to see you, Rosko. Noticed your name just added to the ledger. Ronald must have written it in. How's the big project going? You've got your usual room, number 9. And your friend?"

"Meet Mr. Sheehan, from America," Rosko said before Bret could speak. "Sorry we're early, but the airplane arrived Dublin at half-seven."

She waved off his apology. "It's no trouble at all. Welcome, Mr. Sheehan, sir. We've got you in number 4, just at the top of the landing. I've just finished tidying it, so you're welcome to settle in."

"Thank you," said Bret. "Shall I meet you down here in, say, half an hour?" he asked, turning to Rosko.

"Yes, let's do."

Bret carried his bag up the stairs and entered the empty room 4. The ceilings were very high, and he could see where new walls had been built into one corner fairly recently in order to make a private bathroom. Its tall windows, with many original panes showing their age with rippled glass, faced the back; the view was of a dozen small gardens and, beyond those, a modern yet somewhat timeworn concrete apartment building of four or five stories.

THE FLOW FROM THE SHOWER was a bit unsteady, but the hot water soothed his stiff back. He calculated he had time for an unrushed shower before he'd have to get out and get dressed and go meet Rosko. It was a lucky thing meeting him, Bret thought. Incredible coincidence.

The water ran down the back of his head onto his shoulders, its splattering displacing the other sounds of the world. Bret had never been one to take long showers, because while that removal from human interaction was a respite from being "on stage" for the people around him, he didn't need much of that respite before he began to be aware of how very alone he was. Such a feeling might be comfort for some, but in Bret it induced a quiet panic, as if he himself were rinsing away down the drain. But this day that feeling showed its head only weakly and Bret laughed it off. Maybe because no one here knew him anyway? Maybe because so much of him had been washed away over those many years of very short showers? Maybe he was just occupied with the task at hand, and the old feelings would come back once his business with Uncle Michael was finished. For some reason, that internal query "What would Bret do?" came into his mind. Bret would have stepped out of the shower a long time ago.

After drying off, he shaved and brushed his teeth and then he felt refreshed and ready to go out and get some lunch and investigate the town. Somewhere in the bottom of his duffel was his other pair of shoes. Uncle Michael's metal box was still there, he could feel, wrapped in security tape and a sweater. Funny how Rosko had just nodded silently when Bret mentioned he was bringing someone home in the bag. In fact, now that he thought about it, there were a couple other funny things about Rosko. Like, if he had gotten off the plane by accident, how come he had his suitcase? It was too big to carry on. And how come they already had his name on the ledger at Gate Lodge? Part of it was true at least, because Bret could remember overhearing him tell the agent "Shannon" at the baggage check way back at Cleveland Hopkins. Well, maybe he'd realized his error after getting off the plane, asked to have his bag removed, then called Gate Lodge to make a reservation from the airport. That was plausible.

As he walked through the lower hallway to leave, the proprietress nodded and smiled from a side door.

"Well, I'm a little bit more awake now," Bret offered.

"Nothing like a nice, long American shower to feel at home again," she replied.

THE PRINCESS AND THE WANDERING BARD

The pub had two levels, and Rosko led them right up the stairs to the second floor. Rustic wooden tables filled three or four interconnected rooms, and a stainless steel counter opened through a large window in the wall that looked into a kitchen from which savory aromas wafted. They found a small table by a window overlooking the street. Rosko ordered two pints of Guinness stout, which arrived four or five minutes later.

In the meantime, they visited the counter by the kitchen, where there was a buffet offering a couple of potato dishes, green beans, leek and turnip soup, corned beef, roast beef, salmon cakes, and chicken fingers. Inspired by the sight and smell of food, Bret served himself a sampling of nearly everything save the chicken fingers.

As they ate and drank, Rosko began to ask Bret about his life back home. Satisfied by the food and relaxed by the beer, Bret talked freely. "Well, it's a funny story, really. My Uncle Michael came originally from County Kerry, place called Castle Cove."

"Yes, as I said, I know the place," replied Rosko.

"His health had been failing for years, and I was the only person in the family who lived near him, so I was kind of drafted to look in on him after he moved into one of those assisted living places. Do you have those here?"

"Oh, yes."

"Anyway, it started out as a chore, but after a while, we got pretty close. Or at least as close as you can get with somebody who's about half senile."

"I had an auntie like that, but she passed a number of years ago."

"My Uncle Michael passed away, too. That's why I'm here. Before he died, he asked me to bring him back to Ireland. Then he went and died not more than a few minutes later. But I'm here to do the next best thing—bring his cremated remains back to County Kerry. Blood and bones to water and stone."

"Yes, yes," said Rosko, "quite normal."

"Normal?" Bret paused.

"For an old Kerryman. Sentimental lot."

"Well, he didn't strike me as unusually sentimental. He made it seem like a duty, almost. Very matter-of-fact."

"Do you know the legend," asked Rosko, "of the Princess and the Wandering Bard?"

"The what?" Bret replied.

"Ah, well. Then you must hear it." Rosko paused and took a long drink. "Long ago, in the southwest of Ireland, long before it was even called Ireland, there was a small kingdom. No one knows for certain where it was, but some think it was on the edge of what we now know as Ballinskelligs Bay, all the way out on the farthest reach of the Iveragh peninsula. Then as today, it was a wild region with little tillable land and little protection from the angry sea. Life was not easy, not even for the king. But the advantage was that these very same conditions made the place relatively uninteresting to raiders and plunderers, so life was generally peaceful.

"The king had four sons and one daughter—she was a lovely girl with copper-colored hair, and she was strong, too. Stronger than any of her brothers, it was said. But she was a little bit strange. She liked to walk in the hills, alone. Normally, a woman would not have been permitted to travel about by herself, but she was a willful and persuasive princess and the king had little success in preventing her from doing things she wished to do. Most of all, she liked to climb to a high point and stand there gaze out over the hills and sea. The kingdom was small and everyone knew who she was. Some thought she was enchanted. Others assumed her to be part goddess, because it was said she could call forth storms and fogs and sunshine at will. Therefore she was generally left alone.

"But one day, a band of three ruffians spied her standing upon a high ledge far from the castle and they resolved to disguise their faces and rob her of the golden brooch she carried about her neck. As they approached, she turned and faced them, saying not a word, but smiling. When they were but a few paces away, a cloud of heavy mist suddenly rose up over the edge of the hillside. It was so dense that they could not see the ends of their outstretched daggers. Knowing they were at the edge of a cliff, they all three froze.

"But the fog did not lift. They stood there motionless for many minutes until they heard a woman's quiet laughter. One of them immediately stepped toward the sound, but moments later he could be heard to cry out. Then they heard his body breaking against the rocks far below. One of the two remaining men then bolted the opposite way, but a muffled grunt and the clattering sound of his dagger tumbling down the steep hill told of his demise. The remaining man was not so rash as the others. In any group of people, he was the one who would be telling a story, and so he knew the value of waiting for a tale to unfold. He put his dagger away and stood still until the mist began to clear and then he saw that the princess stood before him. She reached out and clasped each of his forearms in a strong grip. 'I think I know you,' she said. With one hand she reached up and pulled the cloth from his face. She smiled. 'I do know who you are and you know who I am. Unless you wish to kill me, you must leave here and spend the rest of your days far from here, because I must tell my brothers what has happened and they surely will kill you if you stay.'

"'Princess,' he said, 'I do not wish to kill you or harm you. But I have promised my father that when I die I will take my rightful place with our ancestors. I must not break the succession.' And she said 'Then ask of your son or your son's son that your body be burned and the ashes be brought back to these hills of your ancestors. No one will recognize your face in the ashes, but the blood and bones will join the water and stone.' She released him, but he was afraid to run. 'Princess,' he said. 'Why do you not kill me as you killed the others?' She laughed without smiling. 'I killed no one,' she said. 'I simply stayed where I was. I knew the ground on which I stood.' And then the mist cleared and the man wandered off and he never stopped wandering.

"He traveled to many places and composed many poems and songs, but his feet always longed to feel the rocks of his home beneath them. In all that time, he never married and never had a child. So, as the end of his life neared, he began to walk back home. When he climbed over the last hill at the edge of the kingdom, he saw the princess standing on the same ledge. He approached and called out to her. But she was an old woman now and did not hear him. So he walked closer and touched her arm. 'Princess?' he said. 'No,' she replied. 'Queen.' He stood as straight as he could. 'Do you remember me?' he asked. 'Yes, I do,' she replied. 'As you can see,' he said, 'I am still alive. But I have no children, no one to bring my ashes,' he said. 'Do not fear,' she said. They stood there together atop the mountain and a storm came in from the sea. Just as the wind began to blow, a single bolt of lightning struck and their bodies exploded into a cloud of fine ashes. The rain washed the ashes out of the air and back onto the stones where they had been standing.

"That is why, to this day in that region, one sees stone cairns high atop the hills. They represent the princess and the wandering bard, and on stormy nights, if one watches long enough, you can see the lightning strike again."

He stopped and took a long sip from his pint, draining the bottom quarter of the glass. A fine tan foam clung to the sides. "You and I, we have something in common. I suspected it when I saw you in the queue in Cleveland. Something I could see in you as clearly as in my own daughter. I checked the tag on your valise and recognized the name—a good Kerry name. Blood and bones. There are very few of us left whose ancestors were here before the Brits, before the Vikings, before the Celts. And though the blood is much diluted over the centuries, its effect is still strong. A pinch of yeast brews a barrel of beer."

"Yeast?" said Bret. He tried to remember if he had referred specifically to the phrase "blood and bones" as he had recounted his conversations with Uncle Michael, but his mind was somewhat blurred with sleep deprivation and beer.

"It binds us together and binds us to the land," Rosko continued. "It compels us to look after each other."

"It does?" Bret answered. The sounds of kitchen bustle filled a long wordless interlude.

"I must ask you," Rosko finally spoke.

"Yes?" Bret asked.

"Do you recall our meeting before?"

"In the airport?"

"No, before that time. I was on a three-week working holiday with the regional convention association and I'm certain we met at King Arthur's amusement park a number of weeks past. I believe you made a speech for us."

"Oh, yes I remember. You were in that group?" Bret exclaimed. "No wonder you look familiar. My apologies for not connecting."

"It's all right, not to worry."

"We get a lot of groups in—it all kind of blurs together." Bret answered. He hesitated, but didn't feel comfortable telling

Rosko about losing the job. Where would that conversation lead?

"Bit of a showman, are you? That's the Kerry in you as well."

"Well, the job does require presentation skills." Bret paused. "But none of that now. I'm on vacation." Perhaps permanently, a voice in his head added.

"Tomorrow, we shall both go to Killarney," said Rosko, "It's right along the way to my home. I'll help you planning your adventure. And along the way, you can tell me all about American theme parks."

"All I want is a nice vacation. And to put the ashes where they belong. Why do you care about theme parks?"

"I find them a fascinating cultural phenomenon. We've none in Ireland—only places like the West Cork Miniature Model Railway. Not so ambitious."

"Well, there's not much to it," said Bret. "The idea of a theme park is that people will pay a hefty admission fee to get the feeling of adventure without any of the risk and inconvenience of real adventure. You consolidate all these rides and activities in a self-contained park. It's easier and safer than actually climbing a mountain or riding down a river in a hollow log. The trick is, in the backs of their minds, people are aware that it isn't the real thing, so you have to keep upping the ante every year with new rides or marketing gimmicks. The old-style places like Cedar Point or Coney Island were summer resorts before they became theme parks. Newer ones like King's Island or Disney or King Arthur's Kamelot are created with a kind of fantasy image in mind, to sell people on the idea of magic. Although, in point of fact, King Arthur's Kamelot was a much older park and the concept was layered onto it by new ownership. Anyway, you advertise it as a big adventure even though it's actually just a glorified parking lot. It's a rather shallow fiction but only needs to last for a day, and people don't really like to be challenged anyway. Make it easy for them to swallow what you're feeding them and they'll gladly do it."

"Would it work anywhere, or is it just an American phenomenon?" Rosko asked.

"So far, Europe doesn't seem to go for it so much—EuroDisney was a flop—but Japan does. And the Aussies. I think it could work anywhere, though, if the organizers really got the audience nailed down."

"How so?"

"Well," said Bret, "you have to know what they want before you can give it to them."

"How do you find out what they want?"

"Simple. Watch what they do. Ask them. Basic research."

Rosko nodded. "But that assumes they spend their time doing what they want to do, and that they know what they want and are willing to tell you the truth about it."

"Second-guessing yourself," Bret leaned forward, "is the road to nowhere."

Rosko laughed. "Another pint?"

"Should I?"

"As the sign says, it's good for you."

They drank and chatted for another half-hour. Bret indicated his intention to visit Trinity College and see the famous Book of Kells, either this afternoon or the next morning. Rosko recommended today, but begged off for himself. "I've seen it many a time and I need a rest right now. I'm not so young a man as you. And I wouldn't want to color your opinion with my own commentary."

Bret checked the hall clock before he went upstairs to his room. Only 12:30. It would take a little while before his internal clock adjusted. He closed the door and sat down for a moment in the red upholstered chair between the bed and the wall to the bathroom.

HE HEARD A RAPPING SOUND and snapped awake. Where was he? Bret's eyes focused out the window on the apartment building beyond the gardens. A second knock came at the door. "Who is it?"

"Your hostess, sir. I need to check on a plumbing situation and the only access door is in your W.C. May I come in?"

"Yes, of course." Bret pulled himself out of the chair and walked over to unlatch the door.

The redheaded proprietress stood there in her green satin dress, holding a red toolbox in one hand and a very long pipe wrench in the other. "Thank you, Mr. Sheehan. This won't take but a moment."

"Take your time. I was going out anyway. Didn't mean to fall asleep. Have you got the time?"

"Yes, it's about half-three, sir."

"Thanks," Bret dropped his key into his pocket and walked out into the hall. "I won't be back until at least 6:00, so there's really no rush."

"Going downtown?"

"Trinity College."

"Of course. Well, I'm sure you'll have a lovely afternoon. Thank you again."

THE BUS RIDE from the station down to O'Connell Bridge was 20 minutes at the most. After nearly getting killed three times in two minutes because he kept forgetting the cars would be coming from the other direction, he crossed Westmoreland Street and walked into the spacious yard of Trinity College. Closing time was soon, he knew, so he hurried toward a doorway where a sign said the Book of Kells could be found. Entering, he found not the Book of Kells or a scholarly library, but an extensive gift shop full of Celtic knickknacks. After a brief browse, he became overwhelmed by the selection, and went straight to the ticket booth.

The display was on two levels, with educational materials and manuscripts on the lower level, and the Trinity College library itself on the upper floor. Bret was too tired to pay much attention to anything, but he lingered for a few minutes looking at the 1,200-year-old Book of Kells itself, thinking about the strange lives of the men who had secluded themselves away to work on it, year after year, knowing full well that a Viking raid or two could render moot the whole endeavor. But they persevered and, miraculously, those very sheets of handmade vellum and ink had made it intact to this day. Honestly, he couldn't tell much difference between one manuscript page and another. They were written in Latin, which Bret had never studied. Some were plain, some ornate, some just black ink on paper, some plastered with gold leaf. In the margin of one page was a small blue bird, which reminded Bret that he had forgotten to call Leslie about the parakeet; this he would do when he got back to the room, he made a mental note. The manuscripts were beautiful objects, but their writing meant nothing to Bret, so he looked only at the elegant shapes of the letters and examined the tiny, intricate illuminations around the borders. In this way, he thought, I'm like most people were when these things were made: ignorant and illiterate but still able to appreciate beauty and a good picture story. He imagined the wandering bard of Rosko's story climbing the precarious steps to some lofty monastery, rehearsing in his head as he walked and puffed. Or was that before there were monasteries?

He walked up the stairs into the library, a vaulted room three stories high with two floors of leather-covered books arrayed in shelves ascending all the way to the edges of the arched ceiling. A cathedral nave lined with books: whoever built this believed in the power of knowledge. He sat on a cushioned bench and marveled at the scene for a few minutes, then stood up and began to walk to the exit. Two young students were obliviously blocking the doorway as they discussed plans for later in the evening. The slim young man wore jeans and a black sport coat and slouched against the door frame, while his female companion stood facing him, nearly touching, and fidgeted with the hem of her yellow sundress in the slanting window light. The couple stared unblinking into each other's eyes as they spoke.

BRET HAD HEARD that getting a little physical exercise could help the body adjust to jet lag so, foregoing the bus, he walked back to the train station along the river, a stroll that took only ten minutes longer than the halting bus ride had. Along the way, he marveled that Dublin, though an old city in its history and architecture, seemed populated overwhelmingly by twentyish people with cell-phones and personal digital devices, and they all used them constantly. Bret still didn't have a cell phone, and he was beginning to feel that he would be left behind if he didn't get one—but not quite yet. On the other hand, if he had a cell phone, he could call Leslie right now about the parakeet.

As he neared the train station, fatigue hit him like a gusting headwind and he decided it was time to grab a quick supper and then go to bed. By tomorrow morning, the jet lag should be largely dissipated, he hoped—at least that was why he'd made the effort to stay awake until sometime close to when he would usually go to sleep. When he was nearly all the way back to his room, he stopped for a light dinner at a little place called the Parc Bistro, a few doors down from the Nancy Hands. There were only a few tables, and a brief menu of French/Irish hybrid dishes with a short wine list. His pasta with seafood were delicious, tossed with local vegetables and prepared with a light touch that emphasized the freshness of the ingredients. Despite being diluted by food, the one glass of wine hit him like three. He paid his bill and walked the few hundred feet up to the Gate Lodge. The traffic on Conyngham Road was steady, though, so he walked further up to a proper crossing, then doubled back. A few buildings up from the Gate Lodge was a building whose windows were dark and broken out. Bits of graffiti overlapped on the brick walls facing the street, and chunks of rubble filled a deep stairwell that descended from the sidewalk. He didn't see rats, but he knew they were there, along with the echoes of the sad and painful things that had happened in that destroyed space. Bret felt a chill and instinctively veered toward the street.

Rosko was just heading up the stairs as Bret entered. "Back from your travels?" the older man called down.

Bret nodded.

"What do you make of the Book of Kells?"

"Hmm. Magnificent." Truth was, he didn't remember much about it. The image that stayed in Bret's mind was the gutted row house.

PHOENIX
PARK

Bret awoke a little before dawn and could not get back to sleep. This made no sense: his jet lag should have had him getting up late and going to bed early. Nonetheless, he was awake. He decided the plumbing would be too loud to take a shower now, so he put on a jacket and went outside to take a walk. City streets or park? He'd done some streets yesterday, so the park it was. Fortunately, the gate to the park for which the Gate Lodge was named was just across Conyngham Road. The traffic was light, and Bret walked diagonally across the broad intersection.

The map didn't really convey the immensity of Phoenix Park. A low stone wall and formal gate at the entrance implied the kind of groomed landscape one might expect to find in a well-manicured little private garden, but beyond the entrance, the grounds quickly reverted to a much wilder state. It wasn't so much like walking into a park as it was stepping out of the city. Plump deer wandered about the base of an enormous obelisk erected by the British in honor of Wellington not far from the gate, and beyond that were just rolling hills, glades and forest, all shrouded in morning mist. It was perhaps a glimpse at the land as it would be if the city had never been built.

Bret followed a road to the left past the obelisk. The pavement curved around the edge of a hillside overlooking, from a distance, a cramped and dingy-looking section of the city, a view that reinforced the incongruity of the untamed park. After some time, the road dipped into a valley and intersected another, narrower track. On the crest of a hill beyond, a man in knee-high rubber boots was walking two large brown dogs. Bret's mind was suddenly back in Uncle Michael's room, looking out the window across the broad lawn. He could almost hear the old man's faint wheeze, see the slight smile on his white-whiskered face. We're on the way, Bret said to him. He felt peace in the same way he had when sitting quietly in that room, no hurry, nothing to prove, no one to persuade of anything. The man in the rubber boots disappeared over the hill. Bret noticed three brick chimneys sticking up over the grassy shoulder: perhaps some kind of manor house? An old ceramic works? An asylum? He considered walking on to investigate, but decided he should be getting back. To his right, a narrow dirt footpath angled straight up the hill back in the general direction from which he had come. He began to ascend the trail, the long grass soaking his trouser cuffs. Again in his mind he was transported, this time to his walk in the dark just after Uncle Michael had died, after drinking an entire bottle of wine while going through Michael's old photographs. Alone then too, he had stumbled his way into a natural stage and conjured that soliloquy. He'd been drunk enough, but the thoughts had seemed clear, unsettling, terrifying, liberating, exciting. Words about words, a performance yet not a performance. An audience there, but only by accident.

He scanned the woods for a minute. How many others had stood near this spot and looked through trees wondering who else has been here? He turned and proceeded uphill.

The mist was clearing off a bit now, but sheets of it still covered the ground in spots and hovered near the treetops. At the crest of the hill, he found a playing field, marked off in lime.

The sound of morning traffic was beginning to rumble up toward him from the city below, and intermittent cars zoomed down the road that bisected the park a couple hundred yards to his left, little engines revving high. Bret set his own course across the open fields to converge toward that road as he walked, figuring it was probably the street that passed through Park Gate. A bicycle glided down the road toward the city, too far away for Bret to hear the sound. He glanced behind him to see that he was leaving a deliberate though somewhat oscillating trail across the grass in the dew.

After a few minutes he came across a narrow dirt track that ran more or less in the direction he wanted to go, so, to save his shoes from being soaked through, he adjusted his trajectory slightly to follow the trail. He passed a line of trees and then noticed a lone figure standing in the trail just ahead. As Bret approached, the figure periodically gestured as if to be sending hand-and-arm signals to some distant compatriot. Bret saw now that it was a man, short of stature, in a long navy blue coat and matching hat. He could see now that another dirt track intersected the one along which Bret was walking, and that the man was standing just off the trail, inside one of the corners formed by the crossing. The man held out his hand when Bret arrived. Bret stopped walking, afraid that he was perhaps about to be mugged.

"Wait, please," the man said, then paused. "Here they come. Wait until they have passed, please. All right, all right. There they go, there they go. All right." The man turned 45 degrees and motioned to Bret. "You may carry on. Hurry up, hurry up." Bret, the accidental audience of one to this solitary absurdist dramatic production, nodded his head and continued on his way.

I kept my thoughts to myself as Bret wandered that large and wild park. What he was thinking about, how could I know? Strolling alone was unusual for him, and I supposed the thoughts might be similarly unusual. I might have, in an effort to feel effectual in my duties, attempted to push his thoughts in one direction or another, to lead his feet up or down or around. But I became distracted by the wildness of that park and the dense teeming of the city below, by thinking of all the souls who lived down there, of the few who came here to this vantage point where it was possible to see it all. Or, in honesty, more possible to see some of it. One takes care not to mis-estimate the effects of the landscape on the spirit.

IRISH RAIL

Just minutes after they rolled out of Heuston Station, it seemed, the train was out of the city, the building backs giving way to small houses, then open fields. The tracks were set down in a sort of culvert with a lot of foliage on either side, so Bret couldn't see much. Across the little built-in table from him, Rosko sat reading the morning paper. Bret was feeling a little drowsy, as the Irish breakfast—though whiskey-less—had been extravagant with sausages and eggs and all manner of carbohydrates and was now was diverting blood from his head to his stomach. He leaned back in the seat and shut his eyes. The owners of the Gate Lodge had some sort of labor-sharing arrangement such that the lady got to enjoy breakfast with the lodgers while the husband served the food. Bret remembered a circuitous conversation about American politics during which the proprietors took pains not to say anything too directly critical of the current president, while commenting unfavorably on the recent course of world events. "It's unfortunate that it's come to this, isn't it?" the man said as he put down a plate of assorted sausages. "It's just sad, that's what I think," said the woman, leaning across the table to replace a glass cover over a butter dish. The scent of her perfume mingled with that of Bret's marmalade.

A LITTLE JOSTLE in the tracks startled Bret awake, and he opened his eyes to see that the rails had climbed out of the ditch, or at least the ditch was much less deep, and he could see across the countryside. The land was fairly flat here, with hills in the distance and countless cows and sheep between. In the middle distance, a person on a horse emerged from behind a stand of trees, cantering along down a lane. They seemed to be keeping up with the train. Then they disappeared behind the ruin of an old stone tower as it passed by the window, barely ten feet from the track. A sheep was munching grass in what used to be a doorway. Bret had expected the train to pick up speed once it got clear of the city, but it continued along at an unhurried pace. It was a small country: perhaps there was no need to rush.

He looked up the aisle. Passengers who had boarded at the last stop were still finding their seats, each wrapped up in that specific little task. No one looked at him. He could have been there or not; it would make no difference. Back home, his work life was one audience after another. But here? He couldn't foresee any occasion when all eyes would be on him.

"We change trains at Mallow, is that right?" Bret asked aloud, looking back out the window.

"Yes, that's it," Rosko replied. "Should be there in about a half an hour's time."

"So soon?"

"Your eyes have been shut for a good while."

"I see."

"We've just gone through Limerick Junction."

"Sounds like a television show," Bret observed.

"It's not every country that ascribes a mellifluous name to every tiny place," Rosko offered.

"I have noticed that," Bret turned from the window. "Is there a state agency that makes sure every place is quaintly named?"

"Yes, that's it," Rosko replied. "Not only that, they force us all to be unreasonably friendly and hospitable. You never know when someone may want to come here and build Eire-Disney."

"You make your own luck, right?"

Across the aisle, a young woman sat down by the window, placing a small blue canvas bag on the seat beside her. Bret glanced up at her face just as she fixed her green eyes on him. He smiled and nodded a silent greeting. Then she looked over at Rosko, then back at Bret, a quizzical expression on her broad, rosy face. Her skin appeared flushed. Maybe she had just run to catch the train. She smiled very slightly, then turned away to pull a book from the blue bag. Bret glanced over at Rosko, who didn't appear to have registered the presence of their new neighbor. Bret looked back across the aisle. Her hair was long and dark brown and fluffy and draped in front of her shoulders. Every time he checked after that, she seemed wrapped up in her reading, occasional laughs setting her impressive bosom into motion. He imagined actually getting to know the woman, and how, when their relationship ended, he would think back and wonder if she'd been putting on an act for him all along, just as he had done for her.

The train pulled into Mallow station and the other train was already there. The announcer suggested the passengers for Killarney and Tralee make haste to transfer. Those heading on to Cork could stay in their seats. The woman glanced up with a smile and a nod as Bret and Rosko gathered their luggage and made their way to the doors.

They crossed a footbridge over the tracks, then descended a flight of steps to the waiting train. A few minutes after all the passengers had boarded, the doors closed and it rolled off.

If the first train had been leisurely, this one was less hasty still. Even the sound of the rail joints clunking underneath seemed unnaturally slow, as if someone were playing the record at the wrong speed. The view was lovely, but Bret could feel his eyelids falling again. On either side, the hills gradually approached closer to the rail line. Bret could see cairns on the tops of a few barren summits, silhouetted against the gray sky. He leaned his head against the window and the hills began to overlap in his vision.

They went into a short tunnel. In the darkness, Bret could still see the echoes of the passing hills, undulating in time with the rumbling of the wheels on rails. He caught sight of a horse and rider crossing a field to their left, running parallel to the tracks. They jumped a low stone wall almost without breaking stride. As the tracks curved, the horse drew closer alongside. Perhaps local equestrian traditions would account for the rider's odd clothing—leather and greenish cloth, a snug metal helmet, tan-colored leggings. The horse and rider were outrunning the train, so that they were now a hundred feet ahead of Bret's position at the window. How slow was this train? The horse approached another stone wall, this one quite a bit taller than the previous one, and stopped. The rider continued forward, bounced off the top of the wall, and disappeared over the other side. Bret's head bumped against the glass. Obscuring foliage had suddenly come up alongside the tracks.

"Did you see that?" He turned to Rosko.

"Hmm?"

Bret looked out the window at the dense thicket of trees and vines. "Nothing." Bret scanned the faces of the other passengers. No one seemed to have noticed anything. But then, no one was looking out the window.

The reader will expect perhaps that I will interject here a brief aside indicating that this equestrian episode was my doing, but alas, no. I noticed it only when Bret did, and as to why no one else on the train seemed to be paying any attention, I cannot say. I will affirm that, at least as far as possibly helping lead Bret into a state of mind that might be receptive to the irrational or the magical, this peculiar short scene might have been useful. But I could take no credit. In fact, I might have begun to wonder why I was here at all. Increasingly, events seemed to transpire without my explicit action.

"Not far now," Rosko said.

"What?"

"We're nearly there."

"To Killarney?"

"Right. And there we part."

"What? Wait, weren't you going to help me finish my quest?"

"Indeed, but I must travel on home first."

"Home?"

"Even closer to the end of this end of the world," said Rosko. "My most important advice to you is to purchase a good pair of waterproof boots."

"Boots?"

"And drive on the left, of course." Rosko fished in his jacket pocket and pulled out a pencil. "You can get the boots at the equestrian shop along the street to the right as you exit the station, near the corner of Main Street and High Street. Here's my mobile number. Ring me if you get into trouble. I know some people who can keep an eye on you." He scribbled a number on the back of his ticket stub and handed it to Bret. The train slowed as it pulled alongside a platform. "I'll be at home for two weeks' time, then it's off to France."

The cars stopped and Bret stood and gathered his things. "Thank you," he said to Rosko. "Thank you for everything," he elaborated, not exactly sure what he meant.

"Think nothing of it," said Rosko, shaking Bret's hand. "Now off with you, before the train moves on."

There didn't seem to be any present danger of this, but Bret complied. He stepped down onto the platform and walked alongside the cars and past the locomotive to the small lobby.

As he pulled open the heavy wooden door, the sound of the idling locomotive was replaced by a flat male voice on a loudspeaker announcing boarding for the train to Tralee. Bret supposed that must be where Rosko was going.

KILLARNEY

It was already after noon and Bret resolved to get something to eat in town before picking up his rental car. He stopped at the ticket booth to ask if he could put his bag in a locker, but the young woman behind the window said there were no lockers on this side of the station, only at the opposite end where the buses debarked. He could, however leave his bag in the ticket office and she would watch it if he liked. Bret said he would be much obliged and accepted. She stepped to the brass door beside the counter and let him in. Damn, he thought to himself. Must call Leslie about the bird.

"Right longside that cabinet would be just the place, sir."

"Thank you very much. Do I owe you anything?"

"Not at all, sir!"

He thanked her and said he would be back in two hours. Outside, the light gray overcast burning off, revealing Killarney to be a bustling and colorful town. He crossed the busy street that passed in front of the train station and randomly selected one of the three streets that fanned out from there. Within half a block he had located a suitable looking pub and settled in for lunch. Pint of Guinness, potato soup, shepherd's pie, side of potatoes, side of turnips—the sweetest and mildest he'd tasted. Since the pie was topped with potatoes, that made three servings of potatoes in one meal. No blight here recently. A second pint topped it off nicely.

He'd gotten the impression from the little bit of research that he'd done that this part of Ireland was considered the boondocks by Dubliners and other people on the more urbanized east coast, but he couldn't tell much difference other than that people seemed to talk, walk, and generally proceed at a more relaxed pace—and Dublin itself had seemed fairly laid-back to Bret. When he finally got his check and was on his way, it was past 2:00. He'd have to hurry to get back to the station by the time he'd said he would. He wasn't sure how to get to the Avis car rental place, but he figured he could ask the woman at the station, then maybe splurge on a cab.

He pulled open the station doors and went in. The ticket booth was shut. A handwritten sign said "reopen 1415." Bret crossed the room glanced out the window. Maybe she was just having a smoke or something. He didn't see her, but he did note a couple of taxis were parked in the lot. He walked back across the lobby and into the adjacent shopping mall. It was not unlike malls back home, with a tall, glass-ceilinged atrium, food court, and an assortment of what looked to be chain stores intermixed with local businesses. There was a Claire's shop that looked just like the one in the old train station mall back in Cleveland. A mother and daughter stood in the doorway debating, Bret deduced from their gestures, whether the girl should get her ears pierced here, another scene that would have been familiar back home. At the other end of the mall was the entrance to a bus station whose lobby was crowded with passengers waiting to board—much more crowded than the train station.

As he turned to go back, he thought he spotted Rosko walking past, but when he called out, the man didn't look up. No harm done. At least he hadn't run across the hall and tapped the fellow on the shoulder. Then he would have had to explain his error and probably would have stuck his foot in his mouth by saying that all middle-aged Irish gentlemen seemed to look alike in their tweeds and woolen caps.

The woman was back at the ticket window when he returned. His bag was now set aside near the door. "Very sorry I had to close up, sir," she said. She glanced down and noticed that one of her light blue shirttails was untucked from her dark blue trousers. She turned away momentarily to fix it.

"Oh, no problem," Bret responded.

"Pardon?" she said.

"Oh, nothing," he said.

He insisted on leaving a 2-euro tip, despite her protestations. As he stepped outside, he realized he had forgotten to ask her where to find Avis, but decided it would be awkward to go back in at the moment, so he went against his own rule and asked one of the cab drivers.

"Car rental? Yes sir!" In about 30 seconds he was in the back seat as the driver efficiently whipped into traffic, wove through the town center and stopped at a petrol station with a small auto showroom attached. Bret thanked him for the brisk ride (all of about four minutes from the station), tipped the rotund driver generously, and lugged his bag into the showroom as the taxi sped off. Bret walked inside.

"Avis?" asked the pleasant lady behind the counter. No, this is not Avis. Oh, dear. Please wait a moment—I'll try to telephone."

"I've got the number here." Bret pulled the folded paper out of his coat pocket, having printed a copy of the form when he completed the transaction over the internet back home.

"Ah, thank you. Those cabbies are a bit daft sometimes." She shook her head as if the situation were not unfamiliar. "Yes, Avis? Thank you. This is Shirley at Day Leasing. I've got a gentleman deposited here by mistake, says he's reserved a car. Yes, again. Yes. Mr. Sheehan, from America. Yes. Oh, dear. Shall I put him on? Yes, straight away."

She handed Bret the phone, whispering "there's been some sort of mix-up, but it will work out right."

Bret spoke to the woman on the line, who explained without pausing for a breath that she had his car, but it was at the airport ten miles out the other side of town, not in the city centre, and therefore she would have to go get it, and would he mind waiting where he was for about 20 minutes time? He said he would wait and handed the phone back to the proprietress. "Thank you very much."

"Think nothing of it," she said. "Please make yourself comfortable."

He situated himself on a shaded bench just as a large tour bus passed, headed toward the city centre. It seems a bit overlarge for the road. He was just beginning to question how the woman could get ten miles to the airport, pick up the car, and drive ten miles back in just twenty minutes when a tiny red hatchback swerved into the lot. A slim redheaded woman in black slacks and a white blouse jumped out. "Sorry, Mr. Sheehan?" she said breathlessly as she trotted towards Bret.

"Yes, thank you."

"We've got your car back at the tourist centre but it needed cleaning so I left if off there and drove out here to get you. The car should be ready by the time we finish with your paperwork. I'm sorry it took so long, but traffic is a bit heavy this time of day and it's such an enormous car it took me a little bit longer than usual to get through the city. Just put your valise in the boot if you please and we'll be off. Very sorry about the mix-up." She took a breath. "Thank you again Mrs. Day!" She shouted as she waved through the store window.

The ride back to the tourist centre, from the moment the slim Irishwoman leaned left and whirled the car out of the parking lot between two careening tour buses to the ratchet sound of the parking brake as she bounded onto the curb, reminded Bret of Franz Klamer's famous 1976 Olympic downhill ski run—two minutes at the edge of disaster ending in triumph. The real Avis office, it turned out, was no more than a five-minute walk from the train station. As he filled out the paperwork, the agent commented once or twice more about the enormity of the automobile he had rented, which struck him because he distinctly remembered ordering a mid-size compact, a Nissan Almera, which was something between an American Sentra and an Altima. A notch or two above econobox. On the other hand, her Nissan Micra was about the size of a toaster oven, so perhaps these things were simply relative.

She handed him the keys and walked him outside to the car.

He asked what would be the best way to get to Sneem, where he had rented his room for two weeks. "There are two routes," she said. "You could take the highway toward Cork, then go round through Kenmare town, or you can drive the ring road up over the mountains. Three ways, actually. At Moll's Gap, you can either go straight ahead following a very narrow road to Sneem, or go down to the river near Kenmare and take the coastal road. That's not quite so narrow." The way she said "three" was just like Uncle Michael, with only the hint of an "h."

"Which way is longer?" Bret asked.

"All nearly the same, I'd estimate. The ring road is the shorter distance, but the other is easier."

"I'll take the scenic way over the mountains, then."

"You certainly might do that." She seemed to be skeptical. "Follow the main road out of town just past Mrs. Day where you were waiting for me and keep to the right all the way around the lough. And drive on the left, remember! Have a lovely visit!" She stood there waving as he edged the car gingerly out into the main road.

A large sign on the sun visor announced ACHTUNG! DRIVE ON THE LEFT! Presumably the rest of the German was behind the fold with the rest of the English, but it did get his attention. Driving on the wrong side was not as disorienting as he expected, since everyone else was doing it, too. The main thing, he determined, was to sight along the centerline of the road and keep himself to the left of it. About five minutes after he'd set off, the two pints of Guinness notified him that they were ready to leave.

He remembered from his quick glance at the Avis map that there would be some remote territory between here and Sneem, so he figured he'd better find a place to stop soon. He saw a sign for Muckross House, which seemed to be a big tourist attraction, and set his sights on making it there. It shouldn't be more than ten minutes away.

As he drove, three enormous tour buses passed going the other direction. They were so wide that the cars on his side were forced to squeeze right up against the hedges on the left side to let them go by. Each time, the driver nodded and waved in a gesture of thanks. A fourth bus was stopped partway through a sharp corner and this time the driver lifted one finger from the wheel and pointed for Bret to proceed. Bret nodded and waved and went on past. This wasn't so difficult.

He spotted the parking area for Muckross House to the right and slipped in between two clumps of oncoming cars. Once in the vast area, he saw that most people seemed to be heading for Muckross House, but there was a sign that said Muckross Abbey 1448 pointing in the opposite direction. It appeared the abbey would be less crowded, so he parked toward the right edge of the lot and walked briskly down a paved path through the woods.

When he arrived at the abbey, he discovered that it was in fact a ruin—stone walls and no roof surrounded by a cemetery full of Celtic crosses. No toilet facilities visible anywhere. Beyond the Abbey was a dense wood, and Bret saw a dirt path leading into it. He set a beeline for that break in the trees. No one seemed to be around, but he could hear a horse walking along the cindered path off to his left. He remembered seeing horse buggies towing tourists when he got out of the car.

His eyes took a few seconds to adjust to the darkness under the tree canopy, but soon enough he found a broad mossy oak tree to duck behind. Again he heard the horse, a scuffing sound like hooves on gravel, even closer. It seemed unlikely that a buggy could fit down the narrow path, but he zipped up quickly and headed back toward the abbey even so.

Again, I wish I could take credit, but the sound was not of my making. The place seemed to be keeping a few paces ahead of me.

The bright sun was streaking between stormy-looking clouds to the west and illuminating the light gray stone of the abbey with a supernatural glow. He walked through one of the broad arches and found a dark stairway. The spiral steps deposited him on a parapet that gave him a good view of the surroundings. Growing out of an open courtyard was a single enormous tree. Bret concluded that the courtyard never had been covered, as this tree was very old. Through most of the rest of the building the roofs were gone. The abbey was in a small clearing. He heard the scraping sound again and looked down to see that a man was digging a grave in the abbey yard. That seemed strange, that a church that hadn't even had a roof for centuries would still have an active cemetery. The sky was suddenly more threatening, so he made his way back to the car, the sound of the digging slowly receding as he went. It started to sprinkle lightly.

THE
RING
ROAD

Bret swung cautiously to the right out of the parking area, got his car situated in the left lane, and headed on toward Sneem. After a couple of miles, the road began to rise and simultaneously narrowed considerably. And not only did the pavement get narrower, but the thorny hedges and rocks also came right up to the edge of the tarmac, so there was nowhere to go except into the hedge—and giving form to every hedge, Bret soon realized, was a stone wall, so a brush against a hedge was likely to be a scrape against rock as well.

A tour bus loomed up suddenly as Bret rounded a left-hand turn with a rock cliff overhanging his lane. The silver Fiat in front of him slowed, squeezed into the tight space, then squirted out the other side and disappeared up the road. The "enormity" of Bret's car, as noted by the clerk at Avis, became a factor as he realized that his vehicle, perhaps a foot wider than the Fiat, simply would not fit. Bret stopped. The bus driver squeezed a little bit farther to the outside, then stopped and opened his window. Bret thought the man was going to say something, but instead he reached out and folded in his side mirror. Rolling down his window, Bret did the same, then inched the car ahead until he had a few centimeters of wiggle room on either side and was able to get past. The bus driver responded with the universal thank-you gesture of the index finger raised from the steering wheel.

The road climbed more and wove in and out along the edge of the mountainside. Even when there was no oncoming traffic, it took considerable attention to keep the car in its lane. Breathtaking views opened up to the right, with rocky hills that looked both barren and lush at the same time. Every few minutes another enormous tour bus emerged ahead, obscuring the vista. And each time, a polite giving-way occurred on one part or the other, and in this manner Bret eventually made his way to a small parking area and gift shop at a place called Ladies View. He welcomed the opportunity to stop and take a break from the intense concentration. A bicycle whizzed by downhill as Bret closed his door. Now, that was bravery.

He leaned on a railing and looked out over the valley and lakes below. Sheep were scattered over the impossibly green hills while above them, puffy clouds grazed across the blue, their silent shadows wrapping over the contours of the hills and valleys. Bret's heart rate settled back into the aerobic range and he crossed the road to have a look in the gift shop. A small yellow sign on the shoulder said "Leprechauns Crossing." A sheep nibbled grass next to the signpost. It pooped a few turds onto the shoulder.

For sale inside the shop were many postcards, placemats, refrigerator magnets, posters, gift cards, and framed prints showing the view available for free outside, plus all sorts of cheesy trinkets, and, indeed, cheese. Bret bought a small wrapped piece of white cheddar and a bottle of mineral water and, 6 euros poorer, went back outside. His car was no longer where he had left it.

In the next half-second, three thoughts zipped through his mind: someone stole my car; I don't remember where I left my car; I don't remember what my car looks like. These thoughts proved to be moot when his attention was attracted by the honking of a horn to his right. Someone was blocking the road diagonally and a car coming up the hill was trying to squeeze around the outside. Then Bret realized it was his car blocking the way. He trotted down the hill towards it.

Who was driving? He couldn't see anyone in the driver's seat, nor in any other seat. Nor was the door open. An insistent squealing sound was coming from somewhere. He slowed to a walk when he got to within a few feet. The car was indeed empty. Bret stopped down and peered over the hood and through the windows. What was that squealing sound?

Bret heard another sound—air brakes. A tour bus had rounded the corner from the uphill direction and braked hard. Another bus was looming behind it.

The driver of the car that was trying to squeeze around called out through his open window. "Fellow tried to run over a sheep."

"What?" Bret asked.

"I watched it. I come around the bend and I see the sheep trotting down this way and just behind him the car is backing up trying to run it down." The man had close-cropped black hair and a tight, leathery face.

"Where is the sheep now?" Bret was beginning to figure out what had happened and he couldn't stifle a smile.

"It's no laughing matter. Pitiful creature is squeezed against the wall there," the driver said.

Bret looked around the back of the car and saw a plump and muddy white sheep pinned between the right rear bumper and the stone wall, squealing and squirming. Bret walked back alongside the car and made a show of looking in the window. "Keys are still in it, but no driver. Why don't I just move it out of the way? Then I'll go into the shop and see if it belongs to someone."

"That would be a fine public service, sir. No driver?"

Bret shrugged. He hoped the man didn't notice him surreptitiously unlocking the door. He opened it and climbed in, situated himself in the seat, depressed the clutch, and turned the key. The sheep squealed louder for a second, then Bret let out the clutch and the car lurched forward. He parked it near where he had left it the first time, making sure to leave it in gear and pulling back extra hard on the parking brake.

He looked back. The sheep had wandered into the middle of the road and sat down. The driver brushed past it and continued on up the hill, giving Bret a nod of thanks as he passed. Bret waved back. The four or five other cars that had been stuck also passed. Each nodded in thanks, except for the last driver in a red Mini Cooper, who suddenly ducked his head down away from the window just as he approached Bret, perhaps adjusting the radio or something. When the red Mini had rounded the climbing bend, Bret turned to the bus drivers and waved them on. The sheep got up and waddled over to the uphill shoulder.

After Bret was pretty sure everyone who might have seen the incident had left the scene, he walked around to see what kind of damage the car had incurred in hitting the stone wall. Evidently, the sheep had taken the full brunt: not a mark. Bret casually got back in the car and continued on up the road.

SNEEM

At Moll's Gap, Bret decided to proceed along the high road because it seemed the more direct route to Sneem. He also figured that the tour buses would more likely be coming up the other road, since it came from the coast. He figured wrong. The parade of huge coaches continued, and three or four times he had to pull partially off the road to allow one to pass. Once, he nearly hit a sheep that wasn't inclined to move aside. It raised its head just outside Bret's side window and Bret saw the reflection of the bus going by in the sheep's big, dim rectangular eyeball.

But there were also a few moments when he could get a good look at the landscape. The road followed the undulating shoulders of a series of high hills to his right. Straight ahead he could see more high hills and occasionally a glimpse of the sea. At one point he came out into a broad open area and saw the dark blue Kenmare River a mile or two to the left, stretching between this ridge of hills and another mountainous peninsula maybe a mile across the water. He remembered from the Avis map that the river gradually widened into an ocean bay as it reached toward the sea, and it surely seemed more bay than river here. At the shortest distance between him and the river, straight downhill to his left, he could see a couple of small white houses set back from the shore, where a short pier jutted into the river.

When he got into town, he parked the car next to a triangular village green and pulled a sheet of paper from his pocket. Printed on the paper was the e-mail message containing address of the apartment he had rented, which was supposed to be on the second floor of a retail shop in the center of town, as well as the name of the pub where he would find the lady who could give him the key. He unfolded the sheet. Find the Fisherman's Knot and ask for Renée or Cormack. There it was, the Fisherman's Knot, just across the square. He locked the car and walked over. A giant tour bus was rolling away from in front of a Quill's woolen goods store and, just behind it, another was disgorging a load of stiff-legged tourists onto the sidewalk. Bret darted across the road after the first bus passed. Inside the Fisherman's Knot, the white stone and stucco theme of the exterior was reiterated in a series of low arches. The place smelled of savory soup and a familiar herb Bret could not identify. A dark wooden bar ran the length of the room behind the arches, and at one end of the bar he could see a small cluster of men sitting on stools. When he passed under the arches to inquire at the bar, he could see that they were all watching tennis on a television above the bar.

"Vicious backhand, you see that?" one voice said.

"Zinger at the feet. Near impossible," said another.

"Pardon me," he called down. The bartender, a burly, bearded redhead of about 30, looked up toward him.

"Pint?" The man pulled a glass from a shelf.

"Uh, yes, please." Bret paused. "I'm looking for Renée," he said. "Need to get a key for a room I've rented. Or Cormack." A few feet behind the bartender, a small, dark-haired woman leaned out of the kitchen door, looked up and down the bar, and went back in.

"No Renée today, sir, she's gone off to Kenmare Town on business. But Cormack is here."

"Thank you. Could I speak to him?"

"Clearly, you could." He set the glass aside and let the half pour of Guinness settle. Then he reached out to shake Bret's hand. "You are. I'm he. You'll be Mr. Sheehan, then? Letting the self-catering apartment above the glass shop?"

"Yes, that's me. Or I."

Just then the door opened and a tour guide entered, followed by a couple dozen of the tourists Bret had seen getting out of the bus. When he glanced back toward the end of the bar, the television was off and the men were toasting each other loudly and two of them were throwing darts. As the guide led the group past the bar, speaking in German, one of the gents at the end of the bar began to play a jaunty reel on an accordion. Bret looked back at Cormack, who was whistling along with the tune and bouncing from leg to leg and also trying not to laugh, which made the whistling not entirely successful.

Cormack poured the other half of the pint. "Back in just a moment with your key, sir. And that pint's on me. Won't even make you sing for it." He winked.

"Thank you." Bret lifted the glass and sipped the smooth foam off the top and watched the tour group snake its way around the edge of the bar and back out the front door. Most of the people were of middle-age or older, but one couple had dragged along a studiously bored teenage son. Bret caught his eye and smiled. He momentarily broke his expression of ennui in order to roll his eyes at the accordion player, who noticed the gesture and temporarily departed from the Irish folk tune to play "Seven Nation Army" by the White Stripes, a song Bret knew because one of the Indians players used a snippet of it as his music when he stepped up to the plate. The kid caught on after a few seconds and cooly nodded approval. The accordionist winked, his face deadpan.

When the door closed after the last bus passenger exited, the accordion player was back to the White Stripes for a few bars, then folded the instrument and set it down. "Made that one's day, didn't I?" he asked Cormack. "Secret signal to another member of the Resistance."

Cormack replied. "Make it Radiohead next time?"

"Seamlessly, mate."

"My Bloody Valentine?"

"I don't want to break my instrument."

Bret had watched the whole theatrical episode with bemusement as a spectator, resisting his natural inclination to jump in and shape the action himself. He would to wait until he knew the audience better before taking charge of things. He glanced down the bar and saw the television was on again and the men had re-congregated to watch it. After a few minutes, Bret deduced that it must be the early rounds of the French Open. Two Belgian women had advanced, one a French-speaker, the other Flemish. The announcer made a big deal of this, noting that the home crowd was rooting for Justine Henine-Hardene, the French-speaker, since no French woman was likely to make the finals. The announcer said you could walk an hour in Belgium and end up speaking a different tongue. Bret considered how, in contrast, in the States you could drive all day for three days straight and hear the same old English, though maybe with a different twang.

Cormack reappeared through the front door and presented Bret with a key on a leather fob. "Outside the door, bear left and walk just to the bridge, but not across it. It's a blue door on the left with a number 59 marked on it. The gold key opens that door, the silver one the apartment. Not that you really need to lock either one. Now just mind that the cooker is also the heater for the apartment. There's a switch on the left side that controls it, but it's difficult to find and it's not marked very helpfully. That's all. You've paid already with your bank card, so that's settled. Unless you decide you would like to stay longer. In that event you'll want to speak to me or Renée. Or Lee the cook, if we're not to be found. At the moment, the rooms are available until the 13th, if I'm not mistaken."

"Thank you. And thanks for the pint." Bret lifted the glass in a gesture of toast.

Cormack nodded and excused himself, rejoining the crew at the other end of the bar.

Bret drained the glass and set it down on the bar, sliding a few euro coins alongside the coaster. Once outside, he decided to check out the room before getting his things from the car. He opened the outer door and climbed a narrow stairway illuminated by a skylight. The key required some jiggling, but it worked after a few seconds and the apartment door swung open. Bret entered the room. Windows on two sides looked out from the side and back of the building, providing a vista over what Bret figured must be the Sneem River tumbling down over some rocks, then spreading into a meandering estuary. He could see the open water of a bay maybe half a mile away.

The furnishings were not rustic as he had expected. Instead they were of simple modern design, clear finished light woods and metal and glass. The walls were white, with pine floors except for red tile in the kitchen area. The bed was under a high window along the back wall. The window was open and the curtains alongside it swayed a little.

He decided the car was fine where it was, and locked it up after retrieving his luggage. It was now about 7:00 in the evening and it seemed the tour buses were done for the day. Fatigue was catching up with him in a hurry. He figured he'd unpack his things, change clothes, eat some dinner somewhere, and get to sleep early in an effort to readjust his body clock. As he crossed the main road, one bag in each hand, he saw Cormack standing outside the door of the Fisherman's Knot, talking with a tall woman with straight dark hair that was trimmed flat across the back and sides. They kissed briefly, his hand slipping momentarily into the back pocket of her black jeans. She laughed and walked up the street in the opposite direction. Cormack went back inside.

Upstairs, Bret unloaded the contents of his bags into a built-in drawer unit and put Uncle Michael's box on the windowsill overlooking the river. The old man would like the view. With some difficulty (having lost his pocket knife to airport security), Bret removed the yellow tape and peeked inside the box. The chunk-filled light gray powder looked just as it had earlier.

This was comfort indeed. I have found myself becoming progressively more nervous that something may happen to confound the mission. But at the same time it was also becoming more difficult to discern what was happening exactly. The most prudent tactic seemed to be to stay in the background and watch carefully for any moment when an intervention might be in order.

Bret didn't risk the temptation of sitting down for just a moment, knowing he'd likely be out cold for the night, so he slapped the lid back on and set the can on the sill and turned around immediately and went back down the stairs.

He debated having a bite in the Fisherman's Knot, but didn't recall seeing food there, so he set off in the other direction, crossing the narrow town bridge. He found a second village square—a four-sided one—and then a French restaurant, of all things, but decided he was too tired to wonder about that and went in.

He ordered a salmon steak and a glass of wine. The fish was exquisite, its robust flavor suggesting to him it was caught wild rather than farm-raised, but maybe it just tasted better in Ireland. The light lingered long here, though it was still nearly a month to the solstice, and when Bret went back outside and began walking toward his room, the shadows seemed only slightly longer than when he had come in. It certainly was a beautiful little town: lush greenery, bright stone, and colorful painted wood everywhere. Big hills in the middle distance and the smell of the sea. As he crossed the narrow bridge and began to angle to the right over toward the blue door, someone called his name from over his left shoulder. He turned. It was Cormack, standing near a cafe table in front of another pub, not his own. "Good evening Mr. Sheehan. Been looking for you. Take a moment and come hear some of the real thing, real Irish folk music, I mean. Musicians' night once a week over here and we've got a fine group assembled tonight." Standing next to him were the tall woman he'd seen before and another woman, shorter, with extremely thick and wild black hair. "This is Renée, my wife. And this is Lee. Cooks for us at the Knot." Lee tucked her white t-shirt into her blue jeans, and nodded a hello. Her slight build and remote demeanor reminded Bret of the women who used to hang around the modern dance studio back in college.

"I'm still behind the jet lag, but I guess I'll stop in for a little while. Thanks." Bret followed Cormack and the women in through a small front room, down a hallway, and into a larger back chamber where a fiddle player and a man with a hand drum were accompanying a woman who was singing and playing guitar. The music was a plaintive ballad, performed without any amplification. The room was hushed. Bret was somewhere between mesmerized and fading into a stupor. They finished that song and began another, more upbeat tune. Between numbers, Cormack led them to a corner table near the back. Bret and the black-haired woman Lee sat on a bench along the wall while Renée took a chair on the other side of the table and Cormack went for drinks.

"Marion O'Neill, she's the best at this," Cormack whispered in Bret's ear while placing a pint into his hand. "Now, don't try to pay this time. I'll be insulted." Bret shrugged. Marion O'Neill was indeed a fine singer, her voice mellow yet high and pure, breaking sometimes as she shifted notes in a way that echoed the quick double-bounce of the bow on the fiddle's strings. As Bret listened and drank, he felt as if everything that had come before was draining away until all that was left was here and now. She put down the guitar and played a solo piece on the penny whistle. Bret scanned the room until his eyes fixed on a pay telephone near the side door. It suddenly dawned on him that he could call Leslie from here and tell her to go fetch the parakeet, then it double-dawned on him that he wouldn't be able to hear anything.

Then he noticed the mood had changed and there were now eight dancers high-stepping and twirling in an open space while the music went faster and faster. Bret became aware that two of the dancers were Cormack and Renée. He looked nervously at Lee sitting next to him, who returned the glance and smiled. He leaned over and slurred, "I can't do that."

"Nor I," she said, flashing a smile of white, attractively misaligned teeth. Her voice was raspy.

An accordion had joined in, and the drummer was wailing away with a two-headed stick, his hand a blur. The whole crowd in the packed room was vibrating with the sound. Smells of sweat and beer swirled with assorted colognes and perfumes. Then it was over.

Outside, it was nearly dark, but they stood beneath a spotlight beside the building. The two dancers were both drenched in sweat. Cormack's blue shirt was stained under the arms and down the center and Renée's bare shoulders glistened. "Pleasure to meet you," Bret said, reaching out his hand. His head had cleared a little.

She leaned over and kissed him politely on the cheek. "Welcome to knot in Ring of Kerry," she said with a peculiar accent he could not identify.

"Pardon?" Bret asked.

"She's fooling," said Cormack. "It's a phrase the tourist bureau is fond of but it's too awkward to ever say it aloud."

"Welcome to the rot in the dingleberry," said Lee. "See? Impossible."

"I could come up with better than that," Bret said.

"I'm offended," said Lee.

"I meant the original one, knot not rot."

"Say that three times quickly," said Lee.

"Knot not rot not rock not knock knock, who's there?" said Bret, pleased with himself for being so clever.

"Now that will get the tourists piling in, won't it?" said Cormack.

"Based on my drive over here, there seem to be enough tour buses already," said Bret. "Unless it's forbidden to suggest that."

"You can say it, just don't think it," said Lee.

"Do you like the music?" asked Renée.

"Very nice," Bret replied. "Not my usual genre, but it was lovely."

"Punk rock night tomorrow," Lee said. "Then you'll get me dancing."

"If you want to call it that," said Cormack. "Flailing I'd say."

"Envy doesn't look good on you, Cormack," said Lee.

"Fancy a nightcap?" said Cormack. And before Bret knew it, they were all walking back toward the Fisherman's Knot. "Can't sell liquor this late," said Cormack, "but I can give it away."

They stood at the bar and Cormack walked behind and poured each a short glass of straight Irish whiskey. "So, Mr. Sheehan," he said, "What brings you to our little village?"

"An errand," said Bret. The whiskey burned pleasantly down his throat. "I promised my cremated uncle I'd get him back to Castle Cove. I mean I promised him before he was cremated, when he was still alive. I have him here in a convenient metal box."

"Ha!" said Lee. "I told you so!"

"What" said Bret. "You guessed that?"

"We agreed," she said, "that there could be one of three reasons a man like you would be voyaging here alone from America. One, you're a travel writer secretly preparing entries and ratings for one of those silly guide books. Two, you're a businessman looking for some way to buy up a load of property and make buckets of money off it. Three, you're here on some kind of obscure personal errand. I like a mystery. Mine was number three."

"Aha," said Bret. "And how did you other two vote?"

Cormack downed his drink and grinned. "Number one, sir. Guess I can let the guard down now."

Renée blushed. "You must understand that in place I grow up, crazy businessmen always develop wild plans. They never succeed, because government never lets anyone do anything, but still they try. Number two is my idea."

"I take no offense," said Bret. "But if you don't mind, I can't place your accent—where are you from?"

"I am born in Prague, grow up in Bretagne, get in Ireland for college and I am still here with Cormack. Complicated, yes?" She leaned against her husband's bulky shoulder.

Bret was felt that he was getting enough of a sense of who was who now, the roles they played. With that understanding, he was beginning to feel more confident of his ability to shape the story. Shape the story sounds so much better than manipulate people and sling bullshit, he laughed to himself. Cormack, he was the unflappable rock, Lee the studied rebel, Renée the wise and worldly outsider— but she overplayed it. In fact, he thought, all three of them are overplaying. Why?

"And how about miss Lee, here?" Bret was getting a bit of second wind. Or third. He'd lost count of the winds. Or maybe it was the alcohol.

She motioned over her shoulder and angled her head back, causing a shock of thick hair to flip over her face. "Born just round the corner. Me and Cormack went to grammar school together, didn't we Cor?"

"True, that is," he said. "It's like our feet are rooted in these bogs and rocks." He poured another round.

"Never felt a need to wander, like that bard in the old story?" Bret asked, sipping from the refilled glass.

"What bard would that be?" Cormack asked.

"The one in the story with the princess who likes to stand on the hills and they get struck by lightning at the end and their ashes get washed down into the land."

"Never heard that one," said Cormack, looking from Lee to Renée for confirmation. They shook their heads. "Must be an Americanism. There's plenty of fake Irish malarky out there."

Bret shrugged. "Anyhow, before my uncle died, I told him I'd take his ashes back to Castle Cove. He asked me to put him in a holy well. I don't even know what that is, a holy well. What the hell is a holy well?"

"That sounds like some shite Marion O'Neill would sing," Lee laughed. "All about uncles and ashes and holy wells and faeries and sprites." Her black eyes glistened. "Your uncle was a bit feckin dotty, was he?"

"Probably so, probably so," Bret said. "But here I am, I might as well finish what I said I would do, am I right?"

"No harm in it, I suppose," said Cormack. "People done stranger things."

"Tell you the truth, those fuckers my relatives cornered me into this. I was all set to just have him be in the church back there. 'Cause I had already told Uncle Michael I'd get him to Ireland and I think he died a happy man since I told him that, so what difference would it make now?"

"So why are you here, then, if it makes no difference?" Lee asked. "What are you really up to?"

"Like I said, they backed me into a position where I had to come do this, you know just to preserve my good reputation. I'm supposed to be the great persuader, made a life's work of it, but I let my guard down and they walked me into a trap. Amateur mistake. Distracted by skircumskances, circumskant—you know what I mean."

"The unwilling tourist, is he?" Cormack said. "Might as well make a nice holiday of it."

"My attitude exactly," Bret said. "Plus, I don't know . . . maybe there's some small chance . . ."

"That it does matter?" Lee said.

"For me," Renée chimed in, "I am not believing in ghosts, but this is not worth risk of mistake. Come to Ireland, enjoy nice holiday, new friends give whiskey, throw ashes in well. Everybody happy—you, relatives, new friends, uncle ghost."

"That would be the Irish way," Cormack said. "Hedge your bets just in case the magic is real."

"I was watching you and your friends in the pub before," Bret said. "I saw how you can all turn on that authentic Irishyness—boom!—as soon as a busload of German tourists walks in the door."

"Give 'em what they want, oldest story in the book," Cormack laughed.

"And you're playing to me too, am I right?" Bret paused and looked from one to the other, his eyes sloshing unsteadily. "The jolly host, his lovely exotic wife, and the flirty and attractive rebel girl. Just the crast to gab—cast to grab this audience, am I right?"

"You give us too much credit," Cormack shook his head.

"Hey, me I'm just being who I am," said Lee. "Flirty and attractive rebel girl."

"Lovely exotic wife," said Renée.

"And if you assume we're playing to you," Lee said, "then of course you'll be playing to us as well. So what's the story?"

"No story," said Bret. "Just me and a can of ashes."

"You expect us to believe that now?" Lee laughed. "The man without a story, that's who you're pretending to be. We have to wait to find out who you really are. He's more than he's letting on."

"More like less," said Bret, half mumbling. "Or less is more, or words like that, am I right? Do I keep saying 'am I right?'"

"You do," said Cormack.

"I knew it," said Bret. "Right again. You . . ." He lost his train of thought. It was something about getting these people to . . . to something. The overhead lights blurred and weaved as Bret tipped his head back to empty his glass. Cormack began to pour another, but Bret stopped him. "I'm about ready for a pillow. If I can get up the stairs."

"Oh, have one more," said Cormack. "We'll help you up the stairs. Lee will heave you right over her shoulder. Am I right?"

Lee laughed. "I'm feckin strong like an ant."

Bret watched the Tullamore Dew bottle tip once more, the light brown liquid swirling up the sides of the glass.

I might have attempted to intervene here, but a story must take its course. As an aside, I urge skepticism toward the implication that our journey here had been somehow precipitated by certain relatives allegedly maneuvering Bret into undertaking this quest. Rather, I must conclude that my subtle persuasions had taken their effect in a way that simply appeared to have been the result of human agency. I am not offended. I understand that this kind of misattribution of modus operandi is a common characteristic of the taibhse at work, indeed a tactic for remaining unobtrusive.

THE RIVER

The sound of rain on a metal roof woke Bret up. It was well past dawn, though exactly what time it was he didn't know. He didn't remember where he'd put his watch. He didn't remember getting to his room, for that matter. The curtains above his bed were flapping about in a gusty wind. When he stood up to close the window, he winced as his head told him to proceed gingerly. He turned away from the gray yet painful light of the window and realized that Lee was curled up on the small sofa near the table. Her shoes were off, her white shirt untucked and pulled askew off her left shoulder. A thicket of wiry hair covered her face, her chin tucked down against the bare shoulder because of the way her head was wedged into the crease between the arm and the back of the seat.

Bret turned back to the window and reached to pull it closed and that was when he noticed that the little box that held Uncle Michael's ashes was gone. A quick look on the floor of the room confirmed what he feared: with no screen in the window, the box had left the building.

Bret stuck his head out and looked down. There it was, in a small flowering shrub, the lid partially dislodged. Stopping in the middle of the floor for a moment to decide not to wake up Lee, he hurried out the door and downstairs to try to get to the ashes before the rain did. He heard the upstairs door slam itself as the wind gusted again. His head was still thick with sleep and liquor. It wasn't until he was halfway around the building that he remembered he was barefoot, his attention brought to the matter by the coarse gravel that ran alongside the building. On his right, the river had transformed itself from the peaceful babbling brook of last night into a robust rapid worthy of an extreme sports excursion. It was raining a bit harder now but it must have been pouring heavily upon the hills for a while. The air smelled like rocks and sugar.

Around the back corner, he located the box in the bush, frightened off a couple of sparrows who were hiding in there, and squeezed the top back on. Then he walked briskly back around to the front of the building, pushed open the blue door (which had nearly closed itself), and trotted up the stairs. Locked. What to do? Get a spare key from the bar? Surely no one would be working this early. Of course, Lee was inside, he remembered. He raised his knuckles, but the door opened before he could knock. Lee stepped aside to let him in. "Heard that door smack and I thought you'd run off," she said, pushing the black frizzles away from her face with her free hand.

"Thanks," he replied. "Excuse me a second." Closing the apartment door behind him, he crossed the room, placed the box on the kitchen table, and sat down. He pried off the lid.

Some water had gotten into the box. The ashes seemed to be foaming up. Bret slapped the lid back on, coughing. He had a momentary notion that Uncle Michael might somehow reconstitute himself, but he suppressed that. "Well, that was almost a disaster."

"What was?" Lee stood beside him, looking at the box.

"This is the whole reason I'm here," Bret said. "Take Uncle Michael back home. He fell off the windowsill, right outside. Landed in the bushes. If I lose this can, my mission is a failure."

"Your mission?" She raised her brows and looked at him sideways. "Oh, right. The feckin holy well."

"Yes, that's right. I guess that means I talked about it last night?"

"Must have done," she replied.

He paused. "Too little sleep means a little bit of whiskey goes a long way."

"And it wasn't such a little bit, thanks to Cor's heavy pouring hand . . ." she laughed. "Truth is, I didn't intend to go to sleep on the settee. Just having a bit of a rest after carrying you up the stair."

"Carrying me?—" He looked at her and detected a sparkle of mischief in her black eyes. "Never mind," he said.

"Come down to the pub in ten minutes time and we'll have a pot of tea and raisin scones," she said, slipping on her shoes. "Go round back through the alley. Yellow door. The front will be locked. And mind your uncle!" With a wink and a brisk nod of her head, she was gone.

I am still not exactly clear on exactly what happened during these preceding moments, nor indeed, for the later portion of the preceding evening. Perhaps all the whiskey had somehow gone to my noncorporeal head as well. Nonetheless, this day I felt a positive anticipation that progress would be made in our errand.

Bret sat down in the chair next to the table. While his initial plan had been to spend a few relaxed days getting acclimated to Sneem, he now felt a greater sense of urgency about finding the well and properly depositing the ashes. He could have his leisurely vacation after completing that task. Now he had to figure out where the right sort of well might be and get himself there. He looked out the window, as if the answer might be there. And maybe it was: the river. Might there not be a well near the river? Or why not the river itself? Wasn't it just the water from a well that was up in the hills?

He changed out of his wet clothes into dry ones and found his water-shedding windbreaker and a ball cap. Then he put on shoes, picked up the metal box, and descended the stairs. He would start his mission directly after breakfast. It was raining harder now.

A narrow passageway cut through the bank of shops that included the pub, about halfway down the street. Bret assumed this was the alley of which Lee had spoken, so he entered it. The white noise of the rain stopped for a moment, replaced by the sound of water running and dripping. When he got to the light at the other end, the downpour was finished. He trotted through the lingering drops to a yellow door with the image of a knot painted in black near the handle.

Inside, two places were set at a small wooden table near the back window. A teapot steamed under a heather-colored cozy and four lumpy scones sat on a blue-rimmed plate in the center of the table. Holding a crock of butter in one hand and a jar of preserves in the other, Lee emerged through the door to the front of the pub just as Bret approached the table. "There," she said. "Commence the day properly. Please, sit."

Bret seated himself. As she poured tea, she asked, "And what plans have you today, Mr. Sheehan? Perhaps I can help."

"Try to find my holy well, I guess," he said. "These smell terrific."

"They're yesterday's, but still fresh enough with a few minutes of reheating." She nodded. "Today I'm working, but tomorrow I could help you search. Maybe today you should rest and try to get over your jet lag."

"Maybe so. I'd like to walk around the town, too."

"Today would be a very good one for that. Not so many tourists, and the skies should be fair by midday. There's a lovely nature path along the river. And a village full of charming shop proprietors more than willing to help you part with your money."

"Sounds reasonable," he said, but he still intended to look around for a holy well. He didn't like to think about what the water was doing to the ashes and he didn't intend to delay getting them to their final resting place any longer than absolutely necessary.

"Good," she said. "Then let's meet here tomorrow morning, 9:00? Tea and scones, and then a walk in the hills."

He finished his tea, put down the cup, and nodded. "Sure. Sounds great, thanks." He picked up his dishes and looked for a place to put them.

"Right here," Lee said, taking the plate and cup and saucer. "Enjoy your recuperation day. Stop in the Knot this evening if you fancy a pint."

"Thanks, maybe I will," he said. "If not, I will see you tomorrow morning."

A taibhse has very limited self-mobility. The manual, quel surprise, would not touch upon this topic at all. One cannot walk in any traditional manner—only float about following one person or another, or simply "haunt" a particular location. This song you may have heard, Ghost Riders in the Sky or on the Storm or whatever the title is: poppycock. People simply making things up.

THE RAIN HAD EASED to little more than mist, but the river still roared. Along the left edge of it, beginning in a little park dotted with picnic tables, was a gravel path leading downstream, away from the center of town. Bret decided to follow that path.

The river slowed and widened almost immediately, meandering about among clumps of tall grasses. The sea was not visible, but he could smell it on the soft breeze that blew in his face. Soon the footing got swampy and the gravel path was replaced by a boardwalk that led, after ten minutes' walk, past a small marina (where a long-disused, high-prowed wooden fishing boat rested half submerged), and into a kind of arboretum. It seemed like the sort of place where a well might be dug, maybe up the hill a bit. He looked around and spied a little clearing to his left. As he left the boardwalk and ducked under an overhanging branch, a kid on a bicycle zoomed past, the tires rumbling on the boards. Startled, Bret bobbled the box, but did not drop it.

His head was starting to clear better now. It was nice of them to have taken him under their wing last night, but he was paying for it today. Lee was interesting. He'd have to stop in the Fisherman's Knot and have a chat with her sometime. What exactly they had discussed in the bar last night he could not quite recall, but he remembered she seemed to have a pointed sense of humor. Jagged, even. Whether she had actually carried him up the stairs . . . Bret suspected Cormack and/or Renée might have assisted with that.

Finally, he found himself on a narrow lane, and after following it for a few hundred yards, came to the end of a pier marked with a sign showing, in black silhouette, a car plummeting into water. He stopped. No well. He stepped up to the edge of the pier and looked down into the water. It was moving more swiftly than it looked, judging by the strong eddies that formed around the corners of the pier. A metal box tossed in here would be gone instantly, sinking to the bottom perhaps, or simply being carried out to sea if it floated. But he hadn't really considered this. He had always envisioned that he would open the box and pour. He held it up and read the label: Remains of Michael Sheehan, cremated May 17, 2003.

"Don't be littering in my river," said a voice from beside him. The boy on the bicycle had returned. "People always throwing things in off the end here."

"No, I'm not," said Bret.

"What's in it, then?" The boy's voice had the dry huskiness that suggested it would be lower soon.

"My uncle."

"That so? In the box? That's not a very big uncle. Why'd you bring him out here?"

"Well," Bret hesitated. "I'm on a mission to return his ashes back home. I'm to deposit them in a well."

"Oh, yeah," said the boy. "Like I was saying, you can't just chuck him in the river. That's not a well."

"Do you know where I can find a well? A holy well?"

"Holy wells? Yeah, I know a few, up on the hills most of 'em. Do you know which well?"

"No. Just a well. He was from Castle Cove."

"Well, I expect you should take him back there, then, don't you think?" The boy turned the bike around. "Definitely wouldn't be right to pitch him into the Sneem River or the Kenmare if he's supposed to go down a well. Not the same thing at all."

"No," Bret agreed. "I said I wasn't going to."

"You said it yourself. I'm due home. Was I you I'd stop at Cunningham's shop and purchase one of them survey maps that shows Castlecove. I wager it's the same one that shows Sneem." He pronounced "Sneem" with a soft "sh" at the beginning. "They mark every little thing on those maps, you'll see. O something survey." He sped off. That was the third person, Bret thought, who said "Castlecove" as if it were one word.

Instead of retracing his steps, Bret followed the little lane back to town, which he estimated would be a quicker walk. Soon, he could see the main road ahead. He looked to the left and saw that the river level had fallen back down a bit, whether because the rain had let up or the tide was going out, he didn't know. A large stone house with a blue-painted wooden second floor, set farther back from the road than most, overlooked the river from here. Bret spied the boy's bicycle leaning in a carport next to a red mini. The carport was obviously a recent addition, though it didn't look inappropriate. A low stone wall followed one edge of the gravel drive and at the end of it was a short pillar.

On the main road, he turned left and easily located Cunningham's not three stores down. He walked in and nodded hello to the shopkeeper. She smiled at him and resumed a conversation with an elderly man who was wearing a long dark gray coat and rubber boots. "How much is it?," the customer asked.

"Three euro and fifty cents, John Bewley," she answered.

"Eh?" He responded.

"It's three euro and fifty cents, I said John," she replied a bit louder.

"Three pounds and fifty pence?" His voice was deep and gruff.

"That's right, John Bewley, three euro and fifty cents."

Bret located a rack full of maps. The first one he picked up covered the territory but offered no topographic detail. He noted it marked Castlecove as one word. Replacing that map, he looked among the other offerings. On the back side of the map rack was an entire section devoted to a series labeled "Ordnance Survey Discovery Series," each with a number in the upper right corner and a schematic on the back showing which maps covered what areas. He decided that number 83 or 84 would be the one. It turned out both of them included Castle Cove—printed as two words on this map—but number 84 also covered Sneem, so he chose that one. Checking his wallet, he decided he'd try to get a bit more cash as well.

"Thank you, John Bewley, mind well driving."

"Price went up," he mumbled, "used to be 'twas two pounds ten pence."

"That's right, John Bewley, the price went up nine year ago when the tariff changed, you know yourself. And after that we got the euro. You know that too, your billfold is full of them. Good day, John Bewley." The man continued to stand in front of the counter, rummaging through the pockets of his long coat. His face was covered with a week's worth of unshaven white beard, his nose bulbous, the cheeks jowly, the lips thick and held apart. The shopkeeper smiled at Bret, her gray eyes sparkling under a thick tangle of gray-brown hair. "Sorry, will that be all, sir?"

"Yes, thank you," said Bret. "Pardon me, but I wonder if you know where there is a bank machine in Sneem?"

"Ah, no sir, there isn't one at all. Kenmare town would be the closest. Seven euro ten, sir."

"I see," said Bret. "Just this then, please."

"Right. Good day, sir."

Outside, he turned left and his eyes immediately alighted on the phone booth. He walked over and went in and picked up the receiver. He didn't know Leslie's new number by heart, but it was in his wallet. He dropped in all the coins he had and prepared to speak very quickly. It didn't pick up after five rings, and then it went to a warbly answering-machine message, using up precious seconds. "Hey Leslie, don't forget Oprah. I—" his coins ran out. Well, that was probably enough, he hoped.

He nearly stopped in the Fisherman's Knot on the way back to his room but it was still early in the day and he doubted they'd be opening up yet. Come to think of it, it was five in the morning back home. Maybe it was a good thing Leslie hadn't picked up the phone.

Bret took the map upstairs and spread it out on the table. At the upper edge of the map was the lower part of the Iveragh peninsula, with Castle Cove well marked about three quarters of the way out the coast. A few miles inland and uphill from that was something called Staigue Fort. And over the ridge from Staigue Fort was a little red dot and the words "holy well," nestled in Windy Gap and near Eagles Hill. It was adjacent to the Kerry Way, a walking path, also marked in red on the map. Somewhere up there, he felt reasonably confident, he would find what he was seeking. Today, drive down to Kenmare. Tomorrow, off for the hills. He folded the map and placed it on the table, next to Uncle Michael.

On the way out he walked over to the bed and straightened the covers, which were still as he had left them first thing in the morning. A few long, black kinky strands of hair clung to one of the pillows. He lifted them slowly and held them up to the sunlight as a sparrow alighted on the sill. He shooed it away and closed the window.

I was taken aback that I had no particular sense that this holy well marked on the map was or was not the correct one. In fact, I got no sense that there was such a thing as one correct holy well. It would be ironic to get so close and then have to determine a final site by supposition or conjecture. Perhaps any holy well in these hills would suffice. The same stone, the same water.

KENMARE

After about 30 minutes of tense, stop-and-go driving on the narrow and contorted coastal road, Bret found himself entering Kenmare town. A triangular green was the nucleus of the street structure, with the main roads of the town fanning out as extensions of the sides of the triangle. A large number of shops and, more to the point, at least two banks, were visible to the right of the central green, between the center of town and the river. Bret found a small parking lot just the other side of the green, left the car there, and walked into town.

The very first bank had a machine marked with his bank's network. He slid the card in the slot, entered his PIN number, and withdrew 200 euros. That was a relief.

He walked further down the street. Lots of small art shops were mixed in with cafes, clothing stores, and other businesses. He stopped in a music shop and asked if they had anything by Marion O'Neill. "Sorry, no, sir. Did have, but I sold the last one and I haven't called her yet to ask for a few more discs. How do you know her?"

"I heard her sing," said Bret. "Just last night in Sneem. Beautiful."

"Ah. Lucky fellow. They've punk rock night this evening. All the same folk instruments, different repertoire. Spirit of the Pogues, if you will. In any case, in two or three days time, I can get some more discs from Mary. If she's at home."

"Please don't do that just for me," said Bret. "I'm not sure that I'll be around the area that long. But thank you. Anything else in that vein? Local music?"

The shop owner paused for a moment. "You might like this. It wasn't recorded here, but it does feature a few local musicians. It's from the annual Celtic festival across the water in Brittany."

"Where in Britain?"

"In Brittany, France. Finistère. Near Roscoff where the overnight ferry comes in."

"Oh, all right. I'll try it. May I use my bank card?"

"As you wish."

AT THE END OF THE STREET was a post office where one could, for a small fee, use one of a number of computers that offered internet access. He signed out a key card and checked his e-mail (nothing but spam), had a look at the weather back home (partly cloudy in the 70s), and then, on a whim, searched for "Holy well Castle Cove." No matching results found.

He pulled out the card and returned to the desk, noticing a circular stand filled with various maps and guides as he stood in line to pay. One in particular caught his eye: "Hillwalker's Guide to Carrauntoohil and Macgillycuddy's Reeks: A selection of twelve hill walks to the mountains of Killarney, Co. Kerry." He picked it up.

The man at the desk, who had been not uncourteous but brusque when Bret checked out the card, now perked up upon seeing the hillwalking guide. "Going into the hills, are you?"

"Yes," Bret answered.

"Just finished with the annual hillwalking festival last week. Quite a few come a long way for that. Rained only once, the lucky sods. Typically it's quite wet these weeks of the year."

"Actually," Bret paused, "Maybe you can help me. I'm hoping to find a holy well near Castle Cove."

"Oh, that's marked on the Ordnance Survey Map number 84. Very well known."

"Really?"

"Yes, sir. But why would you wish to find it?"

Bret explained about Uncle Michael and the ashes.

"Ah, then again it may not be that particular well. They abound up there. I believe there's another just on the shoulder of Staigue, near the top of the ridge above the fort. That might be your well. Best check both. You could walk past the little one and if you miss it or it doesn't seem right, just continue on to the other. Don't suppose the uncle would know the difference! Very sorry, that was impolite." He opened up his own copy of #84 and showed Bret the spot. "Course, you're crossing private property to walk up that way, but I done it many a time. Just leave everything as you find it and don't disturb the woolies. There's a nice clear way over the ridge, keeping to the left of a row of fences and to the right of a small stream. To find the smaller well, you follow the ridge line to the left perhaps a thousand paces from the low point of the crest. It's not too hard to find in fair weather. But don't be up there in a storm."

"Thanks."

"One more thing," the man said. "That hillwalking guide you've got there doesn't cover the area you're looking at."

"No? Is there such a guide?"

"No, sir. Closest would be the Kerry Way map guide— the Kerry Way circles the entire peninsula and passes straight through the hills above Castlecove. That in combination with the number 84 would suit your purpose."

"All right, then I'll take them both. Many thanks."

LIGHTHEADED WITH HUNGER, he stopped in a small grocer that faced the town green and bought a meat pie and a bottle of ginger ale. Outside, he found all the park benches taken, but settled down comfortably enough on a low stone wall with his back to the green. An enormous tour bus pulled up across the street, blocking his view of all the shop windows he had been scanning. A small crowd of perhaps 25 people was disgorged onto the street (the door of the bus was on the right side, which, along with the "Ligne Quimper" wording on the side of the bus, indicated to Bret that the vehicle was visiting from another country where people drove on the other side of the road and spoke French—France, or maybe Belgium).

As Bret watched, it became clear to him that certain of the party had been imbibing immoderately and these same were now in search of a pub in which to continue said activity. A very red-faced fellow with a big belly draped under an untucked white shirt was pronouncing loudly to his compatriots to follow him around the corner. The bus driver shook his head, slid open his window, and leaned out to call out something in French to the group, the gist of which Bret interpreted to be "Hurry up, you idiots."

Bret finished his pie and decided to walk down a side street near a little sign saying "stone circle." After a couple of blocks, the road crested a hill and the town abruptly ended. He walked downhill toward an open space on the right, just before a bridge. That must be where the stone circle was. But when he arrived at the small green clearing, there was nothing more than a low stone wall and a couple of modern stone or cement statues. The bridge beyond, he realized, crossed the Kenmare River, which at this place emptied from a narrow course into the widening bay Bret had seen farther to the south and west. He wondered if the circle were perhaps on the other side of the bridge, but looking in that direction he saw nothing. He must have missed it, walked past in his haste. He turned around.

At the crest of the hill, on the right, there was a stone church. It was set back from the street and nestled among tall trees. He hadn't noticed it on the way out. Something pulled him toward it now, but he resisted. It was an Anglican church, Episcopal. No one seemed to be there, but churches as a rule were usually unlocked. Wouldn't be much of a sanctuary if you couldn't get in. He envisioned the interior, dark and oaky smelling, with stone and wood everywhere. At the end of a pew he would sit and look around the room, trying not to focus too much on the simple cross at the front. Personally, he was never quite sure what that cross meant, and it made him uncomfortable because it seemed like other people did understand. Those were terms he never liked, being in situations where others understood and he didn't—though this seemed to be his general situation here, on unfamiliar land where he knew no one.

But it was very likely that no one was in the church now. This was a Catholic section of a Catholic country, and this church was probably just a leftover from earlier English occupation. But if he went in and there was someone inside, he would have to explain himself, and he wasn't sure he could do that right now. Especially right now. He took a step to cross the street toward the church and stopped. Maybe later.

Back in the square, he reexamined the "stone circle" sign and determined that it referred to the next street over. The commercial buildings quickly gave way to a neighborhood of low residential structures, brightly painted, many with small colorful gardens inside stone walls that set off the houses from the street. At the end of the block, a little white "stone circle" sign pointed to the right. The paved road gave way to gravel and after a quick minute of walking gradually uphill, Bret found himself at the edge of a grassy clearing in the middle of which was a ring of large stones set upright, with one large rock in the center. He entered the space and looked around. From here he could see the hills he had driven over from

Killarney, plus, in the other direction, the hills he had looked at across the Kenmare River. A few church steeples rose above the trees, but otherwise there was no evidence of the town from here. He leaned against the central rock.

How old was this stone circle? A few thousand years? Such effort must have gone into its construction, and for what? Those people were all gone. Whatever they had believed that drove them to move these gigantic stones into this configuration, that was gone too. Had there been charismatic leaders who persuaded everyone to undertake the task? Or were prisoners or slaves compelled to do it? Was it a place of peaceful contemplation? Had this very central stone been used for human sacrifice? Had thousands of people lived and died for whatever this place had once symbolized?

None of that mattered now. What if some future civilization found the ruins of one of those old roller coasters back home? What would they make of it? Would they marvel at the expense and effort that must have gone into something so ephemeral as a quick, safe thrill? Would they have any idea how many lives were affected by this frivolous contraption? Not just the riders, but the park employees, the people in the building trades, the state inspectors—the marketing guys. But rocks were different. They were real, of the land, planted on the land. The circle showed that once, long ago, some people had determined to change the landscape in a lasting way, and, so far at least, they had succeeded. Maybe that's all it was—that same old quest for immortality that people seem to get sucked into over and over again. That desire to do something that won't be gone the second one's heart stops beating. With that thought, Bret became suddenly aware of the sound of his pulse thumping in his ear.

Motion caught Bret's eye and he glanced up. A couple of black three-speed bikes rolled up the gravel track. The riders dismounted and leaned their bicycles against a wooden bench. They were speaking heatedly to each other, in German, Bret guessed. Behind them came a family of four tourists—two adults, a teenage boy, and a girl of nine or ten. The father wandered around for a minute, then pulled a tripod from a carrying sack and started taking photographs with an old-looking collapsible camera. Bret smiled and nodded at them as he started walking back to town.

EVIDENTLY the bus driver's firm words had taken good effect, because the motorcoach was gone. Bret looked beyond the green, up at the tall hills. Tomorrow, that was where he'd be, hiking along one of those ridges, looking for a holy well. It struck him as funny how he looked forward to that solitary task in a way that he had not only a couple of days ago.

Bret walked to the car and started back for Sneem. Not ten minutes out of town, he found himself stuck behind the French tour bus which, to judge from the reactions of the oncoming drivers, was traveling the wrong direction on the narrow road. By general consensus, tour buses circled the Ring of Kerry in counterclockwise manner, because two buses could not pass each other in many places along the narrow roads. This meant that one could travel the roads around Sneem and Kenmare with little worry until about three in the afternoon, when the excursions that had left Killarney in the morning had made their way all the way around the peninsula. Though this coast road was not on the primary Ring of Kerry loop, it was still assumed, apparently, that motorcoaches were expected to be going from Sneem to Kenmare, not the other way around. Compounding the matter was the size of the coach, which seemed a bit larger than the native Irish buses, and the fact that the driver sat on the left, which make it difficult for him to see around left-hand turns, of which there were many.

About a mile from Sneem, the road made a sharp right turn over a narrow bridge. The bus approached at an impossible angle, got about a third of the way across, and stopped, unable to roll forward. Bret looked behind him to see if there was room for him to move to make space for the bus to back up, but three cars were there already. Now the bus was backing up and Bret realized that the driver probably didn't see his car. He made a snap decision, put the transmission in gear, and scooted off the road onto a little drive to the left. Then he saw that the bus was backing into that very space in order to get a better angle—apparently Bret's car was still invisible. So he continued down the drive just to get safely out of the way. Probably there would be a place he could turn around.

The dirt track sloped slightly downhill through woods and passed a metal gate behind which he could see a large stone house and elaborate flower gardens. He passed the rotted shell of a red wooden rowboat embedded in the weeds at the edge of the path, then emerged from the trees and rolled onto a wide stone pier that projected into the Kenmare River, which at this point in its journey to the sea was more of a broad bay than a river. He shut off the engine and climbed out into the smell of the sea.

A large stream flowed into the larger body to the right of the pier, and the pier angled over into the mouth of the stream creating a protected area inside the elbow where a boat might be tied up. Along the shore, the grass and shrubs gave way to black rocks streaked through with white and gray. At the water's edge, dense colonies of mussels clung inside crevasses in the rocks.

He gazed out over the water at the hills on the peninsula beyond. Had Uncle Michael grown up looking out across that same water? The scene felt so familiar, it made Bret wonder if there was some way that the memory of a landscape could be passed down genetically. On the opposite shore he could just make out the lines of stone walls dividing pastures, and a scattering of whitewashed cottages. The shadows of clouds slid down the hillsides toward him and skated right out onto the water. A line of buoys marked some fisherman's endeavor— mussels? Did they have lobsters here? Suddenly, just this side of the line of buoys, a small, sleek black head emerged from the water, moving briskly upstream. A seal! That was a seal! It continued for another ten seconds, then submerged. Bret scanned the surface for its return but abandoned his vigil after a few minutes when he heard the sound of tires on gravel behind him.

It was the boy he'd encountered earlier in Sneem. The boy coasted up to the water's edge and nodded a hello.

"Hello, bicycle boy," said Bret. "Bit far from home, aren't you?"

"Not so far as you."

"You've got me there," Bret laughed. He looked back out over the water. "This sure is a beautiful place."

"Yes, quite fine. Done a lot of fishing here. It's not a long cycle trip from town, so I come here often," said the boy. "But 'tisn't easy to find. Who told you about it?"

"Nobody. Trying to escape destruction by a giant motorcoach. It threatened to run me over and this was the only place where I could hide."

"Ah, that would be the French visitors. Muppets. I had to wait for the coach to squeeze through before I could come across the bridge."

"You know those people?"

"No, Rosko does. Business associates is what he calls 'em, from France."

Bret looked back out over the bay. "What sort of work does your Rosko do?"

The boy looked up at him. "Him and his business associates want to turn this all into a place like EuroDisney."

"They what?"

"You know, make it popular for the tourists."

"Isn't it already popular with the tourists?"

"He hasn't talked about anything else since he got back from his trip to America to meet the experts."

"Umm," Bret paused. "Did I ever ask your name?"

"No, sir. Sean is my name."

"I am Bret. Bret Sheehan."

"Sean Roche." After a few minutes, the boy rolled the bike back a couple of steps, stepped one foot onto the high pedal, and shoved off. "Good evening Mister."

"Nice to know your name, Sean Roche," Bret called after him. "Ride carefully."

"Thanks, I will do that." The boy stood on the pedals and the tires crunched back up the gravel lane toward the woods. Bret watched the bike roll around a bend and disappear into the trees, the rider standing up the whole way, rocking the handlebars side to side as he went. Soon the only sound remaining was the faint lapping of the water swirling around the rocks. He gazed for a while at the hollow place in the trees where the lane entered the woods. Golden late-day sun bathed the gentle slope before him as well as the taller hills a few miles inland, which looked even more impossibly green in this light.

IT TOOK NEARLY AN HOUR to get back to his room. It wasn't until the line of cars dissipated that Bret saw the bus pulled off to the side beyond the narrow bridge and concluded that the motorcoach full of French visitors had apparently become stuck in another tight spot just—perhaps on the bridge itself—at the edge of town, and created another traffic backup.

Leaving the car on the square, he crossed the street and wearily climbed the stairs and closed the room door behind him. It looked as if the room had been straightened up, the bed made more neatly, his wet clothes draped over chair backs. He removed his shoes then opened up the Ordnance Survey Map #84 on the table near the window. Castle Cove was only eight miles or so to the west. A sequence of tiny roads led up into the hills from the town, doubling back to the north and east until, about four miles from the main road, a winding lane stopped at Staigue Fort. Because of the map's precise topographical markings, Bret could see that the fort was set high in a valley between two mountains, Staigue and Bohacogram. The valley floor leading up to the fort sloped gently all the way up from the shore, but just behind the fort, the hillsides then rose quite steeply. On the Staigue side, the slope gained 300 meters in about a mile to a place on the shoulder of the mountain where it looked like a person could cross, and that fit the description of where the man in the post office had suggested the likely well might be found.

Bret looked out the window and back down at the map. That was probably Staigue that he could see toward the left edge of the range of hills, with Eagles Hill slightly taller behind it. After breakfast, he—and Lee, if she wanted to go—would park the car at the fort, take a stroll out the back and walk up the hill. A mile, even uphill, shouldn't take more than an hour or two. A half an hour looking around up on the ridge, a half an hour ceremoniously depositing the ashes in the well, and another hour back down. If he set out by 9:00 the next morning, he should be headed back to Sneem by 1:00 in the afternoon, still before the first giant tour coaches would be rounding the point.

The curtain billowed away from the window. Wait, hadn't he left the window closed? The maid, or whoever had been in here, must have opened it to air the place out. He looked for the tin containing Uncle Michael so he could put it on the map to keep it from blowing off the table. The can was no longer on the table where he'd left it in the morning. Twenty frantic minutes later he had to conclude that it was nowhere in the room. He leaned out to see if somehow it had been placed on the sill and toppled once again into the bushes below, but no. A sparrow dive-bombed him and he ducked back in. He felt a scratch in his throat and closed the window. Must be allergic to something.

One would think that an entity in a role such as mine here might have some idea of what had happened to the small container which was, after all, the focal object of the entire endeavor in which I was engaged. But I felt myself no more enlightened than Bret himself. I must return now to the topic of the manual. It would seem that a moment such as this would be the manual's opportunity to provide evidence of its relevance, its worth, its reason for existing. But I discovered at this point that the tome was no longer accessible. Perhaps it was improperly reshelved. Some other taibhse checked it out and failed to return it. I did not despair so deeply, however, as I had come to expect very little of the volume when it came to its fundamental utility. Whatever the reasons were for its creation, this evidently was not one of them. Thus, by not being able to find the manual, I am relieved of the likely disappointment of having it fail me.

MIND
YOUR
UNCLE

Why hadn't he just taken the can with him when he drove to Kenmare? Bret chided himself as he walked up to the door of the Fisherman's Knot. He could hear talking and laughing inside. How was he going to tell them about this? Would they even be able to do anything? They'd better. It was their room and they had some responsibility, to be sure. Bret felt the anger rise and he clenched his teeth and pushed open the door.

The television was off and most of the tables were filled with patrons. Cormack stood behind the bar bantering with a red-bearded man seated a few stools down. Wait, thought Bret. Rosko! I can call Rosko. Maybe he could help. He fished out the paper with Rosko's mobile phone number on it from his wallet and dialed. It was loud in the room with the clanking of glasses and silverware. Bret heard another phone in the room, further distracting him. Then Rosko's phone picked up and went to voicemail. Bret didn't think he could explain the situation very well, so he left no message. It was too noisy to talk in here anyway.

Bret walked up to the bar and then thought it might be odd to just ask if Cormack had seen the can full of Uncle Michael, so he ordered a pint of stout. It would give him a moment to think about how to do this. Maybe he could work in the question between the two slow pours that were needed to get the glass full without foaming over. Natural thing for him to do in this situation was to read the crowd and figure out what he could say with sufficient drama to gain the attention of the audience and win them to his cause. He scanned the faces and realized he didn't have that sense of absolute confidence in knowing how they would react. Without that, he knew he couldn't pull off the dramatic turn. Maybe he was losing his touch. Maybe he was just out of practice. Maybe, he thought, I'm changing. The notion took him aback but gave him an unexpected lift. Okay, no acting. Just ask. "I've got a funny question," Bret offered. He smelled lemon wax on the bar.

"Ay, what's that?" Cormack leaned toward him.

"Well, you know how I've got my Uncle Michael here in a metal can, and I'm going to try to deposit the ashes in a holy well?"

Cormack rolled his eyes and nodded as he took an order from another patron.

"Well, the can is missing. It was in the room this morning and it's gone now."

"Gone? What, the whole tin?"

"I can't find it anywhere. I searched the whole room."

"In your car?"

"No."

"Perhaps in the boot?"

"It's not anywhere. I've looked."

Cormack turned away for a moment to take a man's order, then said slowly, "Ah, I expect mother might have—eh, straightened it away someplace."

"Mother?" Bret asked as Cormack turned around to do the second pour for Bret's Guinness and start the first pour of another.

"Mother is the housekeeper. She can't help herself going into the rooms and tidying up, so I more or less made it her official capacity. Keeps her busy, with dad gone. We can ask her tomorrow."

"Tomorrow?" Bret asked. "I really need to know where Uncle Michael is right away."

"Well, you see she lives outside town and she'd be asleep by now." He placed the pint in front of Bret. "Don't worry. I'm sure everything will be fine. She never throws anything away, only moves things to peculiar locations. We'll have your uncle back before day's end tomorrow, I'm sure of it."

"Well, if you're that confident, okay." Bret took a sip. "I guess waiting to the morning won't hurt." He looked around the bar. "Lee in?"

Cormack glanced up at Bret stoically, but a slight grin snuck out. "Nope. She had some special business this evening. Punk rock night up the way. And she's off tomorrow."

"Yeah," said Bret.

"Not so convenient that she's gone, with a crowd like this, but at least she made the soups and shepherd's pie ahead of time and Renée is here," Cormack said chuckling. "How about you? Want a bit of unofficial employment for the night?"

"But I've already been drinking," said Bret.

Cormack bellowed a laugh. "Well, then, we've established our currency. Every twenty glasses you wash is good for another pint!"

Why not? Bret thought. Keep his mind off Uncle Michael for a bit. "Okay, deal." Cormack look surprised that Bret had accepted, but then he handed him a white towel and showed him to the kitchen.

"Serious?" Cormack said. "All right then, join the battle!"

Bret washed a lot of glasses, and quite a few plates and bowls of the patrons who were having a late supper. Renée was cooking as well as waiting tables, but fortunately, not too many people were ordering food, and fewer as the night went on. Bret walked around the pub picking up people's empties, carried them back to the sink, and washed them by hand, a dozen glasses at a time. Then he stacked the plates near the stove and returned the glasses upside-down to their shelves behind the bar. Once or twice, he helped Renée by filling soup bowls, and Cormack even trusted him to pour a few pints here and there. The work was hard, relentless, and sweaty, the reward a room full of happy customers and, no doubt, a good night at the till for the Fisherman's Knot. Bret realized that he hadn't really done anything like this since high school. It felt like real, honest work. He'd almost forgotten. It felt good.

He never attempted to keep track of how many glasses he'd washed—once he was in the thick of the rush, there was nothing but the work to think about. After the crowd thinned, the three of them leaned on the bar and he had one more pint, and a shot of whiskey, and that plus the hard work had the desired effect of making it possible for him to go to sleep. Cormack and Renée sent him off with a grateful thank-you and a pledge of drinks on the house for as long as he stayed. But he was thinking he might actually ask to help out again. That made the drinks taste so much better.

AS SHE HAD PROMISED, Lee was in the kitchen of the Fisherman's Knot at 9:00 the next morning. Bret wasn't at all confident that she would be, especially since the whole thing about the tin of Uncle Michael still seemed a bit fishy to him. He didn't know what, if anything, she might have had to do with the disappearance of the can, but it seemed a funny coincidence that she was called away on unexpected business at the same time that Uncle Michael went missing.

But he saw her through the window as he walked up to the back. She was leaning over the table, placing a plate, her white blouse and black hair blurred and rippled by the old glass. He knocked on the door. Two beats later, it opened.

"Good morning, Mr. Sheehan," she said, motioning him in.

"Good morning," Bret said, resting his rucksack on a spare chair. In the sack he brought maps and some of Uncle

Michael's old photographs in case he might identify some of the locations or people.

"I missed you at punk rock night."

"Ah, next time perhaps. I was helping Cormack."

"Ha. Well thanks for that. I trust our pleasant peninsula suits you?" she said, but with the inflection of a question.

"It's very lovely," he replied, "but honestly I feel like I'm just on the surface of it. I don't know what I'm looking at."

"Well then we've lacked for hospitality," she said, sitting down across from him at the table and placing a plate of scones and two mugs between them. "Tea?" She poured without waiting for a response. "So we're off to see mother, is that right?"

"I guess so," he replied. "Word travels fast around here."

"Cormack told me, yes." She spread jam on a split scone. "I think his theory is right. Mother just put it somewhere. Maybe took it home for safekeeping. She's a bit dotty. We'll find out."

"We'd better. Uncle Michael is the whole reason I came here. You all call her 'Mother?'"

"She is matronly in a way," she sipped her tea. "You must have been close with your uncle."

"I guess we were," he said, "at least, no one else was spending any time with him these last few years. So this lonely quest kind of naturally falls to me." He bit off a bit of scone and chewed it, releasing mixed aromas of butter and blueberry. "It's not my usual thing, though. I'm more of a people person. Spending so much time alone, I'm not sure how to decide what to do next!" he laughed. "Usually I can kind of assess the crowd and go from there. But here, no crowd."

"Ah, a storyteller. Like my dad." She looked out the window. "More than a few storytellers in Ireland."

"Uncle Michael could spin a good yarn in his day," Bret replied. "Is there any more tea? I'd love a little more if there is any. Please."

She filled both cups. "That's not me," she said. "Not one for crowds. No surprise I'm stuck in the kitchen, then, is it?"

Bret smiled and nodded and sipped his tea and they sat silently for a while, both looking out the window. The sun was high enough that an upper band of the trees across the right edge of the open space behind the buildings was lit brightly, though the area just outside the window remained in shade. A fine mist was lifting off the foliage as the heavy dew steamed away. Outside that window was a different world, Bret mused, coexisting with his own. But of course that one out there was real, with trees and water and rocks and sunlight. A startling thought.

"I'll drive," she said, without getting up.

BRET SAT IN THE PASSENGER SEAT as Lee guided the careening car along the high road out of town. Looking past her out the right-side window, he caught a glimpse of the road to Kenmare below and the twinkling water beyond. The town of Cork was beyond the hills on the other side of the water, he recalled from the Avis map, another place of which he would have a vague concept but to which he would probably never go. A triangle of white sail moved along that far shore, heading to the right, out to sea. Then the hedges closed in again and all there was to see was the winding pavement between the close green walls.

A few minutes later, the hedges fell away as the road crossed open pasture. A few sheep bumbled about the fields, but many more gathered along the road as if they were waiting for something but couldn't remember what it was. A few thick clouds rolled in from the left, over the high ridge of MacGillycuddy's Reeks. The peaks were not high in absolute altitude, but since they essentially rose right out of the sea and were the tallest things around, they commanded the landscape. Or rather, Bret reflected, they shared command with the sea. Hills vs. sea was what life was about here, Bret was beginning to conclude: finding some kind of safe middle ground between rugged, treeless hills and the vast water that could lie dead calm or roil itself into tumult. Close enough to the ocean to avail oneself of its bounty, but not so close as to subject oneself to its destructive whims. The hills, too, seemed ambivalent—lush and green and beautiful, yes, but weather-battered and reluctant to yield the produce of, say, a backyard Ohio vegetable garden. People seemed to fit themselves into little nooks or folds in the landscape, and to build modestly there, as if constructing too grandiosely would be asking to be put back in your place. Scanning the hillsides now, he saw no human structures at all. Green and brown hills, gray outcroppings of rock, shadows and sun. Not even sheep.

The road wound higher, then crested a ridge where another road joined from the right. There was a small shop flanked by a couple of parking areas, obviously scaled for tour buses. Lee turned right on the side road, where a sign pointed to Kenmare, then immediately left into a nearly empty lot. She turned off the engine and climbed out. "Come on," she said.

"Does Cormack's mom live way up here?" Bret inquired as he closed the door.

"What's that?" Lee responded. "Oh, no, she lives down on the Kenmare road."

"What?" Bret stopped walking. "Well, then what are we doing up here?"

"Not just yet," she said, grinning. "Too soon."

"What do you mean too soon?" Bret raised his voice. "Come on, I have to find Uncle Michael."

"Mother won't be at home until later. She does her errands in the morning. Don't worry, it will be all right. Now come on, I have to show you something."

He was fuming, but saw no alternative. She had driven and she had the keys. "Fine," he said. "But let's hurry up with it."

She led him up a faint track, around to the back side of a rocky outcrop, and to a ledge that looked out over the gnarled valley between their perch and the Reeks. "Now," she said, "we wait and watch."

Bret waited and watched. He watched a tour bus squeeze itself down the winding road from the pass and thought that it must have started early today to get here by now. He watched a sheep grazing its way toward the pavement and then into the path of an oncoming panel van, which honked its horn curtly and brushed the sheep aside. He watched a long, narrow gray cloud snake its way between two peaks across the valley. He waited for Lee to say what they were waiting for. He watched her chest rise and fall as she lay back on a rock and gazed up toward the ridge to their right. He watched her nostrils contract with each inhalation. He snapped out of it. "For what?" Bret said.

"What?" she turned to face him, but her hair stayed where it had been, and now covered her eyes.

"What are we waiting and watching for?" he asked.

"Ravens," she said.

"Of course," said Bret. "Ravens." He looked back out over the valley.

"Well, one raven in particular," she said. "He's got just one leg and his plumage looks like he lost an argument with a motorcoach. More than once. And he's feckin enormous."

"And why do I need to see this old bird?" Bret asked.

"Why?" replied Lee. "I've got a book at home, a book of photographs. *The Solitude of Ravens*, it's called, by a man called Masahisa Fukase. Japanese. I studied contemporary art in college, you see, before my indentured servitude. This Fukase got divorced and it threw him into a depression and he spent the next ten years traveling between Tokyo and the remote island where he was born, photographing ravens. Then I think he went completely nuts and he's now in an institution. But before that happened, he did this feckin amazing book. Since I saw those pictures it's never been the same looking at a real raven. Ravens mean something more now. And our bird Mono is most meaningful of all, they say."

"Mono?"

"One leg." She continued. "It's as if the bird is a kind of sentinel perched between this world and a vast nothingness—not perched—he flies at will back and forth between the something and the nothing."

"Yeah," said Bret. "Well, he must be in the nothing part now."

"You're so impatient. What's the hurry? Just sit quietly and wait for two or three minutes." She trilled "three" in that same way Uncle Michael had.

"Okay, fine," said Bret.

"Meanwhile," she responded, "I'll tell you the story."

"The story?"

"Of Mono. The raven." She leaned forward. "Years back," she began, "he was a young, sleek raven much like the others. But he was faster and stronger than most. And especially proud of his skills at nicking."

"Pecking?"

"Thieving. Stealing eggs, people's jewelry, things like that. It seemed he enjoyed the thrill of it as much as anything. Appearing out of nowhere, grabbing the thing in his sharp talons, and disappearing into the mist before anyone knew what had happened. But not so surreptitious as not to be seen. It was important to be seen, but only for a fleeting instant.

"As he grew older, he sought out greater and greater challenges. Once he was spotted flying into the open right-side window of a tour bus that was stopped at the Ladies View and moments later exiting the left-side window clutching the driver's keys in his claws. He snatched instamatic cameras when tourists set them down on a stone wall. Took the Prime Minister's spectacles once, they say.

"But he apparently grew tired of frequenting the tourist areas and set off in search of something more. His search took him to the highest peaks, where the creatures more vigilantly guarded their tenuous safety. Pilfering nuts from the stash of a ground squirrel, for example. Then one day, he spotted a tiny figure darting among the rocks, a very young little boy, it seemed to be, but faster and slimmer and surer of foot. Before he could get close, the figure was gone. A few weeks later he was gliding along the cliff edge of Mullaghbeg and he saw the strange creature again, but much closer. Around its neck was a dazzling gold necklace. The raven needed to have that. He swooped down but lost his quarry behind a rock and never spotted it again.

"For months, he never saw it. He never forgot how beautiful the necklace looked, though. Indeed, he decided that if he ever saw it again and managed to pilfer that necklace, he would quit stealing. That would be the ultimate—to have that most beautiful and most elusive thing. There would be no point in continuing thereafter. But summer ended and the cold autumn set in and then the stinging winter. The memory faded.

"The following spring arrived as it often did—at an indeterminate moment on some afternoon when, without warning, the gray damp suddenly dissolves into sparkling sunlight, a change one notices only in retrospect. After being so inured to the elements for so long, it takes a little while to let down the guard and notice that something has changed.

"It was on such a day that the raven, having just come to appreciate the warmth of the afternoon light, settled himself down on a high rock and spread his wings to thoroughly dry them for the first time in months. His eyes grew heavy and closed as the sun slowly descended toward the sea.

"When he awoke, a chill had settled in the air, as the light of day was nearly gone. He closed his wings closer about him and then noticed, not ten feet away, the little figure leaning back against a boulder, fast asleep, the gold necklace catching the last glint of evening sun. No time to waste, he thought. He leapt into the air and let the breeze carry him over his prey, then he collapsed himself like a falcon and plummeted straight down, grabbing up the necklace in a precise surgical motion. Then he flapped his powerful wings twice in order to snap the clasp and be gone.

"But the clasp did not break. He flapped harder, tugging with all his might. Still, it did not release. The sleeping face, meanwhile, did not wake. Its pale, almost transparent skin showed no evidence of strain, yet the force pulling against the raven's fierce effort seemed unnaturally strong, as if a much larger and stronger creature were holding back the necklace. One more pull, he thought, then I'll give up and be off.

"He lighted right on the boyish neck, then sprung back up with all the velocity he could generate and at the same time twisted up and away so as to try to pull the chain over the head. No use. So he released his claws."

She coughed. "But somehow the chain had become tangled on his right foot and, try as he might, he could not separate himself. Now he had no ambition toward stealth. He simply wanted to fly away. But the harder he pulled, the tighter the chain seemed to pull. Soon he was exhausted, and he had to light once again. He stood panting for breath. Then the eyes opened. Bright green eyes. They studied the raven, unblinking.

"Suddenly, the little creature took off running, dragging the raven along behind, half flying, half bouncing along the hard stones. The raven hoped some impact would break the chain and he would be free, but this did not happen. Then they came over the top of a hill and the runner's stride lengthened as their speed increased until it leapt in the air and dove into an impossibly small hole under a large flat rock. The runner disappeared silently into the hole but the raven was too large and his chest and wings became wedged in the entrance to the passage. A tearing pain stabbed up his leg where he could feel the chain pulling harder and harder. Then it eased for a moment. He hopped back slightly and began to extract the leg from the hole, but then the pulling resumed, stronger than ever. His chest was being crushed against the rock and he could not breathe. When the tension eased again slightly, he pulled back with all his remaining strength and then closed his powerful beak down on the second joint of the leg and snapped it off. Severed leg and gold chain disappeared down the hole.

"He hopped away on the one foot, balancing with his wings, staring at the black opening. Then, just as he determined to fly away and never visit this part of the mountain again, the necklace flopped out of the hole." She stopped.

"Well?" Bret asked after a long pause.

"Well what?" she replied.

"Did he pick it up?"

"I don't know," she said. "That's why we have to wait and see him."

"You've never seen this raven?" Bret raised his voice.

"No, not personally. That's why we came up here."

"Who has seen it?" Bret asked.

"I don't know," she replied. "Just people. It's well known."

"Santa Claus is well known," said Bret.

"That's not exactly the same," she said.

"Not exactly," he replied.

The raven Mono did not appear in the next twenty minutes or so, nor did any other raven. But a brown sparrow did hop across a patch of scraggly grass near Bret's left foot. The wind blowing among the rocks and grasses filled the air with white noise.

THEY DROVE DOWN, not the way they had come up, but down the side road, which Bret now recognized as the route he had chosen not to take from Moll's Gap to get to Sneem in the first place, after climbing up into the mountains from Killarney. The road wound its way downhill and joined with the Kenmare road at the edge of the river, not far from the town itself, which Bret could see off to the left as they approached the coast. Lee turned right, toward Sneem, and continued for perhaps ten minutes until just after a sharp hairpin turn over a brook, at which point she slowed down as they passed a sequence of narrow lanes along the left side of the road. The road swung around to the right again. "Here we are," she said, turning onto a dirt track.

The drive curved to the left as it got further from the road, then emerged into a clearing in which a small house of white stone and blue and white wood was situated. The front of the house looked out over a gradual slope down to the rocky shore of the Kenmare River.

Lee parked the car alongside the house and motioned for Bret to follow her to a blue-painted door in the middle of the back of the house. She knocked on the door, but did not wait for a response before turning the handle and entering. Bret followed her in, but Lee held up a hand to his chest and said "Now don't commence right in to asking about Uncle Michael. She might get confused."

"I'm already confused," Bret replied.

"Just let me introduce you and then we'll chat for a bit and get on to business."

"Whatever," he said.

They walked from a central hallway into a bright sitting room with windows overlooking the water. The place smelled like old wood. In front of the window, looking out, stood a tiny twig of a woman, her wild shock of white hair glowing like a halo as the light from outside shone through it. "Nice to see you, dearie," she said without turning around.

Now Bret saw that she held a small pair of binoculars.

"Seals are pilfering those Bantry boatmen's mussel beds again," she called out. "Watch them tug on the pots. Bloop! Blop!" She had the binoculars trained a few hundred feet out into the river, where Bret could make out a row of white buoys. The old woman stood there peering out for the next few minutes, teetering. Then, abruptly, she put the glasses down on the windowsill and turned around to greet them. She paused for a couple of seconds and then said, "Would you like something to read?"

"To read?" Bret turned to Lee.

"She's joking," said Lee. "It's an old line out of Dylan Thomas."

"You're no fun at all," said the old woman, leaning over to peck Lee on the cheek. "And who's this?"

"Mr. Sheehan," said Lee.

"Bret Sheehan, ma'am," he held out his hand.

"American, of course. Oh, my, yes, I know all about you. How's the dehydrated uncle? They may as well do that to me as well. Half way there already." She laughed, a single sharp hoot.

"Now that you mention it—" Bret began.

"Let's have a cold drink," Lee broke in. She began walking out into the hall and toward the kitchen. "Come on, Bret, you can help."

He followed. When they got in the kitchen, she said in a soft voice, "A bit eccentric, she is, but just follow along with her and you may get someplace."

"She seems lucid enough," Bret offered.

"Oh, she's lucid all right!" Lee laughed, handing him a glass as she carried two back toward the sitting room. "Only, let's say—selective."

"Selective," Bret mumbled to himself as he followed her.

"Well," said the white-haired hostess as they settled into chairs, "I assume now you're expecting this time-worn tribal elder to regale you with elaborate tales of Irish lore, magical fables, ancient myths, parables of pride and folly." She gazed into Bret's eyes, unblinking.

"Pardon me," he replied after a dead silence of five or six heartbeats, "but no, I was not. Actually, I hoped—"

"Good! I don't tell stories," she broke in. "Lot of silly fairy dust, that. The poor untethered Irish, only good for spinning tall tales and drinking whiskey, like a whole race of mildly retarded superstitious uncles, good-natured but hot-tempered, incapable of thinking anything new as long as there's some old song to explain everything."

"No," Bret repeated. "Not that."

"Let's hear about the dry uncle." She leaned forward to him.

"Well, it's mostly that the box of ashes—" Bret began.

"Ah, we'll get to that in good time," she interrupted.

"Of course we will," Lee broke in.

"Who was the man? Where was he born?" the older woman continued.

"He was born Michael Sheehan," Bret said, "in Castle Cove in 1916. Or in a Killarney hospital, actually, but they lived in Castle Cove."

"Born in hospital? Unusual for those days, except that it was during the Great War. Complicated years in general for Ireland. All manner of unusual things would happen during that time. An expecting mother might be left alone if her man were off to battle, sometimes even a birth might need to be legitimized after the fact if the father was killed abroad before they'd had the chance to marry. It wasn't much talked about, but it happened. An illegitimate child could have a very difficult time at life . . . a small, out-of-the-way church could make the most of its marginal situation and sometimes save that child a lot of future trouble by post-legitimizing a birth under cover of provincial incompetence in record-keeping, the deacon's illegible handwriting, someone not remembering exactly what year it was. Couldn't get away with it in Dublin, but out here in the wild western hinterlands where the simple people live . . . But I digress. Michael Sheehan is a usual enough name. Very usual. I've known a score of them at least." She sipped her water, holding back the white hair with the other hand so it wouldn't fall into the cup.

"I've got some old pictures," Bret remembered, pulling the envelope out of his rucksack. "Perhaps you'd recognize some people or places." He handed it to Lee, who passed it on with a quizzical frown, as if, Bret later thought, this added an unconsidered factor.

Now, I considered, we might make some progress, if this stack of photographs provided enough clues as to location that this person who had lived here a very long time might point them in a useful direction.

The old woman pulled out the small stack of photographs. "Ah, yes," she said. "Certificate of birth, marriage record the same year, with both parent names on both documents—this might be one of those retroactive cases, you see. A group portrait in Kenmare town, it appears." She held it close to her face. "I don't know these people." She leafed through the prints. "This house on the hill could be anyplace, but the other square one is surely Staigue Fort. My father used to have a camera made square pictures like that—it was a common thing. Not in Ireland, this one, I'm certain. You've got one stuck to the back of another here." She carefully peeled a photo from the back of another of the same size and shape and Bret realized where the missing photo had been all along. She held up the one that had been stuck. Her old hands didn't shake at all, confounding expectation. "Fellow here in the beard looks like a Bantry fisherman. And here's a picnic by the River Sneem—as people have been doing for centuries right in that same spot. A seal by the sea. A boy and his dog near a ruin. People at tea in a dark room. Boy and dog again in another place—same cottage as before." She went back to the first photo of the boy and dog. "This young lad," she held it up in the light. "And the seal." She held up that picture next to the other and shook her head slightly. "I despise telling stories but I'm going to tell you one."

"But about Uncle Michael—" Bret started.

"Yes, it is a story that involves a young boy, named Michael," she said. "This one here, with the dog. I presume this to be your uncle, is that right? I never knew the boy's surname, but I knew the boy."

Bret nodded, suppressing a cough. "Please go ahead." He glanced at Lee, who had reclined against her chair back with an air of resignation, her eyes still on the older woman. She looks more like Lee's mom than Cormack's, Bret thought. That happens when the same few families live in the same place for centuries.

"More universally," the story continued, "it's a story about an adventure that young man once experienced with a local girl whom I knew very well." She cleared her throat. "How to begin? In those days, travel between towns was more difficult, indeed was more easily accomplished by water. That the boy was born in Killarney indicates that either the family happened by chance to be there when the mother began her labor, or that extraordinary efforts were made to transport her across the mountains to the hospital. But that's perhaps not so relevant to this story.

"We used to see this Michael in Sneem town when he and his father, much older, would bring fish to market. I never knew what town he came from, only that the boat always turned right toward the open sea when they left. If he lived just down in Castle Cove, that would be the direction home. But I always imagined he was from Bantry or even farther across the open water. Never talked too much, and he had a very soft voice. Bit of mystery. Curious.

"One summer night about this time of season, when the light lasts long toward morning, a blanket of fog rolled its way up the bay and made everything well-nigh invisible beyond your outstretched arm. One could see nothing, yet it was not dark because the sun was up into the night. When you got close enough, dark shapes and light shapes both would take form against the middle gray. Water contains both light and dark, and I found that when I stood upon the town bridge and looked down at the River Sneem I could see nothing at first, but then the mist would thin a little bit and I could see the foam on the rocks and the dark shadows in the of each standing waves. Nothing else. It was so simple and beautiful and mysterious. This mesmerized me, so this day I stood on the bridge for a long time staring down, until I saw a large dark shape appear where there had been none. I leaned closer to the rapid to try to see better what it was, but it made little difference, and since I did not wish to fall over the railing into the rushing water, I carefully crept around the side of the bridge and down the slope to stream's edge. This would be almost exactly where that picnic picture was taken, on a wide, flat rock near a lawn and the edge of the river.

"The shape was gone. I kneeled and peered out over the churning water, trying to pull it out of the gray again. I looked farther and farther out into the fog. Then, right under my chin, it came back. It was a seal! Swimming upstream to stay in place, just at the base of the rapid. It smelled of puppy and kelp. I don't know what motivated me, but I reached out with my left hand and touched its back. I could feel the muscles rippling with the effort of swimming to stay in place. I let my hand rest there for I don't know how long, then it suddenly stopped swimming and drifted backward downstream. I was just an impressionable girl of thirteen, mind you, but I was sure its open face smiled at me, or at least gave a glance of greeting the way a friendly hound might do.

"I jumped up and immediately started running after it down along the river and almost instantly I was in the river, safely downstream of the rocks and rapids, but being swept swiftly away from town. I was a smart swimmer and I knew better than to try to fight the current, and I also knew that the stream widened and slowed not far from here and I would be able to get myself to the shore near the old marina. It's still there, if you walk down the east side of the stream.

"As I drifted and treaded water, I kept an eye trained for the seal, and it was there from time to time, popping its head above the water to look at me, then diving and swimming away downstream for a while before surfacing to wait for me again. I think it probably wanted me to follow it all the way to France, playing its find-me-now game. Perhaps it had swum upriver to find a playmate. But I was tiring and when I saw the faint shape of a fishing boat off to my left, I swam for it.

Everything was so quiet that when I reached up and grasped the wooden gunwale it made a great splashing and slapping sound and the occupant of the boat startled suddenly to his feet. When he bent down to see more clearly what creature was attempting to board his vessel I saw that it was the boy Michael. 'Hello, miss,' he said in his quiet voice. He blinked and smiled. 'Hand up?'

"I reached up my left hand and he counted 'One, two, three,' and then I was in the boat. I think he was nearly the same age as I, perhaps a year younger or older. He blushed visibly even in the fog. Perhaps he'd never been alone with a girl before that. But I quickly began telling him about the seal and that seemed to distract him. The little black head was bobbing just at the limit of visibility. Michael looked out across the water for a minute and presented a theory. 'Maybe thinks he's a salmon swimming home to spawn.' I said I thought the seal was trying to tell me something, like to follow it to France. Michael just nodded at that.

"Then we decided that, in order to give time to dry my dress before going back home, we would endeavor to follow the seal for a short time, to see where it might be trying to lead us. So Michael untied the bow line from the dock and we shoved off. There was virtually no wind in the thick fog, so the sails weren't of much use, but the current carried us steadily out to sea. I must disclose that, in the damp air, my dress did not dry at all, and we used this as a blatantly contrived premise for further exploration. We drifted and drifted, sometimes seeing the riverbanks, sometimes not, but Michael was very familiar with the waters and the clear channels so I was never in any worry. And the seal led us on like this until we emerged into the rougher water of the open Kenmare. The seal looked back at us, then set off slowly toward the sea. I was quite certain we were going to France.

"But after five or ten minutes, a small island emerged from the mist and the seal climbed out of the water and waited for us there. The island was like a single jagged rock stabbing up through the mist, with only a small flat area on one side where a boat could be pulled up. The whole thing was no bigger than the church on the Kenmare road in Tahilla. Michael by this time was rowing, looking behind, while I sat in the bow and navigated, so, as we prepared to come ashore, it was I who spotted something else on the flat place in addition to our seal.

"I called to Michael to look and he stopped rowing for a moment and turned and looked through the mist. 'Another one. Dead, appears,' he said. Indeed it was. It had not been dead for a long time, but there was no doubt that it was now. We secured the dory and walked closer. Our seal had moved closer to the lifeless body, but as we got close, it bumped the body with its snout and lurched to the water's edge, where it stopped and looked back at us. I looked at Michael and shrugged. The dead seal seemed very old. Its whiskers were white and its body was covered with a long lifetime's worth of nicks and scars. The eyes were closed. I could see no wound nor injury. It seemed to me to have died of old age. The other seal barked, came up to us, then scampered back to the water's edge.

"'I believe,' Michael said, 'it wants us to pull the dead one into the water.' How he came to this conclusion I shall never know, but it seemed natural enough, so we worked together and rolled the dead seal as if it were a log. The other one barked excitedly the entire time. Finally, we got it into the water and it began to float. The other seal barked once more, then swam alongside it, nudging it out to sea. In seconds, both had disappeared into the fog.

"By now it was quite late—I had already had my evening tea before setting out for the bridge—and the air around us was darkening. A cold breeze had begun to blow onshore, thinning the fog, but chilling my damp skin. Michael quickly shipped the oars and raised the sail and, with the cool wind behind us, we sailed straight back up the river without so much as a single 'ready about.'

"When Michael left me off at the docks, I was cold, but the breeze had nearly dried my dress. He steadied the boat against its mooring as I climbed out. I thanked him for helping me out of the water. We had a tacit and unspoken agreement that the rest of our adventure would remain ours alone. Neither of us had to say it aloud. We knew. 'Goodbye,' he said. Then after a few seconds, his voice cracking a little, 'I'm going to America. Father died two months ago and my mother passed when I was born, so I'm to go stay with cousins in Massachusetts, or perhaps Ohio. I could continue fishing the boat myself, but they won't have it. There are lakes the size of the ocean in America. It will be another adventure, my da would have said.' He pushed off. 'But there ever won't be another adventure like this one was, miss Margaret,' he said. I could see him blush. He knew my name. Then he was gone into the mist and I walked home shivering."

Lee gazed at her glassy-eyed. "You've never told anybody that."

The old woman looked up, then turned to face the window that overlooked the sea. "No."

The room was silent for a good while, but Bret didn't want to break it. He didn't need to.

"Mr. Sheehan," said their hostess, turning back from the window, "I mean no disrespect, but could I have a private moment with Lee? There's a nice afternoon sun. It should be pleasant on the terrace."

"Of course." He got up and walked back the way they had come in, through the hall and out the front door. The wind was light, the sun warm.

He wandered around the side of the house in order to better see the water of the Kenmare River and caught the tone of the womens' conversation as he passed by that window. He could make out no words—nor did he wish to—but it was clear that the older woman was exasperated, the younger apologizing.

He glanced away and a new thought settled in his mind. How could it be that Uncle Michael was really Bret's uncle if Michael's father had died before the boy left Ireland and the boy had been an only child? The family resemblances were evident, but there was also the gap in age between Michael and Bret's father—a dozen years. Perhaps Michael had been not the oldest the son of Bret's grandmother, but the only son of his grandmother's older sister, who had never come to America because she had died in childbirth, making Michael a cousin to Bret's father, not an older brother. And one more maybe—if that Bantry fisherman who had raised young Michael had not been the boy's father, but perhaps his grandfather, and the boy the illegitimate child of a father no longer on the scene, well that might explain some of the mystery that seemed to persist around the origins of Uncle Michael. It could also explain why the boy's birth certificate listed the mother as Mary and his grandmother's name had been Dorothy. And why the marriage had taken place the same year as a February birth. If the father and husband's name was noted as Sean, then very likely he was not a deadbeat who flew the scene, but maybe a soldier who died before he could marry and before his son was born. And his family or hers raised the orphaned boy until he was sent to America.

THE DRIVE FROM THE HOUSE back to Sneem was quick. Lee didn't say much beyond that she knew where to find the box of Uncle Michael, and that Bret and his uncle would be reunited presently. She said that Mother wished to invite Bret for a proper tea while he was here and that she was sorry for her imperfect hospitality and she hoped he would forgive a tired old lady. Cormack greeted them as they crossed the street. He handed Bret the box. "Ground floor utility closet," he said. "Don't know why I didn't think to look there."

Bret took the tin and threw a skeptical glance at Cormack. "I don't know why you didn't either," he said. He tucked it under his arm. "I think I'd better sleep with it," he laughed. "With the window closed."

As I recalled those photographs, then left behind those images that so evoked facets of a life, I once again experienced the unmoored feeling. Perhaps I had been mistaken in some assumptions. Could I sustain myself thus unbound by material entities, whether humans or ashes or photographs? To what end?

NOTHING HAPPENS

Later that afternoon, Bret placed the tin on the stone wall beside him and dangled his feet off the edge. The water was a good ten feet down, much lower than when he'd been out here the last time. The tide must be out. Indeed, he could see the river swirling around a couple of pylons, the water massing up on the landward side. The estuary grasses glowed light green in the mid-afternoon sun, swaying like drowsy dancers with the gentle forces of breeze and current.

He lay back onto the cobblestone pavement and felt the heat that had been absorbed into the stone radiating up through his shoulders and neck. Cool air, warm sun, a light breeze, and the sounds of river and sea—Bret would have been happy to lie there for a year. He closed his eyes. Somewhere, one of those small putt-putt motors was running, getting closer. The air was sweet with a hint of ocean and some kind of pollen that Bret theorized had been causing his nose to run ever since he had arrived. Not far away a couple of sea gulls were arguing about something.

He felt his skin get cooler and opened his eyes to see that a dense cloud, white on top, gray on the bottom, had slid in front of the sun. He watched the cloud move silently out of the sun's way, a bright spot growing into a dazzling corona at the cloud's edge, then he turned his eyes away and sat up.

A lone open-top fishing boat was drifting seaward, pushed along slightly by its idling motor. The single occupant, wearing a long oilskin jacket, stood toward the stern, legs apart, one hand on the tiller. Bret watched the shape shrink down the river. The standing figure never switched position the whole time. Then the boat disappeared behind some low shrubs.

The village of Sneem didn't feel like a seaside town at all, yet here it was, this long finger reaching up into the land from the Kenmare Bay. Just looking at the river from the bridge, you'd never suspect that this roiling mountain brook would level out and spread into a tidal estuary in the space of a few hundred yards. Bret got up, lifted the can of ashes, and began walking back toward his room.

With the river to his left, he followed the shoreline along the gravel path and then on the old boardwalk. Minutes later, the pine boards angled left and he came to the small dock where the decrepit wooden boat rested on the bottom, submerged but for the prow and part of the cabin roof. Stringy green algae and snails clung to the sides just above the waterline. Bret sat on a post and examined the wreck.

How long had it been there? Months? A year? A decade? Not that long, he guessed. It didn't seem to take much time for nature to reclaim things. Soil and sun and water nourished the growth of a tree, and men could cut down the tree in order to make boards and fashion a seaworthy vessel. But everything always went back to the basic elements sooner or later. It required continued effort to keep everything from reverting to water and earth.

He looked upstream, where the dock ended and a low stone jetty stuck out into the current, the water curling around the end of it. That could last longer, a stone wall. It was closer to the truth of the land, which was pretty simple: water and stone and tenacious plants rooted in thin soil. Making a wood frame house would be pure fiction here, little more than a temporary arrangement of sticks. A stone house would be closer to true. Better yet, a cave.

He looked down at the tin for a minute, then pulled off the lid. It was getting a little bit harder to remove. Maybe the metal was getting scraped up and that caused some friction. The gray contents looked much as they had. But what else was he expecting? That someone would have tampered with them? He chuckled and cleared his throat and replaced the lid.

But you couldn't very well make a fishing boat out of rocks, Bret thought. The life of a wooden vessel would be a constant losing struggle in the face of certain failure, but at least it would float for a while. And weren't trees and plants fictions, too? Didn't they all fall and rot and return to the land? Maybe fiction wasn't the right concept. Ephemera. Like magazines or newspapers that were never meant to last: the thing itself was less important than the information it communicated or the ideas it shared or the images it showed. All that could be passed on. Once read, the paper itself could be discarded. He stood up and continued walking. The sun was getting low in the northwestern sky, bathing the trees and buildings in a warm gold glow.

He pictured the town of Sneem before him being sucked back into the landscape, the colorful paint and peaked roofs swallowed up in green. It wasn't hard to imagine.

If it seems that nothing is happening, one must look closer. Bret appeared to be gazing at the water, dangling his feet, a can of ashes by his side as if he and his uncle had been sharing the experience. But had not the uncle been in this very spot, many decades before? Who is to say the two were not together now, through shared experience of this swirling water and these waving grasses? Did I persuade Bret to come sit here? No.

He found his own way. One does not have the opportunity to interview the ghosts who have come before, in order to develop a coherent strategy. I do not recall what I had been planning, if anything, but it was not this. Yet this seems important. And the manual . . . now I could not be sure there ever had been a manual. Perhaps it was not so much an actual thing as it was an embodiment of the idea that there ought to be some kind of instructions. Of the assumption that there was a proper way to do this. It occurred to me that everything was, in a way, back to how it had begun. All the way back to the time before the corporeal decease. What if my presence and actions were to have no effect whatsoever? What if I was simply attaching myself to a story that was taking place of its own accord? Persuading myself that I was a cause and not an effect? If I was even that. Maybe I had conjured an enigmatic image here and there, to be sure, but on the other hand, people conjure enigmatic images on their own without the help of ghosts. It was not so much a matter of feeling ineffectual or irrelevant, but rather the notion that I was an image or an expression of something. Rather than my mentoring Bret, he instead was serving me. And doing so without being aware that I even existed. If I existed. What if I never did exist, except as an idea? Was I a figment? If so, whose? Perhaps I am Bret's figment, but so far in the back of his consciousness that he is not aware that he is conjuring me. Or am I a lingering figment of Michael? Still glowing but slowly cooling and dimming like an incandescent light filament. Maybe I am a filament of the imagination. Maybe I am a story that conjured itself. Just to exist, however tenuously. Do stories write themselves?

THE
ROAD
TO
CASTLE
COVE

Bret walked out to his rental car at about 9:30 in the morning, placed the Ordnance Survey #84 map and the box containing Uncle Michael on the seat beside him, started up the engine, and began to roll out of town toward Castle Cove. As he approached the inn where the French business associates were lodged, the bus parked in front turned on its signal and began to pull out. Bret hesitated a moment, deciding whether to zip around it before the oncoming truck arrived or to wait and motion the bus out ahead of him. Castle Cove was only a few miles up the road. There was no huge hurry. All he needed to do was get back by mid-afternoon so he could visit the Fisherman's Knot and talk to Lee, and this way he could spend the day thinking about what to say. He waved the driver on. The bus pulled out in front of him.

It was at this moment that Bret remembered the other day's scene of this very bus making its fitful and laborious way against the prevailing flow of traffic. A moment later he realized that the bus was again proceeding in a clockwise direction on the ring road around which buses always went counter-clockwise. All he could do at this point was be patient and hope that he and the bus would get to Castle Cove before they encountered any large oncoming vehicles. Bret looked up at the back window of the bus. The red-faced man he had noticed in Kenmare the other day was peering back out, his nose pressed against the tinted glass.

Since he couldn't see much ahead, Bret spent a fair amount of the next twenty minutes looking out to the left, where, after they had come out from behind a couple of large hills, the Kenmare River or the sea or whatever it was at this point drew closer and closer as they proceeded. The bus slowed dramatically for each corner in the hedge-lined road, then, after inching through, would gradually work its way back up to about 50 kph.

Soon they were nearly upon the water as the road began to bend around a hill whose flanks went directly down into the sea. The bus slowed to a crawl, began to creep around the turn, then stopped. The reverse lights went on (Bret had learned to leave a decent gap) and the bus backed a few feet, then crept forward about the same distance and stopped again. Then it rolled forward about a foot and stopped. Then six inches. Then nothing happened for about five minutes, at least nothing Bret could see. But of course, the bus was blocking his view.

He got out of the car and started walking ahead. The man's face was no longer in the back window, but the steam marks remained. Bret could not see, but could hear, the French driver conversing with someone, apparently a local farmer. At first, Bret couldn't understand much of anything either voice said. But then he caught the French voice saying "Back up how long?" and the Irish one replying "Haffa mile to Bunnow's Lane, s'wide enough. Naught afore that." Bret turned to go back to his car. Perhaps the map would reveal some way around. As he walked, he noticed a red mini backing around the bend ahead; evidently its driver had determined that this obstacle was insurmountable. "Hallo?" a voice came from behind.

Bret turned. The red-faced man was leaning out a side window. "Hallo sir! The motorcoach it must be backing up! No room in the road!"

"Yes, I gathered. I will move my car out of the way."

"Thank you, sir!" The head disappeared back into the window.

Bret got in the car and started to back up. The road was so narrow here that he wasn't confident that he could turn around without pulling into a side drive, so he figured he'd just keep backing up until he found one. He decided that, though he was pointed the wrong way, it would still be proper to move over to the other side of the road (a very minor distinction in such narrow circumstances) so that he, or rather his car, would be traveling in the same direction as the other vehicles in that lane. It made him quite nervous to proceed in this manner, but he saw no alternative.

As he thought about it, he didn't actually remember how far back it had last been when he passed a drive or lane, but after a couple of minutes of awkward backwards driving he began to wonder if there had been any at all since leaving Sneem. Certainly, he reassured himself, he would eventually come to that Bunnow's Lane the farmer had mentioned. But before that could happen, he heard a screech and whomp behind him, which prompted him to immediately stop the car. After hearing nothing new, he cautiously continued around the next bend and discovered the red mini pressed against the hedgewall with a blue panel van squeezed in between it and the opposite hedgewall. Bret stopped and got out. As the doors of both vehicles were aligned side-by-side, neither driver could get out. Nor could either vehicle proceed forward or backward. He walked closer to the two vehicles and was about to call out to the driver of the mini, who seemed to be leaning down on the passenger side looking for something, when he heard the rumble of the bus approaching behind him. The noise of the engine was punctuated by the insistent "beep-beep-beep-beep-beep" of the automatic warning that trucks and other large vehicles have to let other drivers and pedestrians know when the truck is backing up. A vision of his car being crushed while the red-faced man peered out the back window at the wreckage flashed through his mind. With a zing of adrenaline, he wheeled around and ran back past his car to try to catch the driver's attention before he rounded the bend.

This proved quite easy, as the bus, though loud, was not yet close, nor was it moving quickly. When, after about seven or eight minutes, its hulking rectangular bulk finally came into view, Bret was able to easily walk up beside it and warn the driver through the open window out of which he was leaning in order to see where he was going. Bret noted that the bus was a left-drive model, which normally might have further complicated the situation, though it actually worked out all right when one was driving in reverse, if one could get over the backwardsness.

"There has been an accident, just around the corner," Bret called up slowly and with careful enunciation.

"Zut alors!" replied the driver. "C'est bien fou. I am helping?" He asked.

"I don't know. Je ne sais pas," said Bret, flashing back to high school French class. Jacqueline! Téléphone! Le train de Genève arrive à la gare de Lyon. Garçon! L'addition, s'il vous plaît.

Meanwhile, the bus driver stepped down and walked with Bret around the corner. He was wearing a standard uniform of navy blue polyester slacks and a white shirt open at the collar, and he had an enormous thicket of keys that jingled against his thigh with every step. The driver of the panel van had climbed out through the back of his vehicle and was standing behind the red mini, shaking his head as the driver of that car attempted to crawl out a side window onto the hedge. The bus driver began to laugh. The driver of the car, who was now halfway onto the hedge, turned his head and Bret recognized him immediately. "Eh, Rosko!" the bus driver called.

AMUSEMENT

Rosko nodded subtly to Bret, and then became studiously occupied with the logistics of extracting himself from his automobile, then of his automobile from the hedge. Bret looked back the other way to see that other occupants from the bus had begun filing around the corner. The red-faced man led the group. Behind him came a tall, slender blond-haired man with a beard, a hawk-nosed woman with her dark hair pulled back tightly under a white scarf, two burly and compact red-haired fellows in matching yellow polo shirts, a trim woman with straight gray hair chatting with a lanky, balding fellow of about 30, and a trio of young women who appeared to be in their mid-20s, semi-casually dressed in jeans and snug-fitting, bright colored tank tops, a couple of young men of about the same age shambling along behind in baggy pants and dark t-shirts. Behind these were another five or six people Bret couldn't see yet. Just then the red-faced man came alongside Bret, made a poofing sound through his lips, and shook his head. Then he turned to Bret and smiled, extending a hand, and said, in very proper English lightly accented with both French and what sounded to Bret like a tinge of working-class British, "Good day, sir. I am sorry that we seem to have enclosed you. We have nearly made a sandwich."

"Thanks," said Bret. "It's not quite time for lunch yet."

The man laughed.

"So you know that fellow in the red car, or the one in the van? You said 'we,'" Bret inquired.

"Oh, yes," said the man. "In the car. He is my cousin, or some kind of cousin. But also he is sharing with my friends and me a business proposition."

"Ah," replied Bret. "What sort of business?"

"Rosko is a man of many projects," the man began. "Forgive me. I introduce myself. I am Luc Bernard. I own a small hotel in Roscoff, in Brittany. My colleagues here are also from the Finistère—this is the region of the Breton peninsula. Rosko has a plan for his peninsula to cooperate with our peninsula, so to say, for the tourism."

"Bret Sheehan. Nice to meet you. I have never been to that part of France."

"First, there is the sea. The sea is everywhere in Brittany. It is not so mountainous like here. Gentle hills. Small villages and a few large towns, everywhere the fishing, everywhere the agriculture. And in my town, the thalassotherapie. Seaweed therapy. Many people believe in the healing properties of the seaweed. But for the tourists, it is the sea and the ruins of Carnac."

"Carnac?" Bret was not familiar with the place.

"You see, this is the problem. Carnac is an ancient site of stone rows, like Stonehenge in England, but older. Yet the world does not know of this. And Rosko believes that County Kerry and the Iveragh peninsula especially do not enjoy the acclaim that they deserve, either. So his plan is to make something more to attract the tourists."

Bret nodded. "Everybody wants tourists. Everybody hates tourists. There seem to be a lot of them here already."

M. Bernard agreed. "Yes, but for a man like Rosko, he sees always the potential for greatness. If it is good, then it can be great. Rosko has related to me an ancient fable of Ireland. Long ago, there lived a king who had no kingdom. All of his subjects and his family, all of them lived on three ships only. The ships travel from place to place, but never they find the perfect kingdom because they are too accustomed to their boats. They do not want to leave the boats. The land is too dangerous, they say. We are happy in our small world of the ship. But the king knows they need to make a kingdom on the land because a king must have a kingdom or he is a king of nothing.

"One day the ships come to a small island in a sheltered bay and the king guides the ships in and they put the anchors. On the shore are many trees, and fresh water, and animals to eat and make clothing. So the king commands that a kingdom be built on this island, but the buildings of the kingdom must be exactly like the ships so that the people will feel safe. In time the king's island becomes prosperous, not only making happy the people who live there, but attracting curious adventurers from all around that part of the world. Whenever the new people come, the king builds a little place that is just like their home, so that everyone who comes to the king's island has the small adventure but without the dangerous sea voyage. The people say it is magic, and the king is happy to let them believe it. You see?"

"Yes, I see," said Bret.

M. Bernard continued. "But we do entertain many Irish visitors in Roscoff already, because the Irish Ferries service comes from Cork and Rosslare. The boat of Rosslare arrives at 10:00 three mornings each week, and departs at 19:00 the same evening. The Irish visitors enjoy a 17-hour crossing with music and much drinking. Then they drive their automobiles from the ferry into our town, where they park the car and spend the complete day in the pub or cafe, then they drive back to the boat in the evening and ride 17 hours back to Ireland. To me, this appears as an opportunity that has been missed."

"But is that not essentially what your group is doing here?" Bret responded.

"Of course! Now you understand the problem. The people visit, but they do not leave the bubble of their own habits, you see?"

"Well, people do want to be comfortable. Familiar habits are comfortable."

"Yes, we must present the experience familiar in one way, but with the adventure in another way. So the people want to stay for two days or four days instead of only eight hours."

"So what is the big plan?" Bret and M. Bernard watched as the man in the panel van started the engine and began to inch backward while Rosko stood behind and motioned him left, then right. A spine-wrenching screeching sound accompanied the maneuver.

"Theme parks," M. Bernard laughed. "Amusement parks, like Disneyland."

Hmm, Bret thought to himself. This might be a chance to have a little fun with Mr. Rosko, give him a taste of his own medicine. "You're kidding," Bret replied.

"Not at all. Do you find it a foolish idea?"

"No, it's not that. You see, I myself am a theme park professional."

M. Bernard's eyes widened. "Why, this is unbelievable."

"No," replied Bret, "it is quite true. I have most recently been director of marketing and visitor services for King Arthur's Kamelot in Ohio, USA."

M. Bernard became very animated. "Well, then certainly Rosko must have encountered you, for he has visited this very place and had extensive discussions with a person of this very same description!"

"Hmm," said Bret. "Did he say the name of the person he met?"

"No," said M. Bernard. "I do not think so."

"Well, surely he would not make it all up, would he?"

M. Bernard paused for a few seconds and looked over toward Rosko and back to Bret. "I do not think so."

"So he made a special journey to the US to meet these people?"

"He did not say what he was doing before he left, only after he returned. But Rosko is like that. He likes the drama and mystery. Our meeting was to discuss the modes of tourism, but he kept this idea of a theme park to himself until yesterday. He enjoys to make a surprise."

Bret nodded. "Well, as soon as these vehicles are free of their predicament, you must introduce me to Mr.—what did you say his name was?"

"Rosko."

"Perhaps I can offer some useful advice in your project," Bret continued.

"That would be most appreciated," said M. Bernard.

Bret winced as the panel van finally wriggled free with a metallic shriek. The two drivers exchanged papers while the bus driver explained the situation further up the road. Bret and M. Bernard began walking and approached the three men. The driver of the panel van, a very slight, dark-haired person wearing a light blue mechanic's jumpsuit and calf-high rubber boots, nodded and pointed back over his shoulder, making a sort of sawing gesture to the bus driver in a way that suggested to Bret the back-and forth motion a large vehicle might need to make while turning around in a very confined space. The man's voice became audible as Bret arrived at the scene. "That turn is plenty tight when the coach is coming the right way, but the angle of it is impossible from this side, unless you drive through backways. Which I wouldn't recommend, incidentally," he added, glancing at Rosko, then back to the bus driver. "The only way to get a coach that size out to the point is to go all the way round the other way through Killarney. Road just isn't made to be traveled in this direction. Not for a coach."

Then he stepped away, pausing to examine the deep longitudinal scratches along the entire side of his truck where it had run up against the hedge. "Bit of new paint, that's all. And a bit of ball-peen hammer. I'll be telephoning you, sir," he called to Rosko. He climbed in, started it up, made a deft five-point turn, and sped off back toward Sneem.

Rosko looked up at Bret, who waited as long as he could for M. Bernard to begin introducing him to Rosko, but just then the Frenchman was looking back toward the crowd of passengers and motioning them to return to the bus. Bret had to speak quickly before Rosko could. "Hello, pleased to meet you, sir," said Bret. "My name is Bret Sheehan." He stuck out his hand. Rosko, looking wary, reached and joined the handshake. Bret continued, barely pausing for a breath. "Mister Bernard tells me you're in the theme park business, and I find that such an extraordinary coincidence, because so am I."

"Yes," M. Bernard chimed in. "Mister Sheehan works for the very same King Arthur's Kamelot that you visited."

Rosko opened his mouth.

"I can't believe I missed you," Bret broke in. "What days were you there? Who did you speak with? I'd be glad to give a presentation to your group, more than happy. Mister Bernard told me all about it." M. Bernard nodded. Bret continued. "Well, in any case, I'm charmed to meet you and now we'd better get ourselves out of the road. Let's all get together back in town. Mister Bernard says you're staying in Sneem? Is that right? So am I! What a coincidence. We must have been meant to meet, don't you think so? Wow, that's all I can say. Wow!" Rosko's face bore a bland smile as he nodded courteously to Bret and glanced and nodded at M. Bernard. Then he walked briskly back toward his car.

Bret felt bursting with energy as he climbed into the driver's seat. This was fun. For the first time in a long while, he felt completely in his element.

HE WAS ABLE TO REVERSE his car's direction with a careful multi-point turn, and quickly scooted past Rosko, who seemed to be waiting for the bus. Bret glanced down at the metal container on the seat beside him. Tomorrow? It seemed as if it would be too late to take the ashes up to the well by the time the bus was out of the way—so Bret began to work out his presentation. He could do it on that triangular town green at the center of Sneem. Park the bus along one side and use it as a backdrop so he could enclose the space and better command the attention of his audience.

He rounded a curve and spotted the lane where the bus could turn around, and decided he would stop and wait there, so as to be assured of the opportunity to get the group to follow his plan. Not wanting to block the lane itself, he found a gravel pull-off another fifty yards up the road and waited, drumming his fingers on the wheel. This way he could also see any approaching cars and warn them of the obstacle ahead. But none came.

About five minutes later, Rosko's red mini came slowly around the bend, followed by the bus beeping its way along behind. Rosko parked his car behind Bret's and walked over to guide the bus back into the lane. Bret followed, making a convincing show of keeping a watch out for coming traffic.

When the bus had backed all the way into the lane (with Rosko out of sight and earshot behind it), Bret got the driver's attention and asked him to park alongside the town green in Sneem so that he could make a brief presentation to the passengers. M. Bernard, leaning over the driver's shoulder, nodded in agreement. Then Bret trotted back to his car and waited for the bus to come up behind, which it did moments later. He pulled his car out, waving to the driver to follow him, and led the bus back to Sneem. He caught an occasional glimpse of Rosko's red mini following behind. This was going to be great.

They were still ahead of the first wave of tour buses, so there were two open coach-size parking spaces alongside the green. Bret guided them into the forward slot and got out of the car to greet the passengers as they climbed down. He caught sight of Rosko standing off to his left, watching. Bret shook the hand of each person who came down the steps and said "Bret Sheehan," or "Hello. Bret Sheehan," or "Pleased to meet you, Bret Sheehan," or "Bret, Bret Sheehan."

The tall blond man was a scientist or professor whose identification tag said he worked for some kind of marine institute in Roscoff. The woman with the straight gray hair and the lanky balding fellow were mother and son, Bret surmised. The three young women and two young men were younger than Bret had first guessed—they were more likely college students—but he couldn't yet guess why they were here. The two red-headed men ran a liquor store whose name "Les Vins du Finistere" was embroidered on the breast pockets of their yellow polo shirts. The woman with the scarf, who had looked somewhat severe at first, smiled warmly.

When the group was assembled on the green, Bret stepped back away from them and scanned the faces. They looked eager to hear him speak. He wondered how well they understood English. It almost didn't matter. They were going to eat this up.

Bret glanced over to where Rosko stood under a tree near the rear fender of the bus. Rosko leaned with an aspect of studied nonchalance against the broad trunk, but Bret could detect a twist of unease in the man's spine. Bret felt a twinge of anger. He had thought that Rosko could be a good friend. Ever since he first spoke to him in the airport, then in Dublin, and on the train. It seemed like there had been a genuine rapport. But no. It had been an act all along. And when a relationship is founded on fiction, there's nothing to sustain it when the act falls flat.

He looked back at the faces. They were ready. He looked back at Rosko, who was studying his own shoes.

Bret cleared his throat, and stopped. His eyes traced the hillsides in the distance, then followed the edges of the colorful storefronts into town. A block away, he caught sight of someone walking, black hair bouncing wildly. It was Lee, unmistakably. He glanced back at the hills. Whoa, he thought to himself. Wait a minute. I almost blew it. He understood in that instant that this was a test and he had come to the verge of failing it. Rosko and crowd drifted to the periphery of his attention and his mind locked on something it had been dancing around ever since he had arrived here. His eyes scanned from the dappled hillsides to the figure of Lee as she turned down the little alley next to the Fisherman's Knot. Connection to the land. Connection to another human. Like Uncle Michael had felt with that girl in the boat all those years ago. Like blood and bones to water and stone. It was as if a fog had cleared and, after having stumbled about aimlessly for as long as he could remember, Bret could see what to do—not for effect, but for real. He had to talk to Lee and he had to get Uncle Michael up into those hills.

Time to act fast, he thought. "Good afternoon," said Bret to the crowd. "I am delighted to introduce to you—Mr. Francis Rosko!" He applauded then stepped aside and motioned for Rosko to take his place.

Rosko looked up, wide-eyed.

STAIGUE

Bret ducked behind the bus, crossed the street, and traversed the narrow bridge. Lee would be going in the back door of the Fisherman's Knot. He abruptly turned down a small footpath beside the building and trotted around behind, but she wasn't there. She wouldn't have had time to get inside yet. She must have continued down toward the river. He trotted off that way. The lane turned sharply to the right around a whitewashed stone cottage and ended abruptly on a gravel path along the rocky river bank. Where had she gone? Bret's feet skidded on the loose stones and he found himself on a sure trajectory for the babbling Sneem, landing on his rear on a large, sloping slab of a rock and dunking his left leg up to the knee into the cold water before his foot hit bottom and he managed to arrest his descent.

Crawling out of the water, he scanned up and down the stream and up the path in the direction from which he had been running. Where was she? Bret couldn't have been more than 30 seconds behind. Well, he knew she'd be at the Fisherman's Knot tonight. Maybe he could go take Uncle

Michael to the holy well right now and then see her this evening.

He scrambled back up to the path. A girl of nine or ten and her mother, both light-haired, slim, and tall, appeared from around a bend in the path downstream.

"Good day," said Bret as they passed a few moments later.

"Hi," said the girl in an American accent.

"Hey," said Bret. "Let me ask you a question. You're from the States, right?" They both stopped and nodded. "Would you like this place better or worse if there was a big amusement park here?"

"Yuck," said the mom.

"What for?" said the girl.

"Exactly," said Bret. "Thank you."

BY THE TIME Bret got back to the town green, the tour group had dispersed. This was an immense relief. Relaxed, he trotted across the road and opened his car. He could only imagine the song and dance Rosko had done to get out of that one! He laughed out loud.

It couldn't be past noon, he thought. Maybe that was enough time, especially if he got up there before the buses started coming the other way. He glanced down at the box on the seat. Yes, it was definitely time to take Uncle Michael back. He rolled out of town, back past the place where the bus had gotten stuck and into the not-quite-town of Castle Cove, labeled "Castlecove" on the map but not noted at all on the road. It took less than 20 minutes.

He had the Ordnance Survey #84 half-unfolded in his lap, but was preoccupied with the view as the road came right up to the edge of the sea before veering suddenly to the right. The road then descended a moderate hill and Bret found himself in the little town of Castle Cove, such as it was. The instant he realized he was in Castle Cove, he saw a small brown sign on the right pointing to Staigue Fort. He mashed on the brakes and swerved onto a tiny lane.

Tall hedges lined the narrow strip of pavement and scrubby trees overhung the road from behind the hedges. The road split and Bret had to check the map to see that he needed to bear right. Soon he was at another fork, where he determined to go left. The road began to slope upward as the pavement turned to packed dirt. The noon light painted a bright irregular strip down the center of the lane, where the occasional clump of grass grew between the tire tracks.

As he crested a hill, another car suddenly appeared coming the other way, and Bret's drive-on-the-right instinct was to cut the wheel to his right. The instinct of the other driver was to turn to the left. Thus, they both headed for the same nook in the hedge on the same side of the path. Bret braked hard and the cars stopped just short of contact. In the process, the box of Uncle Michael pitched off the seat and onto the floor. The top came loose but not quite off. Good thing it had gotten stickier. A mess of ashes on the car floor would not have been a good ending.

Bret looked back up to meet the other driver's gaze. A woman with short-cropped black hair looked back at him and arched her eyebrows. Her shoulder hunched as she shifted the car into reverse. Bret did the same, and each backed up about ten feet, then began to roll forward. But again, each angled for the same side of the lane. This time, however, when Bret stopped, the woman continued right off the edge of the track and squeezed her car against the hedge. The she motioned for Bret to go around. He backed up again, then inched past, nodding to the woman, who rolled her eyes and lifted a couple fingers from the wheel. Her straight black hair was streaked with gray, her cheeks red like a farmer's.

The lane leveled off for a few hundred yards, then a side branch angled up to the left. Another small brown sign pointed to Staigue Fort. Over the crest of another rise, Bret caught sight of the fort, a round stone structure uphill and to the right. At first it struck him as just another stone outcrop, but as he got closer, its geometrically curved face gave away the human element. On the left and closer was a farm house and a small parking area. He pulled the car into one of the empty spaces—all of them were empty—and turned off the ignition.

Leaning over to his left, he picked up the metal box and pressed its lid more firmly in place. Should he take the Ordnance Survey #84 with him also? Why not? He folded the map one more time than it was intended to be folded and forced it into the small pocket of his windbreaker. The metal box he just held in his hand, wishing he had thought to bring a plastic shopping bag or something in which to carry it.

He closed the door and started walking up toward the fort. It was set in a wide valley that was shaped like a scoop; its sides sloped gradually away from the bottom, then more steeply up to a high ridgeline and a ring of low mountains that defined the horizon. Hundreds of sheep were scattered across the bowl and up its sides, little puffs of white against the intense green.

He came to a fence. A small wooden gate was marked with a sign asking visitors to PLEASE close the gate behind them and to leave two pounds (crossed out) euros in a slot in a little box that was nailed to a fencepost. This was private property, a text explained, and the small fee would help to offset the owner's cost in maintaining the parking area. Bret dropped a couple of euro coins in the box, then added another, since he was going to be using the property a little bit more than the average visitor. He walked up a curving gravel path around the base of the fort, eyeing the hilltops beyond. That saddle up to the left would be the place he would cross the ridge and, if the man in the post office's description was accurate, a well should be very close to that point. The sky was a pale blue, with faint wisps of cloud blowing across the peaks toward him, north to south.

He walked through the fort's one opening, a low, square doorway with a single slab of rock across the top. The walls had to be 12 or 15 feet thick, maybe 20 feet at the base, just stacked up stones—no mortar, no precise cuts—only stones, rough-edged, each a couple of feet long and 10 or 12 inches wide, and about as thick as the width of Bret's palm. Stairs spiraled up the sides in somewhat arbitrary fashion and there was otherwise no feature interrupting the stacked stone walls except for the entry door and another low opening set into the wall to Bret's left. He walked over and peered into the space. It was a fairly large room, set below grade, extending under the wall on the southwest side of the fort. He stepped down and looked around. What did they do in here? Hide from the rain, maybe. Wouldn't be good for much else. He ascended back into the light.

When he climbed the irregular steps to the top edge of the ring wall, he was rewarded with a majestic view of the Kenmare River widening to the sea. In the other direction he scanned the arc of hills, treeless knobby ridges of grass and stone. As he gazed, he marveled at how the silent passing shadows of clouds could reveal so much more about the contours of the land—ledges, outcrops, and gullies that were invisible under the steady sun. He looked back the other way toward the water. Imagine living in this place. Imagine standing up here and watching friends or foes come up the bay, and preparing to welcome them or to fend them off. What if they came from the other side of the ridge? What was over there? He pulled out the map and looked. Not much was over there. More hills, a few scattered cottages. A deep valley eventually made its way out to a large lake, which emptied itself into Ballinskelligs Bay to the southwest, and there was a footpath over a pass in the ridge—marked as the Kerry Way today, but who knew how old it was—that connected the little town of Castle Cove with Waterville on the edge of the bay. Well, he thought: time to get up there.

He picked his way back down the steps and walked toward the doorway, just as a couple entered. They were young, tall, and blonde, the woman perhaps even taller than the man. They were speaking German or Dutch or some other language

Bret did not understand. He nodded a hello. The young man said, very carefully, "Good morrow, sir."

"Yes, quite," said Bret. Whatever.

UPHILL

Outside the door, Bret took three steps on the packed gravel path, then veered to the left onto the sheep-shorn grass and skirted the fort on the side that was away from the parking lot. As he followed the curving edge, he realized how steeply the land sloped down away from the stone walls. The effort that must have been required to build this two or three thousand years ago, Bret thought, would have been staggering. How long would it have taken? Did they keep working during those long winter nights? He brushed a hand on the stone. This stuff was tough, to last so long in all this wind and rain. He tugged on the stone. It abraded the skin on his thumb.

The sky was beginning to cloud up a bit. He stepped down off the berm of the fort and began to walk away from it. After a couple hundred feet he came alongside a tiny stream course and followed it for a time until it entered a patch of dense scrub that he had to circumnavigate.

It occurred to him that, in this landscape of grass and low shrubs, he would be plainly visible to anyone who might be watching. The guy in the post office had said he'd walked up the same way before, but Bret didn't know all the circumstances. What if the owners of the land actually didn't want people wandering through their pastures? He determined that the best defense was probably to think like a cat—to adopt an attitude of invisibility even while crossing a barren space in broad daylight.

But this space was not so barren as it looked from afar. Large tufts of long grasses half as tall as he were sprinkled across the landscape, along with little paths worn into the grass by the sheep, and delicate pink wildflowers. And it wasn't as dry as it looked from a distance, either. In fact, Bret had to pick his way carefully through the fields to keep his shoes from getting soaked.

All of this kept his mind occupied until he was about ten minutes clear of the fort, when he heard a yell behind him. Very subtly, he changed his direction while continuing to walk and turned his head very slowly to the left so he could glance back, thus turning around while trying not to appear to be turning around.

The two tall visitors he'd recently encountered were standing on the wall, waving, obviously in Bret's direction. He ignored them and carried on. He had enough of a head start that the only problem would be if someone who knew these hills were to try to chase him down, and now, looking up, he saw that he might have another ally in his quest: a long tongue of mist was reaching down the hillside toward him. Under the cover of even a light fog, he could proceed undetected. He heard one more yell and then the cloud was around him.

The mist was thick, but he could still see the ridge crest above because the layer of fog was clinging close to the ground, and the ground, he noticed, was quickly getting steeper. He switched the metal box to his left hand so he could use his right to steady himself on a low stone wall that had conveniently appeared alongside.

He followed the wall until it t-boned against a perpendicular one that was much taller—too tall for him to clamber over it at this point. So he followed it to the left, which seemed the more uphill direction and after a few minutes, the wall abruptly ended in the middle of a steep pasture. Three sheep stood near the edge of the wall, munching grass and eying Bret with their vacant rectangular eyeballs. Bret passed them, then cut diagonally across the pasture to try to correct for the recent detour. Something was bothering his sinuses, causing his eyes to water. He stepped on a patch of dark green leafy groundcover plants and water squished out. A half-second later, he was backpedaling in a futile effort to keep himself vertical over his slipping feet and then, voop-voop-oof! he was on his side in a porridge of spring water and sheep excrement.

"Crap," he said aloud.

Retrieving the metal box from its landing place a few feet away, he retook his bearings and then carefully picked his way to the uphill edge of the pasture, where another stone wall promised to offer a measure of stability. A warmth on his back and a need to squint signaled a sudden thinning of the mist. Leaning on the wall, he looked back down. He was out of breath. The patch of mist slid along the flank of the hill and parted as it passed over Staigue Fort like a wave washing around a seaside rock. Beyond was the hazy green of the shoreline and the twinkling blue water. Out at sea, he could now make out whitecaps and the churning foam of big breakers crashing against the jagged peninsulas. He was surprised by how high up he had gotten in the relatively short time since he'd left the fort. From here, it was clear how close the vast open sea was to the quiet pastoral patchwork of pastures outside Sneem. The town was like a blithely grazing sheep, the sea a pack of wolves waiting in the woods just out of sight. He looked back that way. Sneem was not visible from this vantage point, but it probably would be once he got up to the ridge.

Speaking of which . . . he resumed climbing.

AS HE GOT HIGHER, the smell of the sea became more prominent, which seemed odd, since he was getting further from the water, but then maybe it was just the wind carrying the sea air over the ridge top from the ocean beyond. He had found a natural rhythm, his footfalls steady except where an adjustment was needed to step onto a rock or over a puddle, his left hand holding the box, his right hanging loose except to grasp a stone or root when it might help his progress. And when he did touch the wood or stone or earth, it was familiar to him in a way he could not quite explain. He had never been much of an outdoors type, yet, when his palm settled on a little chunk of moss-covered granite as he hoisted himself over a small ledge, it felt as if the earth were pushing back to help him along. It was like coming to a place where people knew him, where they might invite him to a meal or give him a lift to his hotel.

After a half-hour of very steep climbing, the grade moderated somewhat and he could see that he was coming to the saddle between Staigue Mountain and the next peak over. Somewhere near here should be the well. He paused, turned around, and leaned on a stony outcrop. For a moment he could see Sneem plainly over the lower peak that had obscured his view, then a thick cloudbank closed in over the scene and he was engulfed in a dense fog. He turned and continued up toward the saddle, as far as he could tell. It was difficult to see more than fifty feet.

From the description given by the man in the Post Office, the well should be not far from the saddle, and a little ways up the side of Staigue from there. Bret figured if he kept himself very slightly to the left, he might cut the corner off a triangle and find the place more quickly. But this mist was going to make it difficult to find anything. He decided to go a little farther, then find a suitable resting spot and wait a while for the fog to blow off. A noisy wind was whipping over the ridge and Bret figured it wouldn't take too long before the clouds would part, at least for a while. He found a table rock a few minutes later and sat down to wait, placing the box beside him. That wind was cold, too. He shivered and pulled his jacket more tightly around his neck.

In his left jacket pocket was a Cadbury dark chocolate bar, and now, Bret determined, was good time to eat it. He broke it into thick squares ate them one at a time, letting each piece dissolve on his tongue. From time to time the sky appeared to brighten a little, but each time he looked up in anticipation, a dimmer shade of gray would slide below the lighter ceiling above, often bringing with it a light drizzle. By the time he was down to the last row of chocolate, he was shivering steadily. The rock and wind were conspiring to suck the heat out of him. If the skies didn't change soon, he'd have to head back down. A motion to his right caught his attention.

He stood up and peered in that direction. Nothing seemed to be there, except a little black silhouette at the edge of a rock. Was it a tenacious little plant trembling in the wind? He squinted. No. No, it was a bird, foraging in the lee of the boulder. A large black bird, maybe a crow or a raven. It skirted the edge of the rock, then hopped up onto a smaller stone next to it, where the force of the wind caught under its wings and lifted it airborne for a couple of seconds. Half-spreading its wide dark wings, it darted back behind the larger boulder and alighted there again. Then for a second Bret was sure he saw a human shape, just behind the bird. The bird paid it no notice whatsoever. A trick of the mist?

"Hey!" Bret called.

Startled, the raven flapped its great wings twice, elevated, and was instantly soaring off downwind. Then Bret was pretty sure he saw the figure again, uphill to the right. The colors seemed to be green and brown. He immediately thought of the man he'd seen out Uncle Michael's window that day.

The shape made a beeline up what seemed like the steepest pitch on the mountainside and Bret, his hands numb with cold, followed as best he could, but it was all he could do to keep the dark silhouette in sight. Climbing over the rocks was challenging enough, but it was the wet vegetation that was really treacherous. Twice he slipped and belly-flopped on the slick earth, and each time the form he was following disappeared further into the fog.

Finally, Bret came to an unbroken line of rocks and he summoned his remaining strength to accelerate and close the gap. But the rocks were uneven and he had to keep his eyes down in order to be sure of his footing, and when the skies suddenly brightened and he looked ahead, he saw he was chasing nothing. Bret kept climbing.

The slope eased and the sky became so bright that he had to nearly shut his eyes. Then, in the space of a few steps, he emerged above the cloud. To his left, he could see a raven circling over a lower peak whose summit barely protruded through the cloudbank. He walked ahead for another minute until he was at what he judged to be the summit. That judgment was aided by a cairn of rocks perhaps eight feet high that stood on a flat stone at this high point. Bret's mind immediately flashed back to the train ride, when he'd seen, from a great distance, cairns atop other summits along the ridge approaching Killarney.

His eyes adjusted to the brightness and he surveyed the panorama. The white billows extended as far as he could see, except for a small clear patch straight ahead, where a sliver of open ocean was visible. To the right of that, two sharp rock pinnacles pierced the blanket of clouds, one taller and farther away than the other. Those would be the Skellig islands. All around was a bright world, a simple world of blue above and white below, interrupted only by a half dozen mountaintops. Bret spotted cairns on at least two of them. The climb had warmed him. Steam was rising off his sleeves. He inhaled the deepest lungful he could of the crisp air.

He scanned around and around, circling the cairn three or four times. He couldn't even tell from which direction he had come up. But at least he was here in the bright sun and not sitting on that rock shivering in the drizzle.

He gazed out over the stunning scene and thought to himself, "Oh, shit."

Uncle Michael was still back down there on that rock.

DESCENT

Bret stood on the summit for another twenty minutes, hoping the clouds might burn off and make it clearer to him which way to go, but the rippled white blanket seemed to be settling down for a lengthy slumber. Now he could see no break in the clouds in any direction, and a few of the nearby peaks that had been protruding were now invisible. The clouds were rising and thickening. He'd better go down, now rather than later.

Based on the position of the sun and the direction of the wind, he made a guess at which direction he should walk, and started to descend. The mist rose up around him and soon he found himself picking his way carefully down a steepening slope in increasingly dim light. After ten minutes, he stopped. Nothing looked familiar. How could he find that rock again on this vast mountain without being able to see anything?

He looked around him. If he could find the saddle again, the low place on the ridge where he had first come up, then maybe he could retrace from there. Or at least get back down to the fort. It dawned on him that the way to find the saddle would be to skirt the mountain rather than descending it, spiraling gradually down until he came to a place where the slope leveled into the saddle. It might take a while, but it should work. He turned to his left and began to walk.

His left leg, continually taking higher steps than his right because it was on the uphill side, began to ache. And he could feel blisters forming in his soggy shoes. But he pressed on, walking as briskly as he could until he felt the wind move all the way around his head, from blowing in his left ear, then in his face, the right side and the back, and back to the left side again. That should have been one circuit, but no saddle.

Reversing direction to give his left leg a break, he consciously angled down a little bit more. On the first time around, he had learned that, because the terrain was so uneven, he really had no idea whether he was circling at a steady elevation or going down or going up. This way he might walk down only to have to ascend again, but at least he'd likely find the saddle. "Wait a minute," he said. He pulled the Ordnance Survey #84 out of his jacket pocket and examined it closely. There were two ridge lines that dipped off of Staigue. The one he hoped to find looked to be about 50 meters higher than the other one, which was named Windy Gap. On the back, inland side of the mountain was a very steep section that he guessed to be about 50 meters below where he was now. So if he walked this way, clockwise around the mountain cone, came to the steep section and then, once past it, continued straight down the ridge line, he should find the right saddle. Once there, he might find some familiar small landmark, having just come that way not two hours before.

I guess, he thought to himself, this pretty much proves that it doesn't much matter to me who the guy really was. He chuckled. Uncle Michael.

He made his way around, perceived that he had crossed the bump of a ridge line, and then traversed a steeper section, all the while taking care to descend slightly. But after another half-hour, he found himself with the wind at his left again and still no second ridge line and still no saddle. Maybe he was turned 180 degrees and the ridge line he had crossed was the one he should have descended. His sweat had cooled and now he was getting chilled. He reversed direction again.

This time, when he got to the ridge line, he turned and walked straight down it for a few minutes, then again turned to his left to continue the circuit. The hillside became extremely steep. The fog was so dense that he could not see where the slope leveled or if it got steeper. He continued around. Now the wind was in his face. That didn't make sense. He pulled out the Ordnance Survey #84 again and studied the topographic lines. There was a third, minor ridge hump on the south side of the mountain. Maybe that was the one he had descended. But the steep section wasn't in the right place. And the wind was wrong. But maybe it had shifted. If only the sky would clear for just a few seconds, he could figure out where he was. He sat down on a boulder and pushed the map back into his pocket. There were still a couple of squares of chocolate in there.

In fact, if he didn't figure out where he was, he could really be up a creek. He put a square of chocolate in his mouth. Only one side of the ridgeline led down to civilization. The other side was just wildlands. So if he chose to descend all the way just to get down to safety, he might end up making his situation worse if he picked the wrong place to go down. Still, he might have to take that chance.

But then, miraculously, a hole in the clouds appeared over his left shoulder and as it traveled past, it dipped lower. He glimpsed momentarily a shorter peak maybe half a mile away. Then the clouds closed up and he was enshrouded again. He checked the Ordnance Survey #84. That peak was probably the one on the other side of the saddle, to the northeast, because Windy Gap to the west was flanked by Eagles Hill, which was quite a bit taller than Staigue. Bret got up and made his way to his left.

Then the wind was behind him and he still found no saddle after twenty minutes of walking. If he didn't hurry up he might spend the night up here, except it was June and the sun stayed up forever. The hillside steepened. A sudden bright patch opened up over head and when Bret looked up, his feet went out from under him and he landed with a squishy thud. Then, slowly, he began to slip. Glancing down, he saw he was at the top of a wide swath of grass interrupted by very few rocks. Nothing to hit, but nothing to grab onto, either. He clawed at the vegetation, but his descent accelerated. He rolled over and spread-eagled himself face down and tried to dig both arms and both legs into the soggy ground, but the hillside steepened precipitously and his efforts only delayed for a few seconds the inevitable uncontrolled slide. "Shit," he hissed. Then his right leg hit a rock and he was airborne and tumbling and that was it.

My awareness emerged slowly out of the fog. How long had I been away? Impossible to say. Even now, my connection to the world seemed exceedingly tenuous, intermittent, fading. I was aware only that I was alone. I was with the ash, at least. That was as it should be. But Bret, he was part of the story as well. I listened for a long time, having thought I heard a voice, once or twice. I heard soft footfalls, muttering, nose sniffling. Then I thought that instead of a voice, it was the memory of a voice. Then the call of a bird. So I waited, drifting in and out, more out than in, gradually coming to the conclusion that this would be how it ends. Quietly, in this place. Stories have all kinds of plots, but they all end, and in that they are all the same.

INTO
THE
BEEHIVE

When he opened his eyes, Bret was looking up at a small precipice. Whispering rivulets of water ran down shallow creases. The sky was still a dense cloud. That could be heaven, or it could be Staigue Mountain. Hard to tell. He was on his back. He turned his head to the left and noticed that he was lying in a shallow pool. Water trickled into the pool over the face of a smooth rock. He could see the reflection of the clouds shimmering along the top edge. Lower down, the rock curved inward. Thick moss followed the edge of what looked like a small cave. Inside the cave, small shapes were moving—faint twinkling white lights, a bit of blue, a bit of green. He squinted and tried to focus. A little figure was moving in there, walking toward him. The clothing, green and brown, seemed almost like that of the mysterious man he'd seen far away outside Uncle Michael's window, and Bret's first thought was that he had fallen into some kind of magical fairyland. The lights twinkled and shimmered and the figure steadily grew larger. He heard a sound behind him and twisted himself to see what it was. His right ankle hurt quite a lot. He looked up into the green eyes of a pretty woman. She was wearing a moss-colored jacket and tan slacks, and crouching at the edge of the puddle. A heather knit woolen scarf was wrapped around her head and a few shocks of dark reddish brown hair were blowing across her face. "Is everything all right?" she asked in a hoarse alto.

He just blinked and tried to formulate a sensible response. Was he all right? Well, he was lost, wounded, hypothermic, and he'd misplaced his cremated uncle, but otherwise things weren't too bad. "Maybe so," he said.

"Are you sure you should move? Have you injured your back?" She was also carrying a tan canvas shoulder bag, similar to the sort bicycle messengers use. She ducked her head and lifted the strap of the bag over and put the satchel down next to her.

Bret cautiously shifted his weight onto his left arm and planted his right elbow onto the ground. "I think my back is okay. But I've hurt my leg. My ankle."

"Not a good place to hurt a leg, this," she said, standing. "But if you can walk at all we can at least have you out of the cold. It's but a few hundred meters."

"I guess I'd better try," he replied. He gingerly rolled onto his hands and knees and crawled out of the puddle. His nose was running and his eyes itched.

"Here," she said, crouching beside him. "I'll support you as best I can."

He rose and took a step. A sharp twang went up his leg.

"Come on," she said. "Put some weight on me. I'm sturdy."

She was that, Bret thought. She was a little taller than he and when he rested his arm across her shoulders he could feel solid muscles. They took a couple of steps, painful but not unbearable. "Thank you," he said. "I think this will work."

They made their way slowly along a narrow path with the uphill side of the mountain to the right. Bret felt pretty sure after a few minutes that the ankle was sprained but not broken, or if it was broken the bone wasn't displaced. He'd had the misfortune to break and sprain this same ankle twice before (icy steps, edge of the wave pool), and as he recalled the doctors saying that a sprain was more painful but healed faster. If this was a sprain, he'd need to rest it for a least a couple of days before he could go much of anywhere, and if it was a break, he really needed to get to a hospital.

"Do you think I should try to get to a doctor?" he asked.

"Bit of a challenge, that. We're miles from a road," she replied.

"But I thought we were heading for a house."

She laughed. "It would be a house by some standards, you might say. But there's no road, I'm afraid. I don't need much up here."

"You live up here?"

"Well," she paused for four or five footsteps. "I stay. There's a project I'm working on and while I'm working on it, this is where I stay. But it's not my post address."

"So you're like a hermit monk or something?"

"Not far off the mark, not far off," she said, nodding. "Now, of course, a girl might reasonably wonder why an American fellow like you would be sliding down her mountain on a foggy June afternoon at tea time."

"I slipped," said Bret.

"Ah," she replied.

The path dipped into a steep gully through which a stream flowed. The water was about four feet across—too far for Bret to leap at the moment—but there was one large rock in the middle. She crossed first and held out a steadying hand. He was shivering already and dunking his feet into that chilly water was not a very appealing thought, so he summoned all his concentration and hopped on his good leg to the rock and balanced, then hopped once more to the opposite bank. She released his hand.

"Now if you'll excuse me and wait here just one moment," she said, "I've got to get something." She scrambled up the left bank of the stream to a cluster of large rocks and reached down among them into the water to retrieve a small object which she carefully dabbed dry with a hand towel and then placed in the shoulder bag. Then she walked back down. "Refrigerator," she said as she got beside him again and pulled his arm over her shoulder. "Oh—your teeth are chattering. Let's go. Just over the bank, now, a few minutes' walk."

They made their way up the slope on the other side, then angled slightly uphill until they came to a nearly level sort of terrace about a dozen feet wide between a large vertical outcrop on the left and a thick tangle of vines covering a huge boulder on the right. About fifty feet into this passage, she stopped and said, "here we are. Mind your head." They turned right and pushed through overhanging vines into a round chamber about ten feet in diameter. Light filtered in through narrow slots high up on either side and through the entryway.

"Here," she said. "Lie down on my sleeping pad. I'll see if I've got any dry base layer clothing you can wear."

Bret followed instructions and lay down carefully on a thin foam sleeping pad that was stretched out to the left of the doorway, while she opened a backpack that leaned on the other side and pulled out a large plastic bag. "This should do," she said. "And this. And these." She came back across the room. "Off with the shoes. Off with everything. Then put these on and get into the sleeping bag as quickly as you can. I'll start some water boiling for tea."

She turned away and went over near the pack again, where, as Bret could now see because his eyes were adjusting to the dark, she had a small freestanding backpacking stove set up near the stone wall. He removed his shoes, but was unable to get his leg bent in such a way as to remove his stiff twill pants over his swelling ankle. So he unbuttoned and removed his light flannel shirt and pulled on the thin thermal top she had handed him.

"How's it coming?" she called without turning.

"Okay, but I can't seem to get the trousers off," he replied. "Shall I just climb in with them on?"

"No," she said. "That wouldn't do much good. I'll have to help you." She walked over, knelt by his feet, and carefully worked the mud-spattered olive pant cuff over the swollen ankle, then slid off the other leg. "Okay. You can handle the undershorts?"

"Thank you," said Bret. "I think so." She went back over to the stove and he managed to remove the wet cotton briefs and pull on the thermal bottoms. He put on one dry sock, but the other ankle was too large. Then, still shivering, he crawled into the bag.

A couple of minutes later she came over with a plastic cup of tea and handed it to him. He drank it gratefully and then she took the empty cup back over and made one for herself. He looked around the room again and realized with mild astonishment that they were inside a man-made beehive hut, a conical structure of stacked stone of the type built by reclusive monks a millennium or more ago. He'd seen pictures in some of the travel literature. "This is a hut, isn't it?" he chattered.

"Yes. Don't know if it's an ancient one or not, but it makes a perfect invisible camp site. Can't see it from any footpath or road, not on any map that I've seen. No fires, of course, but with a little stove and a good bag, it does nicely." She walked over and closed up the backpack, retrieving a small flashlight in the process. She was doing something with the light over near the wall and Bret realized she was hanging up his wet things on a string or rope he could not see. It was getting darker outside.

"Now," she said. "It's getting dark and it will be cold, and I've thought about this, but the only way to keep you warm is for both of us to get in there together. I don't mean any discomfort to you and I know you may find it awkward, but it's the only way. No arguing."

He didn't have the energy for even a polite "no thanks," nor much inclination. She unzipped the left edge of the bag, pulled off her fleece sweatshirt and removed her trousers, then squeezed in next to him, zipping the bag behind her. "Oh my," she said, "you're trembling all over. I hope this works."

He nodded, and then said, through clenched teeth. "Thanks. Oh," he stopped to sneeze. "Excuse me. Bret Sheehan. From Ohio. I—what is your name? "

"Oh yes," she laughed. "How rude of me. Caitlin McGowan. Cait." She paused. "From the north originally, County Tyrone. But this is home now. More or less."

"Well," he said. "I'm glad to meet you."

"I should say you are," she said.

After some time, perhaps ten minutes, perhaps an hour, perhaps three, his shivering finally subsided. "It's getting better, I think," he whispered, but she was asleep.

A DOOR OPENED and he walked into a glare. Columns of desks filled a brightly lit room. He approached the desk that was in the very center of the first row and spoke to the person seated there. "I need to report a missing person," he said.

"What sort of person?" asked the woman at the desk without raising her head. Her voice was pleasant, with a western-Pennsylvania twang.

"Michael Sheehan," said Bret. He gazed out across the room full of office workers. No one moved. Everyone was smoking. "Oh, I should mention that he is in a box."

The woman looked up. "What sort of box?" He saw now that, despite the American voice, she looked just like Mother, whom he had last seen in the house down on the Kenmare River. This startled him momentarily, but then he remembered to answer the question.

"A small metal box. Full of ashes."

"Ah," she said, turning around to address someone at a desk behind her. "Hey Mike, come on up here."

A man walked up and Bret saw that it was Uncle Michael, smoking a cigarette. He also spoke as if he came from the environs of Youngstown, Ohio. "What do we got here?"

Bret was intensely aware that the situation could be awkward. He decided to play it straight. "Missing person."

"Missing? Where at?"

"He was here," Bret pointed with his left hand to his right hand. "The box was here, but now it's gone."

"Nope, no box there," said Uncle Michael. "Looks like you're gonna have to fill out some forms."

"Forms? How many forms? I'm kind of in a hurry."

"Just three," said Uncle Michael.

"I'm sorry, say that again?" asked Bret.

"Three." Uncle Michael stacked three forms on the desk, one at a time. They looked very thick. "One, two, three. Take your time, no rush."

"But there is kind of a rush," said Bret. "I've got to find Michael."

"Not much can happen to a guy in a box, trust me."

"Okay," Bret started thinking more clearly now, "what sort of information is it that you need for the forms?"

"Oh, it's just basic stuff," said Uncle Michael.

"Would it include that story about the rowboat?" Bret asked.

"Oh, yes, put that in!" Mother called from behind Michael's shoulder. "That one came out nice."

"She's nuts," said Uncle Michael. "But go ahead and put that in if you think it's important."

"Well, mostly I'd want to include things that would help find him, right? So it ought to be stuff everybody agrees is true, right?" asked Bret.

"Good luck with that," Uncle Michael laughed.

"No, seriously . . . Does it matter if he was really from County Kerry? What if he was from Sharon, P-A?"

"Nothing wrong with Sharon, P-A," said Uncle Michael. "What do you got against Sharon, P-A?"

"Oh, you know what he means, Mike," said Mother. "Listen, young man," she said, turning to Bret, "everybody knows the forms don't really end up being of any use. They just get filed away someplace. But deciding what should go on the forms, that's another matter. So you just do that the best you can."

"You still have to fill out the forms," said Uncle Michael. "All thhhhree." He winked.

Bret squinted at the forms through the smoke and bright lights. Then he realized that he had no pencil. He kept trying to remember where he had put the pencil, but as he was trying to remember, the room disappeared and he was asleep again.

RESEARCH

Indirect light filled the room when he awoke. He could see a sliver of blue sky through one of the high slots in the wall. Cait was still next to him, tilted three-quarters toward the opposite wall with her upper shoulder blade resting on his chest. His left arm was asleep but he finally felt—after a night of only intermittent sleep—truly warm, not just not cold. He moved his injured right leg slightly and it throbbed with pain. That had awoken him countless times. One problem with squeezing four feet into the foot box of a mummy bag is that one foot doesn't easily move without bumping the others. He whispered "Ow."

"Awake?" Cait said.

"Mm-hm," he answered. Another problem with the close proximity was it seemed to have inspired a potentially embarrassing male anatomical response. He twisted his hips away from her as best he could, bumping the ankle again. "Ow."

"How are you feeling?"

"Warm at last, thank you."

"Who is Michael?" She pivoted incrementally onto her back and turned her head to face him. "Why do you need to find Michael?"

"Michael? Was I talking in my sleep? I had the weirdest dream. Excuse me. I have to move this arm." He slid his tingling forearm out from under her. "Ah, thanks."

"Only that," she said. "'Michael. Find Michael.'"

"He's my uncle, or was. But not really."

"Oh. I thought perhaps you were gay."

"Mm. No. Why, are you?"

"No," she smiled. He could see, now that her face was but inches away, that she was a bit older than he would have initially guessed, probably thirty-five. Sun and weather had left fine creases around her eyes. "So what's the story?" she asked.

"The whole story?"

She looked up at the window slot and back down. "Not going out soon, so yes, why not?" She propped her chin on her left elbow and he shifted onto his left hip to make room.

"What, is the weather too nice for you?"

"Yes, that's it exactly," she said. "Please do go on."

"Well, what's the story with that?"

"Ah, well," she paused, "then I'll tell mine first. First point is, we're not actually allowed to be here. To avoid being seen, the only times I travel are in the dark or under fog."

"Not allowed?"

"Let's say that my research is not fully sanctioned by the local authorities, nor by those who own this land. If I were spotted, I could not continue. So I take care not to be spotted."

"Must be serious," Bret offered.

"Oh yes," she replied. "Quite serious. It's about contamination of the watersheds. Kerry rivers in particular have experienced mysterious events in recent years. Fish kills, plants dying off. People becoming ill. I'm tracking for different sorts of contamination in these high slopes to try to determine where the problem comes from. My work is quietly sponsored by a university that shall remain nameless. Everyone thinks I'm on a year's leave from teaching, but that's a ploy to keep from attracting attention. It involves strategically placing small collection vials in water sources, gathering them after a certain amount of time, and chemically analyzing each sample. These are then cross-referenced with topog maps showing the collection sites and dates, and from that we can ascertain what kinds of contamination are coming from what places at which times."

"My," said Bret. "So that's why you camp out here?" His leg was throbbing, so he rolled back onto his back, inserting his left shoulder in the space under her propped arm.

"I leave my car behind a tourist center down in the valley. A friend is the manager and no one thinks anything of a car parked there. After dark, I hike up with a few days' worth of supplies and do as much as I can until the food runs out, then I go back down. Sadly, the food is gone now. Before I stumbled across you yesterday evening, I was about to collect my last sample and come down the mountain."

"Oh. Then you'll need to go down today?"

"More likely tonight, unless the fog rolls in again. I need enough minutes of cover to get over to the Kerry Way and then I can be seen on the pathway and it doesn't matter."

"What do you do in the mean time?"

"Oh, I've spent many a sunny day lying right here, waiting for the weather to turn bad."

"And today?"

She shrugged. "But now, about you. You don't strike me as a biochemist."

"I'm not sure what I am at the moment." He laughed grimly. "But I am here for a reason, I think. A kind of pilgrimage, you might say. My uncle died and I promised to return his ashes back to his homeland. That's here."

"Michael's ashes?"

"Right. But the problem is, I misplaced him yesterday. I was trying to find him when I fell."

"You misplaced him?"

"He's in a small square metal container. I accidentally left him sitting on a rock."

"What were you doing on the top of Staigue in the first place?"

"Looking for a holy well."

"There's one marked on the Kerry Way on the ridge near Eagles Hill."

"Not that one. Another one."

"Maybe. But why?" she frowned.

"Uh," Bret glanced off to the side. "Uncle Michael told me I had to put the ashes in a holy well, so that's what I was going to do. And then this guy at the post office said that . . ."

"A guy at the post office? Just because a guy at the post office told you, you're going to pour human ashes into a holy well? Didn't you think about contamination?" She seemed incredulous, but she was smiling.

"Um, sort of. I figured a holy well wouldn't be used for drinking."

"Well, it's still contamination."

"Could be you're right. But it's a moot point now, because I've lost him."

She rolled to lean closely over him inside the confines of the sleeping bag. "Where do people get these silly ideas? Depositing human ashes in a holy well. Really, it's quite astonishing."

"I agree," said Bret. "I am certainly astonished. Look where it has got me."

She looked down at him and slowly shook her head.

"Okay, look," she said. "As soon as I can I'm going to go down and I'll bring back up some food and something to treat that ankle. I hope it's only a sprain. I may not return until near dawn tomorrow. You will have to stay inside, because if you are seen near here, then my hiding place might be discovered and that won't do. Once your leg is good enough, we'll get you back to where you think you lost your uncle and I'll go about my business."

"Thank you. That's very generous. But I doubt I will ever find the place. It was so foggy. And there was a bird, a huge bird."

"Aha," she said, nodding. "In that case, you may be out of luck. But you could take comfort that, wherever those ashes are, in time they'll be absorbed and he'll be right back where he started."

"Blood and bone to water and stone, right?"

"What?"

"Never mind." In fact, though, he thought, Uncle Michael would likely approve of that outcome. "The water table probably would connect his resting place with a nearby well."

"Indeed," she replied.

"Anyway," Bret said, "thank you for the help."

"I would accept donations for the food."

"I think you already have my wallet."

"Mmm. I must do." She slid her left hand across his chest, her thumb tracing the collar of the thermal top. "But you've got my shirt."

"True," he said. "And your pants. So maybe we're even."

"Maybe," she said.

A
QUIET
DAY

Sometime in the middle of the day, a quick rain shower swept over the mountain. Bret was half-asleep when the smell of impending precipitation focused his mind. He looked up at the slit in the roof, and though the sky was still blue he could already hear the raindrops approaching. Then the bright blue rectangle in the ceiling turned charcoal gray as the torrent washed over the hut. A few fine spatters of water made their way into the interior. Cait was crouching at the door, staring out.

Bret replayed yesterday in his mind. There were plenty of surprises to count, but foremost among them was the way he had surprised himself by walking away from the opportunity to have his way with the French bus passengers. That was certainly out of character. Then again, maybe he was just distracted by seeing Lee and needing to talk to her. But no, he had decided not to make his speech before he had spotted her. So it wasn't that. It was something about this place. It wouldn't let him be his old self.

Every day he spent here, the sensation grew stronger. Every solitary walk, every footfall on rock or grass, every breath of the sea-sheep air—bit by bit, they eroded away the outer shell Bret had built up over the past 20 years. Maybe it was the effect of being in a place where no one knew him and no one expected anything in particular of him, and therefore he had nothing to mirror back to anyone. He was just who he was. That was frightening—in fact, it was a notion that positively terrified him—but it did seem to open up a few options as well. Maybe he didn't have to go back to his old pattern.

Or maybe it was the effect of being a man in the landscape instead of a man in society. Not that Ireland was uncivilized, but Bret had spent most of his adult life measuring himself against other people in social and interpersonal terms. Out here he was just another creature trying to make his way across—or hide in—the abrasive stones and soggy sod. It made his old life seem needlessly complex and silly.

So maybe that was why he had held back on the town green in Sneem. He had sensed that he was at a critical juncture in the music, a place where he could step up and play another tuba solo, but where he could also step back and follow the tune somewhere else. Maybe it was a sign that he ought to try swearing off the bullshit for good.

Cait looked back at him. "Awake?"

He nodded.

"This one's passing quickly," she said. "Don't think I'll be able to set off before nightfall. I'm sorry I haven't anything for you to eat."

"It's not your fault," said Bret. "Besides, I could lose a few pounds."

"When was your last meal?"

"In the morning. Well, yesterday morning."

"You didn't bring food with you for the hill walk?"

"I didn't think it would take very long. Besides that, I was delayed by a busload of French tourists."

"Oh, right. I saw that coach from up the ridge yesterday morning. Appeared to be backing up."

"That's the one." Bret laughed, remembering Rosko's startled expression on seeing Bret in the road. "You know why they're here? You'll never guess."

"I don't know. Stealing recipes?"

"Maybe that, too, but here's the main thing: guy named Rosko is trying to sell them on the idea of building American-style amusement parks to attract tourists."

"What?" She stepped toward him. "Attract them where?"

"Well, to here. And to Brittany."

"That's just bonkers."

"Back home, I worked for such a place, and there's no denying that a theme park can be a powerful economic engine."

"If I ever hear that term again I'm going to be ill," she sneered. "Powerful economic engine. Powerful way to drive the country straight to bloody hell."

"You're right," he said. "You're absolutely right. A week ago I might not have said so, but after having spent a few days here I've come to feel that the earth provides sufficient entertainment on its own. No need to fabricate a lot of fake thrills. And so I had a chance to speak to this group, share my expertise, but I walked away from it. I'm a changed man."

"Changed from what?"

"From a tuba soloist." He laughed. "I used to be a man who could sell anything, and now I'm a man who won't sell anything."

"What's a tuba got to do with it?" She was still fuming.

"Never mind. Main point is, I didn't do it."

"Explain this to me again," she said. "Who's this Rosko?"

"Okay, I first encountered this gentleman—probably in his fifties, medium-short height, tweedy Irish-looking guy—in the airport in Cleveland, Ohio, back home. Actually, I had encountered him earlier, but didn't remember at the time. He'd been one in a crowd. Then we kept bumping into each other in airports and again in Dublin. We had dinner together there and we both talked a lot, and, in retrospect, I think he was picking my brain about the theme park business in the States.

"Anyway, we rode the train together to Killarney where I got off, and I thought he'd gone on to Tralee. So I rent a car, drive myself to Sneem where I've got a room rented, and try to shake off my jet lag while getting ready for my task. While I'm there, I meet some nice folks and have too much to drink one night. The next day I get up and go down and walk around Kenmare because I needed to find a cash machine, and then I get stuck behind this big tour bus full of French people while I'm driving back. Then yesterday comes along. Oh, I forgot—I meet this kid who knows this guy named Rosko who's hosting the French people and that's the first time I hear anything about this theme park idea." He left out the part about finding a woman's black hair on his pillow. "Oh, one more thing. One morning after I drank too much, I realize the box of Uncle Michael has fallen out the window, and I run outside to get it and of course it starts raining and the lid has come off. But I slap the lid back on and put the can back upstairs—oh, this is ironic—I'm just remembering that the box had been wrapped up in security tape because the airport had me pull it out of the bag as a suspicious package or something, and if I had just left the tape on it, the lid would never have come off. Anyway, I put it back and go about my day. And then—this sounds ridiculous now—the box disappears AGAIN, and after another extended episode of malarkey it's finally returned to me so I can at last do what I came here to do. So that brings me up to yesterday.

"I set off pretty early in the morning with Uncle Michael in the can, but almost immediately I get stuck behind the French motorcoach again. When I think back on it, I actually had a chance right then to get ahead of the bus, and if I had, none of this would have happened. But instead I waved him on ahead and twenty minutes later the bus got stuck at a sharp corner. Then there was a mild auto accident behind, involving a car and a truck that had been taken off guard by the stopped bus—and who should climb out of the car but Rosko?

"Meanwhile, I've been talking to the leader of the French group and he's telling me all about the plans for the theme parks and I see an opportunity to use my powers of mass persuasion to get a little payback on Rosko for bullshitting me. I lure everybody back onto the town green in Sneem and I'm about to wow them with my pitch about the great American way of amusement and how this Rosko fellow here really doesn't know the first thing about theme parks, but when the moment comes, I change my mind. I don't want to have anything to do with it.

"And then right at that moment, I spot this woman Lee—and I remember I have to ask her something so I just skip out. But she disappears and I fall halfway into the river, and then I realize I still have time to come up here so I drive to Staigue Fort and start walking up, but then the mist rolls in and I get distracted because I thought I saw somebody walking up ahead of me, and I accidentally leave Uncle Michael on the rock. But I don't notice that until I've already climbed to the summit and I'm standing amazed looking out over the tops of the clouds. Then it hits me and I tear myself away from the beautiful scene and while I'm circling all over the mountain in the fog trying to find Uncle Michael, that's when I slip and fall. Whop, boom! Then I'm sliding faster and faster and I hit a rock and start tumbling. And you know the rest. Here I am."

She was shaking her head slowly. "And you drove to Staigue Fort why?"

"Um," Bret paused. "The guy in the post office."

"Right," she said. "Why didn't I guess." She was starting to laugh. "You know, Bret, I think you did see somebody in the mist." She grinned at him. "You saw me!"

"You? Did you see me?"

"No, but I did hear somebody yell 'hey!' very close and I saw a raven take wing. I was afraid I'd been spotted, so I practically ran up over the ridge top, hoping for the mist to hide me."

"Yeah, that was me," said Bret. "That must have been what happened. And then I decided to chase that figure. Why did I chase? I don't know."

As he spoke, she looked back toward the door and then glanced back at him over shoulder. "And here you are."

WEATHER REPORT

It's not that a ghost doesn't notice the weather, rather that we have no reason to care. A downpour, a gust, a blizzard even—these are factors to a corporeal entity. I, however, am impervious. What does seem to affect my perception and my capabilities is some kind of energy that comes when humans interact. This energy field, if that is how it should be characterized, does not extend indefinitely, so if a ghost happens to spend a length of time apart from other sentient beings, it goes into a kind of dormancy. Now I will say that the presence of a bird or chipmunk does provide some small spark, but it is nothing like when humans are about, especially if they are intensely involved in some discussion or activity. When a place is "haunted," that is, it's not as if ghosts are frolicking about when no one is there. Rather, they sleep, they wait.

Cait left at dusk. The short night seemed barely to have begun when Bret was stirred awake by her return at dawn.

"Troubling news," she said.

"Were you caught?"

"No, no. Nothing like that. First of all, I was talking with my friend about your Rosko character's theme park scheme, and wait till you hear what he wants to call it," said Cait.

"I'm afraid to ask."

"The Legend of Castle Cove."

"Oh, Jesus Christ," Bret snorted. "But . . . I mean it's a strangely awkward name, but in a certain way, it makes sense."

She was getting mad. "How could it?"

"Only in a certain way," he replied. "But we already knew that was going on. Was there something else?"

"Yes," she said. "The bad bit. Seems three tourists and a boat captain went missing two days ago. Hired Jimmy Lawlor's boat for the Skelligs and a rogue wave smashed them on the rocks. Late in the afternoon, not long before I found you."

"Oh. That's terrible."

"More concerning for you is that it's believed you were one of them."

"Hmm." Bret sat up as she arranged the backpack against the wall. "Okay, I give up."

"Well," she said. "From yesterday's afternoon paper." She handed Bret a folded up sheet of newsprint, then went back to unloading the pack.

"Skellig Cruise Feared Lost," read the headline. "Three tourists and captain disappear at sea." He read on. "Police at Waterville report that captain Jimmy Lawlor's cruise boat the Miss Eileen was dashed upon the rocks at Skellig Michael late Monday. Fishermen reported a rogue wave during a mild afternoon squall and it is feared that said wave may have come suddenly upon the Miss Eileen as she circled the island. A fragment of wooden transom molding from the Miss Eileen was found early this morning lodged in a rock near the base of the Skellig stair. Its high position suggested that it had been cast there by a very large wave. Paint residues scraped onto nearby stone surfaces appear to give further support to that interpretation.

"Capt. Lawlor left no log at his office, so it is not known with certainty how many passengers were aboard, but a rental auto charged to the name of Mr. Aki Aldag was found at Capt. Lawlor's premises at Ballinskelligs and subsequent investigation by police discovered that Mr. Aldag and a female traveling partner had rented lodgings at Caherdaniel. The hotel proprietor reported sending the couple to visit Staigue Fort on Sunday, and Mrs. Maureen O'Donoghue, who resides on the Fort property, saw the Swedish couple in the same car, headed for the fort. Mrs. O'Donoghue also reported that minutes earlier, another driver practically diverted her car into the hedge, and that the Swedes had nearly done the same. She noted that the quickest way to identify a right-side driver is to confront their vehicle head-on in a narrow country lane. Natives naturally turn to the left, whereas Americans and Europeans divert to the right. She deduced from this that these individuals were of foreign origin. Later that night, Mrs. O'Donoghue returned home and at that time noticed the first car still there in the car park at Staigue Fort. Monday morning, she rang the police to report the car, and it was traced to an American, Mr. Bret Sheehan, with lodgings in Sneem. It is assumed that Mr. Sheehan, who has not been seen since he nearly diverted Mrs. O'Donoghue into the hedge early Sunday afternoon, accompanied the Swedes to Capt. Lawlor's establishment in their car. Capt. Lawlor had operated the business since 1991.

"The authorities expect that the notoriously strong currents near the Skelligs would likely have carried any floating debris and the bodies of the victims well out to sea. A search is ongoing, but all four persons are presumed drowned."

"But they saw me walking up the mountain," Bret said aloud. "They shouted at me."

"The Swedes did?" She walked back across the room toward him. "Seems as if they didn't tell anyone." Her face darkened and she abruptly took back the sheet of newspaper, but instead of re-reading the passage, as Bret thought she would, she folded it and slipped it into her shirt pocket.

"Well," said Bret. "I guess that means I have to get back down and set things straight. And I think I could try it now."

"I checked the weather forecasts." She lowered herself to the floor crosslegged at the foot of the sleeping pad. "Today sunny and clear, but heavy clouds and mist tomorrow. I'm not confident of your safety in the dark, so I don't want to try tonight, but if we get a good fog tomorrow it shouldn't be too much trouble. I know this old hill quite well."

"What if I can't walk fast?"

She shrugged. "It doesn't need to be fast."

"You know what's inconvenient about a mountain?" Bret asked and then, not waiting for a reply, he answered, "you can't bullshit your way up it. I've spent my working life bullshitting people. You can surmount obstacles simply by asserting your administrative rank and doing a little song and dance for the higher-ups."

"That's what I love about a mountain," she replied.

"What is?"

"If you get up it, you've really done something. Something that can't be accomplished, as you say, by bullshit. You could just sit on your arse back down in the valley trying to convince anyone who will listen that you're on top, but they'd only have to take one look to see that it wasn't true. A mountain—what's that American expression?—a mountain just cuts the crap."

"Hmm." He lay on his back and pulled his leg gingerly from the bag. "It might also sprain your ankle. It might even kill you."

"So be it. Real is real." She smiled, but her eyes did not twinkle.

"Okay, so it's real. You live on a mountain being real all the time. You live, you die—nobody knows. Who cares?"

"I've been thinking about that, yes. If I were here or not here, who would ever know? Besides you?"

Bret couldn't tell how serious she was. "Your friend down by the water?"

"He doesn't have any idea where, only that I'm hiding."

He nodded. "Right."

"Now," she said, "you must be famished. I've brought some things to eat. Nothing too fancy, but it's nourishment." She produced a sack containing some biscuits and a couple of small cheeses. "I've got some oats as well, but they will take a bit of time to cook, so I'll get them on the fire, but if you're hungry now, eat some of this."

"Thanks." He opened a package of biscuits.

"It's only enough food for three days," she said. "If we need more, I'll have to go down again. I'm not used to packing for two. So I hope you can walk tomorrow."

"I do appreciate all your effort," said Bret. "I'd really be in trouble."

"You still are in trouble. After all, you're dead."

"Yes, but I may recover from that." Bret finished a couple of biscuits while Cait put a small pan on the camp stove and retrieved his clothes from the line.

She walked over and handed the clothes to Bret. "These have dried," she said.

Bret sat up. "Just when I was getting used to your clothes."

"Oh, I've found you a crutch as well," she said, producing a tall, crooked stick that she had left at the entrance. "And I found some wrapping to bind the ankle. It's just an old scarf, but it should do. Let's have a look." She crouched near his leg and began unwrapping a wide cloth bandage. "Not so terrible. We can bind this up nicely. You'll want to get your trousers on first, I expect. Shall I tend to the porridge for a moment?"

Bret nodded and undertook the laborious process of removing the leggings and putting back on his own clothing. Cait wrapped the scarf tightly around the ankle and pinned it in place. "We've got no ice. I've brought some aspirin, though. That should reduce the inflammation." She went back to the bag. "And I've got one more important medicinal item," she said. "Bushmill's." She took a swig and passed the bottle. "No worries about passing germs. This will kill anything."

He washed down two aspirin with a couple swallows of whiskey and that, combined with a bowl of warm oatmeal porridge and a few more swallows of whiskey over the next half an hour, put him in an optimistic frame of mind. "I think I should try to walk," he ventured. "Can I go outside at all?"

She stood up. "If we stay between the boulder and the hut, we're invisible. Except from the air. There are some airplane tours that fly over, but I can hear them coming and then I run inside. You can't stray far and you can't risk falling asleep outside." She took another drink. "And if I have too much more of this, that will be a real danger."

"Yeah," said Bret, "What's up with that? I'm the one who needs medication, but you're drinking half of it."

"Everybody's got a pain to kill, right?" She laughed. She took another swig and put the bottle on the ground beside her. "Fact is, I usually sleep in the day so I can work in the dark. And this will help with that." She stepped out.

"Won't someone see your light at night?"

"What light is that?"

"Your flashlight, your torch. So you can see."

"No light. If there's half a moon, that's enough."

"So what have you found out?" Bret asked as he hopped to the doorway. It was intensely bright and he had to pause for a moment at the threshold to let his eyes adjust. Also, he was the slightest bit unsteady from the whiskey.

"Found out?" she said from his left.

"About the water." He squinted over to where she was now sitting, legs outstretched, leaning back on a slanted rock.

"Water?"

"Your secret research project."

"Ah, that. Inconclusive, that is. There's the sheep's waste, the effect it has, but it's hard to trace origin. Pesticides and fertilizers, they shouldn't get to higher altitudes. The agriculture that uses that stuff, it takes place at lower elevations."

Bret made his way to the same rock and propped himself against it. "No contamination up here, then?"

"Nah. All you get is the giardia here and there from human waste, usually a little bit downhill from the Kerry Way. Too many neddys fulla too much shite. Excuse me. Back at the lab, I've got computer sheets of numbers plotting readings for all the sites. Now, if we would check them against the old number 84 . . ." She pulled a weather-beaten copy of the Ordnance Survey #84 map out of the satchel. "The chart would have readings for the samples taken at each site. So you see the numbers for this little stream that down here joins these two other streams and flows past Staigue Fort are almost normal, slightly acidic. That could be from motor vehicle exhaust washing down in the rains." She pointed at a fine blue line on the map and two branches that connected with it. "And here's where we are now. And here's where I found you." She pointed to an area to the north and slightly to the east of the summit of Staigue. "Basically, you fell off the edge of Windy Gap. And now we're over here."

Bret examined the map. "Along this way is where I walked up from the fort, to this flat place." He located the low saddle in the ridge to the north of Staigue where the topographic lines were more spread out. "We're not far from it. And I think where I left Uncle Michael would have been somewhere over here, a little ways up the shoulder of Staigue. And if I was over here when I fell, then I was twisted about 90 degrees. I thought I was over here."

"Good thing. If you'd fallen over there, you'd not likely be talking to me now." She smiled.

"Double dead."

"Twice as dead as dead. I've not passed that place in two or three weeks. You'd be lying there alone, dead and broken."

"But probably some other fair maiden would have taken me in and nursed me back to health."

"Fairy tales."

"Yeah, that is one of my problems." He slid down the rock so that he was sitting next to her. "You know, my family told what amounts to a fairy tale about who Uncle Michael was, but the more I thought about it, the more I realized I just didn't care how much of it was true. The time we had together was real, no matter what the back story was. There's the story, and there's here and now. The story doesn't hold up? So fuck the story. Speaking of which, what is a guy like me, a natural bullshitter, supposed to do with a decent, non-bullshitty person like you?"

"A natural bullshitter?" She laughed. "Americans work out such quaint phrases. If that's what's natural then that's what you have to do, isn't it? Just try to be constructive, right?"

"But bullshit is bullshit. It gets in the way."

"In the way of what?"

"Well for instance, now," he began, "if I'm telling you tales, then you don't really know me."

"But we're really here, right? So what do I care if you've spun me a tale? Everyone is telling tales. You don't ever really know anyone, not completely, not even those closest to you. You don't know me, right? But here we are." She tapped him on the knee. "I could be making it all up."

"That's what's alarming. I could say whatever I wanted and you'd never know if I was sincere."

"Try me."

"Well," he looked over at her. "We're probably getting close to the end of my time here and, at the risk of my having misread things, I would like to make a sincere suggestion that we might go back in there and lie down on that sleeping bag together and, you know . . .

She fixed his gaze and paused a few seconds before speaking. "I do sincerely hope you are sincere about that."

THE DEAD MAN'S CHOICE

Cait picked her way steadily among the rocks, her pace relaxed so that Bret could hobble along behind. The dense mist had brightened with the dawn, but he still had no sense of his bearings. So he followed.

The ankle hurt, but it seemed to Bret, with events transpiring as they had, that he really needed to finish his business with Uncle Michael and then resolve the matter of his own supposed death. After half an hour of slow and deliberate progress, the terrain suddenly leveled and Cait doubled back to her right. It became clear to Bret that they were now walking along a ridge crest. Cait walked a few minutes more, then stopped. "This should be somewhere near to the place where you say you crested the ridge," she said.

Bret scanned the way ahead and it did indeed look familiar. But then, it all looked a little bit familiar. The clouds parted briefly and a patch of sunlight drifted across the mountainside above them, the rocks and grasses glistening with moisture.

They moved laterally along the mountain, climbing a little. Cait led the way, stepping along in a relaxed, sure-footed gait that Bret could only envy. She stopped and waited for him. The clouds parted briefly, revealing a splendid view down into the valley. Cait pulled him into a recess in the rocks, but they could still see. There was the ring shape of Staigue Fort, and the farmhouse beyond. There was the sparkling sea. There was Bret's rental car, being towed down the lane. It would be a pain in the ass to deal with that, he thought. But then, I do have a choice, he considered. I don't have to go down. I could just walk the other way. On the ring road by the shore he spotted the unmistakable profile of the oversized French tour bus, stopped, pointing to the left. That meant they had indeed driven all the way around the other direction. It was hard to see from here, but they seemed to have stopped overnight at a small inn Bret remembered passing just before turning up the lane to the fort. He recognized its bright yellow walls. What other adventures had they had along the way, he wondered. The clouds closed back over the scene.

"Hey Cait," he said. "I don't have to go down."

"What do you mean? Of course you do."

"I mean, everybody thinks I'm dead. I could start a new life from scratch."

"Bloody romantic," she started walking again. "Even I must go down. Eventually. Maybe."

"I mean it. I'd need to get official papers somehow, get a job or at least find some way to survive. But there's no reason I have to ever go back to the world I used to live in."

"If you do that, who's going to go down there and convince those idiots not to turn this into County Disney?"

"I told you," he protested. "I already walked away from that. Besides, they won't pull it off anyway. They don't have a clue what they're doing."

"I'm not willing to take that wager. Clueless people are constantly taking charge of important things." She stopped again. "There have been certain presidents of the United States."

"Point taken. But it's not my job," he said. "What could I do?"

"Use your magical powers to get them to think of something better. Bullshit some sense into them." The clouds rolled back in and they resumed walking. "Not far from here," she said. "If we're lucky."

"What?" Bret asked.

"Your uncle."

"That quest is over, Cait. I think it wasn't meant to be. Or it was meant to be this way. All I need to do is go back down, set a few things straight, and be on my way."

"Well I haven't given up," she said. "Our raven friend always loiters about a certain set of ledges."

He followed her across a gradual slope and around an outcrop.

"Et violà," she pointed. There it was, just where he'd left it, with one difference: the raven was perched on one leg atop the can.

The bird flapped twice and circled and Bret saw that the raven had not only perched with one leg—it had only one leg.

"Good old Mono" said Cait, turning to Bret. "I knew he'd take care of your uncle."

"I don't believe it," said Bret, lifting the can. "So . . . I guess I go try to find that well now."

She laughed. "That's easy." She pointed back to the outcrop they'd just passed and then traced her finger upward. About 50 feet up the slope, in the lee of a small ledge, was a semicircle of stones. "You'd found it the first time around. I just distracted you."

Sitting down on the edge of the well, Bret saw that Cait had settled herself onto the ledge below, up against a camouflaging shrub, looking out. She'd asked if he wanted to do this alone, which he hadn't really considered, but realized he'd always imagined this as a kind of personal, solitary ritual. With gratitude, he'd accepted the offer. His eyes lifted to the glinting flecks of sunlight that speckled to open ocean beyond the wide bay, then scanned the green hills of the Beara peninsula across the Kenmare. A lone sailboat was making slow progress, left to right along the far edge of the water.

He looked down at the can of ashes. As he began to lift it to eye level, it brushed against his knee and slipped out of his hand. It bounced once, and then again, and came to rest with the lid off, near his left foot. He expected ashes to be scattered all about him, but there were none. He leaned forward and half crouched to pick up the metal box. Then he feared that the ashes were gone, that the can was empty. He imagined with horror the raven pecking away at Uncle Michael. But as he lifted the container again, he saw that it was still full. He shook it, but the contents did not move. He used the edge of the lid to try to stir the ashes. It made a dry abrasive sound like a nail on concrete. Uncle Michael's ashes had hardened into a solid mass. His mind flashed back to the rain when the box had fallen out the window. Bret did the math. Blood+bones+water equals stone. It made a kind of sense.

In the reflection of the inside of the lid, he caught a glimpse of his own unshaven face, salt-and-pepper stubble with smudges of mud. He stared at the dull reflection for the better part of a minute and gradually discerned not only himself in need of a clean-up, but the image that had so startled and disturbed him when he had seen it in Uncle Michael's window. Bret sat down and laughed. Doesn't that just figure? He laughed again. But if he had recognized himself at that moment back in Ohio, would he have even set out on this insane quest? The truth was, no matter how crazy the reasons may have been, he was glad he was here right now. A band of sunlight washed down the mountainside, stinging his eyes and warming his body. In his teary vision, the ridgetop threw off a halo. He laughed a little more, then fished a tissue from his pocket and blew his nose and wiped his eyes.

"Okay, Uncle Michael," he said, standing up. "Or Michael-not-uncle, or whoever you are." He leaned over and looked down the well. A faint reflection of sky denoted the presence of water. Bret shook the can, but nothing came out. Then he banged it on the rock. Still nothing. Should he just drop the whole can in? He whacked it on the edge of the well one more time, much harder, and the contents fractured into three or four big chunks and a little wisp of dust, but still nothing came out.

He looked around for a stick. There were none immediately visible, but when he walked a few paces up the path he found what appeared to be someone's discarded make-do cane, stashed behind a boulder as if it were meant to be retrieved. He placed the can on its side on the edge of the well, measured the arc of the swing, and took a whack. The stick snapped in half and two-foot section went spiraling off into the rocks a dozen feet away. Bret took the remaining yard-long section in one hand, picked up the can, and pounded violently on the bottom of it. Finally, he placed the tin face down on the edge of the well and smashed the end of the stick straight down, holding it with both hands as if driving a post into the ground. He held the stick in place and thumped the end of it with a rock. Clouds of dust rose all around. His hands were buzzing as if he'd just taken batting practice.

Bret picked up the battered can and flipped it over to look inside, and when he did, a few chunks flew out amid a wispy cloud of ashes. Two seconds later, he heard a surprisingly loud splash as he watched the swirl of airborne ashes drift and dissipate downwind over the rocky mountainside. Bret inspected the can. The entire contents had come out cleanly, leaving nothing but Bret's dull reflection. Just like that, the job was finished.

My consciousness blinked alive to understand that everything was done now. To tell the truth, I had concluded that it was done some time earlier. I had been intent to abide there on the ledge until the elements had their effects on the container and the ashes, and whatever became of me became. So I wasn't expecting it when Bret suddenly began knocking on the can. I had stopped expecting, stopped waiting. The tale unfolded as it did, as it would have, no matter whether I had haunted the scene or not. I was but a kind of spectator, along for the journey, delusionally thinking it was my charge to lead the way. That would be the only reason for me to be in the story, would it not? To shape the outcome, to make something happen? Or simply to witness? I begin to suspect, now that it is all ending in these few moments of weightlessness, that my consciousness belongs to no one, to no specific person alive or dead. It floats freely, unencumbered. A story without any specific author. A figment pulled out of thin air, looking for something to which it might attach itself. Specter or spectator? That question has spun slowly, inconclusively. But this, this is not so slow. The abrupt fracturing, the weightless fall into the dark, the startling splash, the sudden peace. Will my last thought be wondering if this will be my last thought? Where does that thought go? Does it linger here among the rocks and mist until someone, someday, comes by this place and arouses it from its craggy recess?

Bret stood up and bowed his head over the well. The sound that echoed in there was part water, part stone, part air. And voices. He was sure there were voices, all wrapped in among the other sounds, like the murmurs of a quiet congregation. One of those voices was Uncle Michael's. And his mother's. His father's. And Lee's and Cait's and Cormack's. Rosko's. Donoson Peacock's. They were all the voices he'd ever heard, all the words spoken. He listened until he recognized another sound, much closer, of a man sniffing back tears. He stood up and wiped his eyes with the back of his hand. "Tree fine days," Bret said out into the air. Had there in fact been three sunny days in a row? No. It must have meant something else. He laughed and shook his head. "Time to go." He walked back down to the flat saddle where Cait was waiting.

Cait stood silently as he approached and began slowly to walk. She looped her arm through his, taking care not to dislodge the can he was carrying, as he used the crutch with the other. They descended the way they'd come for a short while, then Cait led them down a sheltered gully. There, she paused and turned to him.

"I've not been," she said, "entirely honest. There's more to my story and I feel I've got to explain it now as best I can, in case there's not another opportunity."

"What would it matter?" he asked.

"Might not," she said.

"But if you want to talk, the least I can do is listen," he replied. "You've listened to me enough."

"Well, that was nothing," she said. "But what I want to say is I am a scientist, but I am also, at the moment, something of a fugitive. And this second role is why I'm up here."

"Fugitive from what?" He asked.

"I'll try to explain," she began.

Suddenly voices were clearly audible nearby, slightly downhill. Cait immediately took refuge behind a boulder, dragging Bret along. The voices came closer and then stopped, just close enough that Bret could pick out a word here and there. He recognized Cormack and Lee.

"I know them," he whispered to Cait.

"They'll be looking for you," she replied and paused. "That means they'll keep scouring the mountain until they find you. Which means they find me."

"It makes sense. They knew I was coming up here. It wouldn't seem right to them that I'd gone off with the Swedes."

The voices came closer.

"Only one thing to do," Bret said. "I stumble out from behind the rock and they rescue me. After we're gone, you can sneak back to the hut."

She looked up at the sky, then up the hill behind them. "That works," she said. "Unless you want to stay dead up here."

"I really would like that. But first I think I have an important appointment with a busload of theme park enthusiasts. It'll be okay." Bret stood up. "Thanks for, you know, saving my life and everything," he whispered.

She smiled and kissed him. He hadn't expected that. He kissed back.

The voices came closer and Bret hobbled out from behind the rock. "Hey," he called. "Have you been following me?"

They were looking the other way, Cormack, Renée, and Lee, but they all three turned in unison on hearing his voice.

I am confused now. Why am I still conscious? Pardon the crude colloquialism, but what the hell?

THE LEGEND OF CASTLE COVE

"Look!" called Renée.

Cormack bounded up the hill as Bret limped down. "He's hurt! Take it easy there, now." One burly arm wrapped behind Bret's shoulder blades and practically lifted him from the ground. Lee appeared and ducked under Bret's other arm and they began walking, angling back down the hillside. Renée walked a few steps ahead, carrying the crutch and scouting for solid footing.

"You'll never believe it," Cormack laughed. "Everybody thinks you're dead."

"Why would they think that?" asked Bret.

"Wild story." Cormack hoisted him over a small stream. "There was a freakish accident. A Swedish couple and a Skellig boat captain were lost to a rogue wave. Because this couple had been seen at Staigue Fort at the same time someone saw you, and because your car was at the Staigue car park but you were missing, it was assumed that you had joined them for the boat tour and you had been killed as well."

"Well, that's a lot to assume," said Bret.

"When we read it in the paper, we knew it couldn't be true," Lee said. "But it got into print before the police had a chance to talk to us, and then it took on a life of its own. But when you didn't come back, we began to wonder. So we organized a search posse. Like on *Gunsmoke*."

"So you're Little Joe and he's Hoss? I get it." Bret glanced back up the hill. The mist already obscured the boulder. Cait wouldn't have too much trouble getting back.

"Little Joe and Hoss, that's *Bonanza*, not *Gunsmoke*. Would you mind saying where you've been?" Cormack changed the subject. 'What happened? How were you injured?"

"Ah. Where shall I start?" He made a snap decision to start the story here and go backwards, so that maybe they wouldn't notice the gaps in recent history. "Believe it or not, I've spent two days up here looking around for a misplaced can of ashes. Luckily I brought a lot of trail snacks, but even so, I'm starving. Yesterday I slipped and hurt my ankle. But, as luck would have it, just as I had sat on the nearest ledge to assess my situation, who should appear but Mono the raven? He seemed to be trying to get my attention, so I found this stick and followed him not more than two minutes, and there it was, just where I'd left it."

"Mono!" Lee chuckled. "I'm not surprised." She pointed at the ash container Bret still carried. "And that?"

"Mission accomplished. Our raven friend then pointed out to me that I had been no more than 50 paces away from the well when I had first sat down there. It's enough almost to start believing in all the mystical poppycock. But I know ravens are smart birds, and I know I'd seen a raven just when I'd lost the ashes in the first place. He just remembered and waited. No supernatural explanation required."

"Not a chance!" Cormack laughed. "Give this story a few years of retelling and it take on its own life as a mystical fable. No worries about that!"

"Anyway," Bret said. "I guess I can go back home now. Walk down this path, get one good night's sleep, and head back for Dublin."

"This brings up a rather obvious point," said Lee. "Why in hell were you climbing up from Staigue Fort instead of just walking off the Kerry Way?" Her shoulder twisted under his arm as she turned toward him.

"Why?" Bret offered. "A few days ago I went to Kenmare to visit an ATM machine and get some money, and while I was there I went into the post office and—"

Cormack finished his sentence "—and that looney bird Dickeen O'Brien started chatting you up about what he and his eccentric hillwalking mates like to do at week-ends. Only O'Brien would tell a foreign visitor to bushwhack across a private property like that." Cormack bellowed out a laugh. "You could be in the next county by now, or having a splash in the sea!"

"Earlier in the first day," Bret continued, eager to get back to the part of the story he could substantiate, "I was driving out here, but my car got trapped behind a giant motorcoach traveling the wrong direction on the ring road. It got stuck and had to turn around and during that process there was a small accident involving a car and a panel van and who should be driving the car, but this fellow named Rosko, whom I had met in the airport, dined with in Dublin, and ridden with on the train to Killarney, but he was traveling on to Tralee."

"Tralee?" Lee roared with laughter. "Rosko's up to his old tricks again, eh Cor? Your man lives smack in the village of Sneem, right on the river. Always has."

"Yeah, I figured out pretty quick that his stories might present a problem to the fact-checkers," said Bret. "Anyway, he's got some crazy-ass scheme to go into business with this busload of French tourists to build theme parks here and in Brittany, where his guests come from. Roscoff."

"Rosko!" Cormack sighed. "Where did he get a dotty notion like that?"

"From me, I think," said Bret. "Not on purpose. But I was in the amusement park business back home, and we talked about it a lot over dinner in Dublin. He seemed pretty interested. On a naive kind of level."

"Forgive me," said Lee, stepping out from under Bret's arm and hopping over a low wall, "but that seems like a perfectly absurd means of employment."

"Oh yes," said Bret. "It certainly is. One thing I know is there's no way either Rosko or the folks from Roscoff are prepared to build and operate a real theme park."

"Why would that stop him?" Cormack grunted. "Never stopped Rosko before. Remember his big equestrian resort scheme, Lee? Remember the marina? He's still got that big tract of land by the river where the old Yellow Brick Inn is. That was going to be a golf course and condolomium development. He's got big eyes, you must hand him that much."

After a time, they paused to scale a stone fence. Renée held out her hand to help Bret over. "What are you speaking about?"

"Monsieur Rosko," said Cormack.

"Ah," Renée said, hissing through her teeth. "Always stories with Rosko." She shook her head. "Lee, my turn?" The two women traded places and Renée ducked and hoisted Bret's armpit onto her shoulder. Since she was closer to Cormack's height, it was a bit easier for Bret to balance. Lee forged on down the slope, skirting the uphill edge of a pasture along a fence, waving Bret's stick about. She walked lightly, a bit bowlegged, her head bobbing side to side so that her black hair kept bouncing up off her neck and shoulders. She seemed to be able to find the dry ground, Bret observed appreciatively.

"A yellow inn, you said?" Bret asked as they followed close behind Lee. "Is that right down here? Could I see it from the mountain?"

"Expect so," said Cormack. "On the sea side of the ring road just on the edge of Castlecove."

"I think he's there now," Bret said. "I saw that enormous coach this morning, parked next to a yellow building of three or four stories. I'm sure it was the same bus. I wouldn't forget that."

"What is the old squirrel up to, I wonder?" Lee called back.

Cormack tilted his head down and to the side. "You know about these things, Bret. How much land would be required to build a theme park?"

"Small one?" Bret considered. "Maybe 100 acres. You could do a lot with 300. That's not close to Disney World, but Disneyland is under 200, Cedar Point is in the mid-300s, and King Arthur's Kamelot in Ohio is a little over 200. Depends how the visitors get there, too. Surface parking takes up a lot of space. But you could do a really little, old-timey style carnival park on as little as 40 or 50 acres. Just wouldn't have the same draw."

"Uh-oh," said Lee.

"Uh-oh is right," said Cormack. "I think Rosko and investors hold near 120 hectares between the Yellow Brick Inn and the river. And I believe the conversion is round about 2.5 acres to the hectare."

The slope was leveling and Bret could see the fort not far ahead. "There's no way you could get that many people out here by car," Bret said aloud to no one in particular. "They'd have to come by coach from Killarney and it would take most of the day. The time economics would kill it."

"Yes, maybe," said Cormack. "But if by boat? Rosko has been scraping about for something to so with the disused ferry terminal at Kenmare Town for years. He's fixated on it because it's nearly equidistant between Cork and Killarney and there is a very large car park. And he keeps talking about how, once you established service there, the possibilities would be endless. You could run a service to Wexford, or Portsmouth, or Cardiff—even Roscoff."

"And if you added to that the drawing power of a major theme park . . ." Bret continued. "I'm beginning to imagine the kind of situation he might have in mind. It's not impossible. This is a fairy-tale place already. You add a perfect little kingdom on the shore of the river and get boatloads of people—literally—seeing all of that as they cruise the river. Build up a whole mythology around it. The Legend of Castle Cove. It would work. From a marketing standpoint, it would work."

"And bring in lots of euros?" Lee added.

"Oh, yes," said Bret. "Of course the park managers and shareholders would make most of the money, but some would trickle down to local businesses. It would cost you, though. You would lose your town, your countryside. Everything would be different."

"Where did you hear that name, Legend of Castle Cove?" Cormack asked.

"I don't know. One of you must have said it," Bret offered. He would have said that Cait had told him, but Cait wasn't supposed to exist.

They walked around the left side of Staigue Fort. "This place, for example," Bret said, asking them to stop. "This is a stunning and magical thing, but you get to it only by finding your way along half-dozen poorly marked unimproved lanes, and when you arrive, there's only enough space to park eight or ten cars. It's in the middle of a fucking sheep farmer's pasture, for Christ's sake, right down to the stinking sheep and the sheep turds and everything. That would end. There would be a nice paved highway right up here so all the visitors could take their easy digital pictures. No touching. No climbing the steps inside. Maybe that would be okay, but it wouldn't be the same. It wouldn't be so personal, just you and the fort and the mountains. And the sheep."

"I could use a bit steadier business, though," Cormack offered. "It's a tempting thought, having a ready-made clientele like that."

"No doubt," said Bret. "That's the problem. You want it but you don't want it. Same story everywhere." They resumed walking.

When they got to Cormack's car, actually a small panel van not unlike the one Bret had seen mashed into the hedge,

Lee spoke up. "But there must be some way to bring in a little bit more money without feckin up the entire peninsula."

"If there is," said Bret, "think of it quickly, because I'm going to ask you to take me to that Yellow Brick Inn so I can try to persuade them of a clever plan. I'm a pretty good persuader, but it would probably go better if I had something in mind."

Cormack opened the back doors. "Okay, sir. To the Yellow Brick Inn it is. You two ride back here if you don't mind. You might prop your leg on the sack, there. Renée can sit with me in the front."

I can only conclude that, rather than being a spirit somehow attached to a specific person deceased or nearly so, a taibhse is a less connected entity. I will begin paying attention to try to discern if I can sense the presence of others. After all, these landscapes have been home to countless humans over the centuries, and to the extent that any taibhse exists in part to connect the lives of the departed to those of the living, then there must be others beyond just myself. Perhaps one might join a guild or other association of some kind in order to expand one's network of contacts. Not that I would trust the leadership of such a guild to meet even the most basic level of competence.

WATER
AND
STONE

The van bumped and lurched down the winding lanes. Braced against one wall with his bad leg over a grain sack, Bret smiled at Lee, who was similarly wedged against the opposite wall. She was humming a tune, faintly familiar, one of those Irish ditties that keep switching between major and minor keys.

"What's that?" Bret asked.

She stopped humming. "What's what?"

"That tune. It's pretty."

"Nothing. Just made it up. Or stirred together pieces from other tunes I can't quite remember." She resumed and went through the up-and-down melody once more.

"I've meant to ask you," he resumed. He figured he'd better just do this right away before he had any time to think twice. "The other night, after the music in the pub—the whiskey really went to my head and I'm not too clear on what happened toward the end of the evening."

"Yeah," she grinned. "Feckin steamboats, you were."

Bret felt himself blushing, a rarity. "Well, I just don't recall. I'd like to know if I did anything embarrassing."

"That would depend on what embarrasses you, wouldn't it?" she responded.

"Oh, come on, Lee. How come I found your hair on my pillow?"

"I thought we were supposed to be discussing a strategy for Rosko and the Frenchies." She closed her lips.

"In a minute," he said. "But first—"

"And why didn't you tell the whole truth about what happened on the mountain? You've obviously had some help, unless you carried a ladies' scarf and a few safety pins with you just in case of an ankle sprain, and then wrapped and pinned it perfectly yourself even though you can barely bend your leg. And you didn't ask a thing about the Swedes, nor what happened to your car—as if you already knew. Plus it was very cold the last two nights. You might well have died of exposure up high like that without any shelter."

That stopped Bret. He looked down at his ankle. The scrap of pink and lavender floral scarf, no matter how faded and threadbare, was a bit of a giveaway. "Look. Yes, I got help, but I can't say any more than that. I can probably explain it later, but for now I just can't." Somewhere in the back of his mind, it struck him that he had not even considered making up an artful dodge. The truth was it. "Please."

"Hmm," she said. "All right. I'll do the same for you. You found my hair on your pillow? I'll explain it later."

"Fair enough," said Bret. "I'm serious. I will tell you later, when I can."

"As will I tell you," she grinned.

The van made a right onto the main road. He looked out the back window at the rugged sunsplotched hills and, as they rounded a bend, rocky bluffs over the Kenmare River.

"Meanwhile," he said, "I'm not getting any great ideas."

"Nor am I. But all I know is these rocks and hills. Blood and bones, water and stone, they say."

"Who says that?" Bret sat up.

"Who doesn't say it? People around here it's every feckin third sentence." She shrugged. "It just means that you shouldn't get too full of yourself. Your blood and bones are no different from this water and stone. All the same stuff."

"That's it." Bret said. "That's it!"

"What?" She frowned. "That's a plan?"

"I'm not going to convince them of anything. I'll make an ass of myself instead."

"Easy one, that."

You may recall that, long ago, I had indicated that by the opinions of some, Bret had a reputation as a so-called asshole. Now that it appeared to me that he had grown his way past a legitimate application of that moniker, it was somewhat distressing to hear him declare his intent to voluntarily revert to that state. Yet, if there is one thing I have learned on this journey, it is that the story will tell itself. Also that the manual is useless, and the home office, if there is one at all, is disengaged at best. I prefer to believe that there never was a home office nor a manual, only the implication of their existence, perhaps to fulfill some perceived psychological need for an objective authority against which the actions of a ghost might be gauged, a notion that I find increasingly preposterous. The other revelation of my recent ruminations was this: if it is always unclear to the humans whether or not a ghost is in their presence and trying to affect events, then does it not stand to reason that it would be equally unclear to the ghost itself? So I held back and let the story unfold or self-validate or whatever it is that stories do.

PERSUASION

The bus was still parked next to the Yellow Brick Inn, and Cormack placed the van in such a way as to block any exit. Lee helped Bret ease himself out the back and onto the grass. The ankle was feeling the morning's effort, despite all the assistance, but he waved off any further help. It would be important not to appear helpless. As they walked toward the building, Bret looked down at himself and realized he looked pretty unpresentable—stained pants, rumpled and filthy shirt, muddy shoes, a bound ankle. He felt his chin: a few days' beard. He'd have to account for this somehow to the crowd.

He could see that Rosko had the group assembled in a large ground-floor room whose windows looked out on the street on the one side, and across a rolling meadow to the water on the other side. He smiled and nodded in case anyone was looking.

Inside, the proprietor greeted them. Bret stepped forward. "Good morning, sir. Very sorry. Mr. Rosko has been expecting me. I'm to give a presentation this morning." Without waiting to be let in, Bret opened the door into a communal dining room where the French visitors, as well as perhaps a dozen others he hadn't seen before, were listening intently as Rosko, at the opposite end of the room, was using a black marker to draw a crude map of the river shoreline on a large pad of paper on an easel. "Good morning Rosko!" Bret called in his best perky tone. "Very sorry to hold you up. You know how traffic can get around here!"

Most of the people turned to look at Bret. Whatever Rosko had been saying dissolved into a general muttering in the room. "We've run some numbers on your proposal and I think we can share some really knockout findings with your people here. This is gonna knock your socks off. This project is gonna be big big big! Hello everybody. Sheehan, Bret Sheehan. US of A. I've spent the last two days bushwhacking all over your lovely countryside—sorry for my scruffy appearance, but true research doesn't come easy, eh Rosko?"

"First," he gently removed the black marker from Rosko's paralyzed hand, "keep in mind that the yield from the 300 acres here doesn't stop here. You're going to get about a 1:3 spillover within a 10K radius, and 1:7 for 30K. That covers here beyond Sneem and to the near side Kenmore metro this way and all the way to Watertown this way for the 1:7. That means these corridors here are going to turn over maybe 40%, and these ones closer in 85% in the first five years, 100% in ten. Really it's more than 100 if you count repeat cyclation. All this substandard mom and pop retail over here will go and you'll be able to get in some real players that can move some real dollars—I mean euros." He took the marker and put an X where the Inn was marked, then he drew a few more boxes to represent existing local shops and homes, and put an X through each of them. "That's going to be a net gain of 250% in cash flow just in the first five years. Most of that goes to corporate, but you'll have local taxes and local jobs created, too, so you'll have some money staying right here in Cattle Cove. Mr. Rosko has got a brilliant strategy worked out here, I tell you."

"Now," Bret flipped the sheet over. "Here's your whole Kenmore Bay with the town of Kenmore down here." He drew a rough map of the shape of the bay, marking with dots Killarney, Cork, and Kenmare as well as the Inn. "You put in the ferry service and you can count on a per capita county utilization of 12% from Kerry—that's 120K, so you get 14K there and 8% from Cork which is about 500K city and county, so that gives you 40K for a total of 54K. Nearby ports of call—Rosslare, Portsmouth, Cardiff, and Roscoff in Brittany yield another 12K combined, so that gives you 66K annually before true international traffic. But international's where your real numbers are going to come from. That's because the theme park lets you offer the one thing that a cute little town like Cattle Cove or Sneem or Kenmore can't do. What's that? Anybody? Anybody?"

Bret glanced up at the back of the room, where Cormack and Renée stood, mouths hanging open. Lee must have been outside still. Bret continued. "Comfort. Comfort. What everybody hates about going to a foreign country is it's so darned uncomfortable. Strange foods, unfamiliar appliance names, and you know the rest. In the theme park, everything can be familiar. You can go to Ireland and it's almost like you never left Hamburg or Kyoto or Dallas. It can be that good. Look out that window." He motioned out to where the river was visible beyond rolling green fields and stone walls. "Imagine it. A brand-new kingdom, shining in the sun, everybody's dream of the perfect kingdom, filled with everybody's favorite kingdom experiences. Now these people aren't going to leave the park, of course, but they love to be waited on and that means jobs jobs jobs. In fact, you'll probably have to import unskilled workers from overseas. The skilled jobs are all filled from corporate, but you always need some unskilleds from the local community. It's a solid formula. It works. And what that means is construction, and lots of it. Most especially, inexpensive housing, and then low-end retail so the low-paid unskilleds have places to shop.

You got O'Hoolligan's Wholesale Club here yet? Ha-ha! Just pulling your leg."

Bret took the pen and started scribbling dark areas along the coastal road, and making bigger blotches and squares around the major towns. "All this area. New housing and strip retail. Now these are transient populations, so you're not going to want to throw a lot of money at this construction. Build for 20-year lifespan, tops, because the power centers are going to move around depending on what real estate opens up. At the fringes here," he scribbled up into the hills near the towns, "these farmers are going to feel the pressure and they'll sell out. Higher and better use. He drew an X over a hypothetical farm. Boom, that's when you move in and create a new power center, capitalize on the profit potential of the value-added factor for the parcel, so you get your unskilleds moving here to here as this growth continues and that's why you don't want to sink the bucks into these places, 'cause they're going to be abandoned anyway." He put Xs through many of the homes and stores he had marked a few minutes earlier.

"Now the key to the successful theme park is containing the experience, so the visitor perceives comfort and safety first, adventure second. You're not going to make this kind of money selling real adventure. Take it from me, the profit potential lies in the lies! Ha! Listen to me! Just kidding! No, really, what I mean is you can't leverage existing social-commercial assets for the shareholders—you got to build new and squeeze out that existing. The more it grows, the more trickle you get for the locals.

"Mr. Rosko here understands that the game is all about the shareholder, and the shareholder likes safety, too. That's why his concept is so brilliant. Now, you might run into some trouble with the treehuggers and preservationists and other people who hate growth, but we all know they just don't get it. They wouldn't know progress if it bit them on the ass, pardon my French. People gripe about crap like green space and biodiversity and authenticity and neighborhood character but they just don't understand what the world is about. If you want green space, build it. If you want neighborhood character, build it. You can't just take somebody else's leftovers. This is all very do-able, very do-able. You got willing shareholders who stand to make a handsome profit, strong visionary leadership with Mr. Rosko, and weak and unorganized local opposition. You can steamroll right over them before they know what's up. Go for it! Thirty years from now, you won't recognize this place, I guarantee it! And I've looked at preliminary numbers for Roscoff, France, and for those of you who are concerned about that we could expect a very similar result there. Very similar." He turned another sheet and drew a thumb-shaped peninsula, working from his vague memory of the little map of the Roscoff ferry station that was included in a brochure on the car ferry service that came with his Avis package. "Here's Roscoff, here's the road to the ferry terminal, here's your major arteries. Growth growth growth." He drew squares and Xs and scribbled all along the coastline. "You can do it, too. Go for it!" He clenched a fist in front of him.

"I thank you for sharing your morning with me and I congratulate you once again on your wise choice of Mr. Rosko. There aren't many like him. Mr. Rosko!" Bret bowed and stepped off to the side. Just in time. His voice was about to croak. He scanned the crowd. Cormack and Renée at the back seemed to have caught on and were suppressing smirks, but the grim and stoic expressions of the people seated at the tables reminded Bret of nothing more than the face of a truck driver he'd once seen in the moments after getting his trailer wedged under a low bridge.

As he walked to the back of the room, he listened to Rosko begin to speak behind him. "Thank you, Mr. Sheehan," he said, "for your enthusiasm and expertise. Don't go too far away. There may be some questions."

"Certainly, certainly," Bret called back over his shoulder. He stopped and crouched next to the bus driver. "Let's take everyone for a ride," he whispered. "Show them what I'm talking about."

"But what you describe is horrible," the driver replied.

"Exactly," said Bret patted him on the shoulder and winked. "Play along." The driver's frowning eyes brightened.

At the front of the room, Rosko turned another sheet. "Of course, Mr. Sheehan's scenario is the extreme case." Bret had calculated that his over-the-top presentation would so horrify the assembled crowd that Rosko would seek to retreat to a much more moderate position. So Bret had to keep pushing it.

"Not at all," Bret called out. "Very do-able."

"Even so, our guests might prefer a more measured progress," Rosko countered.

"No guts no glory," said Bret.

M. Bernard stood from his table at the corner near the front. "Pardon me, Mr. Rosko. When you have described the economic benefits of the theme park, you have not also described these other effects."

"Mr. Sheehan has described these effects in extreme terms," Rosko countered. "He bases his scenario on unlikely numbers, so he—"

"Unlikely?" Bret interrupted. "Not at all. These are very solid, conservative numbers extrapolated using standard industry formulae—it's a straight gravity model based on the acreage of the proposed park, regional population density, aggregated tourism projections, and transportation infrastructure friction models. You're not looking for a smaller local economic impact, are you? Do you want the Sideshow of Suburban Sneem or the Legend of Castle Cove? "

"The goal is to maximize the touristic potential of the area," said Rosko, "and one wonders if the scenario Mr. Sheehan has detailed for us might be exceeding the limit of that potential."

"The potential," Bret replied, "is what you make it. If you want a small-scale rinky-dink tourism where all you do is get more people to take walks in the hills or sail around in the bay or hit a few rounds of golf, then all you're going to get is some happy little rinky dink local proprietors and maybe a little bump in your property values. No big investors, no major international players. It's just a big lumpy sheep farm sticking out into the ocean. Ladies and gentlemen, that's why Rosko's vision is so compelling. It's big. It's bold. It's out of the box. It dares to dream."

"But that's not—" began Rosko.

"Dare to dream!" Bret bellowed.

"Excuse me, sir," came a mild male voice from the back, "but I feel you've not taken a full accounting of the natural touristic value of the landscape as it is." It was Dickeen O'Brien from the post office. "I presume that I was invited to this meeting because I have more than once expressed an interest to Mr. Rosko in engaging more of our visitors to avail themselves of our lovely hillwalks, but I question the value such a walk would hold if the terrain one gazed down upon were transformed in the way in which you describe it."

"I'm glad you said that, sir," said Bret, "because Mr. Rosko's vision is all about progress, not stasis. He's got investors, real money people who are prepared to step up to the plate and capitalize this project, but they expect their return. This is the real world here! Follow me. I'll show you all a perspective on this that will take your breath away. To the bus! Come on, here we go! Allons-y!" The driver was already at the door, waving the guests on.

Just outside, Bret grabbed Cormack. "Quick, what's the fastest way to a high point on the Kerry Way? We need to take everybody for a walk up high—let them feel the land underfoot and get a big eyeful of what they'd be ruining."

"I'd say up Eagles Hill from behind the old Kilcrohape Church. Could get quite far up the hill in 30 minutes' time walking," he said. "Turn left out of the car park, then I believe it's the second right turning. Not marked, but I know just where it is. I'll go now and wait at the turn."

"Okay, we'll look for you," said Bret. "The driver's in on the joke, but no one else. Rosko suspects something, but I don't think he'll act on it yet. We just have to keep moving. Okay, you go. I'll stay with them."

Cormack, Renée, and Lee climbed into the van and sped off just as the guests began streaming out of the inn.

THE
KERRY
WAY

The bus scraped its way uphill through overhanging boughs until it came into a clearing and pulled over next to the remnants of ancient stone church and a small graveyard. Creeping vines seemed to be trying to suck what was left of the building back into the hillside and long grass nearly obscured many of the Celtic-Catholic tombstones. Just beside one stone wall was a cluster of calla lilies growing wild, remnant of the old church garden where funeral and wedding flowers would have been cultivated. The church was a few hundred feet above the level of the sea: the site commanded a stirring view.

Cormack, Renée, and Lee, who were pretending to be exploring the church grounds, quietly folded themselves into the crowd as it assembled. Bret stood next to a small "walking man" sign that marked the Kerry Way pedestrian route. "Who out there wants to be our leader?" he called out. "It's up the mountain to get a good view of the project area." Dickeen O'Brien from the post office raised his hand and stepped forward, then just kept walking right past Bret up the green lane at a deliberate pace. The group quickly straggled itself behind him. The ground was very soggy in places, and increasingly so as they climbed. Bret quietly slid to the back of the group, where Cormack and Renée assisted him in walking. Lee, meanwhile, had positioned herself next to Rosko near the front and was keeping him occupied with nonstop chatter, even matching his bowlegged stride.

Just ahead of Bret, the French woman with the straight gray hair and her lanky balding son chatted, occasionally pausing to point out over the shore of the wide river. Bret could not catch much of what they said, but two words he recognized were "magnifique" and "fou." A large dark bird circled above the mountain top.

Progress was swift until M. Bernard's feet went out from under him on a swampy patch, and then the two red-headed proprietors of Les Vins du Finistere went down trying to get him back up. The pause allowed the stretched-out group to consolidate while Dickeen O'Brien waited somewhat impatiently atop a nearby boulder. "Mind the carcass," he called when they resumed. A female scream followed shortly after, as one of the French college students came upon the gutted remains of a sheep beside the path, its dead black feet still sticking straight up in the air. The rest of the group diverted a few feet to the left as they passed the unsettling sight. "If you don't leave 'em up here for the scavengers, then the scavengers come down to the lowlands and start pilfering the family pets," said Dickeen O'Brien, who then continued his relentless ascent. But he had to wait more frequently as different members of the group experienced delays. These involved such things as soggy shoes, flower inspections, and moments of reverie gazing out over the idyllic landscape.

From time to time a group of three or four walkers would pass going the other direction, greeting the party with unfailing politeness—but Bret also detected a note of bemusement at the task-inappropriate attire—especially footwear—of the tour bus group. Two of the French college student women, for example, walked gingerly along in thong sandals, and M.

Bernard sported a recently shiny pair of brown oxfords. Two of the older ladies wore skirts. One rustic-looking fellow walking alone from the other direction stopped and greeted Dickeen O'Brien with familiarity and then made a point of thanking every person one at a time for taking the time and trouble to leave the tour bus and experience the countryside at first hand.

After nearly an hour, the path climbed very steeply on the diagonal across a rocky pasture and then leveled as it began to pass between a tall hill on the left and a lower one on the right. Bret recognized the place from his map. "Wait!" he called. The party stopped. Some sat on the ground and other milled about as Bret hobbled up to a high place where he could speak. He was out of breath. Walking the generally gradual path wasn't as strenuous as climbing straight up the mountainside, as he'd done from Staigue Fort, but it was still plenty of effort. The group looked happy to have stopped.

"Please look this way," Bret called out, pointing down the hillside toward the loose cluster of buildings that constituted the unofficial town of Castle Cove. As he did so, his shoe slid off a muddy rock and wedged awkwardly. Pain shot up his leg and he instinctively winced and bent over to grab his ankle. He shifted all his weight to the other foot and resumed pointing. "In that clear area there beyond the inn, between it and the water and that row of abandoned farm buildings, that's the theme park. To the left up the river is Kenmare" oops, he thought—accidentally pronounced it accurately, "where the ferry terminal will be, and all along this coast road is where the first wave of new building will be." As he spoke, Rosko climbed up beside him.

"Mr. Sheehan," said Rosko. "You have hurt yourself. Perhaps you shouldn't play outside." Uh-oh, thought Bret. He's had too much time to think.

"That's right," Bret replied. "This would never have happened to me in the safety of a well-designed theme park. You also wouldn't have people falling down in the mud or stumbling across rotting sheep cadavers. That's the whole point."

"But Monsieur Sheehan," said the French lady with the straight gray hair, "you would also not have the beautiful land and water and the soaring birds. What you describe is not real. It is missing something. I don't mind the dirt and the dead mouton so much."

"Look," said Bret, "Mr. Rosko asked me to share with your group how the American theme park concept would work in this setting and I obliged his request. If you don't like his idea, then you should propose a better one. Mr. Rosko owns a large parcel of property and already has his investors lined up. What do you expect him to do?"

"That was not my idea," said Rosko. "Yes, I own the property and I have signed papers of agreement to develop that parcel with a number of investors, but the intention was never to, to create the kind of extreme conditions Mr. Sheehan has described. And I should point out, Mr. Sheehan is employed by—"

"Intention or not, that's what would happen," said Bret. He noticed another solitary walker approaching from the other side of the ridge.

"You toss numbers about, but you have presented no real evidence," replied Rosko.

"Oh, you want numbers and evidence? I have plenty of that. All kinds of evidence. Do you know what causes the fish kills in the Finglas and Cummeragh rivers? Do you know why children get ill swimming in Loch Leane? Why there are no eagles left on Eagles Hill, right there?" He pointed up at the nearby peak. "Pesticides and polluted rain from automobile exhaust. Of course, your actions will have consequences. But who needs a few more fish? Who needs to swim in a stream when you have chlorinated pools? Who needs eagles? Put this in perspective. This is progress you're talking about. You have to accept that things will not be as they were. So what? Grow up."

Dickeen O'Brien stepped up and cleared his throat. "Mr. Sheehan, I'm not sure if you are trying to convince us that the money generated by Mr. Rosko's scheme will be worth the cost to our quality of living, but I myself remain unpersuaded. I think you have done a better job of convincing us that it is a very bad idea indeed." Many in the group nodded in affirmation. "I've never been to America, but after today I can only imagine what a horrid place it must be."

"Well, it's a very big place," said Bret. "So it will take us a while to conquer the entire landscape. But we'll keep trying."

"And correct me if I'm wrong sir," O'Brien continued, "did I not sell you a hillwalking guide in the Kenmare Town post office not a few days back?"

"Yep, that was me. Research, you know." The approaching walker had stopped and stood at the back of the group. Her head was wrapped in a scarf and her face nearly obscured, but he could plainly see it was Caitlin McGowan.

"Mr. Sheehan," said Rosko, "I do not know why you have led us all up here just to argue about fictional scenarios, but our day is growing old and we must go back down and continue our business."

"Okay, if you must," said Bret. "But first, let me conclude our excursion with a favorite American Indian fable of mine. Once there was a great chief named Blue Streak, so named for a blue star that raced across the sky on the night that he was born. Now the Indians didn't have a modern understanding of the land—to them, man was one of many creatures that share the bounty of nature, and there was no concept of ownership of land. Rather, they saw themselves as caretakers of a world that needed to be passed on in good condition to future generations. It was all very quaint.

"Blue Streak had two sons, Wildcat and Raging Wolf Bob. The two sons could not have been more different in character. Wildcat was quiet and hard-working and modest and took only what he needed at the dinner table—well, it wasn't a table, really. It was a big rock. But Raging Wolf Bob was prideful and lazy and always hungry, to the point that he was quite obese even at a young age.

"One day Blue Streak told his sons that it was time for them to prove they were ready to be men. This rite of passage involved trekking alone for seven days into the wilderness and living for one month with only a knife and the clothes on their backs. So the two set off in opposite directions.

"Wildcat was industrious and he soon had fashioned himself a bow and some arrows and had made a fishing line and hooks and a spear. He lived off the meat and fish he caught and on fruits and vegetables he gathered, for he had learned which plants were edible and which were not.

"After two weeks, as he was walking along a remote ridge in a place far from his home, he encountered a wandering bard. They camped and walked together for two days, and the bard told him many stories. One of these was the tale of a king whose subjects lived in three ships until they found an island where they built a kingdom where every building was comfortable and familiar. The people enjoyed living there at first, but over time, a malaise crept over the kingdom because nothing ever happened that was unexpected. There was no wonderment, for everything around them was created because someone had already liked that kind of thing. It became excruciatingly boring. Wildcat hoped he would never see such a place. When his ordeal was over, he went home and sharpened his knife.

"Meanwhile, Raging Wolf Bob had never learned how to use a knife nor what plants to eat, so after a few weeks of living on nothing but water, his ample girth had nearly disappeared. A week later, the fat was all gone, but then, just as he began to wonder if he would starve before the ordeal was over, he came upon a large bay and in the center of the bay was an island. He sat on the beach until a boat came by and the kind rowers transported him to the island. There he found great comfort and a bottomless all-you-can-eat buffet. He was especially fond of the chicken drumsticks. He never did go home.

"As he ate more and more chicken drumsticks, the kingdom had to slaughter more and more chickens. When the chickens were gone, it was ducks and pigeons and housecats. Raging Wolf Bob soon grew to unprecedented human proportions. Pretty soon the other people began to be concerned that Raging Wolf Bob would eat up everything on the island and they would be next. So they made a mast and a sail, and one night, while he slept, they transported him to the harbor on a system of rolling logs, then they set the mast in his navel, raised the sail, and let the wind carry his extremely buoyant body away.

"The rocking of the water was very soothing, so he slept for many days as the wind blew him to a distant shore. By the time he was within sight of that shore, he had become slim again and the mast fell out of his belly button, striking him on the nose. He woke up and drowned because he had never learned how to swim."

Bret paused and looked at the faces. "So there you go," he said.

Rosko eyed him warily. "I'm not sure I see the connection," he said.

"Connection?" Bret asked.

"To our current situation," said Rosko. "It is customary when relaying such a fable that it might have something to do with the current situation."

"Oh," said Bret. He shrugged. "I just like that story."

Rosko turned to the crowd. "We thank Mr. Sheehan for his insights and we wish him a pleasant holiday in Ireland." He began to walk back down the green lane. The group followed, most giving Bret a wide berth and many a skeptical glance.

The bus driver came by last, grinning.

Bret sat down on the edge of the rock and looked up. His ankle throbbed. Cait, her head still wrapped, was conversing with Lee and Cormack and Renée about thirty feet away.

BLOOD AND BONES

Bret tried to discern whether Cait had already known Lee and Cormack, and decided not. She glanced over Lee's shoulder at Bret and fixed his eyes but betrayed no recognition. Then he caught the slightest of smiles between hand gestures after she looked away. Cormack pointed down toward Castle Cove. Lee pointed up toward Bret and motioned him to join them.

"We were attempting to explain what the crowd is doing up here," Cormack offered when Bret arrived. "This is . . ."

"Caitlin," said Cait. "Caitlin McGowan. Pleased to meet you."

Bret smiled and nodded. "Likewise."

"Caitlin says she's never seen so many walkers up here," said Cormack, "and it made her afraid that masses were discovering our little secret."

"Secret?" Bret's eyes flitted among the three.

"The Kerry Way," Cait said. "Our unspoilt national recreation area. Wouldn't want it overrun by the public, would we?"

"Aha!" Bret laughed. "Well you can always count on laziness to keep the crowds down. We sort of coerced these people to come up here."

"You must have some powers of persuasion," Cait laughed. "On what premise?"

"Uh, that's complicated." Bret scanned Lee's and Cormack's faces for any sign that he should not explain, and found none. "We were, uh . . . trying to demonstrate something. Wouldn't you say?"

Lee smiled.

"It will be easier to see if we walk up a little higher," Cormack said.

"Up there?" Cait pointed to a short side path leading to a ledge.

"Perfect," Cormack replied.

Cait led the way with Bret behind and Lee and Cormack following. When Bret got close and the other two were a few seconds behind, Cait said quietly, without turning around, "I was down to Waterville and heading back to the hut when the fog cleared and this group appeared. I couldn't risk being seen off the path. So here we are."

"I don't know how to thank you," Bret panted. "Or how I'll see you again."

"Well, that's my dilemma," she replied. "As long as I stay up here I'm on my own, no one to answer to—but at the same time nothing I do matters much if I stay up here forever. What kind of choice—"

"They're catching up," Bret cut in. "We better stop talking. I'll try to get back up to the hut again before I go."

They emerged on the ledge and looked back out over the vista.

"What we were doing," Bret explained, "was trying to prevent the Tragedy of Castle Cove."

The three of them recapped the events of the day so far, and at the end Cait broke out laughing. "A tour de force! Certainly a creative use of negative capability!" she said. And then, "now I'm afraid I must be going. Very nice to meet all of you, and thank you for your efforts to preserve our peninsula." She nodded to Lee and Cormack, then smiled at Bret and shook his hand. "Au revoir to you, sir. Safe journey to America. Never been, but perhaps someday . . . " As she spoke these last words, she had already turned and begun to stride off back toward Waterville.

Lee looked after her. "Odd bird. What was she doing, just walking up to the pass, then turning around? What kind of a walk is that?"

Bret shrugged. "Takes all kinds, I guess."

Cormack nodded. "Rosko's spotted us. This will be interesting." Cormack chuckled and motioned the two ladies ahead and they began to walk back down to meet the French tourists, who were still assembled where they had stopped earlier. Rosko was standing a little bit uphill from the rest of the group.

THREADS UNRAVELING

Bret caught up to the group at the lower gathering point and politely turned down Cormack's offer to assist him in walking back down.

"We had to tell Rosko we'd brought you," Cormack said. "It was the only explanation for our being here."

"And was he surprised?" Bret asked.

"Didn't appear so, no. Might be he figured it out on his own by now."

"Especially since you all know each other," Bret nodded. "He's quite familiar with these characters, right?"

Cormack shook his head. "Might say that, yeah." He laughed sardonically.

Bret could see Lee ahead of him, picking the best line through the stones and foliage. And Rosko beside her, bouncing along in his similar sprightly gait. Then he imagined Lee's eyes twinkling at him in mischief and flashing black in anger, and Rosko's eyes aglow with a tall tale and glaring when Bret crossed him. Her angled black brows and his, their unruly teeth and unruly hair. Their lilting intonation of "blood and bones to water and stone," a phrase she said came from her father. Bret slowed his stride and stopped. "You idiot!" he muttered to himself. "You're blind!" He raised his arms and pointed at his eyes in a theatrical gesture for which there was no audience but himself.

Cormack looked back and waited for Bret. "Come along, let me help you. We'll get to that pint and a shot all the quicker." This time Bret accepted. He could definitely use a drink, the sooner the better.

"So," Bret asked as they walked, pointing to Lee and Rosko ahead, "how is Lee related to Rosko? Dad? Uncle? Alternate gender clone?"

Cormack snorted but didn't say anything at first. "Just a matter of time, that was. I fancy the game is up. You want the story now or in the pub?"

Bret decided that alcohol would probably facilitate the proceedings. "Maybe we ought to wait. Will they all be there?"

Cormack nodded. "The whole cast and crew."

WHEN CORMACK closed the pub door behind them, Bret was surprised to find inside not only Lee and Rosko and Renée, but also Cormack's mother. He was further surprised that, before he could decide whom to interrogate first, Lee turned on him with a dark glare in her eyes. In one smooth motion she downed a shot of whiskey and slammed the glass down on the counter.

"Funny business," she said. "How closely your leg wrapping matched that lovely and polite redhead lady's headscarf."

"Really?" Bret felt a sinking lump in his belly, but feigned unconcern. "Pattern must have been on sale."

"It's also unusual," said Lee, refilling her glass and emptying it a second time, "that a man would get lost and injured on the mountain for two days alone, and yet appear no worse for the wear, and indeed have his leg expertly wrapped in a cloth that happens to have been cut from the same lot of fabric as the wrap on that girl's lovely copper locks. What's the chance of that?"

Bret shrugged. "You were going to tell me about that hair on the pillow. What's the chance of that?"

"I cannot tell a lie," Lee said. "I put that hair on that pillow."

"Uh-huh," Bret said. "And why would that be?"

"Feckin with your head."

"I thought you liked me."

"Who says I don't? Just 'cause I'm feckin with your head doesn't mean I don't fancy you."

"Well, that's interesting," Bret replied.

Lee continued. "No, her scarf on your leg, my hair on your pillow. THAT's interesting."

"Oh-oh," said Cormack.

"Should I attempt to explain?" asked Bret. "I—"

"I just watched Mr. Sheehan do a fine snow job on a whole coachload of business prospects," said Lee, "so forgive me if I'm a little bit, ah—skeptical of whatever explanation you might improvise."

"Okay. She helped me. Of course. She kept me from hypothermia or worse," he said.

"And how did she do that?" asked Lee. "A warm bath?"

"Of course not," retorted Bret. "Did you see a hot water tap up there?"

"Just her warm body, then, right?" Lee growled.

"Well, yes, that was—" Bret began.

"So that was why you were so concerned about finding my hair on your pillow? Afraid things would get complicated?"

"Things are complicated already." He saw his opening. "How about you and our friend Mr. Rosko, here? Aren't you a bit complicated? I'm a bit dense, but even to me the blood relation is hard to miss."

Rosko stood up and shouted, "Leave my girl out of this. You bolloxed-up a perfectly credible project just to spite me. And worse, the rest of you helped him do it!"

"That's not why I did it," retorted Bret. "I did it because your project was a bumfuck stupid idea. And no offense. I like you. I like the whole lot of you. You just can't seem to tell a straight story."

"Half again of those ideas came from you, Mr. brilliant Sheehan," countered Rosko. "What's wrong with a man just trying to make a better future for his family? You must understand by now that this place yields surpassing beauty but little else—no tillable land, poor soil, no big-city economics. Why do you think everyone left in the last century? Since those years of famine, tourism has come up and thank God for that, but even now tourism is about all we've got. And don't try to pretend that the whole purpose of your visit wasn't to expand your company's American amusement park empire! Returning your uncle's ashes—a likely tale indeed! I couldn't have fabricated a more clichéd story."

"What?" Bret was insulted at first, until it dawned on him that maybe Rosko didn't know that Bret had lost his job. If Rosko really did think Bret was here on professional business, that would explain the shenanigans, the hiding, the lying.

"Rosko," Bret began, then stopped as the laughing took over for a moment. "Is it possible that in all of our conversations you did not learn that I lost my job at King Arthur's Kamelot? Weeks ago?"

"Lost it?"

"Yes, I lost it," Bret laughed. "Quite literally. They canned me. Sacked me. Made me redundant. Only a few days after your little tourism junket came through. I'm unemployed. In fact, I think I'm through with that industry, and perhaps with marketing altogether."

"But then why did you ruin my plan, if not to prepare the way for yourself?" Rosko threw up his arms.

"Like I said, it was a bumfuck stupid idea. Believe me, I have a lot of experience with bumfuck stupid ideas, having dreamt up quite a few myself. I know one when I see it. In fact, I invite you all to come back to America with me and I can show you exactly what I mean, though Rosko has seen it with his own eyes already and evidently didn't perceive it for what it was. In least in that case, it was paving over a piece of relatively nondescript farmland. Here, or in Brittany for that matter, from what I hear, you'd be painting over a—I don't know, a frigging Constable landscape. The land, the people, everything—the thought of destroying it in order to make some pre-fab little cut-and-run profit center seemed just, well, nuts. And you!" He turned to Lee. "Acting like you cared when all you were really doing was abetting Rosko. Although I didn't put it together until just now that young Sean must be yours. I concede that's a mitigating circumstance."

"I'd prefer it," Lee retorted, "if you wouldn't call my cherished son a mitigating circumstance. What's more, we did end up helping you, didn't we? And Rosko didn't tell us what he was up to either. Only that it could help us all in the coming years. I'm a single mum and I can't look out for only myself. And I'm not the feckin hypocrite here, trying to play two women off each other."

"I was not trying to do that," said Bret. "It just happened. Christ, I can't even keep one woman in my life. Why would I attempt two? You know what? I can't believe this. I spend my whole career bullshitting people and just when I think I can walk away from that, I step into a big steaming pile of it."

"Ladies and gentlemen!" Cormack bellowed from the bar. "Please lay down your weapons for a brief intermission while I pour everyone a drink. As you're all cooling down, Mother would like a few words."

A row of full shot glasses had appeared on the bar and pints of Guinness were beginning to line up behind them.

Mother lifted a glass and drained it. "Children," she said, "—for if you have not yet deduced it, Mr. Sheehan, these are all my children in one way or another—this matter has gotten entirely out of hand. Too many fanciful lies, too many tall stories—it's all just too Irish. So let us begin with facts. I, Margaret Roche, am Rosko's mother, and grandmother to Lee and Cormack. Rosko's given name is Francis Roche, and he has a daughter, Lee, and Lee her son Sean. Cormack is the only child of my daughter Bridget, who died in a terrible automobile accident with her husband, Kevin Harper, when Cormack was just a boy. I raised him. My own husband Brian passed seven years ago.

"I was unaware of my incorrigibly inventive son's most recent scheme until Lee asked if I might entertain an out-of-town guest not long ago, to help keep said fellow away from town at a time when Rosko would be there with certain business associates. It was feared that the guest might inadvertently (or deliberately, as it happens) disrupt the proceedings, so I agreed. It seemed harmless enough, and a bit of fun. Besides, I enjoy meeting new people. So that is how I came to entertain Mr. Sheehan at my home that day."

"That whole goose chase for Uncle Michael's ashes was just a ruse to keep me from stumbling into Rosko?" Bret interjected, annoyed. "It's not just some trinket. That was all that remained of a man in there. A real person."

"Not only that reason," Lee protested. "I truly wanted to share some of the county with you, show you things you wouldn't find on your own. And to introduce you to Mother. But I had no idea it would turn out that Mother had a romantic boat ride with the very same person whose ashes were in that tin."

"Where did you learn your manners, girl?" said the older woman, glowering at Lee, then at Rosko. "You see, I sometimes humor Rosko because he so charmingly operates on the assumption that people believe every word that comes out of his mouth, and I find it amusing to let him get well down the winding path before letting him know in some subtle way that no one is buying his bill of goods. You, Mr. Sheehan, strike me as something of the same sort of character—for instance you, like Rosko, undoubtedly thought that everyone was wowed by Rosko's amusement park scheme, and that you had to play the hero and come save County Kerry from its own ignorant populace. I wouldn't be so sure that they weren't just stringing you and my manipulative yet lovably gullible son along because everyone likes a good yarn. But back to my story. When I saw the photographs Mr. Sheehan brought," she continued, "I realized who Michael Sheehan had been and I no longer wished to have anything to do with what has been recently and quite accurately described as a 'bumfuck stupid idea.' I told Lee as much that day, but many wheels were already in motion and it was complicated to get them all stopped. We all know today where that momentum has brought us." She lifted a Guinness and took a long sip. "We all owe Mr. Sheehan an apology. Children?"

Lee, Cormack, and Rosko looked at Mother, then at each other, then all three at Bret. "We're sorry," they said in a kind of perfect unison that hinted at repeated practice.

Bret just shook his head. "Accepted. Thank you. And I sincerely regret the hurtful things I've said. I'm sorry. I think I need some air. Excuse me." He drained the rest of his pint and headed for the door.

"Bret—" Lee called in a pleading tone.

"Let him go, dearie," Bret could hear Mother saying as he stepped outside. "Just leave the man be."

Bret let the door close behind him and took in a cool breath. He felt very tired. All the adrenaline of the fight had drained out of him and now he just wanted to go to bed.

On the one hand, I feel I needn't have tried to shape this adventure at all. Everything that has happened would have done so without my active efforts. To go back to that notion of a collective consciousness, perhaps there are not individual ghosts, but rather one great taibhse gathering up scraps of events and personalities and hopes and fears and wrapping them in the landscape, the landscape in them. The people may not hear my specific ramblings, but they do sense something. They understand themselves as part of a bigger story in a place, even though most of that story is unknown to any one person.

It was never my choice whether to come along, whether to try to put my power to work. I was here already, part of the story inevitably.

PACKING UP

The sea-smell gradually worked its way into Bret's head. He could feel a breeze on his exposed eyebrow. He pulled the sheet away from his face and sat up. The wind had shifted overnight, blowing open the window and carrying in the scent of the nearby open water. He blinked. The room was bright. Must be late.

He pivoted and rose to his feet. The ankle was very stiff, but it didn't hurt as much as it had yesterday. "A walk would help that," he said aloud. He left Cait's improvised leg wrap in place and gingerly tugged a loosened sneaker onto his foot.

Instead of following the boardwalk along the river, Bret limped his way to the east until he saw a small park behind St. Michael's church. He turned right. From the slight rise at the top end of the park, he could see the estuary and the sea breeze caressing the long grasses that lined the watercourses of the Sneem River, Abna na Snadhma, as the Ordnance Survey #84 also labeled it.

Scattered about the park was a group of stone sculptures, made in recent years but obviously ancient in inspiration. One looked like a tomb marker. One was a long narrow crease formed into the ground. Another was a conical form whose antecedent was, obviously, a beehive hut. Bret moved closer. It was about 12 or 15 feet high, maybe 8 feet in diameter, and made of precisely stacked stones without mortar. He squeezed inside. High up, a tiny bit of color tinted a band light, lending the tiny dark space the air of a cathedral. Lower down, a narrow slot window looked out on the landscape. He walked over and put his eye to the window. There was the river, and the high hills beyond. High hills where he had stood, fallen, slept. Where Uncle Michael was dissolving into the water table. Where there was a stone hut, where there was Cait, maybe. All of that mattered, Bret felt sure.

On the way back to Killarney, he decided, he was going to go back up there.

But before he could do that, he had to retrieve his rental car. Probably Cormack would let him borrow the telephone to make the call. Maybe Lee would be there and he could try to set things straight with her as well. He turned sideways and re-entered the bright light of day.

The front door of the Fisherman's Knot was propped open and Bret walked in. As his eyes readjusted to the dim light, he saw Cormack walking from the kitchen door toward the close end of the bar. "Good morning," he called out.

"Good morning," Bret replied.

"Good afternoon, I should say. Is that Mr. Sheehan? Can't see against the light. How's things?"

"Can't complain. I wonder if I might borrow a telephone, though? Need to call Avis and try to get my rental car back."

"Right here." Cormack set the telephone down on the counter. "Sleep well? Lot of energy spent yesterday."

"Pretty well. Finally getting used to it now that it's time to leave."

"Oh, is it?" Cormack put a glass on the bar. "You don't need the rental car for that. We could get you back to Killarny. Even to Shannon airport."

"One more little errand before I go. Requires that I drive."

"Ah," Cormack replied. "Pint?"

"Please, yes." Bret set the Avis card on the bar and dialed the number. "Yes, hello," he said when the customer service person answered. "My car has been mistakenly towed . . . Yes, Bret Sheehan. I'm American . . . yes . . . Nissan Almera, greenish . . . near Sneem, Castle Cove . . . at Staigue Fort, to be exact . . . yes, I can hold."

Cormack set down the glass to let the first pour settle. Bret nodded a thank-you and started fishing in his wallet. Cormack waved him off.

"Yes, sir." Bret said as the man came back on the line. "No, I'm quite alive. Never was dead at all, no . . . Overzealous media, you know . . . right, ha-ha . . . It's not a big problem except now I'm stuck in Sneem without a car . . . well a lift would be fine except I'd like to drive myself to a couple of places yet. Yes, I'll hold." The man said he was going to put Bret's official representative on the line. Mary's rapid-fire voice was next. "Yes, hello," Bret said, "very nice to talk to you again. No, that's right, not at all dead. Yes, I'm very relieved to know that as well. Yes, well I was hoping for a favor. Could someone possibly just run the car out here? I'll give them a lift back . . . or you could send two cars and two drivers, that's true . . . that would work, too, a bicycle in the boot . . . yes, a boat to Kenmare and then a bus transfer would also work, I suppose . . . however you'd like to do it, it's fine with me . . . yes, I'll hold again."

Cormack topped off the glass, the roiling tan bubbles of Guinness slowly congregating at the top. "Ah, Lee was hoping to have a word with you before you left, but she's away today with Sean visiting her mum," he said.

"Yeah, I'd like to talk to her," said Bret. "I feel I've wronged her, or at least that our business isn't finished. Truth is, I'd like to have a word with Rosko, too, if he's around—you say he lives nearby?"

"He's with them as well—always stops in for a bit of grumbling whenever he's got to face his ex," Cormack laughed.

"Can I see Lee in the morning?" Bret replied. "When does she come in?"

"Half-ten on a good day."

"Yes, I'm here," Bret said into the phone. "It should be the same address and telephone as on the original paperwork . . . Yes, that's it . . . Okay, see you in the morning. Thanks. Bye. Yes. Good bye. Of course. Bye. Bye. Absolutely, bye-bye. Okay, bye. Bye." He hung up the phone and handed it back to Cormack. "Thanks. Jesus that woman can talk. The car should arrive mid-morning, so I'll be sure to stop and say good-bye before I go."

"It's only an hour to Killarney and I've not let the room to anyone else," said Cormack. "There's no need to hurry away."

"I've got to leave time to do an errand on the way," said Bret. "A little hill walk."

"Ah," said Cormack. "Bit complicated, that."

"What?"

"The two ladies."

"Just a misunderstanding," said Bret.

"Perhaps so. But complicated nonetheless," said Cormack.

"I wish I'd put it together that Sean would be her son. I figured out that the boy lived with Rosko. I had a couple of conversations with him—very self-possessed young man. What's the story, if it's not rude to ask?"

"She won't mind," Cormack said. "The story is well known. Between Lee and Rosko, one or the other of them is at home most of the time to look after Sean when he's not at school. If not, they work it out for him to visit Mother, or even to come here sometimes. This is, you will have noted, a small town. The kids are cared for outside the family as well."

"And the dad?"

"College boyfriend. He started off well enough, but ended up having too many attention problems. Not enough attention to Lee or Sean, too much to other women. Lee had the good sense to send him packing. He's moved to England. They still communicate cordially, so at least there's that—probably because they rarely see each other. And she hasn't been looking for anyone else. Life is full enough between her dad and her son and helping out here. She's trying to make the best life for them all, and a good future for Sean. They both are, Rosko too."

"So was she not flirting with me? That was just part of the game?"

"Eh, I think it started out as a game and maybe she decided you were okay after all."

Bret had cooled off now that he wasn't so furious at being duped. His main business ahead, he had decided, was to try to find Cait, and if he could not find her, to simply go home. Start over again back there. "You know," he said to Cormack, "It's too bad Rosko had to be such a bullshitter. If not for that, I could even envision working with the guy—not to turn County Kerry and some quaint French town into theme parks, but maybe to find a way for the local people and visitors to, shall we say, make the most of the landscape. Really, the place already is a giant theme park. You just have to meet it on its natural terms. Hillwalking, cycling, sailing, kayaking, horseback riding—wasn't that one of Rosko's ideas, an equestrian center? That wouldn't be such a bad idea for this place. It's too bad they blew it, because maybe there was some potential there."

It seemed to Bret that Cormack wasn't completely paying attention because he was hand-washing glasses and had his back turned for a while. "We already do make use of the landscape, sir, nothing revolutionary in that. And I said it before, Bret." He put a glass on the counter. "You don't need to leave just yet."

"No," said Bret. "I know. But it's time. I've got some things to wrap up there before I do anything else." He looked up at Cormack. "This is lovely, but it's time to get back to the real world."

"Real world?" Cormack walked closer.

"Yeah, instead of this—this fantasy-land."

Cormack stared at him for a second, then said, "Excuse me, but . . ." and he leaned over punched Bret in the upper left arm.

"What the hell was that for?" Bret reeled back and grabbed his throbbing bicep.

"A bit of real world for you, sir." He laughed. "You know how hard people had to work to survive out here? The only thing that grows on these rocky hills is sheep—no vegetation you could eat. If it weren't for the roads, such as they are, this peninsula couldn't support more than a few hundred hearty souls. Fantasy-land, what a load of . . ."

"I meant it in a good way!"

"Then why be in such a hurry to leave?

"Why?" Bret paused. "Because this is over. Now I have to get back to my own . . . my own water and stone."

"Blood and bones, water and stone."

"That's what I meant, yes."

"It's the same rocks, innit?" said Cormack, "just split apart by an ocean. Then you've got to consider the people."

"What?"

"Well, Lee asked me to tell you, just in case she couldn't say it to you herself before you left, that she's sorry for any pain she caused you, that she does care for you. She wouldn't put so much effort into her shenanigans otherwise. I know it."

"Problem is," Bret replied, "that when you start off with lies, sometimes you find out that's all there ever was." The phrase sounded good, but he didn't really believe it anymore—there was always something real, no matter how much shit you shoveled. He stood up. "I'm sorry, that was just a flippant remark. I didn't really mean it. Those come too easily for me. You can tell her thanks, no hard feelings, if I can't say so in person myself. And I will try to see her in the morning. Can I pay you for the pint?"

"Not likely."

DEPARTURE

At 10:00 the next morning, Mary from the Avis office arrived with his car. Bret was waiting outside on the bench in front of the Fisherman's Knot when she drove up. He waved.

"Sorry, Mr. Sheehan," she exclaimed in the same breathless mode of their earlier talk in the Killarney tourist bureau. "Good to see you again. Very sorry about the inconvenience. We've filled the petrol for you, cleaned the car. I'll need to see your driving license again and start a new record, just a formality. I'm afraid that we have not yet been able to update the computer database: apparently it assumes that a deceased person will be staying that way."

"It's okay," said Bret, fishing a stack of cards out of his wallet. The license was behind his old ID card for King Arthur's Kamelot, which—mostly out of spite—he had said was lost when they escorted him out. "This is surely less inconvenient than being dead. Can't complain."

"Right," she replied, handing him back the card. "Though there might be less hurrying about. Being dead, I mean. Though I don't know about that myself for certain. Here you are." She handed him the keys. "We've added another week to the rental for you as well, no charge."

"Thanks, but I'll just be needing it for today," said Bret. "You have someone to give you a lift back? I'm going there anyway."

"Yes, in about an hour's time, my pal will be coming round the other way from Waterville."

"Excellent," said Bret. "Now if you'll excuse me I have to run upstairs and get my things packed. Thanks again." He shook her hand and walked up the street to the blue door. The ankle was feeling pretty good. Accordingly, he'd left the walking stick behind.

HE SPREAD THE ORDNANCE SURVEY #84 on the table and examined his options. He could go to Staigue Fort again and walk up from there. That would be a more direct path to the hut. But he'd have to contend with the rougher climbing and he'd risk encountering the lady who owned the property and she might not be too happy to see him again. If he went back to the old church and walked up the Kerry Way, he'd be less likely to get lost—though the weather was looking clear today, so far—and he might be more likely to encounter Cait, that is if she were walking and not holed up in the hut. The Kerry Way seemed the better choice. It would also be possible, he noted, to drive all the way around the mountain through Waterville, park at the end of a tiny road at a "heritage centre," and then hike up the other side of the Kerry Way, and this appeared a bit of a shorter walk to the ridgetop. But it looked like whatever time he might save walking would be wasted three times over in driving, and then he'd have to drive all the way back around again to get back to Killarney. So that was settled: to the church. He folded the map.

When his bags were packed, he took one last look around the room. The back window was open, so he walked over to close it, and then noticed that the metal can that had held Uncle Michael's ashes was still sitting behind the curtain on

the sill. He lifted it and read the label. He smiled and dropped
the can into the waste basket.

IN THE FISHERMAN'S KNOT, he chatted with Cormack
and Mary until after 11:00, but Lee still did not appear. Then
the door opened and Mary's friend came in to pick her up.

"Enjoy the rest of your holiday, Mr. Sheehan," Mary
called back as she left. "Mind the sheep! Drive on the left!"

"On the left, right." He responded, then turned to
Cormack. "I really need to be going. I'm sorry to miss Lee, but
I've got to run my errand and get to Killarney in time to catch
the late train. I do hope to return here someday. Please give
her my best. And my apologies for all the shitty things I said."
He placed the room key on the counter.

"I'll do that, Bret." Cormack replied. "Best of luck to you.
Come back again. You'll always have first dibs on the room."

"I'd like to," Bret paused. "I really would like to do that.
Carve out some time and really stay a while." He thought for
a few seconds. Truth was, when was he likely to have more
free time than right now? And he still had enough savings
and severance money to stay for months if he wanted—
even fly back and forth a few times. "Anyway, thanks for
everything. Bye." He shook Cormack's hand and stepped out
into the light.

AS HE DROVE OUT OF TOWN, he saw that the French
tour bus was back in front of the hotel on the western edge
of town. "Still here," he said aloud, then he accelerated to get
past it quickly.

He pulled the car up against the tall grass just downhill
from the ruined church and began to walk. It was strange, how
a building like that, which must have been central to the life
of a little town, a space in which many people spent a lot of
time and thought a lot of thoughts, could just be reclaimed by
the land like that. He made a detour to his right and walked
up a steep slope amid tombstones. After stopping to admire the

calla lilies that flanked the rough-cut stones of the outer church wall, he stepped through a narrow doorway into the roofless interior. It was not silent, as he had expected it to be. Sounds echoed in there: the wind, his own breathing, the low static of countryside noises. He imagined being in the building in some earlier day, staring out the window instead of paying attention to the preacher. The voices of all the people who had been here, the things they talked about, worried about, celebrated about, prayed about—Bret got the feeling maybe they were still present somehow in the rocks and vines and grasses, all part of that murmur. Maybe that was what it was about, blood and bones to water and stone. He walked out the other door of the church and stepped uphill.

He turned onto the lane and began negotiating the series of pasture fences along the gradual first leg of the walk, whistling aimlessly to himself. The sheep munched indifferently.

Having walked this stretch in the recent past, he now knew where the soggy places were, and where the prudent walker would place his feet. He laughed at himself for not having taken Rosko's advice and getting rubber boots. Or any boots. His running shoes were a slightly beefier "trail" model, but they were no match for Irish muck. He learned to step on the centers of large clumps of grass, because the root system and the mass of the plant would help support his foot.

Lee seemed to have a knack for that, finding the solid footing. He recalled her leading the way down toward Staigue Fort the other day. Then there was Rosko. Why hadn't the guy just asked Bret to assist him? Why the evasions? Why all the stories? Why make something up when the truth would do just fine? Especially since the truth was a lot easier to sustain than an elaborate lie. That whole charade seemed doomed to crumble right from the start, since it counted on all those people to play along. Then again, had Bret not just happened to encounter the boy Sean, maybe the scheme would have worked. Or if he hadn't hesitated when he could have passed the tour bus in Sneem that morning. But still, what a production. Maybe it was just that perpetuating a fiction was an engrossing challenge, something to occupy your time and attention. Bret understood that impulse. Sustaining the story could be intoxicating, and it certainly did settle the question of what to do with one's time and energy.

About three-quarters of the way up, he stopped to take in the panorama. After a minute he picked out the church far below, an almost unrecognizable bump of green and gray. The first time he had seen the church, it seemed to Bret a pretty obvious symbol of nature putting man's delusions of grandeur in their proper place. But now he felt something different, that the assimilation of the building into the landscape wasn't a denial of human spirit, but an affirmation that the natural world was not over people or in competition with people: it simply included people. Looking down on the landscape from up here, that seemed obvious.

Stone walls and wood and wire fences criss-crossed the sloping pastures all the way down to the flatter area along the shore, and the charcoal-blue water beyond sparkled with whitecaps. A lively breeze swept down from the ridge. He just stood there for about five minutes, panning his gaze up and down the river. A low fishing boat followed the closer shore, near, he thought, the house where he and Lee had visited Rosko's mother.

He realized as he looked down on Castle Cove that the strange little tune had been running in his head as he walked was the same one Lee had been humming in the back of the van the other day, or some variation on it. He began to whistle along with it and continued climbing, filling in randomly the parts he couldn't remember.

AT THE FIRST HOLY WELL, he pulled out the Ordnance Survey #84 and verified that here was where he would want to divert from the Kerry Way. If he went to the right instead of to the left of a small peak just ahead, up out of Windy Gap and then kept to the left of the ridgeline, he should come pretty near where the hut ought to be. Probably above it, because the slope was too steep lower down.

As is often the case, the second time one visits a place the distances seem shorter, and it didn't take very long for Bret to get clear of the back shoulder of Staigue. He started looking down, scanning the terrain for something familiar. It was funny—being up here alone with only the rocks and the earth and the sky made him feel humble, but also more strong and sure of himself than he often felt down there in so-called civilization. He wasn't depressed. He wasn't giddy. He just felt real. He was truly, really, definitely here, picking his way over the real rocks. No acting. Maybe you can't bullshit a mountain, but it won't bullshit you either. A simple bargain.

He laughed aloud at that thought, startling a bird to flight from a nearby outcrop. He looked up. A raven, one with the usual two legs. The bird circled once. Its shadow flitted over the boulders and grasses, then it glided off ahead, following the ridgeline. The crystalline sky and aura of too-calm reminded him of when he had looked out over the city park one recent September morning, a little while before the airplanes exploded through everything. Or maybe he was remembering the strange calm after, when nothing was in the sky at all. But it was too easy to read too much significance into that association. That was the human mind doing what it does—making a story out of everything, whether there was anything there or not. A terrorist attack happened on a quiet, sunny morning. No causation either way. He shook it out of his mind.

Soon, Bret came to a small brook and decided to follow it down for a little while. In a few minutes, he found himself at a place that he recognized as the little stream crossing Cait had helped him to hobble across just after he had fallen. He hopped over and started up the steep little trail on the other side. The path angled uphill until he came to the familiar terrace between the large outcrop on the left and the vine-covered hut on the right. "Hello?" he called. No answer. "Anybody home?" Taking a deep breath, he stepped inside.

He waited a minute for his eyes to adjust, but it was clear to him much sooner that the hut was empty. No Cait. No camp stove. No rope. Really no evidence at all that she and he had ever been here except for the fact that he remembered the terrain well enough to get back to the place. He sat leaning against one wall and stared out the slit window at a passing cloud. Then he let his eyes trace the dark edge of the floor until they picked out something near the door, a piece of paper or cardboard. He walked over.

It was a sheet of newsprint, folded up, a small rock at its center holding it in place. Bret recognized it after a moment as the clipping Cait had brought that detailed the tour boat accident. He unfolded it, held it up, and read the headline, shaking his head. Then he flipped the sheet over. He began reading in the middle of the story, which concerned the search for a missing teacher from Cork who had disappeared from her class after a laboratory session some weeks ago. Bret harrumphed to himself, then skipped over the rest of the article until his eyes settled on the photo at the upper left. The nose and eyes had been cut off. But the mouth and chin he knew well. He stepped outside into the sunlight. For sure, that was Cait.

He leaned against the hut wall and read all that remained of the article. There it was, McGowan. She had used her real name, he marveled. Why? Either his question had happened too fast for her to make something up, he thought, or she really wanted to get caught. He remembered the fleeting startled look on her face as she had reached to take the clip from him. Probably it had happened too fast. She was not so practiced in sustaining a fiction. The reporter suggested (without citing any specific source) that the missing teacher was some kind of whistle-blower in a scandal about water quality and a chemical producer that was also a major funder in the area. He folded the sheet, pocketed it, and sank to the ground, his back against the stone wall. Even Cait had been lying to him. Everybody lied. There were nuances, to be sure . . . Lee lied to help Rosko yet there was still some genuine connection with Bret . . . Cait was the opposite: authentic on the surface, but hiding a secret, though she had been trying to tell him when they'd been interrupted near the holy well . . . Rosko lied because he couldn't help spinning a tale, and probably because he thought Bret wasn't telling the whole truth . . . and Bret wasn't telling the whole truth, but the specifics were not as Rosko supposed. But up here that all seemed irrelevant, just silly affectation. Strip it all away and every one of them was just another organism living in this place of rock and water. He stared at the plain stone face of the outcrop. It seemed impartial, so he spoke to it.

"Is that it?"

The rock did not answer.

Bret stood up and stepped back into the hut, clamping his hand on a protruding rock at the doorframe. As his eyes adjusted, he could see himself, lying on his back on Cait's sleeping bag over near the wall. He could feel his hand following her vertebrae, her warm skin against the cool air. She carefully reaching her leg wide to avoid hitting his injured ankle, easing onto him. His eyes fixed hers directly, and he was startled by the connection. She took in a sharp breath. The vision faded until only the bare floor remained.

He turned and took out the Ordnance Survey #84. Across the other side of the Kerry Way, up the back side of Eagles Hill, away from the sea, the topographical lines got so close together they almost merged. A long, winding cliff edge was marked. Nearly fell and died out here once already. Maybe that was what had been meant to happen all along.

He started walking and followed the stream back up until the slope looked gentle enough to step across the murmuring water, then aimed to the right and began skirting the back of Staigue. Going the other way had been all right, but in this direction, it was torturing the ankle, so he changed his mind and headed straight up again until he reached the ridge crest. It was steeper but it hurt less. Then it was straight down the spine of the ridge toward Windy Gap.

A thick mist was sliding up the hillside from below and to the left. It hadn't been noticeable before, hidden from his view on the other side of the ridge. Within seconds, it had billowed over the crest and enveloped everything. The individual droplets on skin felt cool. He kept walking. For how long was hard to tell, same for how far. Uphill or down? Not sure. But onward. The fog got so thick the ground itself was out of sight. The slope was definitely falling away to the right. The shoe soles kept wanting to slide down that way with each push-off. Then, skirting a large boulder, both feet lost their grip at the same time. There was a weightless gut-tickle.

To die or not? What would Bret do?

He lurched to the left and clamped his fingers onto the jagged porous rock. His left elbow slammed into the stone and his hip found a hard edge just under the soggy grass, but the grip held. What would Bret do? Old Bret wouldn't have been up here in the first place. He gingerly pulled his legs up until he found a solid hold for each foot. On the other hand, Bret was up here now. His heart slowed from a race to a steady thump. No death yet. He tried to watch himself with detached bemusement but found he could no longer distinguish between first-person Bret and third-person Bret. Now he was talking like an English teacher. He wondered if—hoped that—Leslie had rescued the parakeet. He laughed out loud, but didn't dare to move.

Some time later—minutes, probably—the cloud moved off the mountainside, quickly and without drama. He realized he was on a small outcrop not far from the holy well. Had he lost his grip and slid down the hillside, he now saw, he would have stopped after about four feet in a soft flat patch of grass. He would not have died—in truth, he had done pretty well even to scrape his elbow, having landed on the only exposed rock in the vicinity. Bret would have felt extremely foolish except there had been no audience for this little existential drama other than himself. For all he had known, he reminded himself, this could easily have been the edge of a cliff, or a hundred-foot slide punctuated with sharp rocks. He let himself slide down the short slope on his pants seat, then propped himself against a boulder and looked out. He was a couple hundred feet off the Kerry Way, overlooking it. He pulled himself to his feet and discovered that, despite the mildness of the mishap, his ankle had not come through his latest fall unscathed. And of course he'd left the stick behind. He looked behind him, realizing that, standing as he was, his outline would be clearly visible against the blank sky to anyone looking up from below—it had taken only a short time with Cait to begin thinking that way: to be seen or not to be seen?

From this vantage point, the sea reached in two directions—to the left beyond the wide mouth of the Kenmare River and, to the right of Eagles Hill, across and beyond Ballinskelligs Bay. The scene was emphatically green and blue, the verdant hillsides punctuated only by light brown scrub, gray rocks, and white sheep, the cobalt sea dashed with foam, the shores edged by a lace of breakers. The faint lighter green of the trampled footpath of the Kerry Way meandered downhill in both directions. To the right, it emerged from behind a small prominence this side of Eagles Hill, then bent sharply down toward Lough Currane and the town of Waterville. A walker was climbing steadily along from that way, about halfway up the path. The shadow of a cloud darkened a spot on the wide circular bay beyond. He could see a tour bus moving through the town along the waterfront. To the left, the way he'd come up, the trail followed a more gradual line along the outer edge of a shallow trough in the mountainside. Two people approached briskly that way, one following the other so at times they appeared to be just one dark-haired figure, weaving in and out among the clumps of foliage and growing slowly but steadily larger in foreshortened perspective. He knew them. He knew them all. The three walkers converged and Bret watched as they slowed and the two greeted the one. Heads nodded, hugs were exchanged. Cait looked up toward him and pointed. He waved.

Something flickered in the corner of his eye. He looked down. At his feet, grasses had sprouted through a fissure in the rock. The blades and their sharp shadows quivered in the breeze.

THE PEOPLE OF THE VILLAGES rarely strayed from the path. No one could remember a time when the trail had not been there, nor did they know anyone who knew anyone who knew anyone old enough to recall such a day. But long ago, the people of the villages on the Kenmare River and those on Ballinskelligs Bay and Lough Currane would encounter each other only on the seas, because there were no paths across the mountains. Their lives depended upon and were shaped by the water. From time to time, a young man from the Kenmare side would be promised to a young lady from Ballinskelligs, or the other way around, and though the distance between was much shorter across the hills, their courtship would nonetheless take place by water, along the rocky coast, battling swift currents and tumultuous waters around Lamb's Head and Hog's Head.

It was said that some small number of people did live inland. To those in the coastal towns, these were strange and foreign folk, viewed with considerable suspicion. No one had ever seen their houses or learned how they lived, yet if one looked up at the hills at just the right time, one might catch a glimpse of the shadow of a figure atop the ridge, outlined against the sky. Such was the case with a young shepherdess of Castle Cove, who, while calling her father's sheep down to the farm from the high pasture lands near Staigue, caught sight of someone far above. In just a moment, the figure was gone. She walked toward the place, her eyes fixed on the spot, but saw nothing more. The next day, she ventured higher. And the next day. She did not know what drove her curiosity, but still she looked upward.

On the other side of the mountain, another girl also looked up and also saw a figure. She too wandered higher and higher. Whether these two saw the same person, or whether each saw the other at varying occasions—or saw anything at all—is a matter of ancient debate, but everyone agrees that the effect was that each, of her own accord, continued to return to those heights, and in that process trampled a faint foot track into the hillside, and that those paths eventually met at the top of the ridge—the tracks met long before the girls themselves met each other. No one in the villages knew about the paths. Those men and women were always looking toward the sea, and only people with eyes in the backs of their heads would have noticed a lone shepherdess climbing the hill.

One year, however, a storm set in, a storm of such duration and ferocity that the waters remained impassable for a week, then a month. Now it happened that the most important man on the Kenmare River and the most important man in Ballinskelligs Bay had arranged a marriage of their eldest children, a bond that both considered necessary to their mutual and independent fortunes. The appointed date of the wedding fast approached, yet there was no way to get from one place to the other, nor was there way for the people of the two families to communicate with one another. Never mind that each of the young betrothed quietly resented the arrangement, as they had never even met. Yet that was how things were done in those days. And sometimes, unlikely as it may seem, love blossomed in spite of the contrived bonds. As the anxiety rose in the respective villages, and the men began to speak of daring sea-going exploits, each of the two girls spoke to her elders of the high paths. Each reported that one could see the next bay from the top of the ridge. Each speculated that perhaps, once having attained the ridge top, a way down to the water could be found on the other side.

And so, one morning, each girl led a small party walking up, up, up onto the hill, each group climbing away from one bay and toward the other. In each party was the betrothed, the father and the mother, and a holy man, plus each girl leading the way. The paths were so faint that no one in either party, *save the two girls, could follow them, but each girl knew the pastures and trails so well that indeed they did reach the pass. As it happened, the parties arrived simultaneously. Everyone marveled that each group had embarked without knowledge of the other and yet had come to meet at this remote place, and all agreed that unseen and powerful forces must be at work, which was deemed a strong sign in favor of the planned union. The girls had more mundane explanations in mind, but circumstances were such at that time that they had no opportunity to discuss with each other the practical matter of how they had come to trace these paths that so fortuitously converged. Rather, a collective decision was quickly made to perform the marriage ceremony on the spot because, surely, it was meant to be so. The holy men, each having expected that a successful adventure would have ended near water at the intended destination, lacked certain required elements, so they set out to find water that they might consecrate. And lo, not thirty paces from where the parties had met, a pure spring bubbled from the rocks. The holy men collaboratively performed the rites to bless the water and the stone from which it flowed. Next came the melding of the blood and the bone, which the resourceful holy men achieved by rubbing consecrated water and particles scraped from the blessed stones into the hands and foreheads of the living bodies of the betrothed. Then they briskly performed the remainder of the rites.*

Now tradition in this place commanded that the newly joined couple must consummate their union before the water had completely dried from their foreheads. Customarily, the newlyweds would retire immediately to a pre-arranged place that was near the site of the wedding. On the mountaintop, however, these arrangements had of course not been made, so the two had to improvise a solution. They hurriedly climbed the ridge away from the group until they came to a place where the hillside folded into a ravine. Just beyond this place, they found a level grassy patch behind an enormous boulder, spread such garments as they possessed upon the ground, and celebrated the venerated tradition as shreds of cloud whipped the mountain and sharp winds whistled through the rocks. Afterwards, they sought better shelter and resumed the celebration. This was refreshingly unlike life in their villages, and they both began, reasonably enough, to consider if they really wanted to go back. They also began to question which world to which they properly belonged: The village of the bride? The village of the groom? Or this world? Was it necessary to decide? If so, how soon?

The other part of the tradition held that the newly marrieds would after the consummation return alone to the site of the wedding to drink of the blessed water. In observance and anticipation of this ritual, the two parties had immediately upon the conclusion of the ceremony turned to walk back down the mountain. As custom had it, no one was to lay eyes upon the couple before sunrise the day after the next day. When the couple failed to appear in either village at that appointed time, each village assumed initially that the pair had gone first to the other village. But as the days wore on and still they did not appear, the people became concerned. Yet the storm still raged, so there was still no way to travel by sea. Soon it became clear that, unless the weather changed, someone would again need to climb the mountain.

One week after the wedding, the two girls once again set off along their footpaths, each accompanied by a small group of villagers. Once again, the parties arrived at the crest of the ridge at the same point in time, and only then did everyone know what all had feared: that the couple had not appeared in either village. Just then, the stormy skies cleared. As the mists drifted away, they could all see indefinitely in every direction, as is always the case after the passing of bad weather. Confident that there were no more clouds approaching, the group marked the place where the paths had met with a pile of rocks and began to climb in the direction in which the couple had set off. They ascended the ridge, made a stream crossing, then came to a place where a huge boulder created an enclosed space against the hillside. Beyond a flat grassy area, they found *a small, hive-shaped hut made entirely of piled stones. The structure was hard to see, even from a short distance, because the piled rocks blended so naturally into the setting. They looked inside, but there was no outward sign that anyone had been there. They circled the mountain top, taking advantage of the clear weather, but saw nothing except the ravens that always frequented these heights. Once the girl's father was sure he had seen a figure on the crest of the hill, but when they arrived at the spot they found only a cairn of stacked stones. The sun began to get lower in the sky and they determined to return home and resume the search the next day. As a gesture of mutual hospitality, each group invited members of the other party to spend the evening in their village.*

The next day the groups returned to the ridge and resumed the search, but not only could they not find the couple, they were not able even to find the place with the boulder and the hut. They retraced steps from the pile of rocks, and retraced them again, but it wasn't to be found. Perhaps they had all imagined it. But still, the next day, up they went again, and again some went down the other side. Every day after that it continued: at least one person from Castle Cove crossed over to Lough Currane, and someone from the shores of the lake crossed over to the shores of the Kenmare. The more people walked, the more the path was worn and the more permanent it seemed to become. To commemorate the wedding at Windy Gap the villagers and the holy men constructed a basin and dug a deep well at the site of the spring. It became part of the ritual to stop at the holy well and pay respects as one crossed the ridge.

The father of the groom had promised to build a large house in Castle Cove for the young couple, and even when they did not come, he built it nonetheless. It remained empty always. He came to enjoy walking in the hills and would from time to time set off for days at a time, always returning with a bounce in his step and a sparkle in his eye. People said he had gone a bit mad, and his wife affirmed it with a smile. At the edge of Ballinskelligs Bay, the mother and father of the bride no longer cared to live in their formidable castle because it reminded them so of their lost daughter and of a future that would not come to be. Yet the sadness they felt, like that of the family in Castle Cove, was balanced by private notes of delight: at the notion that the two were still alive and experiencing a life of such freedom as they themselves had never felt, and that the day of their return could be today, or tomorrow, or one day soon. That building, too, remained without human inhabitants. Generations passed. The vines grew up. The wind and water did their work. Season by season, crashing storm by crashing storm, green sprout by green sprout, the proud stone edifices were pulled back to the earth from whence those rocks had come. Yet the path—itself not a thing at all, but merely a way of going—endures to this day.

No longer did the villagers look solely to the sea. Indeed, as gazes turned toward the hills, most had the experience of espying at least once a tiny human figure or a pair of figures against the sky, far off the trail. But never a close meeting. It was said that the man and the woman lived on up there, looking down at their former villages, at the empty houses they knew were theirs, until the years fixed them in place and they, like the castles set aside for them, were quietly taken back by the land. Some even said the cairns on the ridge line were all that was left of those souls who occasionally went up and never came back down.

As the years passed, memories faded about what had actually happened, and ancient principles arose instead: The path is there to cross the mountain. Crossing the mountain sustains the path. And so on.

I am sure you will observe that this telling shortchanges the two shepherdesses. They are the essential heroes of the story, but the narrative falls into the familiar tropes with the "blue-bloods" at the center, the offspring of the hereditary leaders mattering most—like all the fairy tales where the orphan peasant is discovered to have royal blood and enjoys a charmed life thereafter. This elitist storyline grows tiresome. Next time, the shepherdesses themselves are the ones who gain freedom and true love and chart their own paths outside the norms of their society. Perhaps they team up to raise the illegitimate child of the pre-annointed couple who have both died or been banished and this child miraculously goes on—not to rule the land because of something special in the blood, as would happen in the version promulgated by the elites who always seek to legitimize their own position of privilege—but simply to live a life as if that were privilege enough. Before too long, no one will remember that the story used to have a different course.

BRET CLOSED THE PASSENGER DOOR and, hobbling on one crutch, circled around to the other window, which Cait had rolled down. "Back in a minute," he said. She smiled and nodded. He patted his pocket to verify that his old ID was there and easy to retrieve, then followed the path around behind the old depot building. If you pushed against the never-latched door, it always swung open. Usually by this time they'd have the rides running, going through the safety checks. But nothing moved: the tubular tracks were still, silent, brightly painted yellow and red against the blue morning sky.

He passed behind the animal pens and came out next to the far bend of the log ride. From here there was a shortcut behind the concessions that emerged halfway down the midway. There wasn't a soul in the place. The plastic-wrapped giant purple dinosaurs still hung from the roof above the bottle ring toss, and there were piles of fresh cigarette butts behind the stool there, indicating that Tattoo Duane had been working yesterday and house-keeping hadn't made it there yet. He looked to his right, up above the faux-thatch roof of the Olde Tyme Emporium—there were the green tracks of Lancelot's Return, still so new that they were free of the dripping rust marks.

At the end of the midway, Bret stopped where he always stopped near the Catch a Holy Grail game stand and settled himself onto the concrete planter bench. He chuckled—in 2,000 years no one had managed to find even one Holy Grail, but here they had a whole rack of them, all different sizes, in sparkly gold-colored plastic from across the sea. He scanned the scene. How perplexing. A breeze kicked up a little swirl of dust over near the base of the big slide. Usually that was where kids tumbled off the end and piled back into the line to climb the stairs and ride down again, bellowing and squealing the whole time. Maybe today was a holiday. Fourth of July? But they'd always been open on Independence Day. Maybe a president had died or something.

The rides and concession stands, spread arbitrarily along the curving shore of a muddy lake in the middle of what once had been someone's hay field, sorely missed the constant motion and noise. Bret chuckled aloud. The silly bravado of the whole enterprise was its chief appeal: the stomach-turning Scrambler, the double ferris wheel that flipped you over, the roller coaster reaching heavenward for the sole purpose of coming rapidly back down to earth. His eyes followed where the car would have traced its winding course against the sky before rolling to a stop back at ground level.

It was easy to see, instead of people, County Kerry sheep queuing up to ride, grazing on the planters. Sheep and mist and rocks kept drifting into the scene, pulling his mind back to the windswept shoulder of Staigue. He could feel the sensation of the soft moist grasses and abrasive rocks through the soles of his shoes. The sea air on his cheek. Warm skin against his chest. The knot in his stomach at the thought of Cait having to decide what to do next, then the exhilaration at the simple audacity of this plan. Details to follow.

Something flickered in the corner of his eye. He looked down. At his feet, a crack had opened and grasses sprouted through a fissure. The blades and their sharp shadows quivered in the breeze. He thought of the church down there in Castle Cove being gently, silently, relentlessly pulled back to earth by vines and flowers. A low cloud drifted across the top of the first hill. He thought he could hear the roar of the surf far away, but of course that was impossible from here. He laughed out loud.

"'Scuse me," a voice called from his left. A wiry little guy in a Guinness cap and striped blue and gray overalls approached, a push broom in one hand and a sheet of paper in the other. "Who let you in here?"

"Let myself in," Bret replied. "Back gate."

"Back gate's chained and padlocked."

"That little door behind the old depot that's always open. What's going on?" Bret asked, pulling out his ID card. "Where is everybody?"

"Didn't catch the news? It's all over, chief. Closed. Just like that. Told us all yesterday afternoon. Bought up by some foreign big shots."

"But the season is just getting going."

"No duh, but that's the deal. Say they're gonna re-brand everything, whatever the hell that means, reopen in a few weeks. Just a lot of name changes, all the knights and armor and fake castle shit can stay. Now you gotta get going. You looking for somebody?"

Bret paused. It crossed his mind to quip something clever like "myself" but that was too glib, and plus, it might not be true. His fingers remembered the plastic card. "I just thought I should turn in my old ID since I don't work here anymore."

"Nobody works here anymore. Now I ain't from HR, but you want my advice, I say turn it in right there." He pointed at the trash can. "Come on, chief. I got to finish this list. Then I'm gonna snag me one of these holy grails nobody never wins. It ain't a gold watch, but it's something." He stepped toward the game stand to his left.

Bret laughed. "A little token of the appreciation they weren't going to give you."

"Damn straight. Sometimes you just gotta take it."

"Self-validation, right? Even if it's fake."

"Want one, too? Now's your chance."

Bret followed him to the game booth and leaned his crutch against the side of it. "Get the grail without even playing the game? Don't tell King Arthur."

"One holy grail, on the house." He pulled a glossy gold plastic vessel from the top shelf where the largest ones were lined up and slid it forcefully down the game counter.

Bret corralled it as it passed. His crutch toppled to the pavement.

"Are ladies allowed to play?" The two men looked up to see Cait walking toward them on the midway. "Sorry," she said. "You didn't come back. We thought you might have fallen."

"Still standing," said Bret, rolling his eyes. He knew another, probably more compelling reason was simply that she disliked sitting and waiting.

"Where did you come from?" The guy threw up his arms in exasperation. "Seriously, you two gotta get outta here. Get the lady a grail if she wants and vamooski."

"What about Lee and Sean?" Cait said.

"We have two more in the car," Bret said. "A mom and her kid. Give him the best one."

"Grails all around," the guy slid a vessel down to Bret, then another.

"Who will ever know? Nobody's watching," said Bret. "All this drama and no audience."

"Hell with who's watching or not watching," the guy said. "I just gotta get my work done. I got personal standards, you know."

"No audience doesn't mean nothing happens," said Cait.

The guy looked at Cait, then Bret, then back at Cait, then harumphed and handed her a shiny golden plastic cup, which glinted blindingly in the sun. "No shit."

THANKS

This book was first written during late nights between 2005 and 2011, then let to sit for more than a decade, then revised in 2023–24. Over the course of that long span, many volunteer readers offered their thoughts, and I am indebted to all of them. No one in my family escaped—my wife EB, our children Andrew and Gwendolyn, my sister Karen, brother Ted, cousin Doug, and mom Carol all read it—along with at least some of their spouses. My museum colleague Barbara Bradley reviewed an early draft with her editor's eye, old friend Stuart Rose provided his curmudgeonly counsel, and County Kerry's own Batt Burns made sure none of the Irish dialogue or cultural allusions were embarrassingly wrong. More recently, friends Richard Brink and Matt Berg read the revised version. And my fellow writers in the Proper Nouns group gave it the treatment as well. To the extent that it turned out to be any good, they are all responsible.

Independent authors rely on reader reviews to spread the word about their books.
If you like this book, please leave a review detailing why on your favorite platform(s). Thank you!

Crombie Hill
A novel
Finalist 2025 American Writing awards

"A captivating blend of literary prose and historical fiction . . . lyrical and immersive . . . a timeless meditation on the connections that bind us together across generations."
—Goodreads/A Look Inside

"The emotions, human drama and intelligence kept me propelled through the whole thing."
—Goodreads

"Having traveled a similar route, it was enjoyable to read of places I've been through. Now I want to travel it again—with the areas highlighted in this delightful book." —Goodreads

Also by G. M. Donley

The Virtues of Alignment
Stories and not stories

The Legend of Castle Cove
A novel

Night Music
Images from dark and noisy places in Cleveland
"Donley's images convey the visceral experience of being at a show in a small, closely packed room."
—Anastasia Pantsios, journalist and photographer.

A Small Book About Design Craft and Practice
"Such an easy and clear writing style. Made me want to really dig into the world of graphic design."
—Don Julien, filmmaker